Nora

by

Eileene Barry McKee

This is a work of fiction. Names, characters, places and incidents either are product of the author's imagination or are used fictitiously, and any resemblance to actual persons, living or dead, business establishments, events or locals is entirely coincidental.

Nora © 2009 by Eileene Barry McKee. All rights reserved. Printed in the United States of America. No part of this book may be reused or reproduced in any manner whatsoever without written permission of the author. For more information or to place an order, write Eileene McKee, 1314 Belmont Drive, Woodbury, MN 55125. 651-731-0129.

ISBN: 978-1-61658-397-2 (paperback)

Acknowledgement

Thanks to all the people who have helped me on this project.

Special thanks to Kitty McMahon-McDonald, the Barry McKee family and The members of the White Bear Writers Club.

And a loving "thank you" to my grandson - Kevin Mergens at Absolute Print Graphics, who so generously agreed to print this book, and to Mary Coughlin for her cover design.

To my family & to the members of the family from which I came.

Preface

    Nora is a collection of stories and one poem by Eileene B. McKee. The stories are about a time long past and a place that has almost disappeared in America, the small town. The stories are unsophisticated and innocent and are being read in a sophisticated and less than innocent time, but in a real sence the stories are timeless.

    The stories are written with sincerity and appear to be autobiographical or they could simply be the words of a woman who has never lost the imagination she possessed during her childhood.

    How do you grow up? When do you grow up? Should you grow up? I can't wait to grow up. I don't want to grow up. It's Nora's story as she finds her way to adulthood. Ms. McKee captures both the simplicity and the complexity of that time in life where you're not a child but you're not an adult, where you're trying to find your way and you can't wait to get there but your heart is asking do you really want to.

    Ms. McKee's characters are colorful and you know that they all have stories to tell if only we had time to listen. Like all good things, you don't want "Nora" to end.

Enjoy.

Barry McKee

FIRST LOVE

Lucy was new in our school
The prettiest girl in class
She sat over by the windows
Reflected in the glass

I watched her when she read her book
Or wrote her spelling words
And when she recited in the class
It was music that I heard.

One day she reached and stopped me
As we were going out
She said, "Billy can you help me?'
"What's Leap Year all about?"

"Leap Year," I said. "That's when girls can ask
Or approach some bashful boy."
She smiled. "I hoped that was it."
Her face was filled with joy.

"I can ask some fellow to hold my hand,
Or maybe give me a kiss.
Since its Leap Year no one will think me bold
Or wild, or find my act amiss?"

"That's the way it works," I muttered
I leaned, stunned, against the wall
She looked relieved and happy
And went smiling down the hall.

"She likes me. She loves me."
I felt strong, and weak by turn
I walked on air the whole way home
My blood seemed to boil and churn.

She often smiled and waved to me
I treasured the special looks
I thought perhaps I'd walk her home
Carry all her books.

Lucy had many, many friends
They'd laugh, and talk and play
She' beckon to me to come join in
But I had naught to say.

The boys would reach and touch her hand
And often sit real close
But she always seemed to brush them off
I knew she liked me most.

One day she gave me a very special smile
And ducked beneath the stair
I knew that I must follow her
For heaven waited there.

My friends all hurried down the hall
But me, I doubled back
I slipped beneath the steps myself
I found Lucy, -- kissing Jack!

Nora

Chapter 1

❧ FORGIVE US OUR TRESPASSES - 1924

Nora stood on the back steps, the wooden boards warm under her bare feet. She watched as Barney left the bunkhouse. He was coming to tattle as she knew he would. She was going to have to chew soap and stand in the pantry corner again.

Barney closed the gate carefully, checked to see that it was properly latched and then started up the path through the garden. He looked at her with sad, reproachful eyes.

She glared at him defiantly even though she knew she was supposed to be respectful to her elders. The freckles stood out on her small nose and she watched with unblinking blue eyes trying to show all the silent contempt and hatred that she felt for him.

"That damn little banty rooster," she thought angrily. That was what Pete and Uncle Jack called him, sometimes to his face, and Nora agreed. "That damn, trouble-making, tattling, scrawny, bow-legged, hateful little blackguard!" She tried to remember all the names Pete called him and she winced a little at the 'damns' because she wasn't supposed to say any words like that. But all she could think of was how miserable Barney always made everyone.

"He's a mean, wispy, cranky old man, and I hate him," Nora thought. "He always means trouble when he comes."

"Mrs. Nolan," he would whine. "That Nora is a little fairy indeed. Today she left the gate open and the bummer lambs got out into the lane. I had the devil's own time rounding them up again."

He would stand on the top step turning his cap in his boney, tobacco stained fingers and look at her with reproachful eyes.

Then an hour later he'd be back again.

"Mrs. Nolan. That Nora is a fright to goodness. Just now she was swearing like an English trooper at that new mare because the poor animal bucked Pete off. Now, I know, Mrs. Nolan, that you'd like to know—that you'd appreciate being told. Ah, indeed. I feel it's a duty I have, Ma'am, to tell you how she behaves. The other two are dear, good children, and the baby is an angel indeed, but that Nora . . ."

Tattle. Tattle. Tattle.

"Why couldn't he be more like Pete, or Uncle Jack," she thought miserably, "and laugh, and play the harmonica, and read to them, and show kids how to do things without making them feel like a nuisance? But Barney! He hates kids—almost as much as he hates Pete."

Just yesterday Barney had left his fencing and had come across through the sagebrush to complain about Pete.

"Mrs. Nolan. Let me tell you now. I know how busy you are, but I must bring it to your attention. Faith, I'd be remiss in my duty if I didn't . . .but that Pete Sullivan is a poor sort, he is, and Nora is much too fond of him. It's his foul mouth and cursing that she picks up, and he supposedly a good Catholic—may God forgive him." Barney had hesitated, then shook his head dolefully and sighed.

"I wouldn't criticize him for the world, you understand. Faith, I wouldn't waste my time on the likes of him, but it's for the child's own good."

Nora was usually sent upstairs to her room, or had to stand in the corner, quietly, while the household noises and the activity of the bright outdoors went on around her. Phil would feed her bummer lambs, and Katie would get to swing the gate for the men as they drove their teams in from the fields. And she now knew every crack and knothole in the entire pantry wall. She remembered all the times Barney had caused her to stand in that dark little room, and she thought of the bitter tasting lye soap that Mother washed her mouth with when she swore. Now he was coming again and she knew she was in for it.

"Mrs. Nolan, Ma'am," he called through the open kitchen door. "Can I speak to you for a minute?" He waited until Mother appeared, a wooden spoon dripping in her hand.

"I'm sorry. Heartsick really. But Nora was swearing again not half an hour ago. She was chasing those two pups and ran in her bare feet into that patch of stickers."

Mother interrupted him impatiently.

"Barney. Are you sure about all this swearing? I never hear any swearing at all from her around the house."

"That's exactly what I'm telling you Ma'am. What I've been trying to

2

tell you for these past weeks. 'Tis that spalpeen of a Pete mouthing curses with every breath. The lass picks it up." Barney moved a little further into the kitchen and lowered his voice. "And you should keep her away from him altogether when he's had a few drinks. Sure, 'tis then he's quite daft. He talks to the child as though she were a woman grown—but sure, he makes no sense at all."

Mother was alarmed.

"Whatever do you mean, Barney?"

"Well. The other night now, he had the poor tyke near to crying. Scaring her he was. Saying, 'listen to the sadness of the wind, like a soul lost, whispering around the empty prairie.' He talks wild to her – and sings sad songs . . ."

"Oh nonsense, Barney. If half the world were as good as Pete Sullivan the rest of us would be much better off."

Barney shuffled uncomfortably.

"Well now, Ma'am. Begging your pardon, but there is very little good about profanity or taking the Lord's name in vain."

Pete was coming in the back door with the evening pail of milk and he stopped short at Barney's words.

"Gossiping again, you old blackguard?" asked Pete. "Discharging your Christian duty?" He turned to Mother.

"Now, Nell. It was I that rescued the child from those stickers, and I heard no profanity."

Mother didn't answer either of them. She called Nora in from the back steps.

"Nora. Were you swearing?"

"Yes."

"Get the soap."

Mother was a no-nonsense, matter-of-fact woman. If one broke the rules, one was punished. No exceptions. No excuses.

Nora stood in the pantry, her mouth and eyes watering from the sharp bite of the soap. She stared at the wall detesting Old Barney with every breath she took. The cream separator whirred away comfortably as Katie turned the handle and she could smell the fresh bread as it came from the oven. She thought of Pete and the wild talk and the singing. It was a little queer, she had to admit, but certainly not a fearful thing. She thought about the 'Irish boys' too. Any man in Ireland who wasn't married, even if he were seventy years old, was called a 'boy'. Here on the ranch they were referred to as *'the boys'* also, and

3

no one thought that was daft.

Nora sighed and shifted her weight from one foot to the other. Then she thought about Pete and smiled. He was as tall as Dad and about as handsome. His blue eyes seemed to be always smiling and he'd wink at her at the most outrageous times.

Pete was nice. She liked him and Uncle Jack as well as she liked Katie and Phil. Better even. Katie and Phil were older and they both went to school in town and they had adventures and wonderful things to talk about, with strange playmates and new books—and they could read. Sometimes she would take one of their books out on the back steps in the warm sunshine and try and try to figure out how one could read. Often Pete would come along and sit next to her.

"Just think," he'd say. "Next year you'll be off to school yourself and you'll soon be reading like the others. Now what the devil do you have there? A history book, is it?" She'd climb happily up on his knee and he'd open the book.

"Great God," he would exclaim. "Look at them silly Egyptians with their slanty eyes and jawbreaker names." While she studied the pictures, he'd read on.

"Great God!" he'd say again. (In surprise, not in swearing.) "Them crazy rulers marrying their own brothers and sisters! 'Tis hard to believe that there were any at all that weren't feeble-minded."

"Pete?" He didn't care if she interrupted. "Pete? What's feeble-minded?"

"Well," he'd think for a minute and then explain in a way she could understand. "Feeble-minded? That's when a fellow is sort of—oh, a little mushy in the head. You know. Not hooked up quite right. Wrinkles in the brain, so he doesn't think as smooth and easy as a fellow should."

Nora would nod her head in understanding. "Like wrinkles in Phil's coat when he doesn't button it up right?"

" 'Tis that way exactly," Pete would say seriously. "But the Egyptians weren't all dumb at all, now. You can be sure of that. Sure didn't they make paper from weeds that grew along the rivers and had some kind of pencils and wrote on funny scrolls—"

Barney was never her friend. Once when Pete was out in line camp, she took a book and asked Barney to read to her. He said it was a waste of time to read fairy tales and such, but he'd see if he could find a suitable book, such as *Lives of the Saints*.

Barney was great for praying. He carried his rosary in his pocket and would bring it out often. He intoned the prayers in a slow and mournful voice always putting much emphasis on 'forgive us.' He could make a christening or a wedding—or even Christmas—sound worse than a wake. Barney was also great for the Catechism—the *Baltimore No. 2*. He made it one of his duties to teach the children their prayers. Nora shuddered. It was with the prayers that all the real trouble began.

When Katie had been preparing for First Communion he pestered her to death. But between Barney and Mother, Katie had been letter perfect in her Catechism and had won a small statue of the Good Shepherd. Then, when he learned that it was time for Phil to prepare for his First Communion, Barney started all over again, except now he tried to teach Nora also.

Normally, Mother would teach them herself, but with four young children and she, the only woman on the ranch to make butter, wash, sew, cook and clean, was terribly busy and perhaps even grateful to have some help. But it was torture to Phil and Nora to have Barney following them everywhere, lurking and waiting to pounce on them the minute they went out the door.

Phil would go off with Dad, or sneak off and hide in the hay mow, and Nora thought of the many times she stayed in her room and played with paper dolls—although she hated paper dolls. But sooner or later, Barney would catch up with them. The 'Hail Mary' wasn't too bad a prayer to learn, and they soon learned the 'Morning Offering.' But the 'Apostles' Creed' was sheer torture.

Every day that pious devil plagued them until they ran like frightened rabbits at the sight of him. And because he watched for them and hunted them so relentlessly he had more to tattle about than ever.

Sometimes Nora thought that Mother didn't like Barney and his tattling too much either. Once she heard her tell Dad that is seemed strange that he often came to tattle just at supper time. Unless it was branding, shearing or haying time, the men cooked and ate their own meals out in the bunkhouse, but if one happened to be at the house for some reason at meal time, he was asked to eat with the family.

But the Irish boys always ate with the family on Sundays or holidays. Sometimes there would only be one or two, but often there might be seven or eight. When everyone came home from Mass, Mother, Daddy, Pete and Uncle Jack would start cooking—putting the meat to roast, peeling potatoes and vegetables, making bread and pies and setting up the long table in the cool dining room. Then Father O'Hagen would arrive, having driven out from town in his buggy. After the greetings they would all sit down and eat, savoring the good plain food and teasing Pete if there were lumps in the gravy. Although there was not always dessert, often a little honey was passed around with the last slice of bread.

Then the Irish boys would clear the table and do up the dishes while Mother bathed and fed the baby and put him to bed for the night. Finally they would all sit in the darkening evening, talking about the price of wool or lamb, about the range conditions, the prospects of a job for one of the 'greenhorns' newly arrived from Ireland, and then – always – of Ireland itself, and the homes and loved ones they had left there.

One evening in late summer, they gathered as usual, after dinner. Phil and Nora showed Father O'Hagen the arrowheads they had found near the hot springs and he cautioned them to save the obsidian points carefully, because someday they would be very valuable. Katie showed the priest the dishtowel she was embroidering, and then the adults spoke as usual of their letters from home and their plans and hopes in this new land.

Finally, as though he couldn't stand the peacefulness, Barney started his plaguing. "Father O'Hagen, you must take a wee minute now to listen to what I've taught these two. Sure, you're going to be as proud of them as you were of Katie."

Phil and Nora were pushed forward and the grownups' conversation halted while Barney prodded and prompted them into reluctant recitation. Phil was very shy, and half afraid of the priest, and he fared even worse than Nora. Although he knew the prayers, he was so nervous he couldn't recite them. He stood there, beet red and stiff with embarrassment, while Barney clucked around like a mother hen.

"Phil. Come on now, boy. Think! Father, I've told the lad a thousand times, 'conceived by the Holy Spirit,' not *received* by the Holy Spirit,' Now where is that Nora? She knows it. She knows the whole prayer. She is the limb of the Devil, Father, but she does have a quick mind. Now, Nora. Say the 'Apostles' Creed' for Father O'Hagen."

The evening was ended. The sweet memories swept away – and by prayer! Nora grimaced remembering those ruined Sundays.

For weeks the old tyrant had grasped for attention and manipulated them all. How she hated him! They were learning to hate prayer, and worst of all, they were beginning to dread the lovely Sundays they had always looked forward to.

"Now this week, Father O'Hagen, we'll start on the Lord's prayer, the 'Our Father.'

Mother and Daddy walked Father O'Hagen out to his buggy, Mother carrying the lamp. Barney trailed along for fear he'd miss a word. Pete put his arm around Phil.

"Sure, pay no attention to that old rooster," he soothed. "Isn't he the greatest stump of a fool I've ever seen? He's a disgrace to the Irish!" Pete's voice was rough and angry.

Suddenly Phil started to cry. He sat down on the bottom step of the stairs, right there in the entry hall in front of the Irish boys and everyone, and he started to cry. Nora knew he was usually a quiet, gentle, methodical, happy little boy and he never cried. Certainly, not where anyone would see him. But he had been tormented, prodded, pinched and tattled on for weeks. Now he cried uncontrollably, the hot tears spilling down his round cheeks and dripping off his chin, his face distorted and ugly as his hurt. This was the ultimate degradation—to sit and cry where everyone could see his complete humiliation.

Nora felt surprise that tears were welling in her eyes. She rarely cried either. Phil must feel as depressed and hopeless as she did. It had only been last Sunday when Barney had embarrassed them so, and now it was only Tuesday and he was already tattling and bedeviling them. Everyone was so mad after the priest left and her parents found Phil crying, that she had expected that Barney would make himself scarce for awhile, but he was back with a vengeance and she knew supper would be a solemn, unhappy meal.

The next morning everyone was cranky. Dad drank his coffee and left for the fields without a word. Phil was defensive and sulky. Mother pretended she didn't hear Barney knocking at the door and calling for the children to come out. Then, when he began knocking louder she stuck her head out and said,

"The children haven't finished their work yet, Barney. They won't be out for quite a while."

It was a barefaced lie and they loved it. The dishes were all done up and stacked in the cupboard and the kitchen was shiny and orderly. The wood box was filled and the ashes dumped and they knew that Barney probably knew it, too. Suddenly they were smiling at each other sharing this small victory over their common enemy. Mother smiled, too. Then she opened the back door and called out,

"Oh, Barney. Mike would like to have you clean out the chicken house today. Put some new hay in all the nests too. It's time those pullets started laying and some clean nests might encourage them."

Barney went mumbling off down the walk, the catechism in his hand. Phil and Nora looked at each other and then at Mother, aglow with joy and reprieve. She looked back at them and smiled.

"Scat!" she said.

They went streaking out into the sunlight, falling over each other in their eagerness to find Pete and tell him.

Pete and several of the boys were in the blacksmith shop, shoeing the new mare. Nora worked the bellows on the forge, watching the coals breathe red, then grey, red, then grey, as she pumped the air. Barney had to clean the chicken house, and they had the whole day free.

Pete listened to their story thoughtfully, paring carefully away at the edge of the horse's hoof.

"Ah, to be sure," he said at last, 'but tomorrow is yet another day. And then the old devil will be back at ye again, prodding and pricking and making life miserable."

"Maybe we could learn it fast – the 'Our Father,' I mean. You could teach us today. We'd say it for him tomorrow and then maybe he'd shut up." Nora felt they had the problem solved.

"No!" said Pete. He shook his head, unsmiling. "Hasn't he a book of prayers bigger than the dictionary?" The boys all nodded in sympathetic agreement.

Pete spoke again, his voice solemn. "And should you learn every prayer in the book, and letter perfect—sure, wouldn't he only start making up some of his own?" Gloom descended again.

"I have a bit of an idea . . . " Pete started tentatively, He looked around at the boys, and Nora knew that they had been discussing the situation since Sunday night. John Reagan looked dubious and turned away – slowly sorting out the horseshoe nails as though to say he'd have no part of it. A couple of the others looked happy and eager, ready for anything. They turned the newly shod mare out into the pasture.

"Now you'll surely get into trouble," said Pete. "You might even get a good thumping." He told them the worst part right away. "But, that whining old devil will never plague you again—about prayer. I promise you that."

Nora stared at him in disbelief.

There was a long pause, and everyone looked from one to the other. Reagan went on with the sorting of the nails, not quite in on the plan, but not completely out, either.

" 'Tis a sacrilege, I think," said Reagan. "Even blasphemy . . . " His voice trailed away.

" 'Tis no worse than that, that cantankerous old maid," said Pete, anger in his voice. "Making them hate prayer, he is, and deliberately turning a bright world sour and bitter. Childhood shouldn't be—wasted!"

"Two wrongs don't make a right," said Reagan stubbornly. " 'Tis teaching them to lie. Small thanks to the father—and he after being so good to us, putting up with all of us until we can find situations of our own. Furnishing the bed and board to all of us. 'Tis poor payment to ruin the children!"

"The father doesn't like it, either," Pete sounded angry. "I knew their father before they did. Didn't we come across together—almost fifteen years ago? Sure, he would have booted Barney off the place long ago except the old fool is kin to Nellie!"

Nora turned in surprise. She didn't know that Barney was any relation and now she hated him more than ever. Making strangers suffer was very bad, but it must be a mortal sin, at least, to hurt your own.

Phil spoke up then, slow and serious. "What do we have to do?"

They weren't committed yet to this plan of Pete's, but they were sliding that way.

Nora was glad. Glad!

"I don't care if we do get a good thumping," she spoke with sudden vehemence. "I don't care if I have to stay in my room forever. They can give me—us—bread and water from now on if we can get rid of Barney!"

The boys looked at her solemnly, then at each other.

Pete sat straighter, then sighed. "Well now," he said. "First we must have an understanding. He looked at them seriously, unsmiling, and then he put an arm around each and drew them close, almost whispering.

"Now, here's the plan. Learn the 'Our Father' from Barney. Do it up in a fine manner, as though your life depended on it. Learn it backwards and forwards, smiling all the time, until Barney thinks he's become an Apostle at least!"

Phil began to look dubious as though he were being betrayed again.

"But…" Pete paused dramatically. "I'll teach you a second 'Our Father'!"

A *second* 'Our Father'? Nora looked at Phil in alarm. She didn't understand.

"Yes!" Pete spoke in triumph. "Now here is the tricky part. Indeed, it is the flame that will singe the old drone's wings. When Barney makes you stand up and recite for the priest, then you'll say the 'Lord's Prayer' I taught you, instead of Barney's!"

"Oh," said Phil in slow disappointment. "It's the reciting that I can't do. The reciting is the worst of the whole thing!"

"Ah, Phil, my boy—" Pete sounded very confident. "It's only this once more! I promise you. Just this one last time." He slapped his knee with finality.

"But!" Pete looked around like a conspirator and the boys closed in around him to show that they were all of a mind and would stick together. "But, there is one more thing! And the most important thing it is, too." Pete became very serious and Nora felt chilled waiting to hear the enormity of this 'important' thing. She held her breath.

"You must swear before God," said Pete, his face grave and unsmiling, "—and before Mother and Dad and everyone—you must *swear* that it was Barney taught you the prayer you recited—*and you must stick to it*!"

Nora knew it was a good plan. She knew it would work. It was a lie alright, but it would work. She laughed and hugged Pete's arm, but he was looking at Phil who struggled manfully with the decision.

" 'Twill be the last time you'll ever have to perform like a trained Russian bear," said Pete. "The very last time. Now, man. Are ye for it?"

Phil sighed and looked into the grey embers now dying in the forge. Finally, he answered with slow reluctance. "Well. I guess—I'm for it."

"Good!" Pete stood and slapped his hands together. "We'll get started right away."

As the week progressed, Nora became cranky feeling and jumpy, but she didn't waver in her resolve. Never had the children seemed to be more willing pupils. Old Barney could scarcely find reason for complaint. He purred and preened and basked in self-satisfaction. He directed the children to recite the 'Lord's Prayer' for anyone who would listen. For Barney himself, many times. For Mother and Dad, and for the Irish boys individually and collectively, and all the while, Barney's delight grew.

"Look. Look now," he would squeal. "By the grace of God, they are finally becoming decent children. God fearing and willing as they should have been all along. With the prayer on their lips, sure, there is no more of the swearing and blasphemy. We must say the rosary now in thanksgiving, so they won't slide back into their old, slovenly ways."

Several times Mother rescued them. "Enough, Barney. Let the children out into the sunshine."

In the evening, after supper, Nora and Phil would slip out into the cool night and walk down along the creek with Pete. The smell of sage and juniper swept in from the desert and the stars seemed to be hanging just above the cottonwoods.

Pete taught them his version of the 'Lord's Prayer' in one night and they nearly died of shock. Throughout the remainder of the week they practiced Pete's prayer quietly, whispering it to themselves.

Now they knew both prayers, letter perfect, but, they were becoming so nervous that even busy Mother noticed the difference in their behavior.

The week flew by and yet it seemed at times to stand still. Nora began to long for Sunday to come so the whole thing would be over and behind them.

They knew they could still back out. All Phil had to do was to recite the prayer as Barney had taught it to them, and several times they decided to do it that way. But then, Barney started on the Beatitudes which no one even needed to know until they were preparing for Confirmation, and then, well, the children felt they had no choice.

Finally, Sunday came and crawled slowly by. Nora's apprehension grew by the minute. There were the morning chores, the long ride home from Mass, the slow restful day, the arrival of Father O'Hagen and the usual family dinner. The boys were quiet as they hurried through the dishes and Pete winked meaningfully at Nora when he saw her sitting on the lower step of the stairs, biting her fingernails. Uncle Jack gave her an encouraging smile.

Then with a cold sickness in her stomach, Nora watched as everyone gathered in the parlor for the quiet evening. It was growing dark and Barney was so eager he could restrain himself no longer. He paced about like a preening rooster, showing off and setting the stage.

"Sit here, Father O'Hagen. Here by the fireplace. And now, two chairs over there. I'll sit here near the children. They can come in there from the hall. Boys, move back there a bit, will you? Pete? Where is Pete? Wouldn't you know now, that he'd be late? Well. No loss. We'll not wait for him either."

Pete was standing in the shadows in the hallway. He smiled wickedly and Nora knew that he'd had a drink or two. She and Phil were close to collapse. At the last minute she had to go to the bathroom and Barney stood at the bottom of the stairs, impatiently tapping his foot.

Father O'Hagen seemed to sense that something strange was happening. The Irish boys who were usually so high spirited and filled with gentle humor were suddenly showing an intense interest and great respect for these children learning their prayers. He sighed and lit a great cigar and leaned back comfortably, waiting.

Finally, Barney pushed Phil forward. Nora could scarcely breathe.

"Listen, now, Father O'Hagen. Just hear what I've taught him. Sure, the lad had done wonderfully this week. Ah, all the vexation I've had with these children these past months—"

It was probably the first time Nora had seen Barney smiling like that in all her life.

"Come now, Phil. Speak up. Don't be afraid. Just speak up. Speak plainly, just as I taught you."

Phil's face was pale—then beet red—then pale again. He fidgeted. He tucked in his shirttail. He swallowed twice, slowly. He closed his eyes and squeezed them shut painfully before he began. Then in a loud mournful voice that mimicked Barney's way of speaking, he intoned:

*Our father, who art in heaven
Came howling down the lane
With his shirttail full of hominy
His pockets full of grain.*

"Mother of God!" Barney screamed in outrage, bouncing up like a rubber ball.

"God in Heaven!" said Father O'Hagen, dropping his cigar and sitting bolt upright almost out of the chair.

"Philip!" Mother and Daddy's shocked voices chimed together exactly.

Nora knew all along what Phil was going to say, but still, she was so affected by the reaction that she started to cry uncontrollably.

*The hominy for food we need.
The grain goes in the still.* Phil's voice boomed on.
*Smooth spirits thus will buoy us up
To do your holy will.*

"Stop! Stop!" Barney screamed like a wild man and clamped his hand over Phil's mouth.

"Oh, Father O'Hagen. My God! Father, I *never* did. That I *never* taught him. Tell him, Phil. I never did it. Phil! Tell him." Barney was shaking Phil, nearly dragging the shirt off his back, meanwhile, rolling his eyes up to heaven as though seeking intervention from on high. Then he rolled his eyes back toward the priest to see if he was being believed. He looked quite wild. Nora wailed louder.

"Stop it this minute!" Mother spoke with fury in her voice. No one paid the slightest attention to her.

"Phil, you devil," Barney was shrieking, and shaking, and pleading. "Ah, Father. As God is my witness. I never said such a thing. Never taught such a thing!"

By this time, Pete had fallen half out the door, weak with silent laughter and the boys were doing a poor job of hiding their mirth. Father O'Hagen seemed to be choking. He covered his face with a huge white handkerchief and struggled and coughed. 'Twas the cigar smoke mixed with all the excitement, Nora imagined.

Mother was rigid with indignation.

Barney executed a weird, wild dance around the room, shaking his fist at each of the boys in turn, his face white and contorted. He shrieked like a banshee.

"You devils," he shouted. " 'Twas you rotten devils that put him up to this!"

The room rocked with laughter.

Suddenly, Barney flew across the room like a scalded cat. Nora had never seen him move so fast. She thought for a moment he was going to hit Phil and the laughter died down.

"Who did it, Phil?" It was a hoarse command rather than a question. "Who was it taught you that foul thing? That terrible, foul thing?"

Phil was slow and deliberate as usual. He seemed a little surprised. He looked around at the 'boys' and then back at Barney.

"Why—you did," he answered earnestly.

Barney was beside himself. It was then he discovered Nora, clinging to the banister and crying, partly from excitement and partly from fright. Barney truly looked like a madman. He grasped Nora by the arm and dragged her bodily out into the parlor.

"Stop!" he shouted. "We'll have the truth." He practically threw the child into Father O'Hagen's arms. "Ask her," he commanded. "She'll not lie to a priest."

Father was uncomfortable. He knew that he was caught somehow in a great joke that was getting out of hand.

"Ask her," Barney cried again. "Oh. 'Twas surely that Pete that put them up to this cruel thing. Why would I do such a thing? I that's always thought only of their own good? Why would I do such a thing?"

Father O'Hagen straightened himself and wiped Nora's face with his handkerchief.

"Stop now," he commanded them. "You're frightening the child. She'd best run along to bed."

"No!" screamed Barney. He stood, his body rigid. "No indeed. She'll answer first! Why would I be guilty of such a thing?" He reached to shake her by the shoulder. "Nora? The truth now—"

Nora looked at Barney. He was red in the face, his features glazed with sweat, breathing in great, ragged gulps from indignation and his wild gyrations around the room.

"I think he's a little unhooked," she said to Father O'Hagen. "You know, kind of mushy in the brain."

Chapter 2

❦ BIG MOUTH - 1926

Mother rushed about trying to do three things at once, as usual. She was changing the baby, trying to button her blouse, and giving orders.

"Nora, hold your hat on your lap while you are riding in that wagon. Be sure it doesn't blow away. Don't put it on your head until you get to the church."

"Katie, take those two pillows for you girls to sit on. Those boxes would be uncomfortable without a little padding. At least Uncle Jack nailed them to the floor boards so they won't shift around on the wagon bed."

The phone rang. One long and two shorts—their signal on the party line. Mother hurried to the front hall to answer it. She had to stand on her tip-toes to be able to speak into the mouthpiece.

"Oh, yes. Yes, Mrs. Blanchard. I'm all ready. I'll walk up the lane to meet you on the road."

The baby started fussing and mother waved a distracted signal to Nora who hastened to bring a bright ball to the crib.

"Yes, Mrs. Blanchard. No. No. None of the children will be riding with us so we can stop to load the flowers. The children are riding in with Uncle Jack on his wagon. Yes. Yes. I think we will have plenty of time. Yes. I'll see you very soon."

Mother hung up the receiver and shook her head. Nora hastened to hand her the button hook.

"Oh, Lord," said Mother. "I would have forgotten those last few buttons. I'm probably the last person in church who still wears high button shoes." She shook her head. She bent to fasten the three buttons at the top of each shoe and handed the hook back to Nora.

"Put it in the sewing machine drawer," she directed, "and turn the machine with the knobs toward the wall. Kevin can't get the drawers open if they are turned away. And Aunt Sue and the children will be here today, too. We don't want her little ones to be hunting through those drawers.

The hired girl came to lift little Julie from her crib and Nora ran to find her mother's purse.

"Thank you, dear child," Mother sounded grateful. She bent to hug Nora. "I'll see you at the church."

Katie was already seated in the wagon and Neil Larkin boosted Nora up to the wagon bed. She adjusted the pillow and sat down on the box beside Katie. Neil climbed up himself and sat on the canvas spread over the dusty boards.

Con Connolly came quietly from the bunkhouse. Newly arrived from Ireland, he was trying desperately to learn and understand the ways of this new country. He climbed up on the wagon also.

Uncle Jack turned back from the high seat in front where he sat waiting to drive them into town. He spread his arms wide and rolled his eyes toward the sky.

"Dear God," he intoned. *"I thank you for your bounty. I'm escorting the two best looking girls in Lake County."*

Katie blushed and looked down at her hands, but Nora giggled with delight. She turned to watch Johnnie Whalen as he hurried from the bunkhouse.

"My goodness! You all look so handsome," Mother spoke from the porch steps. And they did look handsome, Nora thought. The men all wore their dark suits and white shirts with a bright tie. They were clean, and freshly shaven. They no longer wore the heavy work boots but sported dark, highly polished shoes and narrow brimmed felt hats.

Nora loved Sundays.

"Nora!" Mother spoke, her voice sharp. "Where is your hat? You can't go into church bareheaded. Get back in there and get your hat!"

Nora jumped down and ran into the house.

"How lucky now that you discovered the missing hat," said Uncle Jack. "None of us noticed it at all. They should hire you to be a 'pro-hi,' You'd be fine at the job."

The men all smiled.

"What is a . . . a 'pro-hi?' " Con Connolly asked, hesitation in his voice. "I don't think they have 'pro-hi's' in Ireland."

"Indeed they don't," Uncle Jack laughed. "Here in this country, sure, they are men hired by the government to find and catch out the . . . well, the bootleggers."

"Bootleggers?" Con Connolly seemed overwhelmed.

"A few years ago, in this country, they voted through a damn law," Uncle Jack explained, disgust evident in his voice. "The law is called 'prohibition.' It means that no one can buy or drink alcohol. Some damn do-gooders decided drink was the ruin of the country so now we can't even buy a pint in a bar. They don't even call them bars anymore. Now the taverns are called 'pool halls,' and sure, the government hires these fellows to snoop around and try to find out who has a still. It's illegal to have a still, of course. These prohibitioners—they call them 'pro-hi's'—seek out the moonshiners and the bootleggers and get them arrested."

Con Connolly struggled to understand.

"One can't even buy a Guinness?" he asked, amazement in his voice, "even if you have the price of it?"

"You can't!" Uncle Jack said. "And if you find someone who brews a little on the side, and is willing to sell it to you, you must watch out that the pro-hi's don't catch you making the purchase."

Nora returned carrying her hat and Mother abruptly changed the subject.

"But where is Dennis?" Mother asked. "He's not sick is he?"

"He isn't," Uncle Jack assured her. "He's over in the field, closing the gates. The cows are in at the haystacks again."

"Again?" Mother shook her head in dismay. "How in the world do they ever get inside those fences. You're sure the gates were shut?"

"I closed them all myself," said Uncle Jack. "And I rode over last evening to be sure. Those fences are sheep tight, and I know a cow can't unhook a gate. No! Someone with two hands and two feet is opening those gates. I'd like to catch the blackguard at it."

"You'll be going up the track by the railroad then, won't you?" asked Mother. "Oh! Here come the Blanchards. I'll meet you outside the church."

Mother stepped down from the porch and started up the lane. Uncle Jack slapped the reins and the horses were guided in the opposite direction, taking the trail that the men used each day to go to work in the field.

Nora loved the feel of the hot sun on her arms and face. The air she breathed seemed laden with the smell of sage and, of course, the odor of the new-mown hay that lay in the fields. Behind her a great cloud of white alkali dust billowed from beneath the wagon wheels. She hugged herself. She knew that no kid in town was as lucky as she.

Beyond the railroad tracks the road turned right and headed for town. Half a mile further, Dennis Halloran leaned against a corner post waiting for them. He, too, was dressed for church and looked strangely out of place in his dark suit and white shirt as he strolled out across the green of the roadside.

"Both the gates were open," he announced as he climbed up on the back of the wagon. "Those cows are still indignant that I drove them from their feast. And the gate here at the property boundary was open, too. Not just the gates where the stacks are fenced, but this gate, here, at the edge of your fields as well."

"Damn!" said Uncle Jack. "I don't understand it. Someone opens the gates every day for two or three days, and then we have no trouble at all for several weeks and then they hit the gates again." He shook his head, frustration plain on his face.

They rode in silence for a few minutes. Nora wished she could think of a reason for this strange behavior. Maybe it was some mean boys from town. Maybe it was someone stealing hay. But Uncle Jack didn't think so. She wished she could come up with some reason.

Then Neil Larkin started humming. He always started with the same song. He had a wonderful voice and soon they were all singing along.

> *Now the moon shines tonight on pretty Red Wing.*
> *The trees are sighing, the night birds crying-*
> *And afar 'neath the star her brave is sleeping*
> *While Red Wing's weeping, her heart away.*

Nora thought about Red Wing. She felt sorry for the little Indian maiden. It was sad for her to learn that her brave had been killed and would never be coming home again. Nora was glad when they started another song:

> *Where the River Shannon's flowing,*
> *Where the three-leafed shamrock grows.*
> *Where my heart is, I am going,*
> *To my little Irish Rose.*

And the moment that I meet her,
With a hug and kiss I'll greet her.
For there's not a colleen sweeter,
Where the River Shannon flows.

Nora liked that song much better. At least it had a happy ending. Some handsome fellow coming home to hug and kiss his sweetheart. And they would live happily ever after.

Now Neil started a new song. They always sang it and Nora was trying to remember the words. She could call much of it to mind, but sometimes she got the last verse mixed up. Katie said she was stupid. It was a very simple song. But Nora didn't quite understand it and found it difficult to remember.

My wild Irish Rose,
The sweetest flower that grows.
You may search everywhere, but none can compare
With my wild Irish Rose.

Now, that part Nora understood. It was the next part that confused her.

My Wild Irish Rose. The dearest flower that grows.
And some day for my sake, she may let me take
The bloom from my Wild Irish Rose.

Now, that was where she got mixed up. She mumbled and Katie jabbed a sharp elbow into her ribs.

The horses turned and started up Church street. The singing stopped since they were now nearing the center of town.

A big black Ford truck approached. Nora had never seen a bigger automobile in her life.

The logging trucks that brought the logs in to the mill were larger, of course, but this auto was certainly bigger than any of the touring cars one saw about town.

A huge square engine, a square expanse of glass windshield and a square chassis with black canvas side curtains gave the automobile a very distinctive look.

"That's the new grocery wagon that brings in fresh vegetables and fruit,"

Phil announced. "I didn't know that fellow drove on Sundays."

The truck pulled in to the dock behind Jordan's Mercantile Store and the driver climbed down from the cab looking stiff and exhausted. Manny Dietz's big touring car pulled in near the dock as they watched. Manny jumped to the street and went to shake hands with the stranger who had driven the truck into town.

"We'll have to tell mother," said Phil. "She likes to get to the store early when he brings in the new produce. He has melons and strawberries and all sorts of things that no one grows in the gardens around here."

Ahead, Nora saw her mother and the widow Shelby loading huge bouquets of roses into Blanchard's buggy. They were both on the cleaning committee for the church this month, along with Mrs. Blanchard, and it was a matter of pride for them all to have the church beautifully cleaned and decorated.

Nora still struggled with the words of the song:

*"and some day for my sake, she may let me take
the bloom from my Wild Irish Rose."*

She sang the words softly trying to commit them to memory.

"And wouldn't I like to take the bloom from her Wild Irish Rose?" said Johnnie Whelan. "God's truth. She is a beautiful woman." He leaned forward and Nora thought he would surely fall out of the wagon. He was looking at the Widow Shelby and seemed scarcely to be breathing.

Uncle Jack slowed the team. "Can we help you load anything?" he called.

"No. No." the widow answered. "We may need help when we get to the church, though. All these flowers must be carried in and placed on the various altars."

"We'll be waiting to help," said Uncle Jack as he drove past.

"Such pretty, pretty flowers," Nora observed. "Her yard is full of them."

"She has a hundred and fifty rose bushes," said Halloran. "Maybe more. And that's not counting the climbing roses growing there on the trellis, or the ones growing over her door."

"Really?" said Nora.

"'Tis true." Halloran stated. "My brother Tom works for her every now and then. He helps her prune them and water them and clean up the leaves that threaten to choke them out in the autumn. Her husband planted them for her and set up a watering system so she can turn the water from the creek down into the yard if they start to get too dry."

"I thought she was a widow?" said Nora.

"She is. She is." Halloran assured her. "Her husband got gassed over there in France. He came home in bad health and just kept getting worse. He couldn't do much but he did plant all those rose bushes around their little house. Then he died and left her a young widow. I think they were just out of high school when they married, and he went overseas soon after. She's been alone now for five or six years."

"That is so sad," said Nora. "But at least she has beautiful roses to remember him by."

"Aye," said Dennis. "And sure, she gives flowers to anyone who wants them. Anyone who stops by."

"That is so thoughtful of her," said Nora. "She must be a very generous person."

"I wonder," Johnnie Whelan spoke in a tentative voice. "I wonder, has she any—suitors—hanging around?"

Neil Larkin smiled. Dennis Halloran smiled. Even Phil, sitting on the high seat, looked back and grinned. Uncle Jack laughed aloud.

"What's so funny?" asked Nora.

"Poor Johnnie is smitten," said Uncle Jack. "He comes to church each Sunday scrubbed and cleaned and pressed and polished. He pays no attention to the mass, but spends the full hour looking at the lovely widow Shelby."

"Ah, now," said Johnnie. "Not true. Not true." But he blushed up and looked off toward the hills.

"And he drives by her house each time he comes to town. Usually it's several blocks out of his way but he drives by hoping to catch a glimpse of her." Neil Larkin added. "Sure the horses even know of his affliction. When he is driving they don't go up Main Street at all as they naturally would, but they head right for Church Street and even slow down as they pass her house."

"Aw. Will you stop it?" said Johnnie. But he seemed very relieved when the team came to a stop in the small field near the church. He reached to help the girls down and helped Nora tie the ribbons of her hat under her chin.

As they walked across the street, Nora saw that the Blanchard's buggy, filled with flowers, had arrived in front of the church. Mrs. Blanchard seemed to be in charge at the moment.

"There are six large glass vases on the table there in the sacristy," she told her husband. "Fill them all with water and bring them out to the altar rail. We'll put four of them on the main altar and one apiece on the side altars. Oh!

These flowers are so lovely!"

Blanchard retreated into the church as Nora and the others approached. Johnnie Whelan took off his hat and hastened to offer his help.

"Let me lift that bunch down," he told the widow. "Or are there two bouquets here?" He handed his hat to Nora.

"No. Just one," Widow Shelby stepped aside as he lifted an armful of red roses from the tub in the coach. He handed bundles of roses to Mother, to Mrs. Blanchard, to Uncle Jack and Dennis. He handed a bouquet to Nora.

She breathed in the lovely fragrance. "They are so beautiful," she said. "Which ones are the wild Irish roses?"

Everyone stopped and looked at her. Everyone smiled.

"Why—why, I think they are the . . . the deep red ones, there in that bouquet." The Widow Shelby was smiling and she pointed to the flowers that Mrs. Blanchard held.

"Do you have any of them left at home in your garden?" Nora asked.

"Oh, yes. I have a great many of them."

"And you give away flowers to anyone who wants them?" Nora continued.

"Why, yes," said the Widow. "Stop by after church and I'll cut you a special bouquet."

"Oh. It's not for me," said Nora. "Johnnie Whelan here wants them. He said he'd love to take some blooms from your wild Irish rose."

There was a startled silence. Everyone, except Uncle Jack, looked at her in an accusing way.

"Nora!" Mother spoke in that outraged tone she sometimes used. Uncle Jack chuckled.

"What?" Nora stammered. She felt the red rising in her cheeks, but she didn't understand why the adults had reacted in such a way.

The uncomfortable silence was broken when the Widow Shelby spoke. Her voice was very calm and businesslike.

"Are you just going to stand there all day?" she said to Johnnie. "Let's take these flowers into the church where they belong. I'm sure Mr. Blanchard has the vases ready."

"You and your big mouth," Mother hissed at Nora as they climbed up the church steps. "Why don't you think before you speak?"

Nora hesitated at the door. She turned back and made her way down the steps. She crossed the street to the field where the wagons and the buggies were parked. She climbed up on the wagon and sat quietly, miserably alone.

She watched as the parishioners arrived and entered the church. Most were already using their paper fans because of the heat. A few of them even waved at her from across the road. She didn't wave back.

What had she said—what had she done—that made the adults so mad? She tried to understand. The day had started out so beautifully. Everything was going so well, and then this strange, humiliating puzzle. Only Uncle Jack seemed not to be outraged. Uncle Jack. Yes. She would ask him after church. He would explain it all to her.

The bronze bell on the steeple rang out and she knew that mass was starting. She hurried across the street and entered the building.

The crowded church was very warm inside. Outside, the August sun beat down from a cloudless sky, but, at least, there had been a hint of a breeze as she sat in the wagon.

She hurried down the aisle. The pew where her mother and Katie sat was already filled and Mother pointed to the seat directly in front of her. Nora slipped quietly in and knelt to bless herself.

The fellow sitting next to her was a stranger in town. But he had been here to Mass the last two Sundays, and had been present also on Holy Thursday.

He was neatly dressed and his fingernails were very clean. He smelled of soap. She thought he had probably never shoed a horse or harnessed a team. Uncle Jack said he was a 'pro-hi.'

Nora sat very still. Her chest seemed constricted. She had embarrassed her mother again, and she had no idea what she had said that had caused such consternation among the adults. She was always doing such stupid things— and she truly wanted to be good. She wished she could become invisible until she was at least twenty-one. By then, maybe she would have enough sense to know what was right and what was wrong.

The congregation stood for the gospel, and then seated themselves again.

Nora sighed. The priest was starting his sermon. She hoped the sermon would be short. It was so miserably hot in here, and he always spoke for a long time about things she didn't understand. Today she had to sit very quietly. She couldn't even wiggle. Mother sat directly behind her and she was already upset.

Gradually, Nora's mind wandered to other things.

There was 'Dutch' Ferris sitting up there with his brother. Last week when she and Uncle Jack had been in the hardware store, Dutch had come into the store. He leaned against the counter and wiped his face with his handkerchief. He looked quite pale. Then he had flopped right down on the floor and started twitching and kicking—jerking about and hitting his head on the floor and the woodwork.

George Buckle, the store manager, jumped away and looked almost as stricken as the man on the floor. But Uncle Jack had rushed forward, snatched a small brush from a display behind the counter and fell down on Dutch. He flipped the brush around and put the handle into the stricken man's mouth. He shouted at George Buckle to run and call a doctor but George seemed unable to move, let alone run. Uncle Jack then turned and told Nora, "Run and get Dr. Phelps!"

Nora ran.

The doctor's office was across the street and up a flight of stairs, but Dr. Phelps, his black bag in hand, was just starting up the steps when Nora called to him. She grabbed him by the hand, explaining as she pulled him along.

Several people gathered in the store. They parted to let the doctor through, then pressed back together blocking Nora's view. Dutch's brother came running through the door and was soon talking to the doctor.

"He hasn't had nothing like this happen in a couple of years, that I know of. But he didn't feel good this morning. The heat, I think. I wanted him to go up to your office but he said he just couldn't—just didn't feel up to climbing up them stairs. So I went up to get you and . . . "

Other conversations were going on that Nora couldn't understand.

"Dutch is an epileptic," someone said. "I've known him since he was a kid."

". . . stuck the handle of that brush right in his mouth, so he wouldn't swallow his tongue . . . "

"Yeah, he got bit. Look at the blood on his fingers—but that 'mick.' He sure knew what to do!" Nora hated it when the town people referred to the Irish as 'micks' or 'greenhorns.' They always sounded so superior, and she couldn't understand why. Even the children at school acted as though it were painful to have to share their lessons with the Irish children.

Nora sighed again and pulled her thoughts back to the stifling, crowded church. The sermon was over and the ushers started down the aisles passing the collection box.

The stranger sitting next to her suddenly nudged her. He handed her a shiny nickel.

Her eyes widened, her heart rose. She plopped the coin into the collection box with a satisfying clink.

Suddenly the world seemed bright again. She turned to find the stranger smiling at her.

She wriggled in delight. This nice man, who came to church even on the Holy Days, had given her a nickel—and she was a complete stranger! She settled back as the mass progressed. She remembered that Uncle Jack had said the man was a pro-hi. She fervently hoped that wasn't a bad disease. She wanted this nice man to be healthy and happy.

She thought of Danny Truax who had lost a hand in the mill. They called him an amputee.

And John Currier had a new disease no one had ever heard much about. They called him a diabetic.

It seemed to her that men had lots of trouble. There were amputees, epileptics, diabetics and pro-hi's. Maybe men were subject to other things that she hadn't heard of yet.

She had forgotten her handkerchief, as usual, and she felt the sweat dripping down in front of her ear. She wiped at the dampness with her fingers, and then Mother nudged her from behind and gave her a kerchief. It was really hot here in church. She looked around. Everyone seemed to be sweating.

Mass was over at last and Nora wanted to dash out into the fresh air—but, no, they had to stay for benediction. Some of the parishioners slipped quietly out of the church as the many candles were being lit. Now that it wasn't so crowded it seemed somewhat cooler.

Nora turned and looked back down the aisle behind her. Uncle Jack and Phil were gone from their seats in the back pews where the Irish boys usually sat. Nora knew they had gone to look for flasks in the alley behind the pool halls.

Mother nudged her again and shook her head. She didn't approve of anyone turning their backs to the altar.

Nora stood as benediction started, but her mind was on Uncle Jack and Phil. They would put any flasks they found in a gunny sack and hide it in the wagon. Those two would be standing innocently at the foot of the steps when the rest of the family came out of church. She would much rather be hunting flasks than standing here in this heat. But girls didn't do things like that.

Tomorrow or the next day, Phil would bring the glass bottles into the kitchen and wash them carefully. Mother sometimes helped him. She thought he found them on his paper route—and sometimes he did find one or two—but most were found on Sunday morning, especially after pay day at the sawmill. Phil collected a nickel apiece when he sold the clean flasks to one of the town bootleggers.

Nora wasn't sure what a bootlegger was. There were three or four of them around town. She had heard Phil and Uncle Jack talking about them.

Now, as the prayers went on, Nora thought seriously about them.

Mother didn't approve of bootleggers, or moonshiners, as they were sometimes called. She said they should all be arrested because they were lawbreakers.

Uncle Jack disagreed. He said they were fine fellows.

It was all very confusing, especially since Mother allowed Phil to sell them his flasks. The money he made went into his college fund.

Nora had asked Uncle Jack why the bootleggers didn't get arrested since everyone seemed to know who they were. But Uncle Jack had laughed and said,

"Ah, yes. But they must be 'caught.' It's sort of a game. They can't be arrested unless they are caught making moonshine or selling it. They are very careful that no one sees them delivering the 'booze'—and no one knows where they make the stuff."

At last, benediction was over. The smell of incense hung in the air and the sweet sound of the bells seemed to linger as Father O'Hagen left the altar.

The parishioners left the church in quiet groups. They gathered outside, greeting each other, laughing, visiting and exchanging news. Uncle Jack and Phil stood at the foot of the steps as though they had just come out of the church.

Uncle Jack was soon surrounded by a group of Irish men, some of whom hadn't seen him for over a year. The men worked in the distant, lonely sheep camps and rarely came to town for a vacation.

Mother and her sister, Auntie Sue, stood visiting with Ella Murdock. Uncle 'D', Auntie Sue's husband, soon went to join the men with Uncle Jack.

Mrs. Murdock was also new in town. Her husband had been transferred here by the Forest Service. Nora thought she was very pretty.

Nora began to feel happy again. Auntie Sue and her family were coming down to spend the day at the ranch. The cousins always had a wonderful time playing and adventuring while the adults visited.

Nora's hat lifted suddenly and swirled upward. It landed on a tall lilac bush beside the church entrance. Nora ran back up the steps, happy that she could retrieve it when reaching from the landing. As she plopped it back on her head she saw movement over under the trees where the wagons and buggies were parked.

There was Barney Gavin taking a gunny sack from the back of Uncle Jack's wagon.

"Phil's flasks," she guessed immediately. She rushed down the steps to alert Phil or Uncle Jack.

Mother caught her as she dashed past and held her firmly by the shoulder.

"Nora! Behave like a lady," she whispered. "You can't go bursting into that conversation that the men are having. And hold on to your hat. It will blow away again if you aren't careful."

Mrs. Murdock smiled graciously. "Nora," she said. "What a lovely name. "Nora." She repeated the name. "I do hope we will become good friends."

Mother squeezed her shoulder.

"Ah—Thank you, ma'am." Nora answered, demurely lowering her eyes.

"That stinking Barney," she thought. "He's as mean as ever."

She rarely saw Barney any more. He had moved out of the bunkhouse within a week after the incident of the prayers, and had taken a job herding sheep out in the Coyote Hills. He rarely came to town. The story of the Lord's Prayer had followed him, and the Irish often teasingly reminded him of the two children who had put him in his place. Even three years later, Nora felt a warm glow as she thought of his discomfort.

But now the mean little sneak was back, as underhanded as ever.

Again she tried discreetly to pull away, but Mother held her with a firm grip. Then Uncle Jack and the others were gone, hurrying away toward the wagons, still laughing and teasing each other. Phil, too, had gone to the grove of trees. The children piled into the wagon, filling the seats, screaming with laughter. Even Katie, who usually stayed close to mother, was seated on the wagon and reaching to help Uncle Jack to his high seat.

Nora sighed. It was too late now to tell anyone. Barney would be long gone. She'd just have to wait until they got home and tell Uncle Jack then.

Uncle 'D' came driving up in his buggy and Mrs. Murdock said her goodbyes. She went to meet her husband. Mother, Nora and Aunt Sue climbed into the carriage and settled themselves as Uncle 'D' headed for the ranch.

"Nora, you should have talked more with Mrs. Murdock," said Mother. She was trying to carry on a conversation with you."

"I can't think of anything to say," Nora answered. "I—I—guess I'm afraid I'll say . . . you know, say the—wrong thing."

"Well," said Aunt Sue. "Just say . . . oh, something nice. Something they would like to hear. Something maybe a—little flattering. I find that works very well."

Aunt Sue remained thoughtful for a moment. "Sometimes," she added, "you might point out something helpful. Maybe she dropped a glove, or forgot her prayer book in church," she laughed and patted Nora's hand. "I know the feeling, though. I used to be terribly—bashful—when I was young. Didn't I, Nellie? You remember how I suffered." They smiled at each other, remembering.

"That Ella Murdock is sweet, isn't she?" Aunt Sue asked. "And she has such lovely clothes."

"Beautiful." Mother agreed. "That green skirt and those green glass buttons at her throat and on the wrists of her white blouse. So simple and yet so elegant. Every week she comes in another outfit. And they are all stunning."

"And that little tiny waist of hers doesn't hurt at all," said Aunt Sue. "I swear. I didn't have a waist that small when I was ten years old."

"Every week when she comes to church she has a new outfit," said Mother. "It's always beautiful, and it seems to be the latest in fashion. But," Mother paused, then added. "Have you noticed that—tin pan of a hat she wears?"

Aunt Sue laughed. "Such a narrow crown and then that stiff wide brim. It does look like a tin pan."

Nora thought of Mrs. Murdock's hat. She always wore such lovely gowns but always that same hat. It was strange that she had such a way with her dresses but never seemed to think of her hat.

The two women were still talking and Nora half heard that Violet Weldon, who did housework around town, had told Sue that much of the Murdocks' boxes and luggage had been lost when they moved from back East. Although they had put tracers on it, some of their things were still missing but every week or so another box would show up. Much of Mrs. Murdock's clothing had finally arrived, but Mr. Murdock had to go out and purchase a new suit last week because none of his wardrobe had been found. It was truly an inconvenience.

"And the new pro-hi in town," said Mother. "He seems quite devout."

"Yes," Sue answered. "He's a nice looking fellow." She paused. "I don't understand it. I thought those pro-hi's sort of worked on the sly. How do they expect to catch anyone if everyone in town knows who they are? He's supposed to be working for the County Assessor, but everyone knows he's a government man. He even has his name printed on the Assessor's door. It's Anthony

Blaine, but I haven't seen him doing any assessing."

"I know," Mother agreed. "I wondered about that, too. We all knew that the last fellow was a pro-hi. I wonder why he left so soon."

They shook their heads in wonder.

Nora spoke up. "That new fellow," she said. "Mr. Blaine. Anthony Blaine. What's wrong with him? Is it hard to be a pro-hi?"

The women looked at each other. They seemed to be searching for an answer. Nora thought that it must be a tragic thing to be a pro-hi. Probably as bad as being a diabetic—that new disease that the teacher's husband had. He had to get a shot every day!

"Well," said Mother carefully. "The—ah, government sent him here. I think he gets paid well, but . . . ah yes, I think it must be a very difficult—position."

"Oh," said Aunt Sue, after a brief pause. "I meant to ask you. Did you look at the Wilding house?"

"Is the Wilding house for sale?" Mother asked.

"No. We looked at Delmar's house and I think we will buy it. It's so close to the school, and it has possibilities."

"Yes. It's a nice place," said Aunt Sue. "And it's bigger than the Wilding house. It has a lovely fenced yard."

"We talked with Delmar's son. He lives in Klamath Falls now and has no intention of coming back. I think he's eager to sell. We've made an offer."

"I'll love it if you move to town," said Sue. "We can see more of each other."

"We are moving to town?" Nora asked in surprise. "I didn't know that. When are we moving?"

"I don't know," Mother answered in a dismissive tone. "We might, if we find a house we like."

"You mean we'll—leave the ranch?"

"Well, no. We won't leave it. But it's pretty hard to get you three in to school everyday and next year Kevin will be going also, so there will be four of you. We'll move back out to the ranch every summer. Why—most of the ranchers with children have a home in town. Some of them live 30 miles away. They have to live in town if the kids are to get an education. That's just the way it is."

Nora fell silent thinking of this new change in their lives. It was true. Most of the children from ranches had a home in town as well as their home out in the country. And it was difficult for her parents to get the children in to school every morning, especially if the snow were deep. And then, someone had to pick them up in the afternoon when school was out. It was a real problem.

They arrived at the ranch and Nora ran to change from her Sunday clothes. Soon Uncle Jack came driving the wagon, loaded with children, into the yard. He was angry and red-faced as he unhitched the team.

"Those blackguards have been at it again," he announced. "Weren't the gates wide open and the cattle crowding around the new hay stacks as we came from town? Sure, we'll have to hire a man just to stand guard up there."

"Didn't you close the gates as you went in to church?" Mother asked.

"We did indeed," said Jack. "But we had the job to do again just now as we came down." He shook his head in anger and frustration.

The men retreated into the bunkhouse to change their clothes before they started the chores. Mother and Aunt Sue were already hard at work in the kitchen preparing for the Sunday meal.

Nora decided it was not a good time to tell Uncle Jack about Barney Gavin taking the flasks. She went instead to find Phil.

Late in the afternoon, Neil Larkin and Dennis Halloran returned from town. They brought Dennis's brother Tom with them.

Mother pushed the chairs together and Katie hurriedly added several plates to the table where the adults would be gathered. The children were to be seated together at a smaller table that had been set up in the wide front hallway.

As the diners came to their chairs at the tables it was determined that there was an extra place at the grownups' table and Uncle Jack pulled Nora in to sit beside him.

"Here is the sharpest one among us," Uncle Jack announced. "Didn't she catch that old devil, Barney Gavin, up to his old tricks again."

Nora tried to catch his eye. Mother didn't know that he went looking for flasks during benediction, but Neil Larkin saved the day.

"Listen now," he said. "I think we have the answer to the mysterious open gates."

"What? What?" Uncle Jack paused, the gravy dish held in mid-air. "Do you know who is opening the gates to the haystacks?"

"Listen to Tom Halloran here. He works at the mill."

30

Tom reached to take the gravy boat.

"Aye," he said. "Sure, don't the fellows all get paid every two weeks? Those who need a bottle, sure, they have it ordered. They don't want to be seen buying it outright from Manny Dietz. Someone might see them and arrest them both. So, every payday Manny must find a way to deliver the booze in some inconspicuous way. The latest plan, and a good one it is too: Manny puts the bottle down under one of your haystacks. He drives back to town and goes innocently about his business. The buyer, later in the night, goes down and retrieves it. Sure, haven't I heard them speak of it down at work."

"It's under the first haystack," the buyer is told. "Or under the second one, or even as far out as the third one. The fools never thought to close a gate behind them."

Tom paused to look around the table at the rapt faces listening to him. They were impressed at his knowledge, and at the plan.

"Aye," he continued. "And sometimes doesn't old Manny even leave the bottles in a sack under the bridges? I've heard them talking. 'The first bridge,' they will say. Or 'the second,' or even the fence posts along the railroad trail. That fence is yours, of course, but they count off the posts and find their bottle whereever Manny stashes it. Why, they've been using that edge of your ranch for months. It's only a short distance from town and very handy for all concerned."

"My word!" said Aunt Sue.

"They certainly have a lot of gall!" Mother voiced her indignation.

Uncle Jack sat strangely quiet, his face thoughtful. One eyebrow moved up toward his hair line. All waited for his pronouncement.

"When is the next payday at the mill?" he asked Tom Halloran.

"Why, the first of the month."

Uncle Jack nodded.

"I'll take care of it," he said quietly. He changed the subject.

"Nora," he said. "Tell them about that fine man who gave you a nickel in church this morning."

The first of September was always exciting. School started. The rodeo occurred every year at that time. The town was filled with strangers, cowboys, ranchers, judges, carnival people, and visitors from all over Oregon. The single hotel and all the boarding houses were filled with visitors, and nearly every home in town hosted relatives and friends for the three-day rodeo celebration.

Best of all, Dad came down from the mountains where he had been herding the sheep on the summer range.

The bleating, restless band of sheep was turned into the recently hayed meadow where the animals soon settled down into a quiet, contented herd.

September first was also payday at the mill.

Nora was playing hopscotch when Uncle Jack called her to come to the blacksmith shop. She thought she was needed to work the bellows, but instead Uncle Jack gave her his field glasses.

"Climb up there now, on the roof," he said. "Watch up there toward that line of willows. If you see a big black touring car driving out from town, you call me." He gave her the binoculars and boosted her up onto the tarpaper roof. "I'll be down there working on the bridge near the barn. Just watch and call me if you see anything. We'll catch those blackguards that have been fooling with the gates."

He went back to the bridge building.

Nora watched through the glasses. When she looked through one end, everything seemed much closer and the leaves and branches of those far-away willow trees seemed to move right into the yard. When she turned the glasses to look through the other set of lenses, things moved far away. She looked at her feet and her legs had grown so long that it seemed a mile to her toes. That long, skinny extension of overall-covered leg that reached to her bare feet almost frightened her. She wiggled her toes to be sure it was her feet she was looking at. When those far away toes signaled back to her, she flipped the field glasses around quickly and tried to forget how –unnatural—her own body had looked.

She studied the hills that had somehow moved so much closer. She examined the cap of rimrock that topped each hill. She brought her sights down to the mouth of the canyons and the roads that ran out from between the high cliffs. She found herself fascinated by the houses at the edge of town.

And then a big black car came down between the houses and turned left along the alkali road below town. It proceeded slowly and stopped cautiously a couple of times as though it were afraid to proceed.

She called to Uncle Jack.

Jack came running. He climbed up beside her on the hot roof and put the glasses to his eyes. Nora could no longer see the car—only a dark speck that inched along toward the West. Sure enough, the speck turned toward the green meadow where the sheep were grazing.

Uncle Jack gradually tensed and turned to Nora.

"By golly, I think we've got them," he said. He was already clambering down from the roof.

"Come, now." He reached to help her. "Go back to your hopscotch, and say nothing about this to your mother. We don't want to worry her."

He smiled broadly as he hurried to the barn. Soon he rode out across the flat on his bay gelding headed for the meadow's edge. Nora saw the black speck now headed east, toward town.

"Uncle Jack won't get there in time to catch him," she told herself.

Nora was gathering eggs when Uncle Jack came riding back an hour later. He looked happy indeed. He lifted a burlap sack down from the saddle. It clinked as he stowed it behind the grain bin. She was about to ask him about its contents when he turned to her.

"I missed the fellow," he said. "But I shut the gates before the sheep or cows got at the hay." Whistling, he went back to working on the bridge.

That night at supper the men all seemed happy and talkative. Neil Larkin kept repeating himself and Dennis Halloran teased Johnnie Whelan about the widow Shelby until Johnnie left the table.

"They've been drinking," said Dad when the men had all returned to the bunk house.

"Where in the world did they get any whiskey?" asked Mother. "None of them have been off the place for a week or so." She shook her head looking baffled.

Sunday dawned bright and hot. Even the ride into mass in the open buggy was uncomfortable. Nora dreaded having to sit for an hour in the stifling church with everyone else as sweaty and miserable as she.

Mother sat strangely quiet on the ride in from the ranch and she looked somewhat pale as she climbed down from the buggy It was the heat that seemed to be affecting everyone.

As they crossed the road, Nora was stunned to see Johnnie Whelan proudly escorting the Widow Shelby along the sidewalk beside the church. Excitedly, she turned to point the couple out to her mother, but Mother gave her a warning look.

She felt filled with confusion. She had almost done it again. She would never understand what went on in the grownup world. And everyone expected her to know what they wanted or expected. Dismay welled up, making her chest feel constricted.

Many people were visiting outside the church. Mrs. Murdock and her husband greeted Mother who stopped to talk with them. No one was eager to go into the hot church this morning.

"And how are you this morning, Nora?" Mrs. Murdock asked. "It's so nice to see you again."

"Ah, ah, I'm—just fine," Nora answered. She tried frantically to remember what Aunt Sue had told her about carrying on a conversation with adults. Mrs. Murdock looked as though she expected something more from her.

"You are looking very nice, as usual," Nora managed. "That is a lovely dress."

Mrs. Murdock looked pleased indeed.

"Why, thank you Nora," she answered.

"You always look so beautiful," Nora continued. Auntie Sue had said people liked to be flattered.

"That dress you wore last Sunday was—was stunning," she continued. "Those green glass buttons at the throat and at your wrists. It was so simple, yet well—just stunning."

Mrs. Murdock looked delighted, and Mother, too, was pleased. Mother seemed to be almost purring in her ear.

Well! For once she was doing something right—communicating as the grownups expected.

"And that little tiny waist of yours doesn't hurt a bit," Nora felt almost brave as she saw how happy her words made the ladies feel.

"Why, Nora," Mrs. Murdock reached to take her hand. "I should hire you to help me coordinate my wardrobe. You seem to have quite a gift." She was smiling, her face flushed with pleasure. Even Mr. Murdock smiled.

"But why do you always wear that tin-pan of a hat?" Nora continued. "Your gowns are so lovely, and…"

Mother clutched her arm in a painful grip. "NORA!" Mother's voice sounded outraged.

Nora froze. Oh God. She'd done it again! Everything seemed to be going wonderfully well, and then…

The bronze bell atop the steeple rang out, the sound drowning out any further conversation. Mother dragged her up the steps and into the church.

"Why can't you keep that big mouth shut?" she muttered.

This Sunday, Nora didn't have the privilege of sitting next to Anthony Blaine. There was no nickel to put in the collection box, and Mother stood stiff and unforgiving beside her.

Nora sat as though made of stone. She felt chilled although everyone else was visibly affected by the heat. She wished she could hide away. Tears pushed behind her eyes and her chest felt as though a great weight had settled there. She stood, she sat, she knelt with the congregation, but she felt far removed from any of them. She wished she were a jackrabbit out in the desert that could jump away and hide whenever anyone came near.

Benediction was finally over. Mother sat while most of the people left the church.

"She's ashamed to go out," Nora thought. "It's all my fault."

At last Mother rose. She seemed a little shaky. She clutched at Katie and made her way out onto the landing. Nora walked beside her, then stopped to look down at the people eight steps below departing in different directions. The Widow Shelby was holding Johnnie Whelan's arm and smiling up at him.

Suddenly, Mother pushed her. She went flying off the landing, crying out, hitting briefly on the third step, then sailing past all the others to land and slide on the gravel at the foot of the stairs.

Her head, her face, her arm and her knees swelled with agony, but her heart was breaking. Mother had pushed her! Mother had shoved her violently off the steps! She rolled over, shaking. Blood formed on her arm and knees. Her head hurt terribly.

"She pushed me," Nora whispered. "Mother pushed me off the steps." The tears burst forth.

"No. No." Anthony Blaine had appeared from nowhere. "Sit still for a minute. Don't try to move." He had his arms around her. His voice sounded comforting.

"She pushed me," Nora insisted. "She hates me. I'm always embarrassing her!"

"No. No," Anthony Blaine said again. "She fell. She didn't mean to bump you."

"Mother fell?" Nora turned frightened eyes.

"I think she—ah—fainted," the man said. "It was terribly hot there in church."

Others came crowding around. They asked if they could help. They produced handkerchiefs to wipe away the blood. They tried to assure her that her mother would be alright.

Nora fought to see over them to where her mother lay, up on the church entrance. People crowded around her also. Mrs. Murdock led a crying Katie away and Uncle Jack and Mr. Murdock bent over Mother, rubbing her hands, fanning her, trying to restore consciousness.

"She'll be alright," Mr. Blaine kept telling Nora. "It's just the heat. She'll be fine."

Nora pushed herself shakily to her feet. She could see Mother moving now, and trying to sit up. Nora wanted to run to her but she found herself trembling. She couldn't trust herself to take a step. Mr. Blaine took his coat off and put it around her shoulders.

"Oh," cried Nora. "I'll get blood all over your coat. My arm is a mess."

"Nora," her Mother called in a shaky voice. "Nora? Are you alright?"

Uncle Jack came hurrying down the steps. He stopped to look at Nora.

"Great God, child!" he said. "You look like you came through the corn shucker."

"She was pushed down the steps when her mother fell," Mr. Blaine explained. "I think she'll be alright. The gravel there tore up her face."

"Great God!" said Uncle Jack again. "We should have skipped mass altogether this morning. He attempted to give Nora a hug but backed off for fear he might hurt her further.

"I'm just going now to get the buggy," he explained. "I'll be taking them both home. The mother wants no part of calling a doctor."

"Wait," said Mr. Blaine. "I have my car here. I'll give them a ride. It will be quicker, and easier, too—easier to get in and out of."

Auntie Sue came to ride with them. She sat in the back seat with Mother. Nora rode in front with Mr. Blaine. Her face, her arm, the palms of her hands, her knees, all seemed on fire, but she felt a thrill of excitement in spite of her pain. Riding in a car was an adventure.

The hired girl and Aunt Sue helped Mother into the bedroom, but Mr. Blaine took a basin of hot water and a bar of soap and carefully cleaned all the dirt from Nora's injuries.

"You are going to be all swollen on the right side of your face," he told her. "And you'll probably be limping around with big scabs on your knees."

Mr. Blaine told her he had a daughter just about her age. She lived in California with her mother, but they hoped to move up and join him here soon.

Mother was feeling a little better and Aunt Sue invited Mr. Blaine to stay for supper. All the men came in quietly, on their best behavior. They had heard of Nora's mishap and told her how sorry they were that such a thing had happened to her. They seemed to like Mr. Blaine and were soon laughing and joking with him.

"Call me Tony," he insisted. Somehow the name fit him.

"He's a hell of a nice fellow," said Uncle Jack as he watched Tony drive away toward town. "Too bad he's a pro-hi."

Tony stopped by often after that first Sunday. He gave the children rides home from school and brought Nora a jar of salve that he found at the drug store. The strange smelling mixture seemed to help the tight itchy feeling of Nora's abrasions.

Every couple of weeks Uncle Jack would have Nora or Phil sit, with his binoculars, on the roof of the blacksmith shop and watch for cars from town that might go over to the upper gates of the field. If they saw a car headed that direction, or if one stopped, they would tell Uncle Jack, who soon went off on horseback to deal with the shady fellow who was trespassing. Usually he came back carrying a burlap bag and smiling in a contented fashion.

"Where in the world are they getting the booze?" Dad would ask. "I swear, Jack must have a still of his own somewhere here on the ranch."

One day Nora spotted a car from town that stopped by the second bridge. She alerted Uncle Jack who climbed up on the roof beside her and watched the fellow himself. Soon he rode off, a look of anticipation on his face.

When he returned he looked quite sour.

"Did you catch him?" Nora asked.

"No. No. He was long gone."

Nora shrugged. Uncle Jack never seemed to 'catch' them. He just went and closed the gates, she thought.

Neil Halloran walked into the barn as Uncle Jack unsaddled his horse.

"Did ye have any luck?" Halloran asked.

"Hell no!" Uncle Jack sounded disgusted. "It was some clown drowning a bunch of kittens."

Anthony Blaine stopped by to take Nora to ride with him when he went to appraise a farm or a new homestead. She couldn't run and play with the other children at school until her injuries healed. Mother seemed pleased that she had this outlet for her energy.

Nora found Mr. Blaine easy to talk to. She had to call him Mr. Blaine because her mother insisted that it was not respectful to call an adult by his first name.

But she told him everything. She told him even more than she told Uncle Jack and he seemed to enjoy talking to her.

She told him about Barney Gavin. She explained how she and Phil had learned the terrible version of the Lord's Prayer and made Barney leave. She told him about Barney stealing the flasks and said she heard Neil Halloran and Johnnie Whelan talking about some fellow who had a big still out in the Coyote Hills. They figured that Barney was selling him any flasks he could find. She told him about Johnnie Whelan who was now 'sparking' the widow Shelby. She told him that her parents might buy a house in town and they would be moving there before winter set in.

Then she thought to tell him of Neil Halloran's brother, Tom, who worked at the mill. Tom had solved the problem of the open gates around the haystacks that allowed the cattle to get in and tear up the stacks.

She told Mr. Blaine about the bootleggers in town who dropped the whiskey off down by her Dad's haystacks or under the bridges on the ranch.

But, Uncle Jack was taking care of that problem.

"Do I remind you of your own little girl?" Nora asked one day.

"Yes. Very much."

"I hope she comes to live with you soon," said Nora. "I'd like to have her for a friend."

"She'd like that very much," said Mr. Blaine. "I've told her all about you in my letters."

"I don't have many friends at school," Nora admitted, her voice sad.

"Why not?"

"The town kids don't like the Irish much. They are mean. They call us 'greenhorns,' and 'spuds'. The Irish kids are my friends—and sometimes I talk to Gwendolyn Dietz."

"Gwendolyn likes the Irish kids?"

Nora hesitated. "Well. She doesn't have too many friends, either. The kids tease her. You know, they . . . they chant, *'Your daddy is a bootlegger. Your daddy is a bootlegger!'* Like they holler at me, *"Your daddy is a sheepherder! Your daddy is a sheepherder!"*

Blaine turned to look at the child. He couldn't think of a reply.

"Do you think I talk too much?" Nora asked suddenly.

"Why—ah, no," said Mr. Blaine. He smiled and shook his head.

Nora sighed. "Mother thinks I talk too much," she said. "Sometimes she calls me 'Big Mouth'."

When they returned from their trips around the countryside, Mother always insisted that Mr. Blaine stay for supper. He often helped with the chores and the men liked and respected him. They asked him to pick up their mail in town, or buy them cigarette 'makings,' or run some other small errands that would save them a trip from the ranch.

One evening, as they finished their meal, Mr. Blaine took out his handkerchief and wiped at the perspiration on his forehead. Nora immediately ran to the pump and brought him a fresh glass of water.

"Why, thank you." He looked surprised.

"Do you feel alright?" Nora asked, concern evident in her voice.

The others at the table looked on, not understanding.

"Yes. Yes. I feel great," he answered hesitantly. "Do I look—strange?"

"No . . ." Nora sounded uncertain. "I just wonder, though—does being a pro-hi make you—make you real sick sometimes?"

"NORA!" Mother's voice exploded into the stillness. "Nora. Go to your room—right this minute. To your room!"

Nora recoiled in confusion.

Oh, God! She had done it again. What had she said now that had everyone so upset? Mother's face was red with fury. Dad sat with his mouth open. The others around the table seemed equally stunned. Even Mr. Blaine looked terribly uncomfortable.

Tears welled behind her eyes. Her legs turned to stiff pokers. She felt it an effort to walk. She lowered her head and started for the stairway, aware of the stretching silence around the table. She would go to her room—and she would never come out again.

"Wait!" Uncle Jack spoke.

"No!" Mother's voice was strident. "She is to go to her room—now!"

"I think we are all—at cross-purposes," Uncle Jack crossed the room in two long strides and stopped Nora on the bottom step of the stairs. He looked ill at ease and unsure. He never interfered when Mother disciplined the children.

"Nora," his voice sounded reassuring. His hand on her arm gave her courage.

"Nora? Do you understand what a pro-hi is?"

Nora swallowed, twice, before she could answer. She didn't want to sound like a whining baby.

"I don't know what kind of a disease it is," she answered at last. "I think it's pretty bad though. Dutch Ferris is an 'epileptic.' That other fellow is a 'diabetic.' But they can't help it," she added loyally, the tears starting in earnest, "and neither can Mr. Blaine."

She pulled away and ran stumbling up the stairs.

"Oh, my word," said Mother. She rose from her chair and looked around the table, her face registering her dismay. She started to speak, then changed her mind and hastened across the room and up the stairs.

"The poor child," she said.

The next few days brought a terrible tragedy to the town. Both the Pembroke brothers died.

The brothers were ranchers who lived eight miles north of town. They were quiet, hard working bachelors who lived together in a neat little cabin they had built themselves.

They were respected by their neighbors and both were helpful and unassuming. They came willingly to assist at barn raisings. They often helped some unfortunate harvest his crops. Now they were suddenly dead in a terrible and double tragedy.

"Bad booze," the men said.

"Poisoned whiskey," the newspaper warned.

Nora shivered when she saw the coffins sitting side by side in the funeral home. Somehow, death seemed more real to her as she stared at the two wooden boxes. She hoped they were both in heaven. The thought comforted her.

A few days later, Nora loitered in Jordan's general store waiting for Mother to pick out a dress length. She wandered over to the grocery side looking at the beans, the crackers and the dry onions that were displayed in huge barrels near the counter.

She drifted toward a display of leather harnesses hanging on the far wall. She admired a lovely bridle, studded with silver conches and intricate carving.

Outside, beyond the dock, the strange square produce truck that she had seen several weeks before, drove in and backed up to unload. The driver climbed down and Herb Jordan rushed out the door, looking surprised and somewhat upset.

Nora stepped out onto the dock and stood between two huge empty barrels that had been rolled out of the store.

"Benny!" Jordan demanded of the weary driver. "What are you doing here?"

"What the hell do you think?" the man answered. "Where is Manny?"

"We—well, under the circumstances, we—didn't expect you."

"Well, I'm here. Send someone down to get Manny. I have to have some help unloading."

Mrs. Dorsey and Eva Larson were already approaching the truck.

"Oh, I'm glad I saw you drive in," said Eva. "What have you got for us today?"

The driver was already rolling up the canvas side curtains. "I have all sorts of fresh fruit," he assured the women. "Just came in on the train from California last night. I loaded up and drove almost seven hours so everything would still be fresh for you ladies."

Benny pulled a wet sheet of muslin from the top of the produce in his truck. Bushels of apples, tomatoes, grapes, and melons were exposed. Boxes of orange carrots and green vegetables, looking as fresh as if they had just been picked, sparkled in the sunlight. Two huge stalks of half-ripe bananas hung suspended from the ceiling of the truck bed.

The women clapped their hands, laughing in their excitement. "They look like they were just gathered fresh from the garden," Mrs. Dorsey exclaimed. "Jordan always has the loveliest vegetables."

"That's because I spread chipped ice over them every couple of hours as I come across the desert," Benny explained.

"Ladies. Ladies." Herb Jordan said. "Just give us a half hour or so to get these things unloaded. Come around and into the store. We can't sell them to you from the truck. We can't have you standing out there in the sun. Come around and into the store."

Manny Dietz's big touring car hurried around the corner. Manny parked at an angle and hurried to help unload the truck. Herb Jordan and his clerk carried in the lovely fruits and vegetables but Nora noted that Manny and the man called Benny seemed to be unloading heavy boxes which they carried into the adjoining shed. When Manny stumbled and fell with one wooden box, Benny swore at him. He hurried to help Manny lift the box and held the door of the storage space ajar as Dietz struggled in with his load.

"You broke two of them bottles," Benny stormed. "You can take it out of your share." Showing his disgust he threw aside a broken flask.

Nora backed away toward the doorway.

She recognized the smell of whiskey. She certainly recognized the sight of a broken flask.

Herb Jordan pushed past her, carrying a stalk of bananas.

She must run and tell Mother that all this lovely fresh fruit was here. That would save Mother a trip in from the ranch, since she could select the things she wanted while she was here. She started across the store.

"You live out there near the Pembrokes, don't you?" the clerk asked a sun-browned man who was checking his order.

"Poison whiskey," a neighbor said emphatically. "One of them boys got deathly sick, lost his eyesight, curled up like a sick cat. His brother went for help, but by the time he got back with Dr. Phelps he was so sick himself he couldn't walk and his brother was dead. The second fellow only lasted a few hours. Doc tried to find out where they got the whiskey though. The fellow kept sayin' something about Winnemucca so Doc thinks it must have come from over that way."

"Yeah. But who knows for sure?" the clerk said. "Old Manny will have a few lean months after this scare. Who would want to take a chance buying whiskey when a terrible thing like this has happened?"

"Well. I don't want to be next," the neighbor said. "Them were two damn decent fellows, and they didn't die a pretty death. It was terrible. You could hear them screaming . . ." his voice trailed off.

Nora ran back to the yard goods counter. The images of the blind, screaming, dying men haunted her for days.

The tragedies continued.

Ella Bright Sky, an Indian woman from Pine Creek, died of alcohol poisoning, and then Larry Larkin, a young immigrant from County Cork, died out in Willow Valley, also from poisoned liquor.

Irishmen from all over the county and beyond, came into town for Larkin's funeral. Dressed in their dark suits, they made a somber group as they packed the small church and marched four abreast down the center aisle to receive communion.

Then the men walked, carrying the coffin, a full mile to the cemetery where many of them had gathered the night before to dig the grave.

Nora walked with her family feeling cold and somehow lonely and she was stricken to see several of the grown men crying there at the gravesite. She shuddered as they passed the fresh, newly mounded graves of the other recent victims.

The sudden terrible deaths drove the little town to the verge of panic. There were changes everywhere.

Manny Dietz was no longer seen walking the streets and talking to the men from the sawmill. There were no flasks in the alleys behind the pool halls. Pay days at the mill were quiet and uneventful.

Also, there were no more open gates at the haystacks in the meadow and Uncle Jack no longer had Nora sit on the roof of the blacksmith shop with the binoculars to watch for cars from town.

Sheriff Hodges arrested a man out in the Coyote Hills. The fellow was said to be operating one of the biggest stills ever found in Lake County. Anthony Blaine said it only made sense to look near a spring because one had to have water to run a still, and there weren't too many fresh water springs out in the Coyote Hills.

Sheriff Hodges became an instant hero around town. People saluted him wherever he went. They called to him and crossed the street to shake his hand. They offered to buy him coffee, and left cakes and other treats at his office. They all felt 'safer' somehow, even those who didn't drink, now that the big still in the Coyote Hills was shut down.

The first weeks of October passed swiftly. The days were wonderfully warm but the nights were getting much colder. Dad and Uncle Jack started the sheep out to winter in the high desert country, and the Teachers Institute meeting would soon give the children a week off from school.

On Tuesday the bell rang out for the end of afternoon recess and the children trooped toward the school house, reluctant to be leaving the warm playground.

Teddy Gibbs and Clyde Turner hurried from across the street. They had been stealing apples from Nathan Moser's yard and they chewed happily on the fruit while hiding spare apples in their pockets.

Most of the students had entered the building when a sudden commotion erupted on the low hill above the school

Two dogs barked wildly and a man's voice could be heard shouting and swearing.

Suddenly two half-grown pigs rushed down the pathway. One veered off up the street but the second ran straight across the road and entered the school yard.

The animal stopped, grunting and swinging its head from side to side. Then it started chasing Teddy Gibbs, who held a half-eaten apple in his hand. Teddy screamed and ran. The teacher paused on the porch and she started screaming as the pig knocked Teddy to the ground and snatched the apple from the boy's hand.

Nora realized that she could not make it to the schoolhouse door. She saw the squealing pig turn and head her way, and she swung up the steps on the playground slide. Clyde Turner climbed frantically behind her.

From the platform at the top of the slide, she looked down to see Teddy, his nose bleeding, howling in fright and pain as he climbed up onto the wide boardwalk and ran to Miss Burcham. She dragged him inside the door. The pig appeared to rush after the boy, but stopped at the walk. It squealed and grunted wildly as it put its front feet up on the worn boards and tried to hoist its hindquarters up over the high step.

Claude Elliot had been riding his bicycle around the school yard and as he coasted toward the entrance, Miss Burcham shouted at him.

"Get away," she screamed through the partially closed door. "Ride up and get Sheriff Hodges. That pig has rabies. Hurry! Hurry!"

Claude rode off, his legs pumping frantically.

Nora clung to the steel pipes that supported the slide. She felt strangely faint.

Rabies!

Rabies was a terrible plague. All the stockmen lived in fear of the rabid coyotes that sometimes appeared in the wilderness and threatened their herds of sheep and other animals. A single rabid coyote could bite and infect dozens of sheep. Cattle, dogs, pigs and other animals were also at risk. All the infected animals had to be killed.

But how had these pigs come in contact with a rabid coyote? Coyotes were never seen in town.

The pig squealed and grunted. Froth dripped from its mouth. It seemed to be half covered in some milky slime that slithered from its shoulders as it pushed itself along several yards of the board walk, its front feet up on the uneven lumber, its back legs still firmly on the ground.

The second pig suddenly turned back. Nora watched as it rushed down the street then veered to the right and ran up onto Mrs. Elder's side porch. It smashed its head through the lower portion of the screen door leading into her kitchen.

Now the pig in the school yard turned from its attempt to climb up on the board walk. Squealing, it ran to the foot of the slide ladder. The animal appeared to be trying to climb up the steps that the two children had just climbed. Its hooves scraped and rattled on the metal treads. It grunted and squealed in frustration.

Nora looked down into the pigs open, greedy mouth. She saw the white teeth, the red tongue and throat. She clutched the steel bars with all her strength.

Clyde Turner turned to her in wild panic. He tried to speak but no sound came from his terrified lips. He looked with horror at the animal stretching toward them.

With a trembling hand, Nora reached to take the half-eaten apple from Clyde. She dropped it to the earth below. The pig sprang away and crushed the apple in one vicious bite. It returned immediately to the base of the slide and continued its efforts to reach the children.

Nora felt stiff with fright. She looked at the menacing pig. She looked at Clyde and motioned to his pocket. The boy hastened to produce the two remaining apples which he dropped. The pig dashed to consume the fruit and came sniffing and grunting, back to its position below them. It snorted and wheezed, then backed away.

Clyde looked to Nora with terrified eyes.

"I think he can smell that you don't have any more," she told the boy. "I think he'll go away."

The children looked back at the pig below their feet. It slid almost wearily down from the metal steps and lay in the dirt beside the walkway. It grunted a few times and wagged its head from side to side. Nora had never seen a pig act quite that way before. They had pigs at the ranch and she knew that if they were rushing for food, the animals could knock a kid down. This pig looked—looked exhausted. And it smelled so bad. So different! The animal hadn't tried to bite Benny, she reasoned. It just seemed to want the apple he was eating.

Seth Dohering was still shouting and swearing at his dogs. They now stood, barking, on Mrs. Elder's side porch. The dogs ignored their master.

The sheriff's car came hurtling down the road. It plowed to a dusty halt in the street and Sheriff Hodges jumped from the driver's seat, gun in hand.

He cocked the gun and looked up at the children cowering on the slide platform.

"Stay where you are," he directed them. "You'll be safe up there." He approached the pig very cautiously.

"Don't shoot the poor thing," said Nora. "I don't think that pig has rabies. I think it's drunk."

Hodges looked astounded. He searched Nora's face, pity in his eyes.

People gathered on the walk across the street. They shouted and pointed.

"Rabid pigs," they cried. "We need another gun."

Nora was forced to shout above the growing noise.

"That pig is drunk," she insisted. "Can't you smell that stuff that's smeared all over him?"

Mr. Dohering left his dogs and came raging across the street.

"Don't shoot my pig," his voice was almost hysterical. He ran from the walk and threw himself down on the lethargic animal.

"Watch out there, Dohering," the sheriff shouted a warning. "You could be in real danger. I think that animal is rabid."

"No! No! It is not!" Dohering seemed almost in tears. "Let me explain."

The pig struggled to its feet, squealing and suddenly energized. Dohering threw his arms around the animal again, shielding it from Hodges gun.

Nora shuddered at the slime that had been transferred from the pig to Dohering's clothing.

"We can't take a chance," Hodges roared. "Get the hell out of the way."

"No! No!" Dohering begged, hugging the pig even tighter.

Nora let go of the pipe in her hands. She found her fingers stiff and hard to move. She hadn't realized how tightly she had gripped those railings. She eased herself around Clyde Turner and slowly descended the steps.

Hodges stood rigid, shouting at Dohering who refused to move away from his pig. The teacher and several of the students had their faces pressed against the glass inside the windows of the school.

Nora moved hesitantly beyond the slide and stepped quickly up on the walk beside Hodges as he raised his gun. She grabbed him by the sleeve of his shirt and jerked.

"Mr. Hodges," she said politely. "Sheriff. Just look."

Hodges swung angrily toward her.

"My God! Listen child . . ." he began, his voice rough with concern.

"Look," she pointed across the street. "Look at those chickens. Chickens don't get rabies, do they?"

Hodges looked.

Three fat brown hens seemed to struggle as they eased down the path from the hill. They staggered. They fell. They rose again and made their labored way along. One hen spread her wings half open and used the tip of the wings to support herself so she could remain upright. A fourth chicken appeared, walked uncertainly forward, then suddenly fell and made no move to arise. A proud rooster walked unsteadily along the bank, rose, stretching his neck, trying to crow. He fell suddenly and slid down into the ditch.

Mrs. Elder stood weeping over a chicken she held in her arms.

"The poor thing," she sobbed. "My lovely hens. My screen door is ruined, and now my lovely hens. I sell the eggs, you know. Someone is going to pay for all this!"

"What the hell?" Sheriff Hodges breathed in disbelief.

"They're *drunk*," Dohering cried. "I tried to tell you. Your brother, Emil, he poured his mash out there on the hill this morning. I saw him. He threw that mash out there and then the sun got hot, and it started to—you know—to ferment. The pigs smelled it and broke out of the pen. And them chickens too, I guess. "

Sheriff Hodges turned slowly, disbelief in his eyes. He looked at Dohering, who held the now quiet pig in his arms.

"Emil?" he asked. "My brother, Emil? He threw mash out up there on the hill?" There was horror and disbelief in his voice

Dohering lowered his voice. He glanced around to be sure no one could hear.

"Yeah. Yeah. Well. No one else knows who did it. I didn't want to tell you. He's my friend, you know."

Hodges' shoulders sagged. He turned slowly away and walked across the street. Nora walked beside him. She wanted to reach and take his hand. She knew he felt sad.

Behind them, Dohering was calling to his friends to come and help and soon the men were carrying the pig to the pigpen behind Dohering's house. They went then to rescue the pig with its head stuck in Mrs. Elder's screen door.

Hodges and Nora climbed the incline, stepping around the suffering chickens. When they reached the flat above they saw the remnants of the mash that had been thrown out in the cool of the morning and had caused such chaos as it heated in the sun. The smell of alcohol was everywhere. Nora saw puddles of material that looked somewhat like thin oatmeal. Small bubbles formed and gradually, very slowly worked their way upward through the mash and quietly burst. A few chickens still scratched and pecked at the unexpected food.

Emil Hodges, a slight built, unassuming little man, worked with a shovel and a bucket, scraping up the offending mash. He looked at his brother, guilt reflected in his eyes.

Nora had never even known that they were related.

"I'm going to have to arrest you," Sheriff Hodges said.

Emil didn't answer. He bent his head and looked at his shoes.

"Let me finish up here," he spoke at last. "I— I'm—sorry."

The sheriff nodded. He turned and started back down the hill. His shoulders sagged. He sighed heavily.

Two men were nailing boards on the fence of the pigpen, repairing the hole from which the pigs had escaped.

Seth Dohering, filled with energy, came striding up the hill.

"We better take care of these chickens," he said.

Sheriff Hodges looked at him, not comprehending.

"If we don't kill these—ah, these sick ones, they will die and the meat will be no good. Chop their heads off and let them bleed out and they will be fine for cooking. I already talked to Mrs. Elder. She knows it has to be done. She's all torn up over her screen door and now some of her chickens . . ."

"What screen door?" the sheriff asked. He seemed overwhelmed.

"Well," Dohering explained. "Mrs. Elder, she was cookin' a pot roast. It was damn hot there in the kitchen, so she opened her inside door but hooked the screen door and went on with her cookin'. I guess my drunk pig smelled that pot roast and he just plum stuck his head through the screen—tryin' to get inside—you see what I'm sayin'?"

Sheriff Hodges looked numb. He shook his head, then nodded his understanding.

"We'll take care of it," Dohering assured him. "And we'll pay for the screen door, too. So if she asks you—just tell her…"

The sheriff nodded again and started on across the sidewalk. He put his gun into the car and was about to get in himself when Miss Burcham called to him from the school porch and asked him to give Teddy Gibbs a ride home. The boy was pale and shaken and seemed grateful to be climbing into the sheriff's car.

The dismissal bell for the school rang and soon all the children came pouring out of the school. They rushed off in all directions, eager to share the excitement of the day with their parents. Nora realized that she could have, probably should have, gone back into the school when she climbed down from the slide.

Sheriff Hodges looked at her. His eyes seemed weary and defeated.

"I guess you probably got some real lessons today," he said. He seemed extremely weary as he eased himself into the car.

Nora struggled to find a suitable answer. She didn't want anyone to call her 'Big Mouth' again. The sheriff looked so sad, and defeated. She leaned close.

"I think you are the bravest man I ever saw," she said.

The sheriff looked startled. He lowered his head, then raised it and opened his lips to speak. Instead, he swallowed and remained silent. He reached to touch Nora on the shoulder, then slowly he drove away in the warm afternoon sunshine.

Nora watched the retreating car until it was almost out of sight.

"I think I said the right thing that time," she whispered to herself.

Anthony Blaine arrived soon after school was out. They put Phil's bike in the back seat and Mr. Blaine drove them to the ranch. Nora told him of the adventures of the afternoon. Phil was jealous that he had been in class and hadn't had the opportunity to see the mash that was scattered around the hill, or see the chickens staggering around, or the drunken pigs. He did feel bad that Mrs. Elder was crying over her screen door and her chickens. When they reached home Nora told the story again to her mother, to Dad, and to the men. She wished Uncle Jack were there so she could tell him, but he was trailing the sheep out to the desert.

It was almost dark when Tom Halloran came to visit. He told them that Sheriff Hodges had, indeed, arrested his brother. He had no choice. How could people trust him if he made exceptions?

Word had traveled fast around the small town. Everyone knew the story before the sheriff ever went back to pick up his errant brother. As he drove through town with his prisoner, no one stopped and stared. One man bent down to tie his shoe, which didn't need tying, and several others lowered their heads in serious conversation as the sheriff's car, carrying his brother, went toward the courthouse. Emil was lodged in the jail in the courthouse basement.

Seth Dohering hadn't even changed his dirty shirt but went immediately to work salvaging Mrs. Elder's chickens. He set a huge boiler from Emil Hodges house out in the yard and filled it with water. He and the neighbor men built a fire under it and soon had a boiling bath in which they dipped the chickens they had killed. They then stripped the feathers easily from the dead hens and carried the naked birds into Emil's home to finish cleaning them. Every neighboring household had a fine dinner of chicken and dumplings.

Tom Halloran became a frequent visitor at the ranch in the days that followed. Mother invited him for supper several times a week. He would walk the three miles from the mill and always bring the latest news from town. He learned things that were never printed in the newspaper.

Both of Seth Dohering pigs had survived and most of Mrs. Elder's chickens. Teddy Gibbs had become somewhat of a celebrity and was loving the attention. Teddy Gibbs and Clyde Turner both apologized for stealing apples, but Nathan Moser said they could have all the apples they wanted from his yard. They could come and get them any time. They didn't have to steal them.

A few days later, Tom Halloran arrived with a new bit of news. They sent the town marshal down to gather evidence from Emil Hodges' home where he was supposedly bootlegging. He couldn't find a thing.

Seth Dohering and his friends had hired a lawyer who claimed that his client, Emil Hodges, was falsely imprisoned on a misunderstanding.

The judge was scheduled to leave town for several weeks so he called a hearing for early Saturday morning. Tom Halloran had conveniently arrived at the court house in time to sit in on the hearing.

Nora listened attentively as Halloran told his story. She tried to understand all of this juggling that went on in the adult world but she wasn't sure she quite grasped all the details.

One lawyer had called Mrs. Elder, who testified about her dead chickens and her ruined screen door which had been replaced by a brand new one the next day after the pig had tried to invade her kitchen. Mr. Dohering and his friends had installed the new door and had killed, defeathered and cleaned nine of her chickens that would have otherwise been lost. They had paid her for the dead chickens and had offered to pay for any eggs that she might have sold, but she refused to take any money for the eggs. They had all been very kind. No, she didn't think Emil Hodges was a bootlegger. She never heard of anything so ridiculous. He had always been a fine neighbor. Yes, she had heard the rumor that he had poured mash out on the hill above their homes, but again, that was completely ridiculous.

Next, Beulah Moser had been called to testify.

Beulah was thrilled to be the center of attention and gave her testimony in great detail.

She didn't care that the children had stolen apples from her yard. She never canned them anyway. Yes. She had seen the men of the neighborhood taking things out of Emil's house. They brought out a boiler, and made several trips into his house, carrying buckets, to get water for the boiler. They had started a huge fire under the boiler to heat the water. They had been quite noisy but she didn't mind, since Mr. Moser was out there helping the men. She had seen them carrying out boxes that seemed heavy. The boxes could have been filled with flasks, but she didn't actually see any flasks. The men were in and out of Emil's house many times after he had been taken away. They had worked late into the night. Yes. She had seen them stripping the feathers from the chickens after they had been dipped in the scalding water. In fact there were feathers all over her yard that had been blown there by the wind. Yes, she answered for the second time, the wooden boxes that were carried out looked heavy. But it was getting dark and she was busy at her own stove cooking supper, so she didn't watch all the time.

Yes. Some of the men had shovels and she had seen them digging at least one hole. She had heard them digging later, but she didn't know where or why they were digging. No. Her husband hadn't told her what they were burying. She hadn't thought to ask him.

The prosecuting attorney made a big point of the men carrying out the heavy boxes. He also wanted to know why the men were digging holes in the yard late into the night. But none of the men who had done the digging were present at the hearing, and the judge was annoyed and in a hurry.

When they finally called Seth Dohering, he seemed able to clarify everything.

"Sure," he said. "They dug a hole, or maybe two. What were they supposed to do? Let all those guts they took out of the chickens just sit around and smell? They buried them and what was left of that mash that Emil scraped up from the hill."

"Yes," he admitted. "They had carried several boxes out of Emil's house. They broke the crates up and used them to build the fire with. They had to have boiling water to defeather the chickens didn't they?"

But could he explain the fact that Emil Hodges had dumped mash out on the hill?

"Well, hell," said Dohering. "I was upset, really stressed , because I thought the sheriff was going to kill my pigs. Yes, he had said he saw Emil pouring out the huge tub of mash, but he didn't really know it was Emil. It was 3 o'clock in the morning, for God sake! Some fellow poured it out and he couldn't really see who the guy was. He said 'Emil', because he wanted to get the sheriff's attention. It could have been anyone, but he had to do something to stop the sheriff and make him listen. It could have been the prosecuting attorney himself, for all he knew. Just saw some shadowy guy, moving around in the dark."

"And you just told the sheriff it was his brother so you could get his attention?" the prosecuting attorney asked, his voice heavy with sarcasm and disbelief.

"You damn betcha!" said Dohering. "But it didn't really work. Some kid pointed out the drunk chickens and that's what saved my pigs."

"And where is Sheriff Hodges?" the judge asked. "Didn't you tell him he had to be here to testify?"

The prosecuting attorney looked ill at ease. "I just figured he'd be here," he said. "And he would have been, too, except a load of logs rolled off a truck and tore up the bridge out at Deep Creek. He's out there with a crew from the mill, rebuilding the bridge."

The judge had pounded his gavel and told them to turn Emil Hodges loose. He agreed that the man had been arrested and held on a misunderstanding. He said they should all apologize to Emil.

Tom Halloran ceased talking and reached for his now cold tea. There was a moment of silence and everyone took a long refreshing breath

Nora noted that all the men around the table smiled and nodded their approval as Halloran finished his story. Even Mother seemed pleased.

Nora felt glad for Sheriff Hodges.

The next week brought a vacation from school. The teachers all left town to go to Albany for the Teachers Institute. Nora loved the freedom.

Then the newspaper reported that another man had died of suspected alcohol poisoning over in Nevada. This time the town didn't seem so upset. After all, that death was a long way away, and the man could have had some other disease. Alcohol was only suspected.

But Dad and the men were upset. The gates around the haystacks were found to be open again and the cattle were tearing the hay from the bottom of the stacks.

However, another, altogether chilling, detail was discovered. One of the intruders had dropped a cigarette and a fire had been started in the loose hay. The man had discovered his mistake and had stamped the flames out, but several yards of earth had been scorched. If the wind had been blowing from another direction the flames would have engulfed the haystack and much of the precious winter feed would have been destroyed.

"One of us will have to ride over and check those fences every morning and evening," Dad sighed, his face a mask of worry.

On Thursday Nora went in to Jordan's store with her father as he bought supplies for the winter sheep camp. She helped assemble the beans, the slabs of bacon, the canned milk, the onions and the other staples on the counter. Dad was picking out several pairs of heavy socks and some woolen work shirts when she saw the distinctive produce truck pull in to the loading dock. Manny Dietz's big touring car arrived shortly after. Jordan and one of his clerks hurried out to help unload the fruit and vegetables and Nora stepped out on the dock to watch them.

She stood with her back to the wall, wedged behind a 100-lb. sack of potatoes. She watched with interest as the side curtains were rolled up to reveal the treasures within the truck. It was growing late in the season and she realized that one could not expect to have the wonderful fruits and melons that had been brought in during the summer. Yet she knew that Mother would love to get the fresh cabbage, the parsnips and the pumpkins that were being unloaded.

She was about to go to tell her father, when she noted that Benny and Manny Dietz were again hauling heavy wooden boxes to the shed next door. Whenever one of the town ladies approached, the two men would become busy unloading the produce, but as soon as Herb Jordan persuaded the ladies to go around and into the store, the two men immediately started unloading the heavy boxes from the bottom of the truck.

Suddenly she remembered the broken flask she had observed two weeks before. Her hand flew to her mouth. A terrible understanding filled her being.

She thought of the dead men who had died screaming and blind. She thought of Sheriff Hodges who worked so hard and tried desperately to find the source of the poisoned whiskey. The doctor still went about town with a worried frown on his face, and this truck came every two weeks from Winnemucca. Hadn't the dying men said something about the liquor coming from Winnemucca? And, the gates were open again around the haystacks! Uncle Jack had said it was a game that the grown-ups played. They must be caught! Like the children's game of hide and seek. These people must be caught!

Nora slipped back into the store. Her knees seemed stiff and unbending. She felt chilled. What if she were wrong? What if the men had a good reason to unload cases into that shed. Maybe it was boxes of canned goods they were storing there. Canned tomatoes or even canned milk would be heavy. But there had been that broken bottle of whiskey!

Her heart seemed to have sunk into her stomach. Her mouth was dry. They would call her 'Big Mouth' for the rest of her life if she were wrong. But the man called Benny and Manny Dietz only unloaded the cases when there was no one around. They didn't want people to see them putting the boxes into the shed.

The gates at the haystacks were opened again, but this time a careless fire had been started. They could lose the winter feed that kept the cattle alive. And, another man had died, this time over near Winnemucca.

Dad had discovered the fresh produce. He was busily selecting fat parsnips when she approached.

"What is the matter, child?" he asked when he saw her. He reached to take her hand. "Why, you're trembling."

"I'm . . . . I'm cold," Nora stammered.

"Go outside in the sun," Dad directed. "We don't want you getting sick."

"I'll meet you at the wagon," said Nora. "I'll walk around the block."

She hurried from the store, her mind in turmoil. What should she do? Whom should she tell?

Should she tell anyone? What if more people died, and what if the haystacks were burned? It would all be her fault! NO! She had to do something! She strode purposefully along the sunny street, whispering to herself.

And the produce truck came twice a month--always when it was payday at the sawmill! Mother had mentioned that the fresh produce came when people who worked at the mill had the money to pay for the lovely, scarce fruits.

As she turned the corner she saw Manny and Benny carefully loading the heavy crates into the shed. They glanced her way but paid no notice.

"A kid like me doesn't count," she told herself. "If I were grown up and looking for vegetables they'd think they had to be busy unloading the produce to fool me. But a kid doesn't count. And this kid doesn't know what to do."

Then ahead she saw the answer. Sheriff Hodges and Mr. Anthony Blaine were just getting out of the sheriff's big black touring car. The car looked almost like Manny Dietz's car and she thought distractedly that all the touring cars in town looked the same. There were about ten or twelve of them around and they all looked the same. She wished her Dad had one. Then she wondered how she could think of the cars when she had all this other stuff on her mind.

She hurried forward to meet the men as they stepped up on the curb.

Both men smiled as she approached and Sheriff Hodges reached to shake her hand.

"Hello, Nora," he began, but she interrupted.

"I have to talk to you," she said. "It's really important!"

"What?"

"I have to talk to both of you," she said again. "And I might be wrong. If I am—please don't tell anyone."

"What is it, little girl?" Mr. Blaine showed his concern.

"Listen," she clutched the Sheriff's hand, and looked to Mr. Blaine. "Maybe I'm wrong. I could be dead wrong—"

The two men looked at each other, consternation on their faces.

"I think I know where the whiskey is coming from," Nora blurted.

Sheriff Hodges stepped back down from the curb and leaned close to the child. "Nora," he began in a conciliatory tone.

"Listen. You think I'm crazy," said Nora. "And I could be wrong. If I'm wrong, please don't tell anyone. And if I'm right—don't tell anyone either. Please."

She jumped down beside Hodges. She placed a hand on the smooth, black metal hood of the sheriff's big automobile. The hood was warm from the sun, and even warmer from the heat of the engine that had just been turned off. She stretched both arms across the hood and leaned into the welcome heat. She couldn't seem to stop trembling. She hoped no one from the sidewalk would stop to talk to the sheriff. If anyone interrupted, she would run away. And she would never stop running. She took a deep breath.

"The produce truck," she began. "The produce truck from Winnemucca . . ."

She told them of her suspicions. She mentioned the broken flask, the smell of alcohol, the fact that Manny Deitz always came to help the man named Benny unload. She told them of the heavy cases that were hidden in the shed. She explained that they only moved the cases when no one was around. If any of the town ladies came to the truck, Benny and Dietz would unload the vegetables. She told them of the open gates at the haystacks and how Tom Halloran knew that men from the sawmill went down to their ranch to pick up the bottles left there for them. And she remembered that Benny had told Manny Dietz that he would have to take the price of the broken bottles out of 'his share.'

No one came to interrupt her as she told her story. When she finished she found that she was no longer cold and trembling. It was as though telling someone had raised a great burden from her soul. The problem now became someone else's responsibility.

The two men looked at each other in disbelief.

"We'll look into it," Hodges told her. "And if you are right, there may even be a reward for you."

"NO! NO!" Nora's voice rose emphatically. "You can't tell anyone. Not if I'm right. Not if I'm wrong."

"Why ever not?" Anthony Blaine asked. He looked at her, seeking to understand.

"If I'm right," said Nora, her voice sad. "Gwendolyn Dietz is in my class at school." She hesitated for a long moment. "And if I'm wrong—well, I don't want to get called 'big mouth.'"

The following few days passed slowly. Nora waited apprehensively for some news to develop. Tony Blaine came for supper one evening but he acted casual and friendly as usual and said nothing about their conversation

55

a few days before in town. The weekly newspaper came but there was no mention of any arrests or excitement. She decided she had been wrong. She felt embarrassed but somehow relieved too that she had jumped to the wrong conclusions. She was grateful that Tony Blaine said nothing to anyone.

Nora played jacks with Gwendolyn Deitz during recess at school. She knew that Gwendolyn allowed her to win several of the games.

"I'm just not good at snatching up those little metal pegs," Nora lamented. "It's harder to do than it looks."

"Yes," Gwen agreed. "But I play alone for hours. There's nothing much else to do around my house."

One evening Dad surprised and delighted everyone with a big announcement. He was buying a car! Yes, they were getting a house in town, near the school—but they were also getting a new car. The price of wool in the spring had been unexpectedly high, and now he had sold the fall lambs, also for a grand price. Gradually, Nora forgot her uneasiness.

Then two weeks later, Tom Halloran came straight from the sawmill. He didn't even wait to change his sawdust-laden clothing, but practically ran from town with the news. Herb Jordan, Manny Dietz and a fellow named Benny Armstrong had been arrested for bootlegging. Benny Armstrong had been bringing the whiskey into town on his produce truck. Herb Jordan said he didn't know a thing about the fact that the man brought anything but produce. Manny Dietz insisted that Benny hired him to help him unload his truck. He didn't know that the cases contained moonshine.

After several days in jail, Benny Armstrong admitted that he had sold the poison whiskey to the two Pembroke brothers and the Irish sheepherder that died out in Willow Valley. Only he didn't know it was poison! He didn't know where the others who died had got the liquor. And he certainly didn't know that there was anything wrong with the product when he sold it to those customers. A man he had bought whiskey from for months had sold him the liquor. It was discovered that the fellow had used a new kettle or a boiler or something that had copper or lead in it and that metal was what had poisoned the whiskey. The fellow had made good moonshine until he decided to go big time and had bought this new, large kettle. He was the man who died over there in Nevada a few weeks ago—from drinking his own booze. Armstrong himself had been ridden with guilt since the deaths of those several people. He was glad to get it off his chest.

Nora listened to the excited conversation. She pushed her chair back and quietly left the table. It was now too cold to go sit on the back steps so she went slowly upstairs to her room. She wondered what her room would be like in the new house in town. She wondered what it would be like to have an automobile in the family. But mostly, she thought about Gwendolyn Dietz, whose father everyone in town was gossiping about. She cringed to think how unhappy that girl must be tonight.

Chapter 3

🌸 THE CLAY PIT - 1928

Nora jumped from her bed and hurried to the window. The valley below was bathed in early sunlight, fresh, sparkling and cool. The town, lying directly below the sheltering eastern mountains, still lay in shadows waiting for the sun to rise beyond the peaks.

"Everyone is still asleep," she whispered. "I'll run up to the clay pit."

Katie sighed in her sleep and rolled over to Nora's side of the bed, stretching and kicking the quilt away.

Nora dressed, making as little noise as possible. She shoved her nightgown under her pillow and tiptoed down the stairs.

Mother was in the kitchen.

"You're up early," she said to Nora. "I thought you'd sleep until noon. Everyone was so tired and cranky because we got in so late from the ranch."

"I'd rather stay out at the ranch" said Nora. "I like that house much better than this one in town."

Mother shrugged. She was already dishing up a bowl of oatmeal for Nora.

"Think how lucky we are to be able to move in here when school starts," she observed. "Trying to get you all into school in the winter was becoming an impossible job."

Nora nodded and picked up her spoon.

"I'm glad you are up so early," Mother continued. "I want you to run up to the store and get a yeast cake for me. One of the really big ones. I have to set the bread, and I've started the list here that you can give Lloyd Johnson. Tell him Dad will be in later today to pick up the supplies. This is a really big list because we're getting ready for haying."

"The store isn't open yet—" Nora started.

"Yes. They open earlier in the summer. It's been open for almost an hour. It's nearly eight o'clock. Violet Welden will be here soon. She's coming to help me today. We have loads of wash and we must put away the school clothes and get out the summer things and – oh! Here's Violet now."

Violet came up the back steps, her head wrapped in a scarf, and apron tied securely over her cotton dress. She looked ready for work.

"I thought it was much earlier," Nora half pouted. "I wanted to go up to the clay pit."

"No," said Mother. I need the yeast."

"The clay pit?" Violet looked at Mother.

"Oh. It's a spot right up there on the hill," Mother explained. "It's less than a block away—just above the bridge. Phil and the Tatum boy used to play there all the time." She sat at the corner of the table and unfolded her grocery list. "They drove me to distraction. They would make clay figures—you know little dolls, and dogs and horses and even marbles out of the sticky clay they found up there, and then they'd bring them down to bake and dry out in my oven. I'd have to scrub for an hour to get the dirt off my pans—"

"Andy Tatum's boy?" Violet was incredulous. "Andy Tatum had a son?"

"Yes. Tom Tatum. He was about the same age as Phil. They played together all the time. The child died a few years ago."

"I didn't know that," Violet seemed amazed. "How did that cranky old Andy Tatum ever find a wife?"

"He was never cranky until his wife left—" Mother stopped suddenly and looked meaningfully at Nora.

"Tina said the war made him cranky," Nora spoke up in defense of Andy Tatum.

Violet's eyes were bright with anticipation. She sat forward eagerly waiting to hear more.

"Hurry with your breakfast," Mother told Nora. "I must get that bread started."

"Speaking of Andy Tatum," said Violet. "That's some row he's having with Pauline Fitch."

Mother looked perplexed. "I didn't see anything in the paper, but I guess I haven't seen the paper for the last two weeks. Not since we moved out to the ranch. I haven't even got the mail—" She looked at the list she was compiling, then added. "And Andy, well. He keeps to himself so much. He's having trouble with Pauline Fitch?" Now Mother was the one who waited with anticipation.

"Yes," Pauline poured herself a cup of coffee and settled down to tell the story. Nora ate more slowly, listening to the adult conversation.

"It was the week you moved to the ranch that it all started—right after school was out," said Violet. "Andy Tatum lodged a complaint against Pauline Fitch for dumping garbage and refuse into the creek that runs through his property, thus threatening his health and water rights, or something like that."

"Really?" Mother was astonished.

"Yes. Pauline had just bought Tina's house and was cleaning it out. She took all the jars of fruit, the unused flour and sugar, the beans, lentils, oatmeal and anything else that was in the cupboards or pantry and just threw the whole lot out over the bank of the creek. Tatum objected and she told him it was none of his business. Then he went to court and lodged a complaint."

"Good grief," said Mother, forgetting her list.

"Then Pauline said that she was dumping some harmless refuse on state-owned, worthless, sagebrush-covered property that Tatum had no jurisdiction over. The town marshal went up and took a look but didn't do anything."

"That creek does run through his place," said Mother, "and it runs right under the street there and down south to the lake. Lots of children play in the water."

"Oh, I know," said Violet. "But then Tatum, stern as a preacher, dumped a load of dry corn up there beyond the canyon bridge and opened the gate to his pig pen. The pigs all ran up there on the bench, squealing and grunting and rooting around in the rotting vegetables and the dry corn." Violet paused to sip from her coffee and continued.

"Pauline went down and lodged a complaint against Andy Tatum. Said the noise and the smell from the pigs was most unpleasant, since they were rooting around right outside her fence." Violet paused and leaned back, laughing, in her chair.

"Was all this in the paper?" Mother was incredulous.

"Oh, sure," Violet answered. "But who needs the paper? It only comes out once a week and the word flew around town minute to minute. After Pauline lodged her complaint, Tatum stood outside the newspaper office, mad as hell, and said his pigs could forage on state-owned, worthless, sagebrush-covered land without asking Pauline Fitch's permission." Violet reached to refill her coffee cup. "It's the most exciting thing that's happened around here since the fire at the mill."

Mother turned to Nora. "Stop and get the mail and the newspapers when you go to the store. We're going to have to get to town oftener," she observed. "I wonder what will happen next."

61

"Oh. It's already happened," Violet sounded smug. "Pauline drove down to the sheriff's office and convinced him that the wandering pigs were a health hazard. They made Tatum pen them up again. He did go up and pick up all the broken glass and metal cans he could find up there at the bridge though. The parents of the kids that play up there are grateful, I imagine, but I don't think too many children go up there."

"No." Mother agreed. "They don't play up there much, especially in this heat. That trail coming down the canyon is so narrow, and there is nothing much to see up there, and there are no fish left. The water is too low."

"Well. Pauline is having her troubles this spring, I'd say," Violet said. "I see her every Saturday when she and her friends come in to lunch."

Mother looked at her, her expression questioning.

"I still work part time at the hotel," said Violet. "Actually, it gets busier in the summer and I will probably start working full time soon. Anyway, Pauline comes in with her friends and I heard her telling them how she knew people in town were laughing behind her back, and talking about her feud with Tatum. She says she's earned the right to live in peace up there in Tina's house and she wants them to stop calling it Tina's house and they will soon agree with her when they see the changes she's going to make."

"What changes?" Mother asked.

"Well. She's ripped out all the bushes and vines Tina had in her yard, and they have planted lawn seed and smoothed the whole area out and packed it down with a big roller thing filled with water. It must weigh a ton and the fellow that has to push it around to pack the black dirt down is really worn out at the end of the day. Then she had them chop down all those honeysuckle vines below the rock wall, and the bees are still darting around up there trying to find some blossoms or salvage the honey or something. I heard Pauline telling her friends that the workmen refused to work up there until the bees went somewhere else. Several of the workmen have been stung."

"My word!" said Mother.

"Oh. There's lots of stuff you won't read in the paper," said Violet happily. "I can hardly wait to go to work on Saturday when I can listen to Pauline's side of the story. She says she can't believe how stupid the townspeople are that they can't see things her way. And she was very gratified this past week when Andy Tatum went up there on the hill and took most of his beehives back down to his own backyard. She says there are only two left up there and he'd better get them down off the hill soon too, if he knows what's good for him. She wants those workmen back at work!"

"Well. The bees will fly up there from his yard as well as from the hill," said Mother. "Surely she realizes that."

"Yeah," Violet laughed. "She goes around town as composed and snooty as ever when she knows people are laughing behind her back—and it must really gall her that somehow she can't seem to intimidate the bees."

"Nora. Get your shoes on and get on up to the store. The list is almost ready."

Nora hurried through the hallway and up the stairs. She hated that she had to go to town. Maybe Mother would let her take Phil's bicycle. That would help. She snatched up her shoes and returned to sit on the lower step of the stairs while she listened to the adult conversation.

"One thing about it," Violet was saying. "Andy Tatum spends a lot of time talking to that newspaper man now." She laughed. "That makes about three people in town he talks to."

Mother didn't answer. She was making additions to her list. Violet took the paring knife and started slicing a bar of yellow soap into the copper boiler of water steaming on the stove.

"And the editor's kid," said Violet. "He is a real character."

"Who?" Mother asked.

"The Huffmeier boy," said Violet. "He is cowboy crazy. He wears boots, a vest, a big hat and is always practicing his quick draw with that cap gun he swaggers around with." She shook her head, smiling.

"Yes," Mother agreed. "He comes by here to play with Kevin. He came from Portland and never heard of a cowboy until he arrived here. He's delighted with any cowman that comes to town and spends half his life down at the stockyards watching them work the cattle and get them onto the box cars for shipping. He thinks Ken Maynard and Hoot Gibson are the greatest heroes in America. When one of their pictures comes to town, he sees every matinee and tries to persuade his dad to take him to the evening performances as well. It's a good thing the matinees are only on Saturday and Sunday or he'd never be in school when one of their movies is showing at the theater."

Nora took the list and moved reluctantly to the door. There was the clay pit only a short block away. She could be up there, cross the bridge and climb the steep bank in two minutes flat, but no, she had to go to the store.

Two weeks later, Nora climbed steadily along the narrow footpath. The dust under her bare feet felt soft and feathery. She scuffed her toes through the white patches of alkali, watching the little puffs of powder balloon up and then drift slowly higher, disintegrating slowly in the slight updraft from the canyon.

The rye grass and the lower leaves of the plum bushes were already turning dry and falling, their greenery sapped away by the heat and alkali.

It made her sad to see the water in the creek running so slow and sluggish. She felt sorry that many dead silvery minnows floated on the surface.

At the turn of the path beyond the bridge she pushed through the brush and scampered forty feet up the steep bank to the clay pit. She settled there in the deep shade of the cottonwoods and looked back down across the little town.

How different it seemed today. It was the Fourth of July and everyone moved about, hurrying to and fro, getting ready for the big parade that would start at noon.

The Fourth of July weekend was a welcome break from the pressure of haying. Nearly everyone came in from the ranches to spend a few days in town, watch the parade and buy supplies to take them through the remainder of the summer.

She watched Andy Tatum, down below, as he pitched hay to several horses that were being boarded at his barn. He had already fed the pigs and chickens. He must be planning to go to the parade.

And there came Uncle Jack, riding his new pinto gelding. He rode up to Andy's fence, dismounted and led the horse through the gate. The two men shook hands and Uncle Jack unsaddled his horse, putting the saddle and saddle blanket on the top rail of the fence. He hung the bridle on the post and headed off up town, walking eagerly, ready for any excitement.

Nora felt wonderful, sitting there in her private place, observing all the people below. They didn't even know they were being watched.

She noticed some movement to the left and shifted her gaze. There was Pauline Fitch walking about in her usual black dress, gesturing and discussing changes with some poor workman. In spite of the fact that it was a holiday, she had probably pressured him into coming up to her house to give him orders and tell him what she expected when he returned to work tomorrow. Nora could hear the rise and fall of their voices and she watched Pauline duck and strike out at a darting bee.

"The old fool," Nora thought. "That bee won't hurt her."

Pauline continued swatting at the bee, but she never missed a word and continued to gesture toward the house. The workman listened respectfully.

Everyone listened respectfully to Pauline Fitch. They nodded respectfully as she passed down the sidewalk or entered a store. The men tipped their hats respectfully as she drove along the streets. She was the only woman in town who had a private office, who belonged to the businessmen's club and who owned her own car.

Her office was in the Liberty National Bank building and her name was printed in gold letters on the door. Her father had used the same office and her brother, Wilson, had once used it too. But now he sat at a desk out on the banking floor and Pauline called him into her office if she wished to discuss something with him.

Pauline owned part interest in the dress shop on 2nd Street and the hotel on Main Street. She bought up the Maren ranch, the Tatum ranch and the Boggs place on the West Side. She owned a couple of other ranches down toward the county line also. She never got a chance to buy into the sawmill, but she owned a lot of timber options and the loggers had to deal with her before they could get the logs out of the woods. Many of the rental homes in town belonged to her as well.

The first of the month, a line of people waited outside her office door to go in and pay their rent. She accepted their money personally and wrote them a receipt in a large black book with a carbon that always seemed to smear. She kept the original in her book for her files and handed her renters the smudged carbon. No one laughed or visited when they stood in that line outside her office on the first of the month. They waited quietly and patiently, with closed faces, slipping in and out of her presence as quickly as possible.

Emmett O'Connor delivered the Klamath News daily paper to Pauline's office. Nora had gone with him one day when he went to collect for the month. They waited in the nervous line of people but when they stepped into her office she told them to stand aside while she collected from the renters who had followed them in the line. They listened uncomfortably as Pauline dealt with her renters.

"Mr. Reese," she spoke in a firm voice. "I saw your children swinging on that wrought iron gate as I drove past my house." (Mr. Reese never thought of it as his house although he had rented from her for four years.) "Please see that it doesn't happen again. Teach your children to respect property, Mr. Reese." She handed him the smudged rent receipt without a smile or a thank you.

Emmett stepped forward to collect his bill, but Pauline waved him aside waiting for her next renter.

When Roscoe Bell came respectfully in, she didn't even wait for him to close the door.

"Explain yourself, Mr. Bell," she commanded him. "That corner post is still broken and you assured me last month that you would replace it."

"I fixed it, ma'am. Put in a new post just this morning."

"And high time," she answered, her voice cold.

Emmett had been furious because she kept him waiting. He grabbed Nora's hand and strode out the door ignoring Pauline when she called to him in her imperious voice. He went to her home in the evening from then on to collect for the paper. He wasn't intimidated by Pauline Fitch.

Nora smiled. Red Huffmeier wasn't afraid of her either. His dad was the newspaper editor and the family hadn't been in this part of the country very long.

One day Pauline stepped out of the bank and started down the sidewalk. She always walked in the exact center of the walk, head high and face calmly composed. People moved aside respectfully. Red Huffmeier was running along playing with his cap gun practicing his quick draw. The child stumbled over a loose plank. He fell and nearly knocked Pauline off the walk.

"Explain yourself," she commanded, anger in her voice. The people on the walk stopped. They looked at each other uneasily, feeling sorry for Red.

"Cripes," said Red, looking around for his cap gun. "I didn't mean to. I could have busted a leg." Then he looked up and added. "Oh! you're the lady from the bank ain't you? Why don't you guys fix up this sidewalk? Someone will hurt themselves one of these days." Then he ran off, still practicing his quick draw, while Pauline sailed off in a fury to the newspaper office to speak with the boy's father.

No one heard the conversation or knew what happened but Pauline came stalking out of the office, her face a mottled red. The following week, the old plank walk surrounding the bank was torn up and replaced by a grand new cement sidewalk much nicer than the one that circled the courthouse.

Nora heard Mother calling. Reluctantly she climbed down from her perch and ran home.

Nora was going to the parade with Delores, the hired girl, and Delores was going with Jed. She laughed as she wet her hair with the thick liquor from the Chinese shavings jar and combed the little stiff curls around her face. 'Spit curls' she called them but they looked quite nice when they dried.

"I haven't seen Jed for three weeks," she confided to Nora. "You don't mind if he tags along do you?"

Nora felt uncomfortable. Mother didn't like Jed much.

"I could go alone," Nora offered after some thought. "It wouldn't be much fun for you if I were along."

"Oh, kiddo. Would you?" Delores was smiling again, putting her arms around Nora, hugging her. "Just come right home after the parade or your mother will be mad at me. I'll meet you here." She hurried off to help Mother who was busily planning the day, trying to organize the activities for all the family. Who would stay with the baby during the parade? Was Phil's band uniform pressed and ready? Was the dessert ready for the ladies who would be stopping for tea this afternoon? Had Delores dusted all the picture frames in the parlor? Was the good china washed and ready?

It was too early to go uptown so Nora walked back to the clay pit. The bees were quieter than they had been a few weeks earlier, although a few still buzzed aimlessly about. She saw that only two hives remained on the flat spot above the boulders. There were few blossoms anywhere now and she could understand why Andy had removed all the other hives and taken them down from the hill.

Now, as she watched, people came streaming from all directions to the small business section of town. Flags and bunting flew from wires hung across the streets and young boys from outlying ranches galloped about on their horses, showing off to one another and kicking up clouds of dust. The band had been practicing at the high school and now they were hurrying toward the center of town because they were the first unit in the parade.

Nora was about to climb down from her high perch when she saw Pauline Fitch coming across the bridge.

The woman struggled under a heavy canvas tarpaulin draped across one shoulder and she carried a galvanized bucket, balancing it carefully to keep it away from her skirt. Nora stared in disbelief. The bucket was partially filled with oil or tar and a handful of carpenter's shavings was thrown on top.

Pauline crossed the bridge and picked her way carefully up among the boulders.

"What is she going to burn?" Nora asked herself. "She could easily start a brush fire when it's this dry."

She found herself torn between two options. The parade was starting and she wanted to be there, but she was consumed with curiosity as to what Pauline Fitch was doing there at the canyon mouth.

Nora felt afraid of Pauline Fitch with her bold, sharp features and her imperious ways. She didn't want to meet her coming back down the narrow path, if she was merely throwing that oily substance away. Still, Pauline had thrown all of the other refuse over the bank and down into the creek without a thought. Why was she climbing up this side of the canyon trail?

Impulsively, Nora decided to go up along the crest of the hill where she could look down unobserved and see what Pauline was up to. It would only take a few minutes and she could still get uptown in time for the parade. She worked her way slowly upward keeping the crest of the hill between herself and the canyon area below.

She paused for breath, then sniffed, nervous as a rabbit. She smelled smoke. Pauline Fitch was burning something and only a fool would start a fire in the canyon in weather as dry as this. Far away the band started playing "Stars and Stripes Forever." The parade was starting.

She hurried to the summit and looked down toward the creek.

Pauline Fitch had started a smudge fire between the two remaining beehives. The ugly black smoke crept around, close to the ground, feeding on the thick oil that oozed from the bucket and ran in several directions beneath the wooden hives. Then, as the wind fanned the flames a bit, Pauline threw the damp canvas over the hives and the fire, trapping the thick smoke. She rolled several stones over the edge of the canvas, holding it firmly in place on the one side, as she stepped around to the other side and adjusted the tarp to trap the smoke and flames. The dirty black smoke was beginning to billow from beneath the canvas like an ugly flower unfolding.

Nora ran screaming down the hill.

"You'll kill the bees! You're killing them sure!"

She tugged futilely at the edge of the canvas, but Pauline merely stepped around and stood calmly on the heavy cloth. Nora tried to roll the rocks away, but Pauline pushed her roughly to her knees. Now, the smoke billowing up under the canvas lifted the material into a smooth dome over the hives.

Down in the town the band played, "America, the Beautiful," and the sweet notes rose faintly in the stillness as Pauline Fitch stood calmly on the edge of the tarpaulin and regarded Nora with scorn on her face.

"Those bees are a nuisance," she said, her tone cold. "The painters can't work—the yard men haven't finished planting the flowers, and I can't persuade the woman I hired to come and clean the house. They are all afraid they will be stung. I don't have to put up with that."

"But the bees are almost gone," cried Nora. "There's hardly any flowers left for them to gather honey from."

"Go home, child," said Pauline. "This is none of your business!"

Nora turned and ran headlong down the rocky path. She had to find Andy. Had he gone up to the parade? She knew in her heart that it was too late, but she had to try. She looked back as she crossed the bridge and saw Pauline making her way down among the boulders, cool and unhurried.

The band played "It's a Long Way to Tipperary" as she and Andy hurried up the canyon path. She remembered Phil sitting on the wood box in the kitchen at the ranch practicing that tune on his clarinet. He didn't get into town too often during the summer to practice with the band, but he always marched in the parade.

Sweating and gasping for breath, they reached the hives. The canvas had collapsed. Thin tendrils of smoke escaped and the tarp was burned through in many places. Andy jerked the covering away and they both gasped in horror when they saw the scorched hives. The wax had softened in the heat. The wooden frames had burned away. Honey, wax and dead bees oozed out onto the scorched grass.

"That dirty old bitch!" Andy spoke, his voice thick with rage.

Nora winced. 'Bitch,' was a forbidden word in the ladylike vocabulary her mother was trying to instill in her. She felt guilty even *listening* to the word. 'Dirty old bitch,' was even worse. But it sounded so—right!

She tried to put the thought away and turned to Andy and took his hand.

"I'm going down to that newspaper fellow," Andy said. "I hope he prints this." He strode off down the hill and Nora followed, the naughty phrase insinuating itself into her mind again. *The dirty old bitch! The dirty old bitch!*

By the time they reached the smoother path and crossed the bridge, the feeling of guilt was gone. Her mind chanted a cadence with each of her steps:

Pauline Fitch
The dirty old bitch.

Nora didn't go uptown to watch the last of the parade. She sat on the porch waiting for Delores and Jed to return. She heard Katie upstairs reading to little Julie. She saw the silver spray from the sprinkler across the walk. She was shivering with anger and shock.

Pauline Fitch
The dirty old bitch.

How could she do such cruel, rotten things? How could she be so mean to everyone? She liked being mean! And everyone let her get away with it! She'd brazen her way out of this, too. Nora's thoughts ran on in chaos. She didn't even care that she'd missed the parade that she'd waited half the summer to see. Someone should give Pauline Fitch a taste of her own medicine! But everyone was so afraid of her. She was sneaky, too. If Nora hadn't been up in the clay pit no one would have known who smothered the hives. They might have suspected, but no one would ever have accused old Fitch of doing it.

Andy didn't have a lot of friends, either.

Uncle Jack strode suddenly into sight. He hurried to Andy Tatum's corral and was about to enter the gate when he saw Nora sitting on her porch.

Hurrying across the road, he sat beside her on the step.

"I met Andy uptown," he said. "He told me about the bees."

Nora fought back tears. She was too big to cry. She didn't want Uncle Jack to think her a sissy. He put his strong arm around her and drew her close.

"That Pauline Fitch is an ornery old blister." His voice sounded rough with anger. "Wouldn't I love to put my hobnail boot into her skinny backside until she learned some manners!"

Nora slipped her arm around Uncle Jack's waist. She buried her face against his broad chest and let the tears flow. They sat there for a long time in mutual understanding.

"I must go," he said at last. "I'll be sharpening sickles for the mowers for the rest of the afternoon. I'll see you back at the ranch."

Reluctantly, she watched him go. He crossed the street and was soon saddling the pinto and on his way. She wished he could stay and give old Fitch a kick with his hobnail boots. It would somewhat make up for all those poor destroyed bees.

She sighed, thoughtful again. No one would do anything about it, even if it were printed in the paper. Pauline would walk calmly around town feeling perfectly justified. After all, the sheriff had sided with her and made Andy pen up his pigs.

She jerked upright. The germ of an idea was forming. A good idea. She hurried into the house and changed into her worn overalls, planning as she moved. She rushed to the kitchen and selected a sharp paring knife with which to cut the willows. She filled a lard bucket with water and forced the cover tightly in place so she could run without spilling the water. She felt surprised and pleased at how efficient she was.

"I'll give her bees," promised Nora as she ran up the hill. "When I get through with her, she'll be seeing bees in her sleep."

Once in the clay pit, she poured the water on the dry, hard earth and left it to soften. She made her way further up to the flat. Wisps of smoke drifted about from the recent fire. The ruined, dead hives seemed to reproach her.

Taking a stick, she separated a portion of the brood comb filled with larvae and bee grubs. She transferred these, dripping with honey, into the bucket. She scraped up hundreds of dead bees—dry, scorched or smothered in their hives—and scooped them, along with the honey, into the oily bucket Pauline had discarded on the hillside. Then she hurried with the two buckets back to the clay pit.

For the next half hour she dug out chunks of wet clay, rolled it into balls about the size of a jawbreaker, encasing a dead bee in each ball. She worked quickly. She had rolled such balls before when she used to come to the clay pit with Phil and Tom Tatum, although she had never enclosed a bee in them before. She soon had an arsenal of fifty or so missiles.

"Poor little things," she whispered. "They were flying around—so happy and busy—just yesterday. They belonged in Tina's yard and visited all her flowers. They didn't know that the old bitch owned the place now."

With the paring knife she cut a sturdy willow, carefully sharpening one end. She took up one of the clay balls, impaled it on the end of the willow switch, dipped it in honey and flung it far out across the creek in the direction of the Fitch house.

At first her aim was erratic and she missed more often than she hit, but she soon started getting the range and she watched happily as the little balls landed time after time on the roof below. Between the honey and the sticky clay, the marbles seemed to be clinging firmly to the roof. Very few of them rolled down.

She brought up more water from the muddy pools in the creek to pour on the clay to soften it, and sat, rolling the little marbles around the dead bees, smiling all the time. The roof of Pauline's house was beginning to have a definite 'hobnail' look. She was feeling quite proud of herself.

At last she saw Delores and Jed returning from the parade and she knew it was time to go. Mother always checked with the hired girl to see if she had done her chores. Besides, it was Katie's turn now to go up to the carnival and she had to care for little Julie. She hurried down the hill to greet Delores and was soon busily hanging a basket of wash on the line. As she snapped the clothes pins she suddenly thought of the bicycle spokes that she and the boys used to use to propel the clay balls with.

She hurried into the shed and looked about, hoping to find an old wheel from Phil's bicycle. Surely there was one tossed in here. Under the work bench she found a dilapidated wheel from the old baby carriage. The spokes were short and sturdy. She popped two of them out of the rim by stepping on them. They were made of heavier metal and were shorter than the bicycle spokes. She felt that they would work even better. Smiling, she finished hanging the diapers on the line.

Lunch time arrived, but the family members had not yet returned from the parade. She swept the front porch and the back porch, then carried little Julie upstairs to her crib and gave her a bottle of warm milk. She watched as the baby settled down drowsily for her nap. Delores and Jed were laughing in the kitchen and Nora quietly took the spokes and ran up the hill.

From her sanctuary, she looked down on the little clay balls baking in the sun on Pauline's roof. Little clots of yellow bees were already crawling over the honey-smeared dots retrieving the nectar and making the little orbs seem to move in the steady light.

Nora fell back, laughing. She hadn't even thought of the bees themselves coming to re-collect the honey. Now she realized that they would soon be crawling all over the clay pit itself. Some were already here moving about on sticky feet.

"Here's sweets to you, Pauline," she whispered. She started flinging the clay balls again, now using the steel spokes. "Mrs. Fitch, you sticky old bitch." She sent a message with each flying missile, thoroughly enjoying herself.

The metal wands worked ever so much better than the willows. She had to stop to make another arsenal of clay shots and soon the roof of the Fitch house began to take on a strange polka-dot quality. More and more bees appeared to crawl about and cluster around the honey-soaked marbles. The bees appeared to jump and buzz angrily when another clay ball landed nearby, disturbing their work.

Nora had never known such satisfaction. She felt that there was something symbolic about each little bee-filled sphere she sailed out over the creek to land on Pauline's house. Like the Vikings who shipped their dead warriors off in burning glory on the outgoing tide, Nora sent the dead bees soaring on their last short flight to return to plague their enemy.

Finally, the heat from the afternoon sun and the growing number of bees invading the clay pit, sent her scrambling from the hill. She was covered with dirt, streaked with sweat, and felt sticky from head to foot. Now the bees were even following her. Slipping into the yard she washed her hands and face at the hydrant and went to help Delores hang out yet another basket of wash.

As she finished, she discovered that Pauline Fitch's car was now parked in front of Tina's house. She was glad the bees had driven her down the hill before Pauline returned.

Nora threw her overalls in the soaking tub and ran upstairs and bathed. Mother and her friends had just returned and were having a cup of tea in the parlor. Delores served lemonade and sandwiches to the children who had just returned from the parade. Little Julie banged her empty bottle against the crib rails and the voices of the women discussing the news from up and down the valley floated up the stairs. Pulling on a worn housedress, Nora stood braiding her wet hair before the mirror when she heard Pauline Fitch's voice in the lower hall.

". . . that child that runs about up on the hill?"

Nora's fingers turned awkward and suddenly cold. She struggled to put the rubber binder around the end of her braid. She felt sick. How had Mrs.

Fitch guessed it was she? She held her breath, listening.

"Nora?" Mother's voice sounded apprehensive. The ladies in the parlor became very quiet, listening. "Whatever do you want Nora for?"

"Where was she this morning?" Pauline demanded.

"Why, at the parade," answered Mother, and Nora stood frozen with fear, listening.

"Are you sure?" Mrs. Fitch sounded ominous.

"Of course I'm sure," Mother spoke with indignation. She called Delores in from the kitchen. "Nora went to the parade with you, didn't she?" Mother asked, her voice flat.

"Oh. Ah, yes . . . yes!" Delores was flustered, but most people were uneasy around Pauline Fitch. "She was with us—ah, with me – all morning."

"Now what is this all about?" Mother's voice was as ominous as Pauline's and her eyes were hostile. Mother wasn't afraid of anyone.

Pauline threw her head back and raised her chin. "I want to talk to Nora," she said, her voice bold. "I have some questions I want to ask her—some vandalism up at my house . . ."

"Nora," Mother called up the stairs never taking her eyes from Pauline's face. "Come down here, please."

"I'm playing with the baby," Nora called. "I'll be right down." She snatched up a book of nursery rhymes and lifted little Julie from her crib. Her knees trembled and she felt almost faint. How awful! Awful! Mother's friends were listening only a few feet away and Mother didn't deserve to be humiliated in front of them. There would be some new news flying all over town this evening, and all the party lines down the valley would be burning up. It was all her fault. How could she have been so stupid? And she thought she was so smart. And it was a sin to lie! But, she'd be getting Delores into trouble, too—and Delores had lied to save HER! What could she do?

"Nora," Mother called again.

Balancing the baby on her hip, Nora came slowly down the stairs. She turned to her Mother.

"I wanted to keep her quiet while you had company," she indicated the book. Her voice shook. She hoped she sounded innocent.

Pauline impaled her with accusing dark eyes.

"Where did you go this morning after I saw you on the hill?" she demanded, her voice cold. She ignored the other ladies sitting there in the parlor.

"On the hill?" Nora questioned. She was terrified, and her voice trembled.

"Ah, why I . . . I went to the parade right after we came in from the ranch—with Delores and Jed." She lied badly, but then everyone was afraid of Pauline Fitch.

"Oh, yes. Yes, she did," Delores interrupted. "And then she came back to watch the baby while Katie went to the carnival. She's been hanging wash and…"

"Never mind, Delores," Mother interrupted. She was furious now, like a mother bear whose cubs had been threatened. She looked at Miss Fitch with level, unfriendly eyes, and the ladies all leaned forward, seeming to hold their breaths, the tea growing cold in their cups. "What actually did you want?"

Pauline was suddenly unsure. "There was a little girl up on the hill this morning," she said. "Nora, perhaps, or maybe your girl just older. However the child was blonder somehow, but about the same size."

Nora climbed slowly up the stairs. She forced herself to walk casually but she felt weak from relief. She was aware that her hair was still wet and that was why it looked darker. She thanked God silently that Miss Fitch was always so preoccupied that she never paid much attention to children—but she knew too that Miss Fitch was still suspicious.

"Every child that runs about up there on the hills does not belong to me." Mother's voice was sarcastic. "And the girl just older than Nora is a boy—who marched with the high school band."

The ladies were smiling now, giving each other amused, furtive looks.

Mother continued. "I can't think of a child in this town who doesn't have a perfect right to play up there on the hills if they wish." She reached past Pauline and pushed open the screen door in an obvious invitation for her to leave. "Furthermore, Miss Fitch, if you wish to question one of my children, you come here and ask politely. You don't come barging in here demanding *anything*."

Pauline drew herself up and threw back her head preparing to speak, but Mother moved forward, effectively backing her out onto the porch. "Besides, Miss Fitch," she said, her voice cold, "since when did you start running about up on the hill?"

Pauline left without a further word, and the ladies bent double, suppressing their laughter and amazement that anyone dared talk to Pauline Fitch in such a way. Mother came back into the parlor, gasping in angry indignation, her face very red.

"You ran her off too quickly," said Jane Thorson, sputtering with mirth. "I wanted to find out what vandalism she was talking about."

Nora watched from the upstairs window as Miss Fitch retreated up the hill road. She had thought she was so smart, laughing and planning—and enjoying making a mess of Miss Fitch's roof. And then she had compounded it all by lying. Now she was filled with dread. Miss Fitch would surely find out what she had been up to. She could get the marshal up there to investigate, and Mother would die of embarrassment. The buckets were lying up there in the clay pit right now, and the spokes, and the willow wands and all those dead bees. Why there were probably even some of the little balls of clay that she hadn't yet used. She must have been crazy to leave that stuff there so carelessly.

    She tried frantically to think of an excuse to go back up there and move all the evidence, but it was impossible. Mother would never give her permission to go now that Pauline Fitch was on the prowl. Besides, Miss Fitch would see her if she went up there now. She wondered how long it would take for someone to decide to climb higher up the hill to get a better look at Pauline's roof and then discover her sanctuary.

    As she watched, she saw Andy Tatum and the newspaper editor skirt the boulders at the canyon mouth and cross the bridge. Andy had evidently persuaded Mr. Huffmeier to go up and take a look at his ruined hives. The two men stopped suddenly. They had discovered the bees crawling about on Pauline's roof. A couple of other neighbors came over to join them and they all stood on the bridge, gesturing and talking excitedly. Pauline went into her house and shut the door. Nora collapsed into a chair, her stomach roiling, her mind in turmoil.

    Phil arrived from town, perspiring and red-faced in his wool band uniform. Mother immediately sent him up the hill to find out what was going on. As he handed his clarinet through the screen door Mother told him to see what vandalism had occurred at Pauline's house. She ordered more tea for her guests. They would wait, of course, to find out the details for themselves. They all moved near the bay windows, watching. More people were congregating up near the bridge. Occasionally, someone ducked or swatted away at a bee, but no one left. Soon others were joining them.

    Supper time approached but Mother and her friends still waited in the parlor. Myrna Downs suggested that they all go up and join the others near the bridge, but most of the ladies seemed reluctant. It wouldn't be quite proper.

    Finally, Phil came running down the hill, filled with excitement. Nora came down and sat on the lower step of the stairs. She chewed her fingernails, listening.

    "Miss Fitch had burned some of Andy Tatum's beehives up on the hill this morning, and now there were bees busily building little cone shaped lumps all over her roof. " Phil's voice was loud with excitement.

"Andy Tatum was furious about the burning, growling and swearing—but he was also arguing that bees just wouldn't do things like that unless it was some new breed of bees that he had never heard of."

Pauline was as defiant as ever and persuaded some fellow to scrape down one of the little cones from her roof. Inside was a single bee larva.

Andy Tatum snorted and swore and said larvae could never mature under such circumstances. Then they scraped down another cone and found the same thing. Andy just stared at them and said he didn't give a good goddamn. They could believe any damn thing they wanted to. Now he just stood off to the side, frowning as usual, and no one bothered him.

People were arriving from all directions as the news traveled, and now there was quite a crowd watching the bees moving about in little knots up on the roof.

Finally, Pauline, very decisive and important, got into her car and drove down to get the county agent who was supposed to know about such things.

Some people were laughing and saying the bees were getting even, but some of the neighbors were carefully examining their own roofs in case it was some new breed of bees invading the valley. This 4th of July was even more exciting than usual.

"Pauline Fitch burned some of Andy's beehives up on the hill?" Mother asked the question, shock in her voice.

"Yeah." Phil was climbing the stairs, stripping off the hot wool uniform coat. "He only had two left up there, but they were both ruined."

"And she has the gall to talk about vandalism," Mother said. "Were there any windows broken up at her house or anything like that?"

"Nope," Phil spoke down over the upstairs banister, "Just bees crawling all over her roof."

Nora's stomach constricted into a small, hard ball. She was glad it was growing late. When the sun was gone the bees would cease for the night and the people would go home. Then maybe she could run up unnoticed and gather up all the evidence. Tomorrow there would be a real flood of people coming to gawk and wonder. She paced about nervously, watching the townspeople coming and going. She yearned to be up there, listening to what they had to say, but she was afraid Andy would start talking about seeing her this morning. She was glad for once that he was reserved and taciturn.

She climbed the stairs to watch again from the upper window. She was shocked to see the Bentzs and Currys spraying the roofs of their homes with garden hoses—wetting them down to discourage the bees. She felt weak with guilt. McMillians were standing off, looking up at their roof, and even

Mother sent Phil out to check and see if there were any bees around their eaves or shingles. Oh God! She hadn't intended to get the whole town riled up. She just wanted to get even with Pauline Fitch. Now all the neighbors were worried and uneasy. The county agent had gone away shaking his head, with Miss Fitch calling stridently after him that she was going to wire Oregon State College and get someone down here in the morning—someone that knew how to handle an emergency situation.

Andy Tatum, offended because no one was listening to him, was crankier than usual. He knew more about bees than anyone, but people kept on speculating.

The mayor, the marshal, and the sheriff had all been down to look and shake their heads and listen to Pauline, who called them all fools and threatened to take matters into her own hands.

Nora curled into her bed. She pulled a heavy quilt over her shoulders. She felt chilled. She trembled and couldn't stop. "If anyone ever finds out how this all started," she whispered. She could feel the contempt of the community. "Mother will kill me—simply *kill* me."

She remembered Mother's friends in the parlor, earlier, drinking tea and laughing at Miss Fitch. Suddenly they didn't seem friendly at all. They would soon be laughing at her, and Mother, in the same sly way. Or, they would be indignant and furious that she had caused so much trouble, had lied so glibly, had created the 'emergency situation.'

Now that darkness was falling, she decided she had to take a chance—had to sneak up to the clay pit. She started down the stairs and heard Mother's voice.

"Check all the windows, Delores. Upstairs and down. We don't want any bees getting in here and we won't be back in town for at least three weeks."

Delores sounded disappointed. "Aren't we staying in for the weekend?"

"No." Mother sounded decisive. "We're going back down to the ranch tonight. Phil is needed to help with the chores, since all the men are in town. Besides, I'm uneasy about all those bees. And Nora—" she turned to face Delores. "Where *is* that child? We're almost ready to go. She's been pacing around like a nervous cat ever since Pauline Fitch came by this afternoon. The gall of that woman!" Mother was closing drawers, packing up the clean wash, herding the children out onto the back porch. She was tired and cranky and would be glad to get back to the quiet routine. "Hurry, Delores. We're almost ready to go."

Nora slipped out into the soft dusk and ran across to Tatums. She felt

77

quite desperate when she burst into Andy's small, bright kitchen a moment later.

"Andy! You've got to help me," she began. "Pauline . . ." she stopped in confusion. Mr. Huffmeier sat at the table holding a steaming cup of coffee in his hand, looking at her in shocked surprise.

"Oh!" it was almost a wail. She started to back away, looking at Andy's unexpected guest as though she had been betrayed. Mother's voice was calling her, angry and insistent in the growing darkness.

"What is it, child?" Andy was alert and solicitous and he glanced at Huffmeier, who put the cup down carefully, not knowing if he should leave or stay.

"Ah—ah—ah—my—my shoes," said Nora suddenly. "I've lost my new shoes!" She kept looking at Andy earnestly. "I think I left them up in the clay—ah—up on the hill." She glanced briefly at the editor and then turned her attention desperately toward Andy again as she backed toward the door. "Could you possibly go up in the morning—early—and look for them—ah, in the clay pit? I'm afraid someone will take them. Mother will tan my hide!" And then she was gone again into the darkness, her bare feet making no sound.

The two men looked at each other in silence. Then Andy looked away, frowning and thoughtful.

"That girl looked scared to death," said Huffmeier. "Is the missus that hard on the kids?"

Tatum seemed evasive, puzzling over his own thoughts. Finally he answered. "She's strict. She runs a tight ship, but she is a good mother."

Daylight comes early in the desert summer and Andy was already up and crossing the bridge in the still morning dampness. It was not yet six o'clock.

"I'm a crazy old man," he admitted to himself.

Pushing through the bushes along the trail by the bridge, he climbed the steep, forty-foot embankment toward the clay pit. He pulled himself up, steadying himself from time to time on the gnarled roots of the juniper. He had watched Nora scramble nimbly up and down this incline many times but he had never realized how steep it was.

He had been puzzled and uneasy throughout the night trying to fathom her strange behavior. He was convinced that she was trying to tell him something—something she couldn't say in front of the editor. He couldn't believe it was only her lost shoes that concerned her. It seemed to be more pressing than that. She had started to say something about Pauline—but everyone was talking about Pauline. Everyone in town. Still, she had quickly stopped herself and never mentioned Pauline again.

He was puffing slightly when he finally reached the summit, and as he pushed through the brush under the cottonwoods, he stopped and stared about in amazement. Realization came slowly. There was the greasy bucket from up on the flat, half-filled with dead bees, some floating in honey. There was a lard bucket partially filled with honey and bee grubs. He saw the sharpened willow wands, the pile of damp clay marbles and the carriage spokes stuck upright in the earth.

He whistled softly. One metal spoke still held a sticky clay ball impaled on the end where Nora had left it when the heat and the growing number of bees had driven her off. And directly below, across the foot bridge, he saw the broad roof of the Fitch house pock-marked with several hundred dark clay mounds.

He stood for a moment, amusement growing in him.

"I'll be damned," said Andy. "I'll be double goddamned!"

He pulled the marble-tipped carriage spoke from the ground, looked at it critically, bent it far back, aimed at the roof below and released it. The little missile flew in a high arc completely over the roof. He missed the second time, too, but the third sticky marble, larger than the rest, splattered a little and flattened, clinging to the chimney. He smiled to himself as he smeared the cold honey on each remaining ball and flipped it down onto the roof. He was almost sorry when he picked up the last marble in the pile and sent it flying after the others. He hadn't felt so good in years.

Then he walked about, gathering up the buckets of dead bees, the willow wands, the carriage spokes, the remnants of the burned canvas. He carried them far, far up over the crest of the hill. Looking down he saw the scorched flat and ruined hives, but now he snorted and allowed himself a bitter smile. He climbed farther up into the grey reaches of the sage covered hills. Finally, he threw the buckets, one after another, and watched as they bounced and disappeared into the thick, concealing brush.

He walked back down and looked thoughtfully around the clay pit. After a moment he strode around the perimeter, shaking each bush and small tree savagely until the dry and withered leaves showered down and covered the earth like a thick blanket. He stood once more and looked down at the roof of Pauline's house bristling with little clinging dots. It was too cold yet, and too early for the bees and the house looked cold, and silent, too, with the weird little orbs seeming to grow out of the shingles.

"Just like warts on a toad," said Andy happily as he climbed back down to the trail.

Young Red Huffmeier, still wearing his cowboy gear and occasionally practicing his quick draw, stopped in at the newspaper office to talk to his father. He had spent the morning up at the Fitch house and was full of news. The bees were back and were crawling all over the roof and they were building more little round houses all over the place. He knew for sure that there were more of those mounds than had been there yesterday. There was a big one on the chimney and everyone agreed that it hadn't been there the day before. Half the town was standing up there right now watching. They didn't seem to be afraid of the bees too much because no one had been stung, and the bees just seemed to be interested in crawling around that roof. The other half of the town was spraying their roofs with garden hoses just in case.

"Some folks say that Andy Tatum put all those little bubbles up there because Miss Fitch burned his hives."

"Couldn't have," said the editor. "He was sitting right here in this office cussing her out all afternoon. They weren't there when Pauline left and went up to the parade. Pauline said so herself. And Mr. Tatum was right here, urging me to go up and see what she'd done to his hives. The parade wasn't half over when he came roaring in here. And he stayed right here until I finally went up there with him long after the parade was over. Miss Fitch even saw him here."

Young Red was thoughtful and quiet for a long time. Finally, he looked at his father and said seriously, "Some folks are saying that Andy Tatum could have told his bees to build those things."

"Do you believe that?"

"Well, no. I know it isn't really possible, but it would be nice."

Huffmeier laughed. "I wonder what Miss Fitch thinks?"

"Well. She's up there getting ready for those professors from over on the coast. She says Mel Harkins should never have been hired as the county agent, so young and right out of school and all. She says they are a whole new breed of bees that's invading this country, and we'll all be thanking her before this summer is over for stopping them—that is, if she can stop them."

"What do you think?" the editor asked his son.

Red didn't answer. He was staring at the floor and chewing his lip pensively. Finally he asked. "Have you ever seen Andy Tatum smile?"

The question startled Huffmier. He looked at the kid with new interest but he answered casually, "Well. Maybe once."

"Well. He's smiling now," said young Red. "He's sitting there on his porch watching all the people tramp up the hill, watching Pauline Fitch marching around, giving orders and acting important, and he hasn't stopped smiling all morning."

Huffmeier looked over his glasses at the boy, amusement and growing respect reflected in his eyes. "You are going to make a newspaper man, yet." The words were a sincere compliment. "But, I tell you—Andy was right here in this office."

"I don't think *he* did it," said Red, "but maybe he knows who did."

On Thursday, the *Desert Sun* published a carefully factual report of the strange phenomenon of the bees at the mouth of the canyon on Pauline Fitch's house. The excitement of the parade, the prizes won by the various floats and other elements of the 4th of July celebration were also reported. The townspeople showed little interest in the celebration, but they were consumed with curiosity over Miss Fitch and the bees. They talked of nothing else. Theories were discussed and discarded or discussed and expanded. Every development, every detail was breathlessly repeated.

By this time, some of the smaller clay balls had dried out in the sun and rolled down from the roof. The bees didn't seem quite so numerous and energetic, either. Most of the neighbors quit soaking their roofs.

Shortly after noon on Thursday when the professors arrived from Corvallis, Pauline met the two men and took them immediately to her house. There they saw the moving clots of bees crawling about in the hot sun, clustering on the strange dark cylinders that seemed to grow out of the shingles. They looked at each other in amazement and listened with incredulity as Pauline, very important and decisive, explained the details and answered their questions.

"I insisted that you come right away," she told them in her positive way. "You must recommend a spray or something before those bees hatch."

The two men went into the house and set up a laboratory on the kitchen table. They scraped down several of the clay balls and carefully examined them under their microscopes. They retrieved several of the hard little marbles that had dried and rolled down from the roof and examined those also. They found large bees, small bees, scorched bees and bee larvae, all dead and all neatly wrapped in strange blue-black clay balls some of which were now so hardened by the sun that they were difficult to break open. The two scientists dissolved several of the strange marbles in water and shook the mixture. They tasted the liquid sparingly, examined the sediment and dropped chemicals into it.

"It's a hoax, Miss Fitch," they announced at last, and while she raged and threatened, they packed up their microscopes and test tubes and went up to the hotel and the room she had reserved for them.

Andy Tatum heard the news almost as soon as Miss Fitch. The people standing around the kitchen door came streaming down from the hill, bursting with the details. The first person they met was Andy sitting on his porch.

"You were right," they told him. "We should have listened to you. Those professors said that bees couldn't hatch under those conditions. You were right all the time!"

Andy sat there, smiling to himself for awhile and then went and saddled his horse. He tied a half-gallon jug of honey behind the saddle and prepared to ride down the valley. The late afternoon sun was losing some of its intensity as he headed south through town. Workmen carrying their empty lunch buckets were just coming home from the sawmill. They had already heard this latest development and they stood about laughing and talking to their friends.

The wives of the millworkers pulled the cooking suppers to the back of the stove and hastened out to enjoy this latest bit of gossip with their neighbors.

"A hoax," they called to each other. "Someone flim-flammed old Fitch."

A couple of young boys saw Andy Tatum riding down the dusty street on his saddle horse and they started to wave, very timidly at first. But when they saw he was smiling they ran along shouting and waving frantically. Someone yelled "Attaboy, Andy," and although he looked surprised and then rather stern again, people kept on laughing and waving all along the way.

"Can I quit watering down my roof now, Tatum?" someone called after him. Larry Richards pretended to hide behind his gate and yelled, "Don't sic your bees on me, Andy. I'm behaving myself."

He trotted on along the gravel track, the steady crunch, crunch of the horse's hooves sounding gradually louder as he crossed the empty lots below town. It had been a long, long time since he had paid a social visit to anyone besides Tina. Truthfully, he was a little surprised to find himself, after all these lonely years, riding down to visit a child and bring her a present of honey.

"Well," he smiled, feeling suddenly light-hearted knowing he was putting the lengthy, self-imposed exile behind him.

"I have to tell her not to worry. There were no shoes in the clay pit."

Shaking his head, he reached to scratch the back of his neck. He smiled more broadly. "I hope no one introduces her to a sling shot," he told himself. "She could be lethal!"

Chapter 4

🌸 MUSIC APPRECIATION - 1929

"Somebody's coming!" Nora said.

She could see the man walking toward them through the sagebrush. The dancing heat waves distorted his image but she knew she would see the details more clearly as the man came closer.

"I wonder why he's walking around in this heat," said Dad.

"I think he's a bum off the train," Nora pointed to the slow moving train a short distance away.

Dad sighed in frustration and reached again for the level. He placed it along the top of the door frame and moved close to watch the spot of air as it settled slightly off center in the tube of liquid.

"I must be doing something wrong." He shook his head, discouraged. "Sometimes it measures exactly right, yet the catch on the door doesn't quite meet."

Nora didn't answer. She stood watching the stranger as he came through the lower gate. Her dog, Laddie, came to stand beside her. A dust devil swirled across the yard.

The man removed his hat and slapped the dust from his legs and chest. He strode up the path smiling.

"Hello," he called. "I heard the pounding and figured someone was building something. Thought maybe I could get a drink of water. This heat is fierce." His voice sounded friendly and confident.

"Help yourself," Dad nodded toward the pump. "A fellow can't get far in this country without water."

The man picked up the dipper and started the water flowing. He drank thirstily.

"This must be a new well," he noted. "You found good water."

"How can you tell it's a new well?" asked Nora. "It looks just like the one over at the ranch."

The man smiled. "New pipe," he said. "New shiny pump. And no one has stabilized the pump yet. It's too heavy to leave swaying on the top of that pipe for too long. In time it will break the pipe."

"It is new," Dad stepped forward smiling. "Luckily, we found that artesian well just a few weeks ago. I brought out those heavy planks there from the mill last week. I'm drying them out in the sun and I'll build a watering trough and a pump platform in a day or two."

"I'm John Smith," the man shook Dad's proffered hand. "I can fix most anything."

"Can you now?" Dad beamed. "Maybe you can help me with this door."

The two men walked to the unfinished cabin and soon Nora could hear them laughing and hammering away happily. She went to look at the pump and wondered why she had never noticed the new pipe and the shiny pump that swayed slightly when you used it. It was much different than the one back home.

The sun continued its slow descent behind the western mountains and Nora knew that it would soon be cooler. She started into the meadow to round up the team.

John Smith came out of the cabin carrying a two-by-four.

"Holy smoke!" He spoke with feeling. "Look at that sunset!"

"It's like that most every night," Nora told him. "It's beautiful."

"It's sensational," said Smith. "And it's like that every night?"

"Almost every night in the summer—unless it rains."

"I'm going to love this part of the country," the man said. "I've never seen a display quite like that."

"My Dad says it's because there is so much dust in the air out here in the desert," Nora told him. "And a breeze comes up about the time the sun goes down and I guess that blows the dust around." She continued on her way.

"You come along home with us now, and have some supper," Dad invited John Smith. He harnessed the team as he spoke. "I can't tell you how much you helped me here this afternoon."

They rode home though the evening shadows and Dad explained.

"See there," he pointed. "Across the railroad tracks and beyond that alkali field. That is the home place. When we harness the teams, plod across that big field, cross the tracks and get to where we have to mow or rake the hay, we've used up almost an hour that we should have been working in the field. Same thing at noon. We have to take the teams all the way back to the barn, water them and have our meal. Then it's nearly another hour back to the field. So we spend three or so hours just getting to and from our work. That is why I'm building that cabin over at the edge of the field. The men can get back to work as soon as they have finished their meal."

He turned on the seat to point to the flat meadow and the new stacks of hay that stood there. "There are 800 acres of hay there and it takes most of the summer to put it up for feed for the winter. But we waste 18 hours a week going back and forth from the ranch house. Now multiply that 18 hours by six or seven weeks and you can see we aren't being too efficient."

John Smith nodded his understanding.

"And when you multiply that 108 hours by six or eight men you are really wasting time and money," he said. "I agree. You'd better build a cabin."

Nora's mind was in turmoil. She wondered if she would ever be able to do arithmetic in her head that fast. She couldn't keep up if she tried to work it out with a pencil and paper.

Mother hurried about setting an extra place at the table. Dad washed up at the kitchen sink while the stranger cleaned up out in the bunk house.

"He says his name is John Smith," Dad explained, "and he—"

"John Smith!" Mother snorted in suspicion. I'll bet! Why doesn't he just call himself John Doe? I'll bet he's running from something."

Dad was indignant. "I don't care if his name is—is Beelzebub," he said. "I'm going to hire him. I got more done in two hours with him helping me than I've accomplished in the last two weeks."

"He's real nice, Mother," said Nora.

And so John Smith came to the ranch. At first he lived at the home place and stayed in the bunkhouse, but soon he moved over to the half finished cabin and worked at completing it even when Dad had to go to town or to sheep camp. John did most of his own cooking and kept a small supply of groceries in the now nearly finished kitchen.

A couple of times a week Nora and Kevin would ride their horses over to the new cabin to bring John a loaf of bread or some fresh milk. Each time they were surprised and impressed by the amount of work that had been finished and the improvements that he had made. The first week they found a sturdy watering trough for the animals and a stable platform that safely held the new pump erect.

And John Smith found the town dump.

"There's a lot of treasures to be found in that dump," he told the children. "We shouldn't let them go to waste."

One day he carried home a broken screen door. The next day the screen, repaired and painted, hung guarding the front door. He found a cot with two broken legs. He carved two new legs that matched perfectly, then stretched a length of fence wire over the frame and spread his bedroll upon the sturdy cot to form his new comfortable bed.

He brought home half-filled buckets of paint, a half keg of new nails and some tools with broken handles that were soon repaired. He retrieved a hasp for the gate, some discarded sections of stove pipe and many pieces of bicycles from which he constructed a completed bike that Kevin soon learned to ride. He painted the bicycle red with white details that perfectly matched the brand new bikes at the hardware store. He polished the old cast-off handlebars to a glorious shine.

Now even Mother began to unbend a little. She became less formal—almost friendly—and when John Smith occasionally accepted Dad's invitation to come to the home place for a meal, he always brought his oil can along. Now not a cupboard door, not a screen door nor any metal-hinged part of the house squeaked. And he fixed Mother's sewing machine. It ran like new.

One evening as they finished supper, Mother sent Katie into the living room to practice her piano lesson.

"That piano needs a good tuning," she said. "I've sent for the fellow that tunes the piano several times. He comes from Klamath Falls and is much too expensive, and you have to pay for the bus fare over and back as well as the tuning. And I've been waiting for two months or more. Every time he comes over, some people in town will persuade him to tune their pianos and I'm left high and dry again."

"I can tune your piano," said John Smith.

Mother hesitated. "I—I—think we'd better leave that job to a professional," she said at last.

Dad straightened a little in his chair. Mother avoided his eyes as she carried some dishes to the sink. Dad cleared his throat.

"Do you play?" Dad turned back to John Smith.

John shrugged. "A little. I play by ear."

"We'll have to have a little concert after dessert," said Dad.

Mother came with the pie. She gave the biggest piece to John Smith as if to offer an apology for not accepting his offer to tune the piano.

Nora looked at John Smith with new respect. How could he play the piano with his ears? She could hardly wait.

The after-dinner concert was a huge success. John Smith asked for requests. He played *America, Danny Boy, Red Wing,* the *Missouri Waltz,* and many other songs. He seemed completely at ease at the piano and even if the instrument was out of tune, the music sounded wonderful. He played with his fingers like everyone else—not his ears.

"Mrs. Norris should hear you," said Katie. "She comes down to give me my lesson tomorrow. Can't you come over and play for her? She comes right after lunch."

"Oh, that's right," said Mother. "Katie, I forgot that your lesson is tomorrow. I'm going down to Thomas's. We're having a quilting bee. But you'll be OK here with Kevin and Nora. I'm taking the baby with me. And you'll have to practice in the morning. You sounded pretty ragged when you played awhile ago."

John Smith did show up right after lunch the next day. He and Elsa Norris talked about music, the songs they liked, and where they had learned to play. They even played a duet together.

"You play beautifully," Mrs. Norris told him. "You play—well, like a professional. You play with—authority," she finished.

"I've played in clubs all over the country. New York, Chicago, San Francisco, Kansas City and most places in between."

"How come you wind up in this little, out of the way, desert town?"

John Smith hesitated a moment. "Just lucky, I guess," he said.

"This piano is so out of tune," said Mrs. Norris. "I wish that fellow from Klamath would get over here as he promised."

"Let's try something," said John. He took the vase and the embroidered cloth from the top of the piano and folded back the top.

"Hit middle C," he directed Mrs. Norris. "Now go slowly up and down the scale."

"It's really off-key on the E and F," said Mrs. Norris as she complied.

Smith went to his coat and returned with a small case of tools. He went out to the blacksmith shop and brought in a sturdy box on which to stand. He reached into the back of the piano. Mrs. Norris continued to hit the keys he indicated and the sounds slid up a notch or down a bit as he tinkered with the unseen strings inside.

Nora hoped they knew what they were doing. She went to the kitchen and made herself a jam sandwich, then sat in the sun on the back steps and ate it. She threw some of the crusts out into the yard and watched as several chickens fought over them.

At last she went to the porch swing and dozed in the sun. She awoke as John Smith left to return to the cabin.

Inside, Katie and Mrs. Norris laughed and danced about in glee. They sat and played tunes and snatches of songs and laughed even harder.

"It's wonderful," said Mrs. Norris. "He's done a wonderful job. His work is even better than that fellow from Klamath Falls. I know I can get him a lot of work tuning pianos for people in town. Come on Katie. I still have to give you your lesson."

A few days later the children rode over to the cabin to bring supplies to John Smith. He came driving the wagon up close to the cabin and carried a strange burden into the kitchen.

"Lookee what I found in the dump," he sang out. "It's an old Victrola. Looks like the first one that was ever made, and there's a couple of boxes of records out there also. Hope they still work." He placed a strange looking machine enclosed in a weathered wooden box on the table and went back to the wagon. He came in carrying a metal object. To Nora the big metal horn looked like a witch's hat turned upside down.

"It's the loud speaker," said John. "Makes the words on the records loud enough so you can hear them."

"How does it work?"

"Well. I'll have to see if I can make it work. You use this handle to wind up the machine. Then put the needle in contact with the record and it plays until it runs down. Then you wind it up again."

"But where does the record go? The ones uptown in the furniture store have a flat place where you put the record." Nora felt dubious.

Smith laughed. "This is a real antique," he explained. "Really old. It doesn't have flat records."

Don't the records have to be flat? How can they play if they aren't?"

"Look in those two boxes," Smith told her. "I hope they work."

"Are you sure it's a phonograph?" Nora became more dubious by the minute.

"Yeah, I'm sure." Smith examined the machine critically, almost forgetting Nora's presence. "I'm going to have to take it all apart and soak lots of the metal pieces in kerosene. I hope the innards aren't too rusty." He reached immediately for his oil can.

Phil arrived from the field where he had been fencing the haystacks. Soon he and Smith were engrossed in dismantling the strange object.

Nora opened the dusty boxes. Inside were several dozen round cylinders. To her they looked like tin cans with both ends cut out. Some were broken and hopelessly cracked. Some had chunks broken out of them. Several were smashed into shards of dark material that littered the bottom of the boxes. She almost snorted as Mother sometimes did. How could they call these things records?

"Be careful," Smith warned. "There is a little box of needles in that one carton. Some of them are new, I think. They will be great if we can get this thing working. And Nora, do you want to take that clean cloth there, and wipe the dirt off those cylinders? The dirt and dust will clog the grooves and make the sound garbled." He took one of the records and demonstrated how to clean them, pointing out the grooves that made the sounds.

"Just throw those badly broken ones into the wood box," he said. "They are made of paraffin and will burn like crazy."

Nora began to take more interest.

The next week John Smith worked hopefully on the strange machine. He cleaned and polished the cabinet while the small, strange metal pieces soaked in oil and kerosene to remove the rust. He used a toothbrush, sandpaper, toothpicks and even a long sewing needle to pick out the dust and rust from the stationary pieces of the motor. He soaked the removable pieces and cleaned them and laid them out carefully on a clean kitchen towel on the table. Nora wondered if he would ever be able to reassemble that machine again.

The next week school started and the children seldom went to the cabin. The second weekend they rode over to visit with John Smith, who had been absent from their lives.

He met the children at the door, smiling and happy.

"Come," he said. "It's working."

They watched breathlessly as John Smith carefully wound the handle. He slid the record over the round cylinder, then set the needle, with the attached amplifier, carefully on the record.

Suddenly the room was filled with music: Garbled music, but music nonetheless.

"Wow!" said Kevin. "That's 'The Star Spangled Banner' it's playing."

Nora was grateful that Kevin recognized the tune. Now she, too identified the song.

After the lead-in, voices started singing the words. Immediately Smith and Kevin joined in the singing, and soon Nora raised her voice. She sounded a little low so she slid her voice up to join the other two. A happy, unrehearsed concert followed. She forgot that the words and music from the Victrola were sometimes unrecognizable. She understood that this machine was probably older than John Smith, maybe even older than Grandma and that it was the first talking machine ever invented.

"Do you sing at school?" Smith asked her.

"Yes. The whole class sings every morning."

"Does the teacher play the piano for your songs?"

"No. She's got this thing called a pitch pipe and we are supposed to get the key from that."

"I see," said Smith. "Do you like the pitch pipe?"

Nora hesitated. She had never thought about whether she liked it or not. It didn't do much for her. She couldn't seem to adjust her voice to that scrawny note from the pitch pipe.

"I don't know," she answered honestly. "I just wait a few words when the rest of the class starts to sing. Then I join in. Sometimes I sound too high so I slide my voice down until I sound like the others. Sometimes I'm too low, so then I slide up and sing along."

"I see," said Smith. "Once you get the right key, you have a pretty good voice."

He selected several other records and the concert continued.

"Here is a good one," he said. "I've heard them sing this one in Harlem. It was a big hit there. The thing is, I can't seem to remember the exact words. They'll come to me eventually, but…"

He wound the handle on the machine and started the music. He tapped his foot and nodded his head, closing his eyes as the solo began. Nora thought this one was hopelessly garbled. She made out the word 'honey' and maybe 'home', but the rest was just noise.

"That music is really strange," said Nora when the record ended. "It seems to be going along just great—then all of a sudden there's a bunch of noise and drums that—well, the drums interrupt the melody."

"Yeah," Smith agreed. "That's called 'The Blues.' In Harlem they have a whole—well, sort of different kind of music. They have jazz, and the blues and others. It's not just there in Harlem anymore. Lots of people all over the country are picking up on it."

He started the record again, and hummed along. Nora liked the melody, but hated when the drums interrupted. She wished she could make out the words.

That evening she asked Mother if she knew anything about 'jazz,' or 'the blues.'

"It's nonsense," said Mother as she scrubbed the sink. "Some of the words to the songs are rotten…well, really suggestive. There is so much lovely music around that one doesn't need to bring themselves down to that level! I hope they aren't introducing jazz into the music at school."

"No." said Nora. "I just wondered about it."

"Don't waste your time," said Mother.

On Saturday, Nora took her tablet and pencil with her when she and Dad went to the cabin. The men went to replace some beams on the bridge and she stayed alone in the little house. She played the new song over and over on the Victrola and tried to make out the words. As the hours passed she became more familiar with both the music and the garbled words. Sometimes she now was able to catch a whole line. The word 'honey' was repeated many times as someone called a child, or a girlfriend or someone 'honey.' She felt that if she recognized some of the words, John Smith might be able to fill in the others.

She showed the tablet to Smith when he came into the cabin after the work on the bridge was finished. Dad was harnessing the team for the ride home.

"I figured out some of the words," she said, "and I even got two whole sentences. Maybe that will help you remember. Listen to this."

Oh, my honey. The skies are black
Oh, sweet baby, won't you please come back?

John Smith's face lit up.

"Yeah. Yeah. That's part of it. Did you get anything else?" He looked at the scribbled words that dotted the page.

"'Oh, 'my honey' is in there a lot," said Nora, indicating the words on the sheet. "And at one place, right there—" she pointed, "The song says, 'I'll do the washing' – at least that's what I think it said."

"Yeah. That's right. 'I'll do the washing, I'll mend the clothes—The way I need you, nobody knows.'" Smith did a little jig across the room. "This is a big help. I'll work on it. Your dad is calling, so you'd better go. You've done a really good job here." He was already winding up the machine. "I'll work on it."

* * * *

The school year slipped away. Halloween was approaching and it was nearly Mother's turn to entertain the Altar Society. Mother washed all the lovely 'good' china and cleaned the house from top to bottom. She worried about the decorations and decided she would bring in some of the bright colored fall leaves. Then she remembered how well John Smith played the piano and decided to ask him to come and entertain the guests. He agreed, and they decided that he would play background music while the ladies ate their lunch.

The children rode over to the cabin and found that Smith had remembered or retrieved all the words to the song and the children sang along with him as he played the record on the restored Victrola.

On Saturday, when the Altar Society was to come for the meeting, Mother was up early, giving orders before she was even dressed.

"Nora, put new, fresh bars of soap in the bathroom. Phil, set up two card tables in the dining room. The dining room table isn't big enough to accommodate sixteen guests. Katie, those linens and napkins are all ironed and ready. You set the tables and don't forget the napkin rings. Dad, I've made arrangements for Sadie Noonan to take care of the younger children. Take them in to town anytime this morning, and don't forget to pick up ice at the creamery."

At last the guests started arriving. John Smith came from the cabin and at first Nora didn't recognize him. He wore a suit and tie and a white shirt that make his tanned face look remarkably handsome.

"You look wonderful," Nora told him. "I'll bet you didn't get that suit in the dump."

"Nora!" Mother spoke in annoyance. "I should have sent you into town with the baby."

When the meeting was over and luncheon was served, John Smith sat at the piano and softly played a medley of songs. The ladies were delighted. They loved the music. They appreciated the wonderful food. The weather, the decorations, the renewed friendships, the relaxed atmosphere—all helped to make the day a grand success.

Katie, in a pretty white apron, helped with the serving.

Nora tried to stay out of sight. She wore her best dress and hoped to remember to be ladylike at all times. She was glad that Mother only had to entertain the Altar Society once a year. She sat quietly listening as Smith played *I'll Take You Home Again, Kathleen.*

Suddenly, he launched into a snappy, happy sounding tune that Nora had never heard before. The ladies sat alert and some of them swayed in their chairs. Some snapped their fingers in rhythm with the piano. They smiled and nodded in approval. Many tapped their feet as though they were dancing.

"By golly," said Smith. "Most of these ladies seem to know the modern music." He played a little louder, a little faster.

"I've never heard that song before," said Nora.

"It's called 'The Charleston.'" Smith whispered. "Look. They love it!"

The ladies did seem to 'love it.' The dining room became completely animated, and they cheered loudly when the tune ended.

"Let's sing our new song," Smith suggested suddenly. "You sing it."

"Oh. I couldn't," Nora protested. "I always start out either too high or too low."

"Never mind. I'll just move up a note or two," Smith promised.

He launched into the beginning bars of the song from the Victrola. He smiled, softened the music and nodded to Nora to begin.

> *Oh, my honey, she sang, where you been so long?*
> *There's no fun here now. No light, no song.*

Smith adjusted the music, moving up a key or two to match Nora's voice.

> *Oh, my honey, the skies are black*
> *Oh, sweet baby, won't you please come back?*

The conversation in the dining room stuttered to a halt. Nora felt proud that the ladies liked her voice. She wished Phil were here to sing with her.

> *Oh, my honey, if you would, you could*
> *Make me feel better, make me feel good.*
> *I'll do the washing, I'll mend the clothes*
> *The way I need you, nobody knows.*

In the dining room across the hall, Nora could see many of the ladies where they sat at the tables. They were being very quiet and staring at her with interest. Mother put her napkin aside and seemed to be rising from the table. Nora sang on.

> *Oh, my honey, won't you come back home?*
> *I'm going crazy just being alone.*
> *Your red kimono is all I've got*
> *Without you in it, it ain't so hot.*
> *Oh, my honey, the skies are black*
> *Oh, sweet baby, won't you please come back?*

Mother's heels beat a swift tattoo across the hall floor. There was anger and outrage in her voice.

"NORA!"

"What? *What?*" Nora felt a paralyzing horror growing within her. What had she done? She thought she was adding to their enjoyment. She turned in desperation to look to John Smith for him to explain to her mother.

John Smith was gone. The front screen door was just swinging silently shut on its well-oiled hinges.

Chapter 5

❧ HALLOWEEN

"Don't leave your room," Mother said. "Well, you can go down to the window seat. But do *not* go downstairs or have anything to say to Mrs. Baldwin."

Nora nodded.

"I want you to stay in bed as much as possible," Mother continued. "You have been pretty sick for two days and the doctor said you should rest." She searched Nora's face for a moment, worry reflected in her eyes.

"I wish I could take you into town with the other children," she said. "but, Aunty Sue was afraid her little ones might catch whatever you had." She turned away and started down the stairway, then she turned back. "Tonight is Halloween," she reminded Nora, "and there is no way you can go out if you look the least bit tired or under the weather."

Nora nodded again.

"I'll leave your lunch in the icebox and when you go get it, don't stop and talk to Mrs. Baldwin at all. Bring your food and milk right back up here with you—and do it quietly. Understand?"

"Yes," said Nora. She hesitated. "Mother, I just forgot that she doesn't want to be called Minnie. I just said 'Minnie, do you want to go see my little heifer?' and she got mad! We always called her Minnie—and I don't even remember that name she wants to be called."

"She's decided she wants to be called 'Minerva'," said Mother. "But don't you even call her that. You call her Mrs. Baldwin. That is how a respectful child should address her!"

Mother hurried off down the stairs and Nora stood, undecided, in the hall. She was always getting into trouble. She'd better not make any other mistakes today or she would not be going out for Halloween. It was such a fun night. She'd die if she had to stay in.

Suddenly Mother hurried back up the steps.

"Nora! When Phil comes in, tell him to study that lesson in the catechism or he won't be going out tonight either. The lesson on the Beatitudes! He doesn't know the first thing about them and he's supposed to have them memorized by Sunday. Help him if you can."

"I'll try," Nora agreed.

She slipped down a few steps beyond the window seat and watched as Mrs. Baldwin tinkered with the sewing machine. Mother brought out a basket of sewing and threw several spools of thread on top of the fabric.

"These quilt pieces are all cut to size," she told Mrs. Baldwin. "I have to make up two bedrolls for the men to take to camp. These are wool pieces and will be easy to work with. Make five blocks across and seven down. That will make a fine large quilt—and I'm going to have to leave you here on your own for most of the day." She hurried to find her purse and returned. "My husband has hired two new men and neither of them has a bed roll. I just hope they don't have lice." She looked about distractedly. "I hate to rush off like this, but …Oh, they're waiting! Just look in the icebox for your lunch—" Her words became indistinct as she hastened down the steps and out to the waiting car.

Mrs. Baldwin stood at the window and watched as Mother was driven away. She looked at the basket of sewing and shrugged. She walked to the front hall and wound the handle on the telephone. Nora heard her giving the number to 'central' and then talking to some friend. She made a second call and returned to the dining room where the sewing machine was set up. She shrugged again and went to the kitchen. She returned chewing on a cookie, with an additional cookie in her hand. Then she sat down at the sewing machine and started to work.

Nora slipped back up the few steps to the hallway and went to her room. She lay on the bed and thought about Mrs. Baldwin. That lady was a wonderful seamstress. She made her living going about the country sewing for overworked housewives or those women who couldn't sew. Often she would stay for a week at some lonely ranch way out in the desert and catch up on all the mending and sewing that had to be done. She sewed for many of the women in town also, but she always went to their homes to sew—never allowing them to bring their mending or dressmaking to her house.

Nora knew where she lived, even delivered the paper to her house there in town. But she disliked old Minnie with no reservations. Most of the adults that she knew were nice, friendly people. When she delivered the paper route for Phil, most people smiled and thanked her, but not old Minnie. And she wasn't really that old, either. But she was mean. She told lies and exaggerated little incidents until they became almost mortal sins. She told Mother one day that she had seen Nora going into the saloon and talking with the men there. Which was a barefaced lie. Mother had warned her not to go into the pool halls and when Nora said that she had to deliver a paper there, Mother said, "Go the two steps in the door and put the paper on the counter, whirl around, and come straight out again. Don't speak to anyone, and let Phil go collect when the month is up." Nora had done that and then the old biddy had told Mother that big tale about her going in and talking to the men.

Last night she had told Uncle Jack that Minnie was coming to sew today and he said, "Good Lord! Mrs. Newsy Paper herself. She knows every bit of gossip in the valley and loves to spread it around, and add a bit here and there to make it a little juicier. I'm keeping out of there tomorrow."

Pete had laughed and teased Uncle Jack saying, "I wish I weren't leaving for camp tonight. I'd hang around just to watch her in action when she's around you. Sure, she has a great crush on you, a real throbbing heart when you are near."

"Go on," said Uncle Jack, but he blushed up just the same.

Nora picked up the catechism and found the chapter on the Beatitudes. She started reading, sounding out the hard words.

> *Blessed are the poor in spirit*
> *For theirs is the kingdom of heaven*
> *Blessed are the meek*
> *For they shall inherit the land.*
> *Blessed are those who hunger*
> *For they shall be filled.*
> *Blessed are the peacemakers*
> *They shall be called the children of God.*

Halfway through the lesson, she put the book down and shook her head.

"Wow!" thought Nora. "Phil had better settle down and learn this stuff in a hurry or neither of us will get out tonight."

Nora was dozing off in the quiet room when she heard voices. She sat up in the bed, wondering if she was hearing things. She heard laughter and more voices. She jumped from the bed, slipped down the hall and descended a few steps to where she could look through the banister.

Two women she had never seen before were greeting Mrs. Baldwin and settling down near the sewing machine. They must be the friends she had called right after Mother left. Soon they were talking and laughing.

"Oh by the way," said the chubby lady called Vera. "You remember the big wedding Carol Higby's daughter had. Four bridesmaids, banks of flowers and all the trimmings. Well, guess what. She's pregnant!"

"Already?" Mrs Brewster squealed.

"She's showing," said Vera. "And laughing and talking about it as though she were all excited."

"Well, what do you know…?" said Elsie.

"It always takes nine months for the second or third child," said Mrs. Brewster, 'but the first one can come any time."

"Well, this one will have sore feet from running so fast to get here," said Elsie. The ladies dissolved into gales of laughter.

The three women slipped from one subject to another without missing a moment. Nora learned more from them in half an hour than—well, her head was spinning.

Each of the guests reached into the basket of quilt blocks and carefully placed two of the blocks together, then handed them to Mrs. Baldwin. She quickly sewed them together and reached for the next pair. The sewing was progressing very rapidly. So was the conversation.

Dan Bellows has a bad case of the gout, but then he's had a drinking problem for years and it finally caught up with him.

Ted Rogers wrecked his new car. Yes, the one called a Studebaker. The only one of its kind in town, and he had paid almost $500 for it. He was probably drinking, too. And guess what? Mrs. Brewster had heard that he had Catherine Tolby in the car with him. I wonder what Mr. Tolby thinks. Those two have had a 'thing' going for many months, but think no one knows.

And that Brewer boy? The one that played basketball and had his name in the paper all the time? Well he was sporting a big black eye that a neighbor fellow was supposed to have given him when he came home and found the kid talking with his wife.

"I'll bet it was more than talking—" Elsie passed more quilt blocks.

"Oh," said Mrs. Brewster, "I made curtains for Eva Harrier last week. She has painted her living room the most awful shade of green."

More quilt blocks were passed.

That Chester Rowe was a smart aleck kid. His team ran away with him, and one of the horses wound up with a leg in the watering trough and the horse is too badly injured to work. Mr. Rowe was trying to borrow or rent a horse so he'd have a team to finish the field work, but he couldn't find a horse anywhere. He should give that kid a good whipping!

Nora listened for almost an hour. Then she heard her own name mentioned.

"Yes," Mrs Baldwin was saying. "Her name is Nora and she's the meanest little girl I've ever seen. She's bold as a brass monkey and fights with her sister Katie all day long. Those two don't agree on anything."

Nora sat, stunned. She and Katie did disagree on some things, but they often played together, sang together, had fun together. They played cards with Uncle Jack and Pete and Phil, and sometimes teased each other.

Mrs. Baldwin was just returning from the kitchen with a plate of cookies.

"Eat up," she told her friends. "Mrs. Nolan will never miss them, and if she does I'll just tell her the kids ate them. Nora and Phil will be home before she gets back."

Mrs. Brewster seated herself at the sewing machine again.

And then there was a handsome fellow, right here, named Jack. He owned half this big ranch and half of all those sheep. No. He didn't just work for his brother. He was in partnership with him. Mrs. Baldwin was sure. And guess what? He had shown some real interest in her. Yes, in Minerva herself. She hadn't had much of an opportunity to talk with him. He was really very shy. He would be coming in for lunch in an hour or so, and she would talk with him then. It would be nice to have him all to herself for a change instead of having all that big family around, interrupting and butting in.

Nora remembered Pete teasing Uncle Jack last night and telling him that Minnie-Minerva had a great crush on him. And now the old biddy was waiting for him to come in, hoping she would have him all to herself.

The ladies were preparing to leave. They laughed and chattered as they gathered their belongings and went down the front steps, giving Mrs. Baldwin all kinds of advice about how to handle the handsome young man.

Nora retreated quietly to the window seat and looked down over the garden and across the barn yard. There in the distance she saw Uncle Jack, coming on horseback from the lower field, headed for the barn. She wished she could warn him.

She slid back to her place behind the banister and saw Mrs. Baldwin looking through the bag she had carried in when she arrived. The woman took a comb and brush from the bag, and a ruffled garment of some sort. She retreated into the bathroom.

Nora ran down the stairs, tiptoed to the kitchen, retrieved two sandwiches from the icebox and started out the back door. She turned, hurried back and took two sugar cubes from the bowl. She arrived, breathless at the barn, her bare feet making no sound as she ran through the granary. Uncle Jack, just unsaddling the horse, looked at her in surprise.

From a stall, a half-grown calf came mooing a greeting.

"Minnie Baldwin is waiting for you to come in for lunch," Nora said. She fed a sugar cube to her calf, Peaches. "She told her friends that she would have you all to herself for an hour or so."

Uncle Jack blinked in surprise.

"If you want to talk to her I'll take the sandwiches back and put them in the icebox, but if you don't want to talk to her you can eat them out here and just let her wait."

"What else did Mrs. Big Mouth have to say?" Uncle Jack reached for the sandwiches.

"Oh, so much I can't even remember." Nora said. "Sue Higby is pregnant and—showing. I don't know *what* she's showing, but the baby will be born with sore feet because it's in such a hurry to get here."

Uncle Jack blinked again and took a huge bite of his sandwich.

Peaches mooed again and Nora fed her the second sugar cube.

"Oh, yes. Ted Baker wrecked his new stew baker. I think he hit Catherine Tolby, but I'm not sure. I've got to get back to the house quick, before Minnie gets through in the bathroom. I don't think she even knows I'm home, or she has forgotten."

Nora started for the door but stopped again.

"And Chester Rowe. He's a nice kid in school. Is always nice to us. His team ran away, and one of the horses hurt its leg and can't work. Now his Dad is having a terrible time trying to find another horse to make a team so they can finish the field work. Have we got a horse we could loan him? He is really a swell kid and they said Mr. Rowe would even rent the horse."

Uncle Jack swallowed and was about to answer, but Nora was gone. He stepped to the door to see her running through the yard and mounting the back steps into the ranch house. He shook his head, hoping Minnie Baldwin was still in the bathroom.

Nora snatched her sandwich and milk from the kitchen and mounted the stairs silently, her bare feet making no sound. As she ate her lunch she could hear Mrs. Baldwin pacing about downstairs, and finally the hum of the sewing machine started again.

She went to her place behind the banister and was surprised to see Mrs. Baldwin wearing a lavender colored blouse with a deep ruffle around the neck. Her hair was swept up to the top of her head and little curls peeked out above her ears. The woman kept looking toward the back door, and then toward the clock. If she heard a sound from the yard she would pinch her cheeks and smile, then settle back in disappointment when no one came up the steps.

Nora felt a great rush of satisfaction.

It was almost dark when Mother arrived home. She was happy to see that Phil and Nora were busily studying the Beatitudes. Nora didn't tell her that Phil had been home only a few minutes before she arrived.

"What time did Mrs. Baldwin leave?" Mother asked.

"About 4 o'clock, I think."

Mother was impressed. "She really got a lot done," she said. "She works fast."

"She had help," Nora told her. "Two of her friends stopped in this morning and they put the blocks together and handed them to her so all she had to do was guide them through. They did work fast."

The Halloween parties at the school were always a huge success, and Nora was happy she felt well enough to attend. Mother was on the committee for the third grade and the mothers and the children made huge popcorn balls for all the students and anyone else who stopped in for a treat. Mother prepared the hot, sweet syrup that was poured over the popcorn, and the children buttered their hands and formed the mixture into balls.

Johnnie Proxmeier came to help. He stirred the syrup into the popped corn with a huge wooden spoon and soon had the mothers laughing and relaxed as he made the task look almost easy. He helped the children, and soon had them laughing as well. He excused himself and said he had to go play a ghost for the sixth graders.

"He's outrageous!" Mother was smiling. "He isn't intimidated by anyone. I hope he gets back soon."

And he did come back. He brought a bucket of hot suds and started cleaning the sticky tables and desks. He gave the bucket to two of the boys and showed them how to wash the door handles.

"These knobs are so sticky that you kids may never get out of the third grade," he told them.

Nora slipped out as the clean up went on and was soon joined by Johnnie Proxmeier, his sister June, and Chester Rowe. Nora hurried them along her paper route and pointed out where all the customers kept their trash. They soon had two gunny sacks full of empty cans, broken toys, crushed boxes, raked up leaves and many pounds of plain garbage, potato peelings, apple peelings, carrot peelings, meat bones and leftover food. They hurried past the North school, down the road past the bakery and soon saw Minnie Baldwin's house. Johnnie and Chester each took a gunny sack, sneaked behind her house and turned the sack over. Then they ran, dragging the sack behind them as the contents spilled out all over her yard. Nora and June struggled to suppress their laughter as the boys came running across the street to join them. Minnie rushed out of her house, screaming and swearing in a most undignified way. She still wore her lavender blouse with her hair swept to the top of her head.

Johnnie lifted the metal gates from the gate posts of Burch's home and Sanders' home. He slid them under the foot bridge only a block away, and the four walked innocently along as they saw the town police car headed for Minnie Baldwin's house. Several times they saw groups of older, high school boys struggling to move or tip over an out-house.

Johnnie hurried back to help with the third grade clean-up.

"They'll never know I was gone," he said.

Nora loved Halloween!

The next morning it was fun all over again as, on the way to school, the children saw the results of last night's pranks. There were innumerable soaped windows. There were many missing gates and disturbed outhouses. A one-horse buggy rested atop the court house, and people wondered how anyone ever got it up there or how they would ever get it down. Several yards were trashed and a wicker baby buggy hung from a wire stretched high above Main Street.

Nora smiled as she hung her coat in the cloak room and carried her books to the desk. Everyone else seemed in good spirits also. They finished geography and were well into the arithmetic class when there was a knock on the door and the teacher was asked to send Nora to the high school office.

What in the world? thought Nora. It was bad enough to have to go to the grade school office, but she must really be in trouble if she had to go over to the high school office! She walked hesitantly along, down the long hallway, up the stairs, across the second long hallway that led to the high school. The door leading from that hallway was usually locked, but this morning it was open. Through the window she could see the sheriff's car parked at the entrance of the high school.

She saw Mr. Niederman, the high school principal, standing at the end of the next long hallway. He was always friendly toward her and knew her by name, since he was on her paper route. He even gave her a tip when he paid the monthly bill. He didn't seem to be smiling now.

"Come in," he said. It wasn't an invitation. It was a command.

Nora stepped into the room and sucked in her breath. There was the sheriff, his badge hanging prominently on his vest. Phil and Johnnie Proxmeier were there, and Chester Rowe. None were smiling. The biggest surprise was Uncle Jack, who rarely even came to town.

Nora was baffled.

In the silence it began to dawn on her that the room seemed to be in a terrible mess. The waste basket was overturned. Papers and books were scattered all over the floor. The plant that had stood on the desk lay in a shattered mess, the broken pieces of the vase strewn across the rug.

Nora looked in disbelief. There, too, was cow manure. It seemed unreal. Cow manure in the principal's office! But she could smell it now and it was—right here in this office.

She looked around in bewilderment.

"We know it's your calf," said the sheriff. "It has your Dad's brand on it."

"What calf?" Nora managed.

At the sound of her voice there came a wild, plaintive 'mooo' from across the room and Uncle Jack was hurled aside as Peaches jumped from the corner where her uncle had been holding her. The animal bumped the desk, overturned a chair and slid to a stop in front of Nora, a length of rope dangling from around its neck.

The sheriff and Mr. Niederman bumped into each other as they sought safety.

"Peaches!" Nora draped her arms around the calf. "Oh, Peaches. What are *you* doing here?"

"That's what we want to know," the sheriff spoke, trying to compose himself. "What *is* Peaches doing here? He's been here all night."

"How do I know?" Nora felt indignant. "Who brought *her* in from the ranch? Has she had her breakfast?" She continued to pet the sniffling calf.

"We think your brother put him here for a Halloween joke," said Niederman. "Phil and his two buddies." He nodded toward the boys.

The boys shook their heads in denial.

"Peaches is *not* a *he*!" said Nora. "Phil would never do such a thing!"

"Somebody did," said the sheriff. "And your ranch is close by."

"Well, we never did," said Johnnie Proxmeier.

"Whoever decided to do such a rotten thing," Nora voiced her anger, "they certainly wouldn't go to Pine Creek or Silver Lake to steal a calf. Of course they'd go somewhere close." She continued stroking her pet. "Poor baby," she whispered.

"What were you doing last night?" the principal asked the boys.

"Why we were at the party at the school," said Johnnie. "Ask anyone."

"Before the school parties?" Mr. Neiderman insisted. "Phil, where were you *before* the school parties."

"Studying," said Phil. "Nora and I were studying the Beatitudes."

"The Beatitudes?" Mr. Niederman looked puzzled. "Nora? Is that true? What are the Bea—Beatitudes?"

The sheriff was chuckling to himself.

"Yes," said Nora. "We worked on them until it was time to come into town."

"What?—What?" The principal asked again.

"You know," Nora explained. "*The Beatitudes*! 'Blessed are the poor in spirit; theirs is the kingdom of heaven.' Tell him, Philip. You know them better than I do."

Phil grimaced. "Blessed are the meek;" he intoned, "they shall inherit the land."

"The meek shall get kicked around," said Johnnie Proxmeier.

The sheriff laughed aloud. Mr. Neiderman gave him a cold look.

"Blessed are they who hunger and thirst," Phil continued, "for they shall be filled."

"Tell that to the calf," said Johnnie.

The sheriff laughed quietly now, but even the star on his vest jiggled up and down. "The Beatitudes," he whispered, "I haven't thought of them for years."

"Well, think about this," snapped the principal. "How are we going to get that animal out of here without further tearing up the school?"

"I'll just walk her down the stairs and out the door," said Nora, "but we have to get Peaches some milk. She hasn't had anything to drink, or to eat all day and all night."

"Go to the cafeteria," Niederman looked at Chester Rowe. "Tell them to give you a quart of milk."

"Better make it several quarts," said Uncle Jack. "That little heifer has to walk two miles back to the ranch. And bring a pan to pour it in."

Nora grasped the rope in one hand, but continued to pet Peaches with the other. She walked out the door and down the hall. Phil and his two friends walked with her. Uncle Jack stayed behind to help clean the principal's office. The sheriff rushed ahead to open the doors. He looked concerned when they approached the stairway, but Peaches followed Nora without any hesitation. Soon the group stood relaxing in the sunshine.

"Won't you need a bottle to feed the milk to that calf?" the sheriff asked.

"No. I taught her how to drink out of a pan. She hasn't had a bottle for a long time."

Chester Rowe arrived with three quart bottles and a pan. The calf drank thirstily and licked the pan when the last of the milk was gone.

"She's half starved," said Nora turning to the sheriff. "Can't you give her a ride home in your car?"

The man winced. "I'm afraid she'd mess up the inside of my car," he said.

'She'll never make it back to the ranch," Nora worried.

"She'll be alright," Phil spoke.

"You shut up," Nora snapped at him.

Phil's surprise turned to puzzlement.

"Wait a minute," said the sheriff. "There's the truck from the box factory." He stuck his fingers in his mouth and blew a startlingly loud whistle. The calf plunged and bawled aloud. The sheriff flagged the driver to a stop.

"We'll get a ride for you from him." He went to explain the situation to the man from the box factory.

"Let me help you with the calf," said Phil. "Peaches is almost too big for you to handle."

"You get away from me," Nora snapped. "She sure wasn't too big for you to handle, was she?"

Phil stopped short. He looked at his two friends. They stared at Nora in alarm.

"What are you talking about?" asked Phil. "You don't think we put her in the school, do you?"

"I know you did," Nora asserted. "And I lied to Mr. Niederman before I knew you did it."

The boys looked at each other again. Finally Phil asked.

"What makes you think we did it?"

"The rope," said Nora holding up the end of the tether around Peaches' neck. "I don't think some stranger would come in on the back porch and take my jump rope and take it out to the barn to steal Peaches with. It's my jump rope—and you are the one that took it." She stopped abruptly as the sheriff came back across the yard.

"He's just going to dump off that load of blocks up there a couple of houses and then he'll come back and take you and that calf down to your ranch." He looked at the boys. "Do you think we can boost that animal up into the truck?"

"Wait a minute!' said Johnnie. "Phil! Chet! Come with me."

The boys went off around the school, and by the time the empty mill truck came back, the boys were returning, carrying a heavy wooden picket gate. They placed the gate as a ramp and Nora and the calf walked up into the back of the truck with little trouble.

Nora settled down on the sawdust-covered floor and Peaches flopped down beside her. The sheriff closed the tailgate. He went to the driver to give him instructions.

Phil came and looked in on Nora. He seemed strangely subdued. He fidgeted for a moment. Nora knew he was afraid she would tell Mother about the bad joke they had played on the principal.

He spoke at last.

"Blessed are the merciful," he said, "for they shall obtain mercy."

"Blessed are mad little sisters," said Johnnie Proxmeier, "for they will surely get even."

Chapter 6

❧ THE RIGHTEOUS COMMITTEE - 1931

Dad helped Grandma up into the wagon. She had to step first on a wooden box, then higher up onto a sturdy stool. Finally she made it into the wagon as Dad held her chubby arm to keep her stable. Nora hurriedly slid the corduroy pillow across the seat for her to sit on.

Grandma was mad. Ever since she had her stroke she was sometimes very unpredictable. Now she stared straight ahead and jerked her black shawl tighter around her shoulders, although the desert sun beat down relentlessly and there wasn't a cloud in the sky. Mother didn't come out to say goodbye, but Nora could see her hovering behind the dining room window. The two women had a terrible fight the night before and had said cutting, sarcastic things that Nora knew would not soon be forgotten.

Grandma was upset because she was leaving the ranch and going to her little house north of town. Dad had a load of hay on the back of the wagon that he would pitch off into her barn, and Phil would walk her cow back into town this evening when he had finished in the field.

Dad put Grandma's suitcase under Nora's feet and then loaded her bicycle atop the mound of hay. Kevin climbed up to sit as high as he could on the load. Dad took the reins in his hands, climbed up and settled on the high seat. He turned the horses up the lane that joined the town road. Nora felt squeezed between the two adults. She wished she could ride back there with Kevin. She was sure it would be cooler.

Dad was ill at ease. It seemed that every time Grandma came for a visit it ended with her going home mad. Grandma was always nice when she first came and she would joke and tell the children stories. Then she'd begin to get crabby and critical and very bossy as time went on. Finally, the visit would be over and she would go home mad and not speak for several months. The same thing happened when she went to stay with Aunt Sue.

Dad tried to start a conversation. Grandma didn't answer.

Yesterday, Grandma had insisted that she was going to eat her supper with the hay hands. She said the food was always cold if she waited to eat with the family after the men left the table.

Then, at the table, she had told Ray Griggs not to pile so much food on his plate and Ray's face had turned beet red. She told Pete Sullivan to get his elbows off the table. He blushed up, too, getting a wounded look in his eyes. She criticized Phil for chewing too loud and said that Mother was stingy with the whipped cream on the rice pudding. She turned and smacked Kevin because he ran noisily through the dining room. It had been a terrible meal.

"Your mother is getting old," Dad told Mother. "She is like a child, trying to see how much she can get away with; looking for attention."

"Well, she's not getting away with anything else around here," Mother had snapped. "She's going home tomorrow."

Nora didn't even like to remember how unhappy she had felt last evening. She wriggled on the hard wooden seat and watched the swaying rumps of the horses as they trotted along the dusty road. She couldn't seem to think of anything else except the fight she had witnessed the night before between her mother and her granny.

Supper had been barely over when Mother went upstairs and dragged Grandma's suitcase out of the closet. She threw it on the bed. She opened the dresser drawers where Grandma's socks and nightgowns were stacked and started pulling them out.

"I can pack my own things." Grandma sounded like a stranger.

"I'll do it," Mother retorted.

"You can't wait to get rid of me," Grandma sounded bitter. "And I can't wait to leave. I won't stay where I'm not wanted."

"Who wants a contrary old blister around?" Mother answered. "Isn't life hard enough at this time of year with everyone trying to cooperate? Hired men are hard enough to find and keep around without you criticizing their table manners!" She slammed a drawer shut and continued. "And I don't need anyone deliberately making me look like a fool. Saying I don't give them enough whipped cream! Maybe that was all the cream there was!" She slammed another drawer.

"Get out of here," Grandma shouted. "I'll pack my own things. You don't have to stand watch. I'll not be taking any of your towels, or sheets, or soap!"

"Take whatever you want," Mother retorted. "It will be one thing less I have to take care of."

Nora had slipped out of the room to sit on the stairs. How could they talk to each other that way? Mother had taught them all to be respectful of older people. But Grandma was mean to Mother, too. Nora tried to understand.

"And I'd almost rather walk back to town as ride in that wagon," Grandma had continued. "Why doesn't Mike buy a car like Sue's husband did? It's so much more comfortable."

"We'll get a car when we can afford it," Mother snapped. "And Sue's husband doesn't feel so comfortable when he's stuck in the mud, or in the snow. He calls for Mike and our team to pull his precious car out—at least three or four times a year."

Nora fled out into the yard. She, too, wished Dad would get a car. They were about the only family who still drove a wagon into town and sometimes the kids at school made fun of them. But her parents had bought a house in town because they now had four children in school and it was very difficult to get them in to their classes each day.

Remembering last night, Nora wriggled again on the hard seat and looked sideways up into her Grandma's face. The old lady looked straight ahead, her jaw set, her eyes unblinkingly following the road. She looked almost like an Indian, Nora thought. She sat there without a trace of feeling on her face. Her mouth was a tight little slit, all puckered, because most of her teeth were gone.

Nora felt sorry for her. She slid her hand across the old lady's lap and found Grandma's hand. She was almost afraid that Grandma might slap her hand away. Instead, Grandma grabbed her hand and held it tightly.

Nora smiled. "Grandma," she said. "Your hands are so cold – you must have a very warm heart."

Grandma smiled.

Dad stopped the wagon in the middle of town. He jumped down and helped Nora and Kevin to the ground.

He pointed to the clock atop the tower of the courthouse.

"I'll meet you back here at noon sharp." he said. "That will give you a good hour to look around. Don't get into any mischief, and keep an eye on Kevin."

"I'll watch him," Nora promised.

"I'll be good," Kevin said. "Bye, Grandma."

The two children walked sedately across the street until they were out of sight behind the mercantile store. Dad could no longer see them now. They ran happily along the sidewalk.

"Come on over to the five-and-dime," urged Nora. "They've got the cutest little dolls…"

Kevin interrupted. "I don't want to see no dolls," he said. "Dolls are stupid."

"I don't like dolls much, either," Nora told him. "But these are so different. They are little dolls that are sleeping in a peanut shell. You take the top off the peanut, and there they are—little cute, celluloid things, wrapped in a tiny blanket."

She stopped speaking. She looked with keen interest at a truck parked at the end of the block, right next to the park. Several men were unloading all sorts of household goods. Two fellows struggled under the weight of a davenport as they strained to carry it up the long flight of stairs to the upper apartment.

"C'mon," said Nora, the dolls forgotten. "Some new people are moving in. Maybe I can get them to subscribe to our paper." She dragged Kevin along the street as she hastened to offer her help.

Phil had taken over the paper route when Emmett O'Connor had broken his leg. Nora went with Phil every day when he made the deliveries and she would love to get a new customer, all on her own.

Several cases, along with two kitchen chairs, were unloaded and waiting in the street. As Nora approached, a handsome blond woman threw an armload of clothing over one of the chairs. The hangers on the garments banged and clattered against the chair and a silky robe slid to the ground. Nora jumped to retrieve it and slapped the dust from the skirt.

"These are beautiful," she breathed as the woman approached her. "I'll stand here and hold them on the chair so they don't all slide off. They are really silky."

"Thanks, honey," the woman smiled at Nora. She was chewing gum and sighed as she looked around.

"If they would hurry up and get the big stuff moved in I could start taking those clothes upstairs. I don't want them to stay out here too long. The sun will fade them."

"You renting this place?" Nora asked. "It's been empty a long time."

"Yeah. I know. I'll have to finish scrubbing it out, but I'm starting to settle in." The woman was smiling at the workmen. "And the landlord has promised to fix that railing on the stairs. It looks like a hazard to me."

"Ah. He won't fix it," said Nora. "It was broken for months before the

Statler family moved out. He promised and promised to get it fixed—but he never did."

"Really?" The woman stopped chewing her gum for a moment and looked at Nora. Then she said, "I think it would be best if he tore off all those boards that are walling in those stairs." She turned to look up the dark stairway. It makes those steps so gloomy."

"Oh. But when it snows those steps would be so slippery that you wouldn't be able to get up and down them. They used to be uncovered, but after a couple of people fell on them, the landlord built that enclosure."

"I see," the woman sounded thoughtful.

"Did you move over here from Klamath Falls?" Nora asked.

"No. I came up from California. I heard this is a very nice little town."

"Oh, it is," Nora assured her. "Most people here are real friendly."

The woman turned back. "What's your name, honey?"

"I'm Nora, and this is my brother, Kevin."

"I'm Claudette," said the woman. "It's nice of you to help."

Claudette wore lots of rouge on her face, and a bright shade of lipstick. Her blond curls were piled high on the top of her head and gold earrings swung against her neck. Nora thought she looked as though she were all ready to go dancing instead of preparing to scrub out Statler's old apartment. But the woman climbed up into the truck to search through some boxes. She finally emerged with a scrub bucket and a sturdy brush. She hurried away up the long flight of stairs and Nora hoped she wouldn't forget about the clothing that was heaped on the chair. It would soon be time for her to meet her father and get down to the station to pick up the papers. And she hadn't even asked the lady yet if she wanted to subscribe. She squirmed around to look at the clock above the courthouse. She had about half an hour left.

Nora found it exciting to watch as the men moved the heavy pieces of furniture into the apartment; a huge brass bed with a heavy spiral springs and a thick mattress, several easy chairs, one of which matched the davenport that had already been carried aloft. There were four large, heavy mirrors and Nora wondered where they would be hung. Mrs. Statler hadn't had any mirrors that Nora could remember, and very few pictures.

Nora hunched against the chair and tried to keep the bright garments from slipping.

Claudette appeared and made her way down the stairs. She retrieved a garment bag from the truck and turned.

"Oh dear," she said and Nora realized that a rose-colored blouse had slipped from the pile of garments and now lay in the dust.

"I'll just take these up," the woman said. She slid her arm along the seat of the chair and lifted the clothing. Nora snatched up the blouse and hastened along beside her. holding up some of the trailing skirts.

The apartment looked crowded and cluttered. Most of the furniture was piled in the middle of the rooms and several men were busily scrubbing down the walls of the bedroom. The kitchen and living room had already been scrubbed down and the walls painted.

Nora turned with a smile of approval on her face. "You are really getting this place fixed up," she said. "I thought you just got here this morning."

"No. I came into town a couple of days ago," Claudette smiled. "The truck with most of my things just came in this morning.

She turned to give instructions to the workmen and movers. "That mirror should be hung right there," she pointed. "And take the others into the bedroom. We'll have to wait until tomorrow to hang them. The paint should be dry by then."

Still burdened by the clothing, Claudette moved past Nora and into the bedroom.

"The bed will go right against that wall," she pointed with her chin. "And the dresser over by that window." She surveyed the small room off the bedroom and said, "At least there is this big closet. I hate a small closet."

"Why this is where Mrs. Statler had her baby's crib," Nora told her.

"Really, honey. Well, it's going to be my closet—and I'll have to send one of the workmen to get some long rods so I'll be able to hang my things up."

"Boy! It sure looks brighter in here with all that new paint. Did old Hal Steele do the painting?"

"He had someone do it, I guess."

"Mrs. Statler couldn't get him to fix anything," Nora volunteered.

"Really?" Claudette gave Nora a quizzical look. "Did you know Mrs. Statler well?"

"Yes. I delivered the paper to her. I used to stop and play with the baby." Nora hesitated, then asked. "Would you like to take the paper from me?"

"You have a paper route? A girl with a paper route?" Claudette looked up in surprise.

"Well. It's actually my brother's route. But he has to work in the hayfield so I deliver his papers for him in the summertime."

"I see." Claudette looked thoughtful for a moment. "Sure, I'll take it for a month. It will be nice to have a newspaper around. We'll see how it works out."

"Oh, good. I give really good service and you live so close to the stage office that I can deliver your paper the very first one. Right after noon. The stage gets in right about noon."

Nora felt pleased. The boys who delivered the Portland papers would be calling before the day was over to see if they could get a new customer, but, for once, Nora had beaten them. She watched as Claudette shook out the clothing and hung it carefully over the backs of several chairs.

"I have to go check on Kevin," said Nora. "I don't want him to wander off."

"You've been a big help."

"I could still carry things up," Nora offered. "Could Kevin help, too?"

"Well. Yes. There are lots of pillows down there. For the davenport and chairs, and some throw pillows. Lots of small things you two could handle. My hat boxes and some small pictures. Pots and pans for the kitchen. They won't be too heavy for you. But tell Kevin to be very careful. I don't want anything dropped or broken."

Nora ran down the stairs. She saw Kevin swinging on the new swings in the park next door. She called him to her side.

"Come on," she said. "Help me carry some of these things upstairs for Miss Claudette. But, she said for you to be very careful."

The children made numerous trips from the flatbed of the truck up to the apartment. They carried all sorts of household goods and murmured with surprise at how different Miss Claudette's furnishings were from the familiar objects in their own home. They sighed with pleasure when the strange woman carefully unwrapped the tissue paper that protected a frilly lampshade. She placed it on a waiting lamp. She tightened the screw that held the shade in place and set the lamp atop the nearby dresser. The shade was trimmed with a thick layer of scarlet beads that winked and sparkled in the sunlight.

"It's so pretty," Kevin clapped his hands. "And the red cloth on the sideboard matches it."

Kevin admired the lamp for a moment and then dashed for the door. He stopped abruptly on the landing as a portly gentleman made his way up the stairs.

"Hi, Mr. Bushnell," Kevin greeted the man. "Did you come to help us?" Kevin never forgot a name or a face.

"Well, I just might help," said Bushnell. He frowned, trying to remember who the children were.

"I'm Nora, and this is my brother, Kevin," Nora hastened to remind him. "You came down to the ranch a couple of times trying to sell my Dad a car."

"You gave us a ride almost to the state line," Kevin added.

"Of course, of course," Bushnell answered. "It's just kind of dark here on the stairs."

"I wish you would talk my Dad into buying a car," Nora interrupted. "We are about the only ones who still drive a wagon into town."

"I'll do my very best," Bushnell laughed as he continued up the stairs.

When Nora struggled across the threshold carrying a box of silverware, Mr. Bushnell was helping Claudette position the dining room table. The apartment was beginning to lose the crowded look and was becoming quite attractive.

"There's a big box down there that I can't lift," said Nora. "I think it has curtains and drapes in it."

"I'll go down and get it," Bushnell offered.

"Will you look at your watch and tell me what time it is?" Nora asked. "I have to go get my papers at noon."

Bushnell consulted his pocket watch. "Well. You have about ten minutes," he said.

"We can bring in a few more things," Nora decided and ran down to the truck.

Kevin was talking with Perry Carson who used to work at the ranch. Nora liked Perry. He was always laughing and joking and he got along well with the other men. But he and Mother had a falling out. He had some 'rotten magazines' Mother called them, and he had given them to Phil to read. Perry had left the ranch and got a job in town in one of the pool halls.

"Nora. It's nice to see you," Carson said. "Boy! You are growing right up."

"I'm helping Miss Claudette move in," Nora announced with pride.

Carson raised his eyebrows in surprise. "I'll bet your mother doesn't know you are helping her," he observed.

"Well, no. But she'd want me to help. She says we should always be neighborly."

Carson turned and caught Bushnell's eye. They grinned.

"Do you think Mrs. Straight-laced would approve?" Carson muttered to

114

Bushnell. They laughed.

Nora frowned, puzzled. She didn't like it much that Carson had called her mother 'Mrs. Straight-laced.'

Kevin climbed down from the truck. "Lookee here," he cried, balancing a box of cosmetics.

A red, heart-shaped bottle with an atomizer attached caught Nora's attention. There were several smaller bottles of perfume, a rouge pot, and a box of bath powder, minus the cover. A huge powder puff kept the contents from spilling. There were jars of creams and bottles of lotions and several tubes of lipstick. There was a cunning blue bottle marked 'Evening in Paris' that sported a shell-shaped stopper. Nora could imagine Claudette touching a drop of the scent behind each ear as she had seen a screen star do once in a movie. The noontime sun struck prisms of bright light from the assembled glassware.

"Oh, they smell so—wonderful!" Nora sniffed, thrilled.

Carson and Bushnell looked at each other and grinned again.

Nora grabbed up some books and followed Kevin up the stairs.

"Oh, Miss Claudette. Those little bottles are so pretty and they smell so wonderful."

Miss Claudette settled the box on the dresser beside the colorful lamp and smiled.

"Wait a minute," she said.

She hesitated, making a careful selection from the box. She chose the red bottle, holding its heart shape delicately in her hand.

"Hold up your wrist," she invited Nora. She pushed the bottle close to Nora and squeezed the bulb of the atomizer. A magic spray of heavenly scented mist burst forth to settle on the girl's wrist and lower arm.

"Oh!" Nora breathed. "It's so…so lovely!"

Kevin moved closer to sniff. He seemed impressed.

"I should have washed my hands and arm first," Nora inhaled deeply, savoring the perfume.

Claudette smiled and gave a small shrug. "It's called toilet water," she said. "I do like the fragrance."

"*Toilet water*?" said Nora. "That's an awful name! This smells—well, wonderful!"

"We have to go," Kevin reminded her. "Dad will be waiting for me, and your papers will be in."

He clattered off down the stairs, but Nora didn't hurry. She placed each foot daintily on each descending step and held her head high, with her arm drawn up and resting against her chest so she could smell the delicious violet odor.

They found Dad's wagon parked in front of the post office. It was piled high with supplies: rock salt, harness, groceries, several fence posts and a small keg of nails. Nora's bicycle had been carefully moved to the back and she lifted it down easily.

Dad came out of the building carrying a letter in his hand. They didn't get much mail and Nora was instantly curious.

"Is it from Ireland?" she asked.

"No." Dad answered. "It's for Mother. It's from right here in town. I wonder what that can be?"

Nora crowded close, the letter forgotten. She stuck her arm in Dad's face.

"Smell," she commanded him.

Dad looked his surprise. He sniffed. "Very nice," he commented.

"It's violets," she told him. "I'm never going to wash my arm again. We helped a new lady move into her apartment and she subscribed to the paper. I got a new subscription."

"Good for you," Dad approved. He swung Kevin up onto the high seat and waved as Nora pedaled away.

"Violets," he smiled. He wondered what the letter could be about.

The letter was about jury duty. Nora heard all the details as the family ate a late supper after the hay hands had finished their meal and gone off to the bunkhouse.

"I'm going to have to serve," said Mother. "It took them three weeks to get a jury to hear that theft case last month. The judge said that from now on he wasn't going to excuse anyone who wasn't dead."

Dad still looked doubtful, but Mother hurried on.

"The newspaper had an article saying that the courts are going to insist that people serve when they are called. Really. We have an—an obligation, you know."

"But it's such a busy time," Dad objected. "We are in the middle of haying here. Who is going to cook? Who will care for the children? Surely the judge will understand."

"My sister, Sue, will take the two younger ones," Mother said. "Katie will have to handle the cooking." It was evident that Mother had given this a great deal of thought. "I'll prepare the pies or other desserts for the next day, when I come home each evening. And we can have the vegetables ready, too."

"I don't think…" Dad began, but Mother cut him off.

"Katie can handle it," she said. "I guess it will have to be roasts and stews. And the other children can help. I'll set the bread before I leave—"

"It won't work," Dad threw up his hands. "Tell them you have small ones at home, and lots of responsibilities. You can't serve on a jury! Let some of those ladies in town who run to their card clubs or their dressmakers…"

Mother tossed her head. She set the platter of bread firmly on the table. Actually, she almost slammed it down.

"I *want* to serve on that jury," she announced. "I'm sorry that this is happening at an inconvenient time, but I have no control over that. Besides, there isn't a time around here that *would* be convenient. If it isn't the haying, it's the shearing, or the branding, or the lambing, or the fencing. There is *never* a time that is convenient!"

"You—you—*want* to serve on the jury?" Dad's voice betrayed his astonishment.

"Yes. I want to serve. I want to go into town. I want to go every day for a week or two, or for however long it takes. I want to see other people and talk to other women—see what some of the new styles are. I want to eat meals that somebody else cooks—and buy some bakery bread instead of making rolls and loaves here every day myself. And as far as the men go—why Katie's cooking is as good as any they get in sheep camp, or any they do for themselves out there in the bunkhouse when they aren't haying." Mother looked almost out of breath, and the family stared at her as though they were seeing her for the very first time.

"Besides," she added. "I'll be home every day before the evening meal."

Mother turned away and busied herself at the stove while the family members stared at her back and then turned startled eyes to each other.

The silence stretched. Mother turned back suddenly. "I go to church once a week," she reminded them. "Straight in to Mass. Straight home again. It will be good for me to get away."

"But," Phil asked with some hesitation, "is serving on a jury—*fun?*"

"Probably not," Mother snapped. "But at least I can sit down on a chair most of the day while I do it."

Quiet prevailed around the table. The children had stopped eating and now they looked at Dad. He remained silent.

"I have it all planned." Mother sat down again and folded her hands in front of her on the table. "I'll make a list with all the chores on it. Who fills the wood box. When they do it. Who brings in the water. How much water each must pump. Who feeds the chickens. Who washes the dishes. Who sets the table, and when. And many more chores. I'll have it all written out by tomorrow, and we will start practicing all the jobs that must be done. We will have it all down pat by the time I have to show up there at the courthouse. Besides, they may not even choose me when they do start to empanel the jury."

Without a further word, Mother left the table and went to give little Julie her bath.

The following week, as Nora left to ride her bicycle into town, Mother called after her, "Be sure to stop down and ask Auntie Sue about watching the children tomorrow. If they choose me, I don't know how long it will be—but she understands."

Nora nodded and waved goodbye. She hoped to see Miss Claudette again. The apartment near the park now looked so different from when the Statler's had lived there. It was so bright and lovely with all the new paint, the polished floors, the starched curtains. Nora felt surprised every time she saw it.

She hurried around her paper route, pedaling furiously between her old customers, hoping to be able to spend more time with her new friend.

She clattered up the long flight of stairs and then spent two hours helping Miss Claudette finish papering the bathroom. The bathtub with its claw feet looked the same, but a miracle had occurred with regard to the rest of the room. The dark and peeling paint had been scraped away and the woodwork and ceiling were now a pristine white. Miss Claudette had chosen a light wallpaper with tiny lavender violets scattered across it. The border displayed darker violets with touches of green and scalloped edges of true purple.

Claudette climbed up on a chair and reached to pat the last of the border into place. Nora held the wet strips for her and handed her a clean, wet cloth with which to wipe away the excess paste.

"It's beautiful," Nora squealed. "I've never seen such a beautiful room. It's so much nicer than when the Statlers lived here."

Claudette climbed down and the two gathered up all the scraps and trimmings from the paper and stuffed them into a box which Nora carried down the stairs. She covered the box with a wire screen, then touched a match to the contents and waited until all the papers had burned away. When she returned to the apartment, Claudette was just finishing scrubbing up the paste spots from the new linoleum.

"It's so fresh and clean," said Nora. "Doesn't the room look bigger?"

"Yes, it does." Miss Claudette was also very pleased. "I'll make us some lemonade," she said. "I think we've both earned it."

They sat in the kitchen while Claudette squeezed the lemon.

"The floor is almost dry," she said. "When I finish this I'll put down the rug. And I have to hang a couple of pictures that I brought from my last house. Then the room will be almost finished. Only the curtains left to hang."

"What color is the rug?"

Claudette laughed and stirred the lemonade. She laughed again and gave Nora a teasing look from beneath her long lashes.

"Purple," she said. "Passionate purple."

"Purple," said Nora. "Yes. I guess that would go well with the lavender in the wallpaper."

Nora sipped her drink and Claudette took a tack hammer from a box on the cabinet and went into the bathroom. Nora could hear her pounding as she prepared to hang the pictures.

"That should be about right," Miss Claudette seemed to be talking to herself. "I don't want to get them too high."

Nora stared around the transformed apartment. She wondered what it would be like to live in a place so clean and beautiful. Perhaps Mother would let her pick out some wallpaper for her room. Of course she would pay for it herself. But fresh wallpaper would make such a difference.

Also, Miss Claudette had thrown out all those dark green window shades that Mrs. Statler used to keep pulled halfway down. Now the rooms were wonderfully light. She couldn't believe the improvement. She sighed, appreciating the beauty.

"Come and see," Miss Claudette called. "The pictures are in place."

Nora placed the empty glass on the table and hurried down the hall to the bathroom. Claudette stood aside looking very pleased with herself.

"It's beautiful," said Nora. "It's just right. I was afraid that a purple rug might make the room look dark, or smaller, but—it's just right."

"And the pictures?"

Nora turned to look. Her hand flew to cover her mouth and she gasped in shock. She could feel the hot blush spreading upward across her neck and face.

The pictures showed two young women completely unclothed. Their feet, their legs and thighs, the flat rosy stomachs, their pointed breasts, their throats and faces were—naked. One of the ladies reclined on a wrought iron bench holding a shimmering sort of scarf in her hands. The other stood languidly in a background of yellow sunlight, a bower of green branches overhead. Both young women looked out of the pictures with a teasing sort of smile on their lips and a bold flirtatious invitation in their eyes. The pictures were placed so that they were reflected in the wall mirror. There seemed to be four naked ladies instead of two.

"Oh!" Nora turned shocked eyes toward her new friend. "You can't leave those pictures hanging there. If anyone comes in to use the bathroom they will see them." She raised her hands in an effort to cover the prints.

"You don't like them?" Claudette asked. She didn't appear to be offended. She smiled and reached to straighten the lady on the iron bench. "It's just a different kind of art."

"They have some nice little flower prints at the Five-and-Dime," Nora told her. "They probably have Iris or Violets. Either would look nice in here."

"I'll have to think about it," said Claudette. She went into the kitchen and poured herself a glass of lemonade.

"I have to go," said Nora. "Mother will be wondering where I am." She hurried down the stairs and picked up her bicycle. She pedaled away, her mind in turmoil.

How could Claudette be so stupid? People in this town would talk about her the way they did about Perry Carson whom mother had sent packing off the ranch over the dirty magazines. Claudette was her friend and she had tried to warn her, but the woman thought those pictures were art.

Nora stopped pumping and coasted for awhile. Maybe those pictures *were* art!

She turned slowly and started back along her route but steered away from the center of town. She rode very slowly now, wondering if she should, if she dared, go and talk to Grandma. Maybe, if the old lady were having a good day… maybe she could talk to her. She couldn't talk to Mother. Mother would forbid her to go near Claudette again. And if she talked to Auntie Sue, Sue would tell Mother. After all, they were sisters. She hoped Grandma was in a good mood—was having a good day.

She hadn't seen Grandma since the day Dad had brought her into town—the day Claudette had moved in. Filled with apprehension, she approached Grandma's little house.

Her Grandma was sitting in her rocking chair on her little porch when Nora maneuvered her bicycle through the gate. She jerked erect when she saw Nora.

"Hi, Grandma. Are you busy?"

"Do I look busy?" Grandma snapped.

"I need to talk to you," said Nora. "I need to talk to someone." She approached the porch with a hesitant step.

"Why don't you talk to your mother? She seems to have an answer for everything."

"Oh. I can't talk to her—or to Auntie Sue, either." Nora thought she had said the right thing when Grandma sat up straighter in her chair and her lips curved in a satisfied little smile.

"Come. Sit on the step here, child. Out of the sun. Now. Tell me what is bothering you?"

"Well." Nora took a deep breath. "I have to find out about art."

"Art?" Grandma looked at her with a puzzled frown. *"Art?* You can't ask your mother about art?"

"Not this kind of art," Nora explained. "This is the kind of art where—where—well, where—people don't—they don't—don't have any clothes on. These people are—stark naked." She finally got it out.

Grandma jerked upright in her chair. She turned to stare. Nora thought she looked like a surprised frog as she blinked twice, then swallowed twice, and finally exhaled two long breaths.

"Begin at the beginning," she said at last. "Tell me all about it."

Nora told her about Claudette. How pretty she was. How she had ordered the paper for a month. How she had let Nora use the heavenly perfume. She told Grandma how lovely her furniture was, and how she had fixed up Statler's old apartment and got Mr. Steele to paint the rooms and how he was supposed to fix the stairs. Grandma learned about the perfume bottles and the mirrors and how they had worked together putting the pretty new wallpaper in the bathroom. Then she explained how uneasy the pictures on the wall made her feel.

"Those ladies in the pictures look like Elva Rudd when she's looking for a fight," Nora finished.

"Elva Rudd? Old Nate Rudd's granddaughter? When did you fight with her?"

"Oh. All the time. She called Dad a 'dirty old sheepherder' one day—and her eyes looked just like those ladies in the pictures looked. Sort of challenging and bold, and naughty. Like she was saying, "I'm bigger than you, and what are you going to do about it."

"What did you do about it?"

"I smacked her a good one. I'm stronger than I look. She ran and tattled on me. The teacher whacked my hands with a ruler, but I didn't cry."

"What did your Mother say?"

"Oh! I didn't tell her. She'd have told Dad and he would feel bad."

Grandma stared at Nora for a moment and then looked off across the yard and up toward the far mountains.

"Sure, old Nate Rudd is a bigoted devil himself," she murmured. "The child, Elva, knows no better."

Nora watched as Grandma's face grew pink with anger.

"Old Nate is a sharp tongued little spalpeen," she said. "Wouldn't he criticize the Lord himself? And he has no call to criticize anyone. That sneaky little bootlegger has been making his living selling that swill to anyone and everyone for years! And his son…" she stopped abruptly and waved a hand as though to erase what she had just said. She straightened the buttons on her waistcoat and cleared her throat. When she was satisfied that she had everything in order she turned again to Nora.

"Dear child," she began. "Don't pay any attention to Elva or any other person who says hateful things. Sure, wasn't the dear Lord himself a shepherd? Don't feel ashamed that your father cares for sheep."

"I'm not ashamed!" Nora was emphatic. "But she tries to make me feel ashamed."

"Bugger her," said Grandma and she turned away muttering to herself.

"What about the pictures?" Nora reminded the old lady.

"Come along, child." Grandma pushed herself up out of her chair and humped along for a few steps until she worked the stiffness out of her legs. She led the way into her parlor. Dust lay thick on everything in the room. It looked as though it hadn't been disturbed in years.

When Grandma raised the green window shades the dust billowed out, then drifted toward the floor. Grandma stepped to the bookcase along the wall and raised the hem of her apron to wipe along the spines of the volumes there. She muttered and read the names of the books half to herself.

"It's here somewhere," she told Nora. "I haven't thought of it for years—but, Dan'l, he set great store by that book. The pictures in it are quite wonderful."

"Were they art pictures?" Nora asked. She watched the individual motes of dust that remained to dance in the sunlight. She wondered why these little specks didn't fall and settle like most of the dust that had been disturbed.

"Ah. Here it is." Grandma took the book down, dusted it and opened it with care.

"There are pictures here of David and Moses and several others," Grandma told her. "They were painted and sculpted by Michelangelo and everyone knows that he was the greatest artist that ever lived."

"Really? Are they naked?"

"Child. Child. The human body is a beautiful thing. It's not something to be ashamed of. The sin is when people make jokes, belittle it, use it for uh, uh, purposes God never intended..." Grandma raised her eyes from the book and looked seriously at Nora. "Do you understand?"

"I think so."

"Look at your hands. You can fold your newspapers with them. You can button your blouse.

"You can wash the dishes, play the piano, hook a screen door, write a letter..."

Nora looked at her hands. She felt ashamed that they weren't too clean. They were already very brown from the summer sun and the fingernails were uneven and broken.

Grandma continued. "Hands can be wonderful things. They can heal the sick, comfort a child, plant crops, shear sheep, weave yarn, write books and newspapers, and, unfortunately, they can do terrible things."

Nora looked up in surprise. Wow. Grandma was really having a good day. She made Nora think of hands—and art—in an entirely different way.

Grandma kept talking.

"If a person's hands should stab someone, or deliberately destroy another person's work, or sneak around and set his house on fire, or write lies and gossip to ruin another man's reputation—do you understand what I'm saying, Nora?"

"Yes. Yes. Now I do. I understand about my hands anyway."

"Well, it's the same thing with your—your lips and your tongue. They can sing, read fine books, teach or say things to amuse or maybe comfort another. Or those same lips can lie or curse or belittle.

"And your feet. They can take you to school, or to church or to help others, or those same feet can kick and hurt, or carry you to places you know you aren't supposed to go."

Grandma paused, frowning. She looked at Nora doubtfully. She shook her head and took a deep breath.

"Nora," she began. She sighed again. "Nora. I don't know exactly what to tell you. We are all trying to raise you to be a nice, modest, innocent girl. The *world* will try to make you something else." She paused again.

Nora waited. She wondered if Grandma was losing her train of thought.

Grandma closed the book. The little motes of dust near her danced away.

"Nora. If a picture makes you uncomfortable—if you *feel* that it's not right, then just walk away from it. As you grow older, you'll be able to *know* if it's truly art or not."

The old lady paused, then sighed. "Trust your gut feeling!" she said. "That feeling is usually right!"

Frowning, she led Nora out again onto the porch. She settled into her rocking chair.

"The business part of town is really torn up," Grandma changed the subject. She was obviously through talking about art. "I hear they are putting down huge sewer pipes or pipes to carry the water from the canyon down under the streets so we won't have any open creeks running along the streets or across people's yards."

Nora wheeled her bicycle out the gate. She peddled slowly back through town. She wished Grandma had been more specific. But then—the old lady hadn't seen the pictures on Claudette's bathroom wall. How could she really answer?

The trial started Tuesday morning at 9:30. Breakfast was over and the men had gone to the field. Mother rushed about, setting the pans of milk in the cold room so the cream could rise; peeling the potatoes and vegetables; getting the breakfast dishes washed and set to drain and dry. She gave orders like a drill sergeant all the while. Katie and Nora rushed about, helping and determined.

"Nora. Pack the bag for baby Julie. Put in 5 or 6 diapers, a couple of toys, a change of clothing, and a couple of bottles of milk. And don't forget her little blanket. You know she won't go to sleep without that 'blankie.' And help Aunt Sue all you can. Don't go off playing with her children and leaving all the work to her. You take care of Julie until you have to go on your paper route, and then get right back to her house as soon as you finish and help her again. Do you understand?"

"Yes, Mother."

Nora was filling the second shiny bottle with milk when she suddenly remembered. She had forgotten to tell Aunt Sue that Mother was going to serve on the jury and wanted her to watch the children. She had been too interested in Claudette.

Dad came in from the field with the team which he hitched to the wagon. Nora, Kevin, baby Julie and her parents clambered aboard and waved to Katie as the horses pulled them up the lane. Nora felt sick with apprehension. She hoped Aunt Sue wouldn't tell her mother that she hadn't been told that the children were coming.

Half an hour later Dad pulled the team to a stop.

"Holy Smoke," he said. "Look at how deep that trench is. And look at the size of those huge cement pipes! I knew they were piping the water from the canyon underground, but I didn't realize how big a job it was going to be."

"Well, don't spend too much time looking," said Mother. "I must be at the courthouse before 9:30."

"We'll have to go all the way up to the North bridge and around," said Dad. "The road down to Sue's house is a trench right now."

"Drop me off at the courthouse first and then go around," said Mother, consternation in her voice. "I can't be late!"

"Wait a minute," Nora spoke. "I'll take the little ones with me. We can walk right through that trench. They aren't working right here. It's only a block on the other side to Aunt Sue's house. We will be just fine. I peddle around that ditch every day when I deliver the papers."

So the baby was handed down. Nora retrieved her bicycle. Kevin carried the sack with the diapers, bottles and Julie's blanket. Her parents went on their way to the courthouse.

"I'll meet you right here at five o'clock," Nora called after them.

She hurried the children through the trench and up the other side so she could wave to her parents from the opposite bank. They looked back and waved. She thought they were happy to see that she was so close to Aunt Sue's home. She skipped along pushing her bicycle with little Julie riding in the basket. Kevin struggled to keep up.

Aunty Sue's house was locked and quiet. Nora banged frantically on the door.

"They aren't home," Mrs. Tate, the neighbor, called. "They left yesterday for their ranch. They are haying out there and very busy."

"Ohhhh—" Nora's voice betrayed her dismay. "Oh, well, thank you." She turned away.

The children played for awhile in Aunt Sue's yard. Nora took them in out of the hot sun onto Sue's porch and they played with the toys her cousins had left there. She took them down to the dry creek bed and they played in the sand. All the while she worried about what she could give them for lunch. What would happen to them when she went to deliver her papers? How had she gotten herself into such a mess? What should she do?

Grandma, she thought. Even though the old lady was angry with her mother, she had been interested in and kind to Nora when she went to ask her about the art the other day. And the baby could sleep there. She could take them back to Aunt Sue's when Julie awoke from her nap. They could play in Sue's yard and be waiting to meet Dad at 5 o'clock.

Sighing, she put the baby into the basket of her bicycle, and, followed by Kevin, she walked the eight blocks up to Grandma's house.

As she approached the house Ted Hamblin came out the gate. Nora was surprised to see him.

"Hi, Nora," he said. "Where are you headed?"

"Why I'm coming to see my Grandma. I—I want to see how she is doing."

"Oh, she's gone," Ted told her. "She left to go out with your Aunt Sue to their ranch. I'm just checking on her cow."

"Oh, dear," Nora's consternation was reflected in her voice.

"Oh, she's OK," Ted hastened to reassure her. "She seemed fine when she left with Sue." He smiled and shrugged. "The other day though—she walked right up and boxed my ears. Said I'd stolen all her chickens. She hasn't had any chickens for ten years." He laughed and shrugged again. "I don't care, though. She was so damn good to us when my Dad left when we kids were little. We got all our milk and eggs from her for years. She may be a little— well, confused now from time to time, but she's one of my favorite people, no kidding."

Nora smiled and nodded. She heard his words but somehow they weren't registering the way they should. Nervous frustration rose unbidden. She nodded her goodbye as Ted walked away. The baby struggled to get out of the basket. Julie was cranky and hungry. Nora felt herself becoming frantic. Now what could she do?

Claudette!

Unbidden, the name popped into her head. Yes! Yes! That was the answer. Claudette was her friend. She would help her out in this time of need. Even if the court case went on for several days, Claudette wouldn't mind. She was a friend.

Pushing her bicycle, Nora turned and strode back toward the center of town. The baby struggled for a moment in the basket and then settled down. Kevin hurried silently behind.

"I'll take them to the Penney's store and get them both cleaned up," Nora thought. "That way they won't have to use Claudette's bathroom. But Kevin probably wouldn't look at the pictures anyway."

She hurried along the sidewalk and lifted little Julie from the bicycle at the side entrance of the store. She felt quite efficient as she changed Julie's diaper, scrubbed the baby's hands and face with warm, soapy water and saw to it that Kevin, too, looked clean and fresh. Then she rushed the children across the street to the park entrance and the stairway that led up to Claudette's striking new apartment.

She placed the whimpering toddler on the bench at the foot of the stairs and hurried up to knock on Claudette's door. It was almost noon and the door was locked.

She knocked again.

"Just a minute," Claudette called from inside.

Nora waited impatiently. She heard rustling from inside the apartment. Claudette finally opened the door. She wore a silky white robe that reached the floor and emphasized her tiny waist.

"Oh Claudette," Nora began. "I'm so glad you are home. I'm in real trouble. The baby is down there with Kevin and she's hungry." She pointed down the stairway.

"I thought we would be staying with Aunty Sue but she went out to her ranch. Grandma's not home either and Mother will kill me when she finds out I forgot to tell Aunt Sue that those two little ones would be staying with her, so, of course—Sue went out in the country and I'm left in town with them." Her voice rose in panic.

"Where is your Mother?" Claudette asked.

"Serving on the jury," Nora answered. Remember, I told you—but the kids, they have nothing for lunch and the baby needs to take her nap and..."

She stopped. She had pushed partly into the room and was surprised to see a strange man sitting in his shirtsleeves in the big soft chair. He had a drink in his hand. His shoes were off! He looked surprised—yet interested in what she was saying.

Claudette didn't look too happy. She somehow didn't seem as friendly as Nora expected. She hesitated, then said, "Well, I can make you a couple of sandwiches, but—I have other plans for this afternoon, so the baby can't sleep here." She hesitated. "Take her to—to—one of your little school friends." She turned away to the kitchen. "I don't have any peanut butter," she said. "You'll have to settle for butter and jam."

Nora stood at the door. She felt uncomfortable. This stranger had heard her rattling on like a banshee. No wonder Claudette seemed upset. She hadn't even introduced the strange man. Nora wondered who he was. He might be a relative of Claudette's.

Now the baby was wailing, her little voice reaching all the way up the stairs. Claudette came without saying a word and handed her three sandwiches on a paper plate. Nora thanked her quickly and hurried back down to the landing.

Little Julie and Kevin ate hungrily. Even the crusts were gone. Julie drank her bottle, settled down on the bench with her blanket and was soon asleep.

Nora gave half her sandwich to Kevin and explained that they would save the other half for Julie. She would be hungry before Dad came to pick them up.

"Ain't she going to sleep upstairs on Miss Claudette's bed?" Kevin asked in surprise.

"No. Claudette's got to go out, I guess. Julie will have to sleep right here and you'll have to watch her until I get back."

"I can't watch her," Kevin objected.

"Sure you can. She won't wake up and I'll hurry around the route. I'll be back before you know it."

Kevin looked doubtful.

"I'll get you a bag of marbles if I sell a paper," Nora promised. "And if I don't sell a paper, I'll tell you where Mother hid that bag of marbles at home. She was afraid the baby might find one and put it in her mouth and choke on it."

"Awright," agreed Kevin, "But hurry back."

Nora rushed around the paper route, all the while berating herself for the mistakes she made. No other girl that she knew of got herself into such messes. And they would have to bring little Julie into town tomorrow and for however long Mother had to serve on the jury. She'd have to sneak some food for their lunch out every day, and get the marbles for Kevin. She couldn't believe how strange and distant Miss Claudette had acted.

"I must have done something to make her mad," Nora decided. Her mind skipped from one idea to another in dizzying haste.

Kevin would be okay, though. He could get some of the town kids to come to the park to play marbles with him. Maybe Grandma would get in a fight with Aunt Sue and come back to town. If Mother had to quit serving on the jury they would probably arrest her and throw her in jail.

"It's my fault," Nora moaned. "It's always my fault."

Kevin sat on the bench with the sleeping baby. He looked happy to see her. He jumped up and dashed into the park and she could see him helping the workman who had come to water the little shafts that she knew would grow into mature trees in a few years. There should be lots of shade in the park then. Those little shoots were from cottonwoods and those trees grew fast.

When the man left, Kevin sat and told her that the fellow had explained that they would be planting some elms and other trees there, too, but the cottonwoods would be the first shade.

Perry Carson came walking up from the pool hall where he worked. When he saw the sleeping baby on the bench he sat on the edge of the board walk and stretched his feet down into the street.

"Hey there, kids," he greeted them. "What are you doing out in this heat?"

"My mom is working on the jury," Kevin told him. "And I just helped a fellow water them new trees. That's going to be a real nice park when they get some shade."

Little Julie stretched and stuck her thumb in her mouth. They could hear footsteps approaching along the board sidewalk.

A man stepped on the landing, then started up the flight of stairs.

"Hi, Mr. Griggs," said Kevin.

"Huh!" The man turned startled eyes toward the children. "Do I know you?"

"Yeah," said Kevin. "I know you. You've come to school a couple of times. Your little boy, Nate—he's in my class."

"Oh. Oh, yeah." The man glanced up the stairs again and then looked toward Perry Carson.

"That kid knows everybody in town," Carson shrugged and smiled, then added. "He even knows Miss Claudette."

"Umm." Mr. Griggs stepped down onto the landing again.

"The saddle shop and that shoe repair place are on down the walk about half a block," said Kevin. "Were you looking for one a' them?"

"Ah—yeah, yeah—the shoe repair," said Mr. Griggs. He hurried off, his footsteps echoing on the dry planks of the walk.

Nora wondered why Perry Carson seemed so amused.

When the baby awakened, Nora walked with the two children back down to Aunty Sue's house. At least there was shade there on her lawn, and Nora waited until the whistle from the mill told her it was 4:30. She washed the children's hands and faces at the hydrant and then took them through the trench to wait for Dad to come to pick up Mother. She felt so exhausted that she nearly fell asleep in the wagon on the way home.

The next morning she managed to sneak some sandwiches and a precious banana into her newspaper bag. She packed the items for the baby as her mother directed and then slipped into the pantry to retrieve the bag of marbles that her mother had hidden there.

They left the wagon and crossed the trench where the pipes would be laid as they had done the day before. Kevin was happy and cooperative since he now had his bag of marbles.

"I'm going to go get some kids to play with me," he told Nora. "I'll meet you at the park."

Nora entertained little Julie in the shade on Aunty Sue's lawn, then walked to the center of town pushing the child in the basket of her bicycle. She found Kevin already there with several of his friends. Kevin was happy. He had won two steelies and a cat's eye and was concentrating on his game.

A neighboring house cast a shady area into the park and the boys had drawn a huge circle near the entrance where the marbles were lined up. As the sun rose, the shaded area became smaller and the boys moved their game closer to the walk. Nora took little Julie out into the park and played with her on the swings until the heat of the sun drove her back under the awning. Julie objected and wanted to stay on in the park but Nora feared the child would get sunburned.

Occasionally a strange man came along the sidewalk and went up the stairs. Nora was surprised that Claudette knew so many people. She had only been in town for a few weeks.

Just before noon, Nora took little Julie to the Penney's store and washed and scrubbed her hands and face. Kevin came, too, because the boys playing marbles with him had to go home for lunch. They returned to the bench at the park entrance and ate their sandwiches. Julie grabbed her bottle of milk, pulled her blankie under her head and was soon asleep.

"I'm going to deliver my papers," said Nora. "Kevin, you keep an eye on her, although I'm sure she'll sleep until I get back."

She hurried around her route. Today things had gone much better. She began to feel more at ease with the fact that she was responsible for the two children. Mother had said that she thought the trial would only last a few days longer and she was sure that she could manage for another day or two. She still couldn't figure out what was wrong with Miss Claudette. Sometimes Claudette came out on the landing and looked down the stairs as if to check and see if they were still there. She never came down and she never invited them up. She barely said 'hello.' Nora wondered what she had done to offend her.

When she returned, Kevin was playing marbles again with two friends. They had abandoned the circle they had drawn in the dirt of the park. Now they had scratched a circle in the boards of the walk, directly in front of the bench where Julie slept. The cracks between the boards made the marbles take some unexpected jumps and routes and these changes were now part of the game.

Perry Carson came strolling along carrying a canvas bag.

"I've got to take these bar towels up to the Chinese laundry," he explained. "It's sure quiet down there at the pool hall. Haven't had a customer all afternoon. It's just too hot."

"Must be 90 degrees in the shade," Nora agreed. "I'm about ready to join Julie there and take a nap."

"Yeah. It's 90 in the shade alright. My thermometer out back says it's 101."

"Really? No wonder I'm so drowsy," Nora answered. "I hurried to get all the papers delivered so I could get back here with the little kids, and I'm all in."

"She's sure a cute little thing," Perry nodded toward the sleeping baby. "You aren't taking her out there in the sun on those swings when she wakes up are you?"

"No. I brought a book along. She likes to have someone read to her."

They heard someone approaching down the walk and a well dressed man rounded the end of the bench and started up the stairs.

"Hi, Uncle Ed," Keith Baldwin looked up from his marble game.

"Oh. Uh. Hello there, Keith," the man said. He came back down the two steps and took out a handkerchief to wipe his face. "What are you doing out in this heat?"

"Playin' marbles," Keith answered. "I gotta go home after this game though. I gotta help my mom get ready for dinner. You're comin' to dinner tonight ain't you?"

"Huh? Oh. Yes, yes. I'm coming."

Miss Claudette came out on the upper landing and looked down the stairs. Uncle Ed looked up, saw her and shrugged.

"Hey. What are you doing out in this heat?" said Keith suddenly. "Hardly anyone is out walking around."

"Well, ah, I was just headed—ah, headed down to Perry's place," he nodded toward Carson who still stood with his bag of towels.

"Thought I'd have a game of pool."

"Oh. Well just go on down," said Carson. "The door is open and I'll be along soon. Just gotta drop these towels off. Have a good game."

Uncle Ed went off down the street. Miss Claudette went back into her new apartment. Perry Carson strolled away up the street, smiling. Nora wondered why, lately, Carson always seemed to be thinking of some private joke.

The next day Nora allowed baby Julie to walk along beside her as she went from Aunty Sue's up to the park. Kevin had gone on two hours before to play marbles with his friends and she felt that the exercise would make the baby sleep more soundly if the boys made any loud noises at their marble game.

A little before noon the boys went home to eat and she took Julie and Kevin over to the Penney's store to clean them up for their lunch. When she returned across the street, a strange man sat on the bench with a newspaper spread out around him. Nora was surprised. She hesitated a moment and then asked him politely if he could move down to the end of the bench.

"No. I'm not going anywhere," the man growled. "You should find another place to feed those children anyway," he said. "It's hot and dusty around here and not too healthy for little ones like that to have to eat here."

Nora couldn't think of anything to say. Kevin sat on the steps going up to Claudette's apartment and opened the sack that held the sandwiches. Little Julie sat beside him. Neither one seemed to care whether the fellow sat on their bench or not. They hungrily ate their lunch.

But where could Julie take her nap? The poor little thing couldn't lie on the steps to sleep. And the strange man had no intention of moving. Besides, the stage carrying her papers would be coming into town at any minute.

Little Julie stood up, reached for her bottle and her blankie and approached the bench. The man made no motion to move. Instead, he put one leg up along the bench to almost completely cover it. Julie looked at him for a moment, her eyes heavy with sleep. She sat down on the planks in front of him, grasped her blankie around her shoulders and rolled under the bench. She sucked happily on her bottle and was soon asleep.

Nora felt anger rising. She stepped toward the stranger.

"The park is supposed to be for everyone," she said "Why do you think you have a right to use the whole bench?"

"I choose to use the whole bench," the man said. "I told you it wasn't a good idea to have these kids here all day."

"You better get going with your papers," Kevin interrupted. "I saw the stage go by."

Nora snatched up her bicycle and pedaled furiously away. She wished she could punch that fellow in his stupid face. She wished Auntie Sue were home. She wished Claudette wasn't mad at her. She wished her mother was not serving on the jury.

When she returned, the baby slept on the bench and the man was gone. Her brother played marbles with two friends.

"I put her up there to sleep as soon as that fellow left," Kevin told her. "She didn't hardly wake up."

Nora sat beside little Julie on the bench. She found herself dozing in the shade of the awning. The boys' voices sounded mute and far away, although they moved about the landing directly in front of her. Occasionally she heard Kevin greet someone who came along the walk.

She heard footsteps coming down the stairs and looked up to see Perry Carson descending from Claudette's apartment.

"Hi, Nora," he greeted her. "You back from delivering your papers already?"

"I really hurry," said Nora. "I don't want to leave Julie alone too long."

Perry sat on the edge of the plank walk and stretched his feet down into the street.

"Kevin is getting pretty good at winning those marbles," he observed. "I used to play marbles a lot myself."

They heard someone approaching along the walk and two men rounded the end of the bench and started up the stairs.

"Hi, Mr. Norris," said Kevin. "Hi, Mr. Turner."

"Whoops." Mr. Norris stepped back down onto the entryway, but Mr. Turner stood where he was and looked very annoyed.

"What are all these kids doing here?" he asked, anger showing in his voice. The children looked their surprise.

"Why, we're playing marbles," said Kevin. "We are playing here on the landing 'cause it's too hot out there in the sun in the park."

"Well, you don't belong here," Turner growled.

"They play here every day," Perry Carson interrupted, laughing. "They don't know it but they are sort of a—moral committee."

"A what?"

"A—well, a—Righteous Committee, you might say." Perry met Turner's eyes and smiled. "It's been good for my business. Do you want to come on down and have a game of pool?"

133

"Hell no!" said Turner. He turned and stamped off up the stairway.

"I'll go have a game with you," Mr. Norris told Carson. "I was headed to your place anyway."

When little Julie awoke, Nora read her the nursery rhymes she loved and showed her the pictures in the book she had brought from home. The boys playing with Kevin decided it was too hot even on the landing and they went off to their own homes.

Miss Claudette came out and looked down the stairs a couple of times. She wore a blue satiny robe and high heeled blue slippers. She hesitated a moment but didn't greet the children or invite them up.

"Don't she ever get dressed?" said Kevin. "It's almost time for supper and she's still wearing her nightgown. I bet she don't even own an apron."

The next day when Julie awoke from her nap, Nora took out the book and started to read to her. Kevin was bored, but happy, too. He had won two pretty agates.

Suddenly Miss Claudette appeared upstairs at her entry way.

"Nora," she called. "Kevin. Come up here a minute. I have a surprise for you." The children hurried up the stairs.

"Here is a quarter for you," Miss Claudette smiled. "I worry about you sitting down there in this heat. Take the quarter and go down to the Sweet Shop and get yourselves a nice, big dish of ice cream. Just sit down there where it's cool, and enjoy it. Little Julie will love it, too. Then you'll be half way down to your Auntie's house where your dad picks you up. When you finish your ice cream you can go on down to her cool, shady lawn and yard."

"Oh boy!" said Kevin.

Nora reached to touch Claudette's arm.

"Are you mad at me?" she asked. "Did I do something to—to—something wrong?"

"Why, no." Claudette answered, but she didn't wait to discuss the matter further.

Nora again took the children to the Penney's store and scrubbed their hands and faces with soapy water. She wanted them to look presentable in case they met someone they knew at the Sweet Shop.

The ice cream was wonderfully satisfying. Little Julie sat quietly while Nora fed her. She was so well behaved that their waitress stopped to compliment the children as they left the shop.

The following day went very well. Mother said that the trial wouldn't last much longer and she should be through serving by the end of the week. Kevin's friends all went home out of the heat before little Julie awakened from her nap. Mr. Norris came back again. He hesitated, then walked on down the street to play pool at Perry Carson's place. When Nora started to read to Julie, Claudette came down to give them another quarter and send them to the Sweet Shop.

The following Monday, Claudette again called them upstairs to give them a quarter. Kevin and baby Julie were delighted to go to the Sweet Shop, but, Nora felt strangely uneasy. Claudette didn't seem very friendly at all. She gave them the money, but seemed a little reluctant, Nora thought. But why did she want them to leave their place on the landing? Why didn't she ever invite them up? And why wasn't she as friendly as she had once been? Nora couldn't understand.

Tuesday was the hottest day that Nora ever remembered. She returned from her paper route to find little Julie sleeping soundly, but with drops of perspiration on her forehead and face. Kevin moved about the landing practicing his marble shooting. Nora slumped on the end of the bench and dozed.

Abruptly, she was awakened. Clyde Turner stood at the top of the stairs pounding on Miss Claudette's door. He was angry and swearing.

"Open up, damn it! I know you're in there!" He pounded some more, then kicked the door. No one answered.

Turner turned suddenly and lunged down the stairs. Twice he nearly fell. Nora realized that the man was drunk.

"It's your fault," he thundered, shaking his fist at Nora. "You damn kids—sitting here all day, keeping watch. Why don't you get the hell out of here and find somewhere else to play?" He kicked at Kevin's marbles sending several flying out into the park.

Nora jumped to her feet and stood protectively in front of the baby.

"We have as much right to be here as you do!" she shouted. "This park is for everyone—even the people who come to town as visitors."

"Well, your visiting time is over," Turner staggered toward her in a menacing fashion. "Take that sleeping kid and go find someplace else to squat."

"I will not!" Nora drew herself up to stand as tall as she could. She could see Miss Claudette hurrying down the stairs. Little Julie whimpered in her sleep.

"Don't you sass me, missy!" said Turner.

"I'll say anything I please."

"Don't even answer him, Nora," said Claudette.

"Are you taking his side?" Nora asked, indignation in her voice.

"She better take my side, if she knows what's good for her," Turner swayed closer. "Now take those two brats and head out of here."

Claudette reached to swing Kevin toward her. "Go get Perry Carson," she told him. "Run! Quick!" Kevin jumped down into the dusty street and ran.

"I'm not going anywhere," said Nora. "I'm not afraid of you."

"Maybe you're just waitin' for me to give you two bits so you can go get ice cream," said Turner. "Well, I ain't buying you off."

"Buying me off?" Nora stammered. She thought of the several days they had gone to the Sweet Shop. Understanding flooded over her. But Turner still stood in front of her, threatening and angry.

"I'm going nowhere," she told him again. "You are just a big bully!"

"A *bully*?" Turner roared. He drew back his hand and slapped Nora hard across the face. She half fell, landing on her knees beside the park entrance. Claudette screamed. Little Julie awoke and her screams joined Claudette's.

People seemed to spring out of nowhere. Perry Carson arrived and pinned Turner to the bottom step where he struggled and cursed. Two other men came to help Perry and Turner turned suddenly docile. The town marshal arrived from his office in the courthouse and Turner was taken away.

Trembling, Nora took Julie on her lap and tried to comfort her. Gradually the people left until only Claudette and Perry Carson remained.

"Kevin, put Julie's bottle and her blankie in my paper bag," she said. "We'll go down to Aunty Sue's yard where it's shady. She can play in the water at the hydrant."

"Wait until I get my purse," said Claudette. "Stop at the Sweet Shop. A little ice cream will make her feel better."

"No," said Nora. "I won't stay where I'm not wanted. You can save your money."

Miss Claudette looked stricken. Nora almost felt sorry for her. And she felt acute bewilderment. A short time ago she had insisted to Turner that she wasn't going to be made to go anywhere she didn't wish to go, and now she was insisting that she wouldn't stay where she wasn't wanted. There seemed to be a giant balloon where her head had once been. Now she couldn't sort out her thoughts. And she couldn't lift Julie. She tried twice to raise the child high enough to settle her into the basket on her bicycle, but her muscles refused to react.

"You're shaking like a leaf," said Perry Carson. "Let me carry little Julie. You and Kevin come along."

The baby nestled into his arms. He stepped down into the street and crossed to the Penney's store. Nora, pushing her bicycle, tried to keep up, but her legs felt like rubber.

"I wonder if this is how people feel when they faint?" she murmured.

"Park that bicycle right here," said Carson. "You *are* going to the Sweet Shop—and right now! You have to sit down where it's cool and where you can get some ice water. You'll be OK, but you have to rest a while."

Nora nodded. There seemed to be a huge weight in her chest that was growing heavier by the minute. She felt that if she spoke she would burst into tears.

They found an empty table at the Sweet Shop and Nora was soon sipping icy water and feeling less faint. She was surprised that little Julie laughed and allowed Perry Carson to feed her ice cream. Her own treat melted untouched in the dish in front of her. When Kevin finished his sundae, Nora pushed her dish over to him and he attacked it with pleasure.

Nora leaned back in her chair and closed her eyes.

"I am feeling better," she told Carson. "How did you know I needed ice water?"

Before he could answer, there was a commotion at the front door and Mother appeared in the room. People nodded and pointed and Mother made her way to their table.

"Nora. Are you alright?" she bent to put her arms around her daughter.

"How did you know?"

"We were just coming out of the courthouse when they brought Turner in," she explained. "Half a dozen people told me some version of what happened. They said Turner beat you up, half killed you, threw you down the steps—all sorts of things. I've been worried sick!"

"I'm just fine," said Nora. "I felt sort of—weak—but then Perry brought us here and got me out of the sun and got me some ice water, and I'm much better."

"But why were you at the park? – and with the little ones? Why weren't you at Aunty Sue's?"

Nora pushed her chair back. She felt sick – and faint again.

"Sit down, Mrs. McCarthy," said Perry Carson. "I'll just tell you what a special child you have there. Truly outstanding. Now, here is what happened."

Nora turned away. Mother would be humiliated. She would be horrified. Nora knew she should have told her the very first day that she had forgotten to ask Aunty Sue about the children staying there. She heard Perry's smooth voice telling the story. Somehow it didn't seem so bad.

Aunt Sue had been called away suddenly. The child wanted to spare Mother the work of having to find someone to sit with the children. She thought that Mother might be thrown in jail. She had done a wonderful job of looking after the children. Had cared for their every need. No one she could have hired could have done a better job. What a mature, caring person for one so young.

"But . . . but . . . that Claudette person," Mother said. "I've heard some disturbing things about her."

"Claudette?" There was surprise in Perry's voice.

"Is she—is she a. . . a . . ."

"She is a widow," Perry's voice held a trace of sadness. "I understand her husband was killed down in California a few years ago."

"But—how does she make a living?"

"I think…I believe she is independently wealthy," Carson sounded thoughtful. "Possibly insurance money. And Nora spends no time with her. Why, I haven't seen her go up to Claudette's apartment at all. Not even once. She is such a kind and thoughtful child. She wouldn't presume to impose on Miss Claudette. She would no more impose on her than she would come into my pool hall. She's never been in there, either."

Perry paused as though in tribute. "You've done a wonderful job raising those children, Mrs. McCarthy. I wish some of the other children in this town had parents like you."

"Why—why thank you, Mr. Carson," Mother was obviously pleased.

Nora listened in disbelief. How she had worried all this past week and a half, and to hear Perry's smooth explanation—well, it didn't seem possible. And she had been wrong about Miss Claudette, also. She wondered how old she would have to be before she could think and act like the adults expected her to.

Nora continued to look away. The balloon in her chest continued to grow upward. She had been afraid she might cry if she tried to speak. Now she felt she would howl!

"We must go," said Mother. "Dad will be waiting."

She nodded pleasantly to Perry Carson and reached to take the baby. Kevin slipped his bag of marbles under the table to Perry and skipped ahead out the door. Mother looked at Nora with pride in her eyes.

"Just wait until I tell your Dad!" she said. "He'll be so proud!"

Chapter 7

❧ REDECORATE - 1932

"I hate her guts," Nora stated, "and her stuck-up daughter, too."

Uncle Jack paused in his whittling. His eyebrows raised in surprise. He held the knife poised above the piece of wood.

"And why would you hate her?" he asked, his voice mild. "Why would you hate anyone?"

"I know Mother says it's a sin," said Nora. "But she never has to listen to those two—"

"Ignore them," said Uncle Jack quietly. "Ignore them and walk away."

"I can't," Nora explained. "I have to deliver the paper to Benson's house every day, and she sets down the rules."

"The rules?" Uncle Jack's voice sounded calm and reasonable. "What rules?"

"Well. Madam Benson says I must deliver the paper within a few minutes after the stage brings the paper over from Klamath. She wants to be the first one in town to get the paper. She says it must be there when her husband comes home for lunch. And I can't just throw it on the porch. It might blow away. So I must put it behind the screen door. But half the time the front screen door is locked, so then I must take it around the house and put it behind the back screen door."

Uncle Jack started to speak, but Nora rushed on.

"The sprinkler is always on, watering the grass in the side yard and the walk is muddy. If I track any mud on her porch she makes me scrub it off and I wind up scrubbing her whole back porch. She even has the pail of soapy water waiting—"

"A pail of water waiting?" Uncle jack sat forward and spoke, his voice no longer calm and reasonable.

"Tell her to go to hell!" he advised.

Nora smiled. Uncle Jack understood, as she knew he would.

"But then she'd quit the paper," said Nora. "She said she'd quit and she'd also write the paper in Klamath and tell them what a bad job I did. Anyway, I hate to lose a customer."

"Let her quit," Uncle Jack was almost shouting. "Let her get her news from somewhere else—or from the other gossips around town."

Nora laughed. Uncle Jack didn't even know Mrs. Benson, but he called her a gossip.

He spoke again, his voice ominous. "Now. What about the daughter?"

"Clarice is a brat," Nora said. "She and her two friends, Ethel Sandquist and Myrtle Hodges, think they run the school. They make fun of everyone, especially the Irish kids. Call us 'greenhorns,' 'sheepherder's kids,' and 'cat-lickers' – all that kind of stuff. Make fun of me, being a girl and having a paper route."

Suddenly her indignation faded and she smiled. "But, guess what?" she said. "Clarice has a mad crush on Emmett Casey. He can't stand her because she used to make fun of him and treat him as mean as she did the rest of us."

"Emmett Casey? Old Jack Casey's boy?"

"Yes. You should see him now. He's got so tall and good-looking. He's the best ballplayer in school, though he's only a sophomore. Plays basketball and baseball. Phil says the coaches love him. He's written up in the local paper almost every week."

"Last time I saw Emmett Casey he was just starting school."

"Well he really *grew* over the summer." Nora said. "When school was out last spring and he went out to the ranch, he was a little taller than I am. But when he came back in this fall—I almost didn't know him! I didn't know anyone could grow that fast in three months."

"And Miss Sweetie Pie Benson has a crush on him?" Uncle Jack seemed to relish the idea.

"Yes. She simpers around and tells him how great he looks, how great he plays, how much she admires him. She invites him over for supper because she tells him the food in the boarding house where the ranch kids live must be terrible."

"And does he go to supper there?"

"No. Just says 'no', too. And right to her face."

"Good." Uncle Jack nodded his approval. He leaned back in his chair, thinking.

"Now," he said. "We must solve your problem."

"I don't want to lose a customer," Nora warned.

"Well. That old blister is getting a great bargain," Uncle Jack remarked. "The paper delivered every day and a maid to scrub her floors in the bargain."

The man's whittling was forgotten. There followed several moments of complete silence as he pondered the problem. Finally he sat forward and spoke.

"Mrs. Hoity Toity says her husband must have the paper when he comes home for dinner. Where does he work?"

"Why, he has an office up in the courthouse."

"Fine." Uncle Jack nodded. "Deliver the paper to *him*. Either in his office or hand it to him on his way home."

"Yeah," Nora was delighted. "I see him walking home every day. I can give him the paper and all I have to worry about will be the weekends."

"Ah, yes," said Uncle Jack. "But Mr. Benson will probably be home then and you can knock on the door and hand it to him, or—better still—roll that paper up—don't fold it. Roll it up as tight as you can and put a rubber band around it. And leave it on the front porch. The wind will never pick up a paper rolled that tight."

"Yeah." Nora's eyes sparkled.

"Or," said Uncle Jack pausing a bit. "Hell. The country is full of rocks. Just pick up a good sized rock and anchor the paper down with it. Put the paper held down by the rock on the FRONT porch. Don't ever go around to that back porch again."

"I tried that rock business once before," said Nora, "and she yelled at me for putting rocks on her porch. But that rubber band should work."

"Yell back at her," advised Uncle Jack. "Tell her you won't walk through that mud anymore." He dropped the piece of wood he had been working on and his face grew very red. Nora decided to change the subject.

"I wish school was out," she said. "I can hardly wait to move back out to the ranch for the summer. It's so nice there."

"Yerra. You have a nice home here in town," Jack reminded her.

"Oh, I know. We are very lucky. And it's so much easier to walk to school and not have to be driven in each day. Mother loves it, and we can all come home for lunch. But I do miss the ranch—all the animals, playing in the creek, racing Phil down the lane, and hunting for arrowheads."

"Aye," agreed Uncle Jack. "But you are very fortunate. Think of those poor young ones like Emmett Casey. They have to live in that boarding house and sometimes don't get home to see their families for weeks, or even months if the snow is deep."

"I know," Nora sighed. "It must be very hard."

Uncle Jack's suggestions worked wonderfully. Nora either delivered the paper to Mr. Benson's office or handed it to him as he walked home at noon. For three weeks in a row, Mr. Benson was in the yard on Saturday and she handed him the paper.

Besides, the Bensons had some sort of a remodeling project going on at their house. Workmen worked there each day, tramping, about the yard, hauling lumber and supplies into the house and piling large amounts of destroyed walls and even broken windows into the waiting trucks. The debris was hauled away each evening and the trucks returned again each morning to be filled.

Charlie Wilder installed a lovely white picket fence with large square white gateposts.

"I'm going to have my very own private bathroom," Clarice bragged, "and we're making the back porch much larger. It will be big enough for a table and we can eat out there in the summer. We'll have awnings and everything."

Two bathrooms in one house! The whole town buzzed. Half the people in town didn't have one bathroom. They had outdoor privies. Now the Benson's would have two bathrooms. It was unheard of.

"That is a beautiful picket fence," one of the girls said. Toby Wilder, who stood nearby, blushed up with pleasure to hear his dad's work being praised.

"Oh, it's okay," said Clarice dismissively. "But my mother planned the whole thing and she had to watch Mr. Wilder all the time to be sure he got it right."

Toby walked away without a word.

"Well, it's true," Clarice called after him.

Nora coasted on her bicycle down toward the Benson's house. The sprinkler watered the side yard. The workmen were gone. Everything looked sparkling and new. She hoped the screen door was unlocked. There was no rubber band in her pocket.

She heard voices as she hurried through the new gate and up the walk to the house. The screen door was locked. Defiantly she searched about the yard, looking for a stone.

"But I thought you'd be glad to see me," one voice said. "I've been so eager to see you again."

"Well, you thought wrong," Mrs. Benson's voice was unmistakable. "You spoil my wedding, run off with that—that—scoundrel, Ben Devlin, and then expect me to welcome you with open arms?"

"Spoiled your wedding? What are you talking about? I stayed until after the wedding." The strange voice came again, hesitantly. "I was a bridesmaid, remember?"

"Oh I remember. You stayed for the wedding and that same night eloped with Devlin. Instead of talking about my beautiful wedding, the whole countryside talked of nothing but my sister eloping with that—that—low life."

"I was so happy when Ben's job sent him here," said the voice. "I thought your daughter and my Gracie could be great friends—not just cousins."

"Well. Think again. Tell Miss Gracie here not to even speak to Clarice. My daughter has her own friends, her own place in this town and she doesn't need Gracie hanging on her coattails."

Nora crept slowly about the yard. She picked up, then discarded several stones that would hold the paper down. She knew she shouldn't eavesdrop but somehow, she just couldn't walk away.

Mrs. Benson had a sister? A sister who had moved to this town, and Mrs. Benson hated her. Mrs. Benson was treating that woman like a *thief* or something. Nora discarded another rock.

"And Ben Devlin is no low-life," the voice suddenly showed anger. "You liked him well enough yourself."

"Yes. Until you stole him away."

"You drove him away," said the voice. "Miss selfish, self-centered, can't-see-past-yourself big sister."

Mrs. Benson's voice rose and became cold and bitter. "Don't speak to me. Don't nod to me. Don't even pretend to see or know me if you meet me on the street."

Nora reached for yet another rock, but was knocked to her knees as a young girl came rushing around the corner of the house.

"Sorry. Sorry," the child mumbled as she ran out the gate and turned along the sidewalk. Tears streamed down her face.

The angry argument in the backyard continued, but Nora thought only of the sobbing little girl who ran down past the new picket fence.

She picked up a rock, set it to hold the paper down on the porch and went to her bicycle. She pedaled slowly along, her thoughts in turmoil.

She delivered two more papers and wondered where the strange child had disappeared to. She delivered the Scroggins' paper and rode slowly past their long green hedge.

There at the end of the hedge, she saw the child, huddled at the corner, on her knees, her shoulders shaking, her hands clenched in the dirt.

Nora brought the bicycle to a quiet stop. She didn't know exactly how to proceed. She, herself, didn't like to have anyone see her crying. Yet she felt such an overwhelming pity for the strange little girl that she couldn't leave. She lowered the bicycle to the sidewalk. She dropped down on her knees and reached a hesitant hand to touch the child's shoulder.

"Don't cry," she whispered. "It will be alright."

The little girl jerked in surprise.

"Go away," she whispered. "Go away." She lowered her head, hunched her shoulders, seeming to be pulling away.

"I'll go," said Nora, "if you want me to, but don't pay any attention to that old blister. She's the meanest old—old fat toad in town. She makes everyone feel bad." Nora's voice rose a little in indignation.

"What?" The child turned to Nora, wiping her wet face with her fingers, leaving streaks of dirt across her cheeks.

"She's mean to everyone," Nora hurried on. "Or almost everyone. She doesn't even speak to half the people in town and she treats most people like – like – well, like I wouldn't treat my dog."

The tears started again as the little girl spoke.

"She said terrible things about my father," she hiccupped. "And my mother was so looking forward to seeing her again. Mom said I had a cousin…" the child's head dropped.

"Well. You don't have to tell anyone that you are related to that stuck up Clarice." Nora spoke. "I'm glad she's not related to me."

The little girl rose to her knees and turned toward Nora, confusion mirrored in her eyes.

"I'm so…mixed-up," she said.

"Yeah," Nora agreed. She looked at the child for a moment. She found her really lovely. Dark, soft hair, beautifully curled to make a good impression when she met her aunt and cousin. Huge grey eyes, still swimming with tears, and an oval face that didn't look at all like Clarice Benson, Nora was glad to discover. She knew she shouldn't stare.

"I've got lots of cousins," she said. "I get along with them. They are all pretty nice. Just a couple are sort of…pills."

"And I have to start school on Monday," the little girl said. "I have to start a new school—"

"The kids will love you," said Nora, sincerity ringing in her voice.

There came a whispering of rushing footsteps along the sidewalk. The little girl rose quickly to her feet and was enveloped in her mother's arms. They both cried together for a moment, then hurried away, still weeping. Nora rose slowly and picked up her bicycle.

On Monday morning Nora waited by the school door until the new girl arrived. She took her by the arm and started introducing her to some of the other students.

"This is Grace Devlin," she told Johnnie Proxmeier. "This is her first day here and she's a little nervous."

"And I'm completely overcome," said Johnnie. "This school is finally getting some class. I think I'm in love." Gracie blushed, then smiled, and was quickly surrounded by many other young people. Everyone knew and loved Johnnie Proxmeier.

Even Clarice's friend, Myrtle Hodges, drifted over to the laughing group. But then Clarice called to the girl.

"Come on, Myrtle, we're going to be late for class."

"Come on, Gracie," Johnnie mimicked. "We're going to *be* the class."

Clarice tossed her head and rushed off down the hall.

Gracie was a hit. With her lovely big grey eyes, her soft voice, her modest ways, the other students soon accepted and loved her. With Johnnie Proxmeier escorting her about, they welcomed her at once.

"She's so stupid she can't find the study hall without someone leading her there by the hand," said Clarice.

The last hour of the day, all the interested students went to the music room. Nora went to music every day, although she knew she had a very ordinary voice. She loved the choir when everyone sang the song, but she completely avoided any solo. Now she persuaded Grace to go to the class also.

Mr. Vernon announced that they were in the process of selecting the spring operetta and that they would soon start tryouts for the leads. Then he sat down and played several favorites to warm up the class. Gracie hummed along.

Grace looked around. "Someone has a really wonderful voice," she said. "He's bound to get one of the leads."

"That's Ben Welch," Nora explained. "He does have a great voice."

"That's tangle-tongue Welch," said Clarice from the row behind them. "He stutters like a drunken chipmunk."

"He never stutters when he sings," Nora defended.

"Well I'd never trust him in front of a big crowd," said Clarice. "Mother says he'd get nervous and just go to pieces."

"Come on, Gracie," said Nora. She took her friend by the hand and they moved across the room to a different row.

"She'd make anyone nervous," said Nora. "Ben won't even talk at all if she's in the same class he's in. She says the meanest things and it does upset him. When he's with his friends, or playing basketball or something, he never stutters."

Tragedy struck when Gracie had been in school only two days. Her father was hurt in an accident at the mill and remained in the hospital for several days. He returned home, pale and weak, with a cast on his leg from his hip to his ankle.

"He looks terrible," Nora told Mother and Uncle Jack. "And now her mother is going to take in boarders or something until he gets back on his feet."

"How sad," said Mother. "I'm going to send something over there for their supper. Most people in town don't even know they have moved in, so there won't be too many people helping."

"Well," said Nora. "A couple of fellows from the mill have rented that empty house down there by the highway. It's only a few doors from Gracie's house. They are fixing it up and about four mill hands are moving in. They will live there, but go over to Gracie's house for meals. There is another fellow from the mill, named Stumpy that will live in Devlin's house so he can help Mr. Devlin move around with that big cast on. He says he's worked with Ben Devlin for fifteen years and never had a better boss."

"Stumpy?" said Uncle Jack. "His name is Stumpy?"

"Stumpy Hayes," said Nora.

Uncle Jack smiled happily. "Sure, don't I know him?" he exclaimed. "He comes up to the pool hall nearly every night and is great company. There can't be two Stumpys."

"This one has a tattoo on his arm," said Nora. "A tattoo of a snake."

"He's the very one," Uncle Jack slapped the table. "And it's like him to figure a way for that family to survive the bad luck that's come to them. He's a fine fellow and keeps us laughing all the time." He paused suddenly to look closely at Nora.

"Does he use any – any – bad language around you?"

"No-oo-o. Not really, but Mrs. Devlin is always warning him to watch his mouth around us girls."

Uncle Jack rose to his feet and reached for his hat. "I'll see that they get a nice leg of lamb this week," he promised. "That family will find that they have lots of friends." He paused, still smiling, then turned to Mother.

"Do you happen to have a grease pencil around here?" he asked. "I must mark some wool sacks before we send them into the storage shed."

"I think so," said Mother. "I had to rescue that pencil from Kevin. He wanted to write numbers on all the houses in the neighborhood." She retrieved the pencil from the sewing machine drawer. "That greasy ink is hard to scrub off."

Uncle Jack stuck the pencil in his breast pocket and sauntered off.

Every day at 3:30 when the music class was over, many of the students went over to the gym to watch the basketball team practice. They cheered or jeered, good naturedly, at Johnnie Proxmeier, Toby Wilder, Emmett Casey, Terry Moore and even Nora's brother, Phil. The coach didn't mind the audience because he said the players would have to get used to people calling to them and even insulting them when they played at other schools.

Terry Moore was an excellent player and often guarded Emmett Casey. The two were great friends and learned much from the rivalry.

Clarice Benson and her friends came every afternoon to sit in the bleachers and watch the practice. Clarice, however, seemed to feel that Emmett Nolan was the whole team and she made cutting remarks to the other players. She called Toby Wilder 'Shrimp,' because he was rather small. She ignored the fact that he was remarkably quick and often stole the ball.

She referred to Johnnie Proxmeier as 'The Movie Star' and belittled all his efforts.

Nora was appalled when Clarice started calling Terry Moore 'Tangle Tongue.' It was true that Terry sometimes stuttered but who could be so downright mean as to make fun of him for this handicap?

Then one day Clarice referred to Gracie as 'Miss Mouse.'

"She's so quiet and shy," said Clarice. "—sort of sneaky. She slides around without making a sound—just like a mouse." She and her friends referred to 'Mousy' for several days.

At first Gracie didn't realize that Clarice was talking about her. But then, in the gym, Clarice moved closer to where Nora and her friend were sitting and soon everyone was aware of the nickname that Clarice had chosen for Gracie.

"Just ignore her," Nora whispered. "None of the boys pay any attention to her and she's been calling them names for weeks."

Gracie said nothing, but deep red color crept up her cheeks. She looked at the wall clock.

"I must go," she told Nora. "I have to help Mother with the supper. We have five men from the mill that take their meals with us now." She rose and gathered up her coat and books.

Hickory, Dickory Dock, sang Clarice and her friends.
Miss Mouse ran up the clock.
When the clock strikes four
She's out the door
Hickory, dickory, dock.

The three girls laughed aloud as Gracie hurried along the sidelines and out the door.

Suddenly the basketball came whistling across the court. It caught Clarice squarely on the side of her laughing face. Her head jerked. Her glasses flew across a row of seats. She screamed in surprise and pain. Nora threw the ball back onto the playing floor. The game went on. No one stopped or apologized.

The next morning as Nora hurried to school she was surprised to see Mr. Benson standing on the sidewalk in front of his newly remodeled house. Mrs. Benson scowled on the porch and Clarice cried hysterically in her mother's arms.

"Cover it up," she screamed. "If you can't scrub it off—cover it up!"

"What's wrong?" Nora began, but stopped when she saw the words written neatly on the square white gate posts that Toby Wilder's dad had finished only a few weeks before.

Clarice is a poet
But she don't know it
But her feet show it
Cause they're LONGFELLOWS.

The words were neatly printed, using black grease pencil. The first two lines of the poem were written on one white pillar, the last two lines on the second post. Mr. Benson stood with a scrub brush in his hand and a steaming bucket of sudsy water at his feet. He looked utterly defeated as his efforts had not removed any of the paint.

"Get Charlie Wilder up here," screamed Mrs. Benson. "Tell him he has to paint over that—that rubbish."

"Cover it up!" screamed Clarice.

"I have a meeting with the judge in about ten minutes," shouted Mr. Benson. "You call Charlie Wilder yourself. I have to get going."

"Don't you dare walk off and leave us stuck with that mess!" Mrs. Benson yelled from the porch.

"It's just a bunch of kid stuff," Benson said dismissively as he picked up the bucket of water and hurried around the house.

Nora hurried away.

She wanted to laugh. She felt like crying. She couldn't understand this mixture of feelings. She thought she heard Mrs. Benson calling to her but she pretended not to hear. If she was calling, she probably wanted her to go find Charlie Wilder and she would be late for school. Besides, Uncle Jack had asked Mother for a grease pencil just last night. But then, Stumpy Hayes had a grease pencil in his pocket at all times and many of the other mill hands had grease pencils. She had seen Toby Wilder buying one for his dad at the mercantile store just yesterday. Lots of people had grease pencils—but who would use it in such a way? She smiled again through her worry. Someone would surely get into trouble for this. She hoped it wasn't Uncle Jack. And that poem didn't sound like Uncle Jack. She had heard it around school several times. She doubted if Uncle Jack had ever heard it. He'd make up one of his own.

Mr. Wilder refused to come and repaint the gateposts. He said the grease paint would probably bleed through a new coat of paint anyway, and he was building a huge dock for a new building down near the railroad terminal. He couldn't take time off from that job.

It seemed that everyone in town found some excuse to walk down the street where Benson's lived. They wanted to see for themselves the crude poem written on the gateposts. Finally the druggist told Mr. Benson about some liquid called solvent. That evidently worked, because the gateposts were now clean and repainted and the excitement around town had died down.

Mrs. Benson too, was back to her normal bossy self. She had the front yard plowed up and smoothed down and new grass seed was sprouting. She had ordered a new cement walk to run from the gate up to her front porch, but the workmen hadn't arrived yet from Klamath Falls to do the work so she had several planks put down so a person coming to visit wouldn't sink into the soft earth.

And now there were many visitors coming to the Benson home. She invited the bridge club to come and tour the remodeled home and see Clarice's beautiful new bedroom and bath. She invited the teachers at school, some of the clerks at the Penney's store, all the tellers at the bank, and often stopped an acquaintance walking along the street and invited them in to see her home. Clarice invited many of the girls from school, and even some of the boys.

Emmett Casey said he was too busy to come, but all in all the visitors were duly impressed and the word spread around town about the lovely pink bedroom, the sparkling private bath that Clarice could enjoy and the other changes made in the home.

"Mrs. Benson didn't invite me in for the grand tour," Tillie Garson laughed as she visited with Mother one Saturday afternoon. "After all, I'm just a waitress."

"She didn't invite me, either," said Mother, "and I go past her house every time I go up to church."

"We'll have to mend our ways," said Tillie. "We don't seem to move in the right circles."

They giggled together like school girls, then Mother excused herself.

"I must call Nora," she said. "Miss Bishop wants her to go to the store with her this afternoon. She says she has quite a list of groceries and she needs help carrying them home."

"Is she still around?" asked Tillie. "She taught me in first grade and that was—was—what? Forty years ago. I haven't seen her for years."

"She's around," Mother answered. "She doesn't get out much any more. She gardens, though, and keeps her house spotless. She reads a lot and loves to have company. I think she taught most of the people in this town. It's an all day job to go to the store with her. People keep stopping her on the street to visit—and she remembers all their names."

"She taught for fifty some years, I think," Tillie said. "She must be in her seventies."

"And she's been a big part of this town all those years," said Mother.

She stepped to the bottom of the stairs and called up to Nora.

"Miss Bishop is just coming in the gate, Nora. Come along and don't walk too fast. She may not be able to keep up."

"I'll remember," Nora promised.

"Stop in when you come back," Mother invited Miss Bishop. "We'll have a spot of tea."

"That will be lovely."

Nora remembered to hold the gate for Miss Bishop and reminded herself to walk slowly. They crossed the main street and turned toward the business district. Sure enough, there was Mrs. Benson, sitting on her porch watching them approach. She rose from her rocker, turned off the sprinkler and called to Miss Bishop.

"It's so good to see you again," she said. "You must stop in and see my remodeling."

"I have heard that it's wonderful," said Miss Bishop, "but I have a helper now and she may not be available later on. She probably has plans of her own."

"Oh. She can come in, too."

"Well—" Miss Bishop looked at Nora. "Do you mind seeing it again?"

Nora shrugged. She had never been invited to see the new rooms and she rather liked the idea.

"Sure." She said.

They walked carefully along the wet planks. There in the mud, half covered by a pool of water, Nora saw a grease pencil. She smiled.

"Wipe your feet, Nora," Mrs. Benson commanded as they reached the porch.

Nora had delivered papers to this house every day for three and a half years, yet she had never been inside before. She was very familiar with the back porch, but the soft carpeting, the muted colors, the well-placed mirrors, the tufted furniture, the elegant draperies, and the complete lack of clutter gave her a feeling of unreality. In her mind she contrasted this room with her own home—the linoleum floors, the tattered furniture, the children's toys scattered about, the plain curtains at the windows. She reached to take a firm hold of Miss Bishop's hand.

"We'll just go down this hallway," Mrs. Benson said. "I'll show you Clarice's room first—and her bath." She opened the door into a pink paradise.

There were lovely pink walls with rose colored drapes at the windows and a rose colored ruffled spread on the bed. The ceiling gleamed in soft white and the rug seemed to be white, or very light, also. Across one wall stood a pink ruffled dressing table with a shiny mirror above it that reflected the treasures of the room, making it look large indeed. Nora could scarcely catch her breath. Clarice slept alone in that big bed while Nora shared her bed with her little sister.

"I have ordered a very nice painting for that wall there above the bed," said Mrs. Benson pointing. "It's an oil painting of a ballerina. I'm sure Clarice will love it."

A polished desk stood in the corner where one could study undisturbed, with a floor lamp beside it. Nearby a pink padded, white painted rocker waited. Soft light filtered from the windows and seemed to fill the room with a rosy glow. Nora knew she had never seen a more beautiful room – even in the movies.

Still holding her hand, Miss Bishop dragged her along into the bathroom. It, too, was lovely. Polished fixtures, white shining walls, huge mirrors, and a white porcelain, strangely-shaped tub positioned along one wall. The tub had no feet but sat squarely on the floor.

But the most remarkable surprise in the whole room was a stunning little closet with a glass door where one could stand a take a shower with water cascading down over you, yet none of it spattering or washing over the bathroom floor.

Mrs. Benson explained at length that the windows were set high in the wall on purpose. They didn't require any curtains and they were made of a mottled glass so that no one could peek into the bathroom.

Beyond the bathroom was a laundry room where the washer stood with its own set of faucets for hot and cold water. Nora thought everyone did the washing in the kitchen or maybe on the back porch in the summer, but the Benson's had a special room for laundry with a special big tub for rinsing, and numerous wooden racks that could be set up to dry the clothes in the winter time.

Then came the kitchen with the shiny new stove, the flat, linoleum-covered counters and the numerous cabinets and shelves. Nora could see the porch beyond and it was indeed much larger. She shuddered.

The front door slammed as Clarice came in from the afternoon matinee.

"Come say hello to Miss Bishop," her mother said.

"In a minute," Clarice called back.

Mrs. Benson opened the back door and was about to step out onto the porch when there came a wild scream from the end of the hall. Everyone stopped abruptly. Then came another scream, followed by a series of strangled cries and screams that sent the adults rushing across the kitchen and down the hall. Nora rushed after them.

"What's wrong? What's wrong?" Mrs. Benson was roaring in terror.

Clarice stood in the middle of the lovely room, rigid, on the soft carpeting, screaming and pointing at the wall above her bed. She seemed unable to speak.

Nora looked. Her hand flew to her mouth. She felt she was about to scream herself.

Muddy footprints were planted in the midst of the ruffled spread. The pillows were flattened where someone had stood. Printed on the pink wall in black grease pencil was a nasty little poem.

> *Girls are lucky as they can be.*
> *They only have to squat to pee*
> *But the men, poor sons-a-bitches*
> *Have to undress—or shit in their britches.*

Mrs. Benson's face turned a mottled red. She whirled about the room as though looking for an intruder. She started to comfort Clarice but whirled again and pointed at Nora.

"You did this," she accused. "While we were busy you sneaked in here and DID THIS!"

"No. No!" Nora denied, tears distorting her voice.

"You did! You are a jealous, spiteful little brat. You can't stand it that Clarice has such nice things. You—you—"

Miss Bishop stiffened and drew herself up until she seemed to tower over the others in the room.

"Now, stop this nonsense," she said. "I have held this child's hand since we entered this house. She hasn't been out of our sight. How could she possibly have done such a thing?"

Mrs. Benson drew in her breath and opened her mouth as though she were about to argue. She seemed to think better of it and suddenly burst into tears herself. Clarice, seeing her mother crying, threw herself on the bed and started screaming again.

"They're howling together," Nora thought. She felt like howling herself.

Miss Bishop cleared her throat. She put a hand on Mrs. Benson's shoulder.

"Calm yourself," she said. "This can be cleaned up. It's not the end of the world." She looked at Clarice. In her school teacher voice she said.

"Screaming is not going to help, young lady. You are too big to act like a baby."

The Benson women struggled to pull themselves together.

"Don't tell anyone," Mrs. Benson begged. "I couldn't bear to have everyone gawking and talking again."

"No need for anyone to know," said Miss Bishop. "Nora and I will say nothing. We'll just go on now and do our shopping. And I advise you to say nothing either."

She paused for a moment. "Clarice if you tell one person, one girl friend, you might as well put it in the paper."

She took Nora's hand and started for the door.

"Mrs. Benson," she said. "I have never seen a more beautiful job of decorating a house. You should be very proud." She squeezed Nora's hand.

"It's lovely," Nora managed.

They found their way to the front door and stepped out onto the porch. As they made their way across the planks that served as a walk, Nora noticed that the grease pencil she had seen as she came in no longer floated in the water.

She was very quiet as she accompanied Miss Bishop. It couldn't have been Uncle Jack. He had been gone now for three days out on the trail to the mountains with the sheep. It might have been Toby Wilder. She saw him buying a grease pencil the other day at the store. It could have been Johnnie Proxmeier or even Terry Moore whom Clarice called Tangle Tongue. Anyone could have found that grease pencil lying beside those planks. And lots of people disliked Clarice. Or it might have been Stumpy Hayes. He hated the way Gracie was treated by the Bensons.

She wished Uncle Jack were here. But no! She couldn't even talk it over with him. She couldn't tell anyone. And she wouldn't tell anyone. Miss Bishop would not approve.

As they neared home and Miss Bishop prepared to stop in to their home to have tea with her mother, Nora had a sudden thought.

"What if whoever did it, tells?" she asked.

"Don't worry about that," said Miss Bishop. "I doubt if we'll hear any more about it."

Nora sincerely hoped she was right.

Chapter 8

❧ SUMMER OF SADNESS - 1933

Raymond Morgan was a large, hearty man with a loud laugh and a soft handshake. He came driving across the green of the meadow in the early afternoon leaving two vivid tracks where the hard rubber tires bruised the grass.

Nora thought that it was probably the first time an automobile had ever come up that steep mountain trail. Now, as Raymond came bumping through the long grass, making his own trail, she could see that he was mighty proud of himself.

"Here comes Jester," said Dad.

"Smiling, no doubt," Mother answered sarcastically. They didn't go to meet him.

Raymond maneuvered the car through the creek and up to the little rise in front of the cabin. He swung down from the wide running board and pulled some grass from the wooden spokes of the wheel.

"By God, she made it, Mike," he sang out jubilantly. "She's steaming a little, but she sure as hell made it." He looked around and caught Mother's cold, disapproving eye.

"Pardon me, ladies," he murmured, looking at Mother and Nora and Katie, but he didn't look sorry for swearing. He was still smiling.

He took the briefcase from the back seat and followed the grownups into the cabin. Dad and Uncle Jack looked grim and uncomfortable. Mother followed along reluctantly. They looked unsure and troubled. Nora decided that the grownups were frightened. That made her afraid.

Hesitantly she moved closer to the big touring car. It was so shiny and bright. She decided that Jester must be very rich. Everyone she knew was now very poor because of the depression. All of them still drove horses and wagons—except the sheriff and the forest rangers, of course.

She looked toward the cabin. Nora thought with sadness that nearly the only topic of conversation these days was the Depression and what the new President Roosevelt was going to do about it. Everyone seemed sad and uneasy. No one had any money.

Nora hoped they would never have to move and she wondered where they would go if the bank took their house. Now, birthdays came and went without a cake or a present and they used lots of rice, and beans and oatmeal. She shivered. They never got a loaf of bakery bread anymore, and they never bought fruit. No one was embarrassed anymore if they had to wear boy's shoes to school. Nora always wore Katie's hand-me-downs. Very few kids had any new clothes. Lots of other children at school had linoleum soles in their shoes, too.

She sighed and turned away to watch as Phil came dashing across the meadow. His brown legs churned through the meadow grass and his eyes were bright with anticipation. He ran around the car, twice, and then jumped right up on the running board and settled himself into the driver's seat. He was older than Nora and she thought him much braver. He turned to look back down the steep trail.

"I'll bet he even started out from town after breakfast," Phil said. "It took us three days in the wagon to get up here with those slow old workhorses pulling. I wish Dad would get a car."

"He can't even afford a hired man," Nora answered. "That's why he's up here herding the sheep himself. We wouldn't even have Tim helping, except he's related—and he can't find a job anywhere." Phil was not listening. He was pushing the three pedals on the floor with his bare feet and making noises like an engine.

Nora slipped unnoticed into the cabin.

Jester Morgan sat at the rough plank table looking strangely out of place. His shoes were polished, his shirt was neatly pressed and looked surprisingly fresh considering he had just finished a long, hot ride up from town. He wore a gold watch on his wrist and occasionally the watch strap would catch on some of the papers spread on the table and move them around. Nora had never seen a man wear a wrist watch before.

She realized that the adults had been arguing. Mother looked white with emotion.

"Kill a fourth of the sheep?" Mother's voice was shaking and incredulous. "Why, that is 300 head."

"No!" It was terrible to see Dad shouting. He was always soft spoken. "I'll not do it. There is some mistake!" The sound of his outburst quivered in the air.

"Mike," said Jester after a pause, "Mike—It's the law." He looked around gravely at everyone in the room. Then he continued. "You're an American now. Sometimes Americans have to make terrible sacrifices. It's always been that way. That's what makes this country so special."

He knew that Dad and Uncle Jack had only recently become naturalized and he always acted somewhat superior. Once Nora had heard him refer to the Irish, sneeringly, as "foreigners." But now Jester was very earnest. He was being very patient and persuasive.

"Now, Mike. I know it's hard to believe—but it's certainly true. Why would I drive all the way up here? Spend half a day? Now, would it be reasonable for me to make such a trip if what I'm telling you was untrue? If I weren't absolutely sure? Dammit, Mike. But this is hitting the whole country. Not just you people. Why there's folks suffering from this Depression in every state. Every single state!" He paused to look through some of his papers.

"I showed you the pictures. The bread lines, and the soup lines in the cities where people—actually—they don't have enough to eat." He paused for a long moment and then said again.

"It's the law!"

Dad snatched up the pictures. "If people don't have enough to eat, why don't they use these animals to feed those that are hungry?"

Nora cringed. She wished she had stayed outside in the sunshine.

"Well, Mike," said Jester unhappily. "Who is going to drive the stock to the railroad? Who is going to pay the freight? Who will pay to harvest the crops and grind the—that there—grain into flour?"

"Of course it wouldn't be easy," Dad began thoughtfully, "but.."

"Mike. Mike," said Raymond. "We don't make these decisions. People smarter than we are figured out this plan. Our congress, and the experts down there in Washington—they passed this law. We must abide by it."

"But Raymond," Mother struggled to be calm. That's 300 head of sheep!"

"I know! I *know!*" Jester emphasized the last 'know' and his voice purred with understanding. "And believe me when I say I'm terribly, terribly concerned. Why, I know how hard you people have worked." His voice was very grave and he looked from one of the adults to another. He shook his head sadly.

The adults looked at each other, dismay registered in their faces. Nora had heard them read some of the proposals of the new government aloud. She had listened while they discussed them. She didn't understand these proposals, but neither did the grownups. The government wanted to create shortages to relieve the Depression. But, the stockmen just couldn't believe that the law was insisting that they kill healthy animals. Besides, all the sheep were mortgaged and now, as she listened, Nora began to understand why Jester had driven this long way up to this cabin. He wanted to be sure that Dad and Mother understood the process, filled out all the necessary papers and returned the papers to the bank. The government wouldn't be paying her parents for the sheep they destroyed. The sheep were all mortgaged, and the *bank* would get the money.

Jester smiled now and said, "The ranchers all over the country will be compensated by the federal government for any crops or livestock they have to—a—part with. Really, friends, it could be much worse." Jester stood. He shook hands all around. The adults looked at each other incredulously.

"Now, Mike. You and Jack just cut out the worst sheep, the lame ones, the old ones—whatever. And just—well—decide how you want to –er—a— dispose of them. You can get any government official to go with you—or it's legal for them to make their headcount after the animals are all dead, too. Arrange with the sheriff, a ranger, the town marshal—just be sure that they get the complete count and that they sign these papers. You want to be sure that the government pays you for every one of those sheep—and they must have the proper signature or you won't be able to collect. When we get the papers, we'll credit your account with the entire amount."

He turned, smiling, and stepped out into the sunshine.

"Beautiful day," he observed, taking a deep breath and looking around. "You folks are lucky to be able to live up here in the summer. Fishing and hunting right handy. It's so quiet and peaceful too." He gazed around at the wide sky, the stately ponderosa, the brown-green of the meadow.

"Oh, yeah. And, Mike—we arranged for a store in town to get a whole supply of shells of different kinds to the ranger station, in case you need them."

Jester swung down the steps, his briefcase in hand.

"Phil, you're just growin' like a bad weed." Nora watched as he approached his car and Phil climbed out reluctantly.

"Wish I'd thought to bring my Sid along," Raymond spoke. "He's whining and complaining that he can't find nothin' to do. You could have taken him fishin'."

The next few days passed with a nightmarish quality. Nora had rarely seen her mother cry, but now her eyes were always red. Everyone seemed short tempered and irritable. Phil came down with a terrible summer cold and ran a high temperature.

Dad and Uncle Jack ran the sheep through the chute and swung the gate dozens of times, shunting the sheep from side to side, trying to pick out the ones to keep, the ones to drive away.

Three days later, the men had made their choices. Uncle Jack and Tim drove the doomed animals across the meadow and down through the timber. Dad turned away. It had been decided that he would take the wagon and necessary supplies around by the road. He would stop at the ranger station and then meet the two men east of the little town of Bly.

Nora watched as the men threw their bedrolls, the grub box, and the extra clothing, into the wagon. She ran and got her coat and bedroll and threw them into the wagon also, not really expecting to get away with it.

Mother was annoyed.

"Nora! Get those blankets back on your bed. Where do you think you are going?"

Nora knew she should have asked permission, but she knew also that Mother would have said "No!" She felt so useless—so confused. She wanted to do something helpful—hoped to understand. There was a painful tightness in her throat and tears stung her eyes. She jumped to take her coat out of the wagon. Dad looked at her and then turned to Mother.

"Let her go," he said, his voice quiet. "It will be alright. She can open the gates and hold the horses, since Phil is sick and can't go along."

With slow reluctance he put the guns and the boxes of shells under the seat. He covered them with a piece of canvas. He hesitated a long moment as though he hated to start. He climbed up to the high seat of the wagon and Nora clambered up the other side. Mother and Dad looked at each other without smiling or speaking. Reluctantly Dad signaled the team. They drove away without looking back.

The doomed sheep were already moving across a grassy hillside a fourth of a mile away. Nora listened to their faint bleating. It sounded like thin nervous complaints. She thought that sheep were dumb, but they were smart too, in a way. They knew this was an unusual drive. They usually stayed, peaceful and undisturbed, in the mountains, until the cold weather started to close in. They didn't like this move.

Nora sat, alert yet quiet, on the high seat. They drove around the edge of the Lee Thomas meadows and past the Forest Service Lookout Tower. At each range boundary she jumped down and opened the gate. Dad would drive the team and wagon through and wait while she closed the gate and ran to climb back to her place on the wagon seat. Neither could find anything to talk about. They skirted the edge of the marsh and reached the ranger station about noon.

The station was a neat, modern building, well cared for, with flowers planted in neat rows around the porch. It seemed a strange surprise when one came upon it suddenly in this silent wilderness.

A flag hung on a tall pole in the yard. Today it looked limp and lifeless, barely moving in the slight breeze.

Dad stopped the team and the two climbed down stiffly from the high wooden seat. They crossed the plank porch, Dad's footsteps sounding loud in the forest stillness. The wooden boards felt hot under Nora's bare feet.

Ray Hacker sat at the cluttered desk. He turned as they came in the door.

"'Lo, Mike," his voice was firm and friendly but his eyes looked wary. Nora had seen him every summer for as long as she could remember.

Dad nodded and fished a paper out of his vest pocket.

"I have the count here for the sheep kill." His hand shook a little as he unfolded the paper and handed it to Ray. "112 ewes, 20 bucks, 168 wethers."

Ray shook his head. "Mike," he said. "I hate to see this." He took the paper and looked at it, not really seeing the few words. He searched for something to say.

At last he sighed and picked up a folder from his desk. Without moving from his chair, he reached over with his foot and pulled a chair out from under the adjoining table.

"Sit down, Mike," he invited. He tapped the pile of folders stacked against his ink well.

"You're the second one that's been in. Con Kiely killed 180 head yesterday over behind Cougar Peak."

Suddenly Nora felt very sick. Until that moment she had been expecting that somehow the killing would not really have to take place. Now she began to know that it would. She could tell by the look on Dad's face that he felt the same as she.

"Hell, Mike," Ray's voice sounded ragged and angry. "I've arrested people for shining deer and killing antelope and taking too many fish, but By God! Now I'm being told I have to arrest them if they won't kill their own livestock. Good Christ! I'm ready to quit this damn job! I would too, except I'd never find another."

Dad sat stiffly on the straight backed chair. He leaned slightly forward.

"There's no way around it, then? Has it really come down to killing them?"

"The orders are clear." Ray sounded tired. "All the farmers must plow under one fourth of their beans, peas, corn, potatoes, all crops—tobacco, cotton, grain crops. Every fourth acre is to be burned or plowed under. Livestock is the same. Pigs, cattle, sheep. One out of every four animals must be destroyed."

Dad cleared his throat. He started to speak. His face was dead white. He stopped and cleared his throat again. Ray swung away and looked out the window. He started talking.

"It's crazy, Mike," he said. "If they were going to have a program like this the president should have had this plan announced last fall, or else wait until next year. The expense of planting crops, the expense of lambing and calving, the money spent for seed, and hired help—those expenses don't even seem to have been considered." Ray kept looking out the window giving Dad plenty of time to pull himself together. And he kept talking.

"Old Seth Bailey drove 270 head of sheep down off the rimrock yesterday, right into the Chewaucan River. Drowned them all! Now we've got to send a crew to clean up the mess and pull the carcasses up out of the river or the water will be fouled for the rest of the summer." Ray slapped the arm of his chair, anger and frustration showing on his face.

"Hell. I'm not going to arrest him. Seth said he didn't have the money to buy the shells to shoot them and Roosevelt could come out and cut their throats himself if he wants them dead. He said the president just said to 'kill them,' but didn't tell him *how*. So, by God, he killed them. So now we're going to have to drag them all up out of the water so we can verify the count on them and he can get paid." The ranger sighed and shook his head. "Or the *bank* can get paid!" he added, bitterness apparent in his voice.

"Now, my friend," he turned back to Dad. "What can we do? Where are you taking the—er," he glanced at the paper again and shook his head, "the 300 head?"

Dad swallowed, then answered quietly. "We thought we'd take them down to the Devil's Garden. We've already started trailing them over that way. It's pretty desolate there and no one goes through there this time of year. We'll push them back a half a mile or so from the road. In this heat -- in a few days--"

"Yeah, yeah," said Ray. "The damn smell…" He rubbed his jaw and continued. "Well, ah—when are you going to kill them?"

"Tomorrow afternoon," Dad answered. "They are headed west through the timber right now."

Ray looked away again. "I'll be down to get the count along about evening."

Nora felt she couldn't stand any more. She slipped out the door and went to sit in the wagon. Her teeth chattered, although the sun was warm and bright.

Dad came out of the ranger station, his shoulders slumped, his steps slow. Nora thought he looked like an old man.

Dad climbed into the wagon and they started on their way. Now they took an unfamiliar road that Nora had never travelled before. They were headed for the Bly cut-off. They dropped below the timber line and rode in silence most of the afternoon.

In early evening they stopped at Mustang Springs and made camp. They watered the horses and took the grub box and the bedrolls from the wagon. Shortly after, Nora saw the sheep break out of the forest and into the little meadow nearby. The sheep drank at the stream, grazed a little and bedded down for the night.

Dad had coffee ready and they brought out the sandwiches Mother had prepared before they left. No one seemed very hungry, although Nora remembered that they had not eaten all day. No one spoke.

The men hobbled the team and everyone turned in about dark. Nora watched as Dad put a dry log on the fire and filled the water bucket. His movements were stiff. His eyes glistened strangely in the firelight. Nora wished someone would speak. Even the dogs slipped around in silence. She couldn't think of anything to say. She put her bedroll next to Dad's and crawled, shivering, into the blankets.

She lay there, trying to sleep and trying to understand. She looked up into the cold, dark sky. Tonight there didn't seem to be any stars—just the black abyss above.

She thought of the new President Roosevelt in faraway Washington and wondered how this event could really be true. It had to be a ghastly mistake—a long, bad dream that would end with the new day. But how could it be a dream when she was wide awake and wishing she were asleep?

Could a good man, a president whom everyone loved and respected, really have ordered this terrible killing? Dad and Tim and Uncle Jack had all come from Ireland and she had heard them talk about the hunger there, and the injustice. Here, in America, where there was nothing but hope and opportunity, people were now hungry. Nora had seen the pictures of the bread lines and the desperate people in the cities. How could the government insist that you kill sheep? Waste meat?

The darkness of the night pressed close around her and for the first time in her life the night sounds terrified her. In desperation, Nora thought of the solid ranch house back down there in the valley. Cool in summer, warm and protective in the winter—filled with good cooking smells, and familiar voices and faces. The fantasy comforted her, brought her a feeling of security. Finally she slept.

The sheep moved about, grazing, as usual, as they broke camp in the chill dawn. The men moved the herd in a diagonal direction across the low foothills. That route would bring them East of Bly and Nora thought sadly of their destination.

The Devil's Garden is a strange, forbidding place. The earth is literally covered with rocks, small, large and wicked. Nora had ridden though The Devil's garden twice last summer. She thought that in some distant past a terrible upheaval of the earth had caused the skies to rain down rocks, like giant hail, and they had covered the area for twenty square miles. She remembered the adults talking about the challenge it had been to build the road through the impossible rocky terrain. A few twisted juniper trees and an occasional clump of sagebrush grew there, but people and animals avoided that section of the country because of the uneven, closely packed stones that made walking difficult and riding horseback torture. There was nothing for miles except breathless, shimmering heat and black unyielding rock. Now, Nora knew that they would arrive in that hellish place in early afternoon.

She threw the remnants of the morning coffee on the nearly dead campfire as Dad hitched up the team. They checked to see that everything was packed into the wagon, threw a last bucket of water into the fire pit, then broke camp. They traveled the faint, rarely used track that joined the gravel highway just west of the tiny town of Bly. The dust now rose in a choking cloud as the green of the forest was left behind.

Bly had been a lumber town and the huge dead mill, with its tall, rusting smoke stack and silent buildings, stood eerie and tragic. The battered sign at the edge of town read, "Population 388," but some of those people had moved away. Abandoned houses stared with empty eyes out over weed-choked yards.

As they drove down the curving main street, Nora looked about expectantly. A few men stood silently outside a store. One fellow leaned against a post on a porch. They looked at the passing wagon with listless, indifferent eyes. No children ran in the streets or played in the yards. They sat quietly on their doorsteps or in the dusty yards. No one spoke. No one waved. That was unusual. Most folks in this country were friendly and spoke even to strangers. Now they weren't even speaking to each other, as there were no conversations going on that Nora could see. There was no—spontaneity. There seemed to be no animals about. The grocery store was empty. There were no cars in front of the small, one-pump gas station. A few men sitting on the plank benches in front of the store or the pool hall looked apathetic and weary; their shadowed faces and sunken eyes seemed to belong to sleepwalkers. Two children sitting on a sagging step outside their home barely moved their heads as they drove by.

Nora and her father passed two more boarded up houses at the east end of town. They crossed the hollow sounding bridge. That was the most noise they had heard since they entered Bly. Nora turned on the wagon seat and looked back.

"What's the matter with everyone?" she asked her father. "They all look like they just came from a funeral!"

Dad looked at her for a long silent minute. "They're hungry," he said, his voice bitter.

Nora stood up on the floor boards. She braced herself against the swaying of the wagon. She stared back at the ghostly quiet town. She was filled with a terrible understanding.

Suddenly, Dad pulled to the side of the road and stopped the team. He sat there, chewing on his lower lip, frowning slightly and looking out across the sun-scorched sagebrush. He looked at the band of sheep, moving like a low, gray cloud shadow across the hillside. He looked back at the quiet town. He looked for a long, thoughtful moment at Nora.

"Listen", he said at last. "Go back to town and tell—someone—what's going to be happening out there." He gestured toward the Devil's Garden, now only a few miles away. He sat for a moment longer, hunched forward, holding the reins, still chewing on his lip. "I don't think we can get into any trouble." He added. He shook his head, doubt registered in his eyes.

Nora felt apprehensive, but she was already climbing down over the wagon wheel.

"I'll wait for you up there, under those trees," Dad said. He pointed ahead a few dozen yards to where a couple of cottonwoods hung over the road. "Just tell someone and come on back."

Nora nodded. She started back along the road. At first she ran. Then, after she crossed the bridge, she slowed to a walk and wondered what she would say. She worried about whom she would tell. She felt frightened. Would they get into trouble? Old Jester had kept saying "It's the law!"

She saw the two children still sitting on the step. She approached them with slowing steps. They looked a little surprised when she hesitated and finally entered the gate.

The boy was older than Nora, probably about twelve, and he looked at her, curiosity mirrored in his eyes.

Nora paused for a minute. She swallowed—then blurted.

"Do you guys want some meat?"

The boy appeared stunned. His look changed to quick hostility. He turned his head slightly and shouted, "Ma!"

Nora wanted to run, yet she stood there, scared but resolute.

A bony looking woman pushed the screen door slowly open. She stepped out.

"Yes?" she questioned.

"Do you guys want some meat?" Nora repeated, hating herself because she had thought of no nicer way to say it.

Hostility flared in the woman's eyes also.

"You wicked, *wicked* child!" Her voice trembled with anger. "Get out of my yard!"

Nora retreated outside the gate, but turned stubbornly to face them.

"No. Really," she insisted. "My dad's got to kill all those sheep. And they are good sheep, too," she added, her voice shrill.

The woman continued to look angry and dubious.

"You can *have* the meat!"

The woman's eyes didn't move from Nora's face. She raised her head a little and shouted, her voice cracking.

"Stokie!"

Nora felt desperate, clinging to the gatepost. She heard Stokie's footsteps as he crossed the wooden porch of the store next door and hurried down the steps.

"What's wrong now?" he asked.

"Listen to this kid," the woman spoke warily.

Nora turned to look at the wiry, brown-faced man approaching. He stumbled a little in his hurry.

"It's true," Nora was beginning to get mad. "They are going to kill all those sheep…there in the Devil's Garden," she repeated, her voice sounding shrill. "Dad said for you—I mean, he wants you…" she stuttered. She was afraid she was getting them into trouble. "He doesn't care—if you come and get the meat."

"My God," Stokie breathed. He beckoned to his friends watching from the store front.

"What the hell is going on?" one of the men asked as he scrambled across the walk. The other two followed, dubious concern evident on their faces.

Nora told her story again, slowly now, and in more detail. The adults looked at each other in a stretching silence.

"I can't believe such a damn thing," Stokie sounded uncertain.

"No! Wait a minute!" His friend was beginning to show some excitement. "They got the radio over at the store working. I think I did hear something about the stockmen having to kill part of their animals. I thought it was some damn, rotten joke! Thought I'd heard it wrong."

"Hey. Get Hodges over here. He gets a newspaper over there at his office every day. He'll know what's going on."

Without being told, one of the children ran off to get Hodges. Nora clung uncomfortably to the gatepost. She knew they were staring at her tattered overalls and her bare feet. She wished she had worn her shoes.

Soon Hodges came down the street, surrounded by a silent group of men. Nora felt a hopeless dread invading her being when she saw the star pinned to his chest.

"We don't want to get into any trouble," she blurted to those around her. "We just thought maybe we could help you out." She started to back away, but Stokie caught her by the shoulder. She winced and twisted aside and he let her go, but by now the men were all around her and she couldn't run.

Hodges hunkered down on his heels so he could look her in the face.

"You aren't going to get into any trouble," he assured her, his voice kind and unhurried. "Now, just start at the beginning and tell us all about it." He pushed his hat back on his head and smiled into Nora's face. Then he added, his manner reassuring, "It's never been against the law for folks to give each other a helping hand, as far as I know. But I'll tell you if it's lawful or not, before we do anything."

So then Nora told them the whole story. About old Jester Morgan telling them it was the law. About the president saying you had to kill every fourth animal. About Seth Bailey driving his sheep into the Chewaucan River. Even about Phil being sick so she came to open the gates. She described the long ride around to the ranger station and this morning, coming down off Bly Mountain with the sheep already moving ahead to the Devil's Garden—and the guns and the shells under the seat of the wagon, hidden by the canvas. She was feeling a little better when she finished.

"Well, I'll be damned," said Stokie, almost in a whisper. "What the hell is this country coming to? Do you think she has the story mixed up somehow? This can't be true."

"It's true alright," said Hodges. He stood up slowly and took off his hat. He wiped his forehead with his handkerchief and looked around. "I'm going up about 40 miles this side of Silver Lake tomorrow. The Breen brothers are going to have to kill 640 head of sheep and I have to take the count." He wiped at his forehead again and slowly put his hat back on. He scuffed at the dirt with the toe of his shoe while everyone watched him with concern. He looked at Nora thoughtfully and finally spoke.

"Now, as far as I know, no one can get into any trouble. All the officials have to do is take the headcount." He spoke very slowly, scratched his jaw in further thought. "If the hind quarters are gone—well –we still only count the head. Now me, I'm taking the day off from around here. I'm going up to the Chewaucan to look over that mess of sheep that's plugging up the river. I can't see nothin', or hear nothin' that goes on around here for the rest of the day. I may be back this evening to help Ray Hacker get the headcount."

Nora slipped away while they were still talking. She knew Dad would be worrying that she was gone so long. She ran all the way across the bridge and back to the wagon.

They reached the Devil's Garden about two o'clock. Uncle Jack and Tim had dismounted and were waiting by the side of the road. There was no shade here and the heat rose in shimmering waves over the black expanse of blistering rock. Nora couldn't see the sheep, but a cloud of dust still hung in the air where they had passed. The men tied the saddle horses to the wagon. They took up the guns and shells without a word and started hopping and limping away through the impossible rocks, almost hurrying as though they were now determined to get the job over with as soon as possible.

Nora watched them out of sight and then unhitched the team. She drove them to a small knoll that lay to the north of the road. There was a patch of green there and a few trees for shade. She walked back to get the saddle horses and was just swinging into the saddle of Uncle Jack's mare when the shooting started. She began to cry.

"Poor Daddy," she thought. "Poor Dad."

Suddenly the sheep dogs came flying and yipping with fright, seeming to drift out of the heat haze without their feet touching the ground. They were frantic, groveling in the dirt beneath the wagon and whimpering as though in pain. They had been bred and trained to protect the sheep and help the herder. Now the shepherds were killing the sheep. It took Nora a long time to quiet them. The shooting continued.

At last, Nora got back on the horse and rode it up the little knoll. She slipped the bridle and walked slowly back. The shooting went on and on. It sounded like firecrackers off in the distance. She rode the second saddle horse up the rise, then rode further on up the foothill until she could no longer hear the distant shots. But from here she could see the milling herd of sheep, dispersed now, the cloud of dust growing ever larger. She couldn't bear to watch that, either. She brought the horse, now nervous and shying, back down and tied him near the others. She used a long rope that she found tied behind the saddle so that he could move around and graze. She walked back to the wagon, crying.

The dogs still cringed under the buckboard, whimpering in fear. The shooting continued. Nora sat in the scant shade thrown by the wagon seat and put her fingers in her ears.

Then she saw them coming. A rickety little Ford came pulling a long hay rack, the side rails still in place. Hitched behind the first was a second rack, this one with the side rails missing. The three vehicles, chained together, looked like a strange, slow moving train. It had to maneuver carefully around the bends in the road because of its great length. Every man from town seemed to be riding on it.

Nora stepped out to meet them. The men carried knives and saws of every description. The dogs howled again and ran back under the wagon.

Stokie came forward and looked at Nora with sympathy. She merely gestured toward the ragged sound of shooting.

Some of the men started down through the ditch, but Stokie called them back.

"Come on. Get these wagons turned around and headed back toward town," he told them.

Quickly they unhitched the hay racks, first one and then the other. They pulled at the tongue and cramped the wheels of each, pulling the vehicle forward a few feet, then backing it again until they were able to tug each rack into place. They waited while Stokie turned the Ford back toward Bly and drove it to the front of the line. The men soon hooked the unwieldy train back together again.

Now they took up their sharpened knives once more, and, holding them carefully, they hobbled and picked their way off through the treacherous rocks. Soon they were out of sight.

As she turned away, Nora discovered a group of black, carrion birds already wheeling high against the blue sky. Many were flying, unafraid, above the dust cloud. Vultures were gathering. The shooting continued.

Nora sat and waited beside the wagon, wretched and alone. She felt glad that the people had come out from Bly. At least they wouldn't be hungry for awhile. She thought of the boy on the steps with the hostile eyes, and of his little sister. She imagined their faces filled with anticipation and pleasure as their mother cooked supper and she figured that he might be smiling and thinking happily of her.

The shooting went on and on. She thought of the sturdy ranch house down in the valley again and she clung desperately to the thought.

Suddenly she heard a voice. The sound was thin, yet vibrant somehow, and she realized that the men from town were coming back. Some of them carried haunches of meat between them. Some carried smaller pieces, a front or a hind quarter or a length of loin. Some fools had left the wool on the meat and didn't know any better. Several of the men had thought to bring a clean cloth or a sheet to wrap the meat in. They loaded their precious burden onto the hay racks and went back for more. They were dirty, bloody and smelled of sweat, but their apathy was gone. Back and forth they went through the stifling afternoon heat until both wagons were piled high. The blood dripped over the sides and through the floorboards. The dry earth beneath the wagons was soon dark with moisture. Nora realized that the magpies and vultures now drifted over the wagons as well as over the dust cloud half a mile below the road where the shooting continued.

At last the men from town could load no more meat. The wagons were piled high and they had trouble finding room for themselves to board. Stokie came over to Nora as they prepared to leave. He shook her hand, his face grave.

"I'm awfully glad you came out," she spoke politely.

"And I'm awfully glad you came in," he answered with a wry smile. "And tell your father how much—tell him he'll never know how much—how he's helped…" He let the sentence trail off. Nora nodded. Stokie backed away, turned and ran to get into the Ford. They all waved as they pulled out of sight.

Shortly after, Nora saw the Ranger truck coming. It was getting late and the shooting was quite sporadic now—an occasional shot instead of the steady reports that had been evident earlier in the afternoon. The sun was far down in the west and it was getting cooler. A flaring red sunset climbed up the sky and the departing birds showed black against the crimson background. The birds were going to roost somewhere, but Nora knew they would be back in the morning.

Hacker stopped the truck and jumped down. He saw all the blood thickening in the gravel where the hay racks had been standing and he looked up in surprise. Just then Nora realized that the shooting had stopped completely. She began to cry again. She didn't know why.

"I guess they're—finished," she said. "I guess I'd better go up and get the horses."

She didn't hurry. She made three slow trips, and when she came back the last time and backed the team into place, all the men were back up on the road. Ray Hacker had gone down and taken a quick look. Now he was signing the papers. He handed them to Nora. Dad was dirt and blood from head to foot. Only his eyes and teeth looked clean.

Nora waited while the men decided that Tim and Uncle Jack would take the horses and the wagon back up to Gearhart. Dad and Nora would ride into town with Ray Hacker so Dad could turn the papers into the bank in the morning. Ray was going back out to the ranger station the next day and they could ride with him back to the Gearhart camp.

When they were ready to leave, Nora climbed up into the cab of the truck with Ray but Dad crawled into the back of the pickup and sat down on a coil of rope. They pulled out onto the road and turned east, toward town. Behind them to the West the drifting, dissipating cloud of dust floated in the fading light, turning the sunset to a mottled red.

"Dad looks so lonesome back there," Nora said to Hacker. "Why don't you stop and let him ride up here in front with us? I don't care if he's dirty."

"I don't care, either," Ray answered. "But he said he just wanted to be alone for awhile." He hunched down over the steering wheel and headed on toward home.

Chapter 9

✤ TWO WORLDS - 1934

Nora stalked, seething, down the alley, pushing her bicycle. That stinking Rollie had cheated her. She leaned the bicycle against the brick wall and threw herself down on the only spot of shade around. The high gable of the building across the dusty alley cast this small area of shadow and even that would be gone in a few minutes as the sun rose straight up toward noon.

She was glad there was no school this week because of the teachers' meeting.

"I can't believe it's this dry and hot," Rollie Fitch wiped sweat from his forehead with his handkerchief and put his hat back on his head. "It's only the middle of May but you'd think it was August, it's so damn dusty, and that bitchin' hot wind just never quits."

"And you never quit talking," Nora thought. She looked at Rollie with disgust. She wished the stage would arrive with the papers so she could get on with her route.

"Be a hell of a time for a range fire," Rollie continued. "Why, even the damn sagebrush is a dryin' up. A fire would burn all the way to Winnemucca, or down to Reno, depending on which way the wind was blowin'..."

The Benson boys, who delivered the *Oregonian*, sat on the curb also, waiting for their papers. They looked meaningfully at each other but didn't say a word.

"The damn stage is late again," Rollie was saying. "And another thing. Why the hell do they keep on calling it a 'stage'? You'd think they still used a six-horse team or something. And that big 'RED BALL' sign that's painted up there on the baggage rack, why that's just plain stupid!"

"Not as stupid as you are," Nora thought.

"Why, people around the country must have a good laugh when they talk about the big old Red Ball Stage. You'd think the guy that owns it would think up a more modern name."

"Had the same name for sixty years or more," said Nathan Cox, the stationmaster. He stood in the open door of the freight office and looked at Rollie with disapproval.

"They called it that when it was a stage coach and the horses pulled up right there where you're standing. I hope they never change the name."

"Well, ah—ah—" Rollie stammered.

"Now he'll start talking about the Depression again, and I'm sick of hearing about hard times," Nora thought. "He'll be telling us how FDR is going to fix everything."

Rollie was...different. He talked a lot, and if you answered him he would pick up on your answer and be off in another torrent of words. He came every day to meet the stage, hoping to pick up some money by delivering any packages that came in and were destined for the merchants in town. He would call the store and announce, "Say, Mr. Moss, there's a package here for you. It might be important. Would you like me to bring it on down to you? It would save you a trip." He didn't have any other job that Nora knew of, but lots of people didn't have jobs.

Nora figured he might be lonely, and she was sorry if that were true—but today she hated him.

She was often lonely herself and she knew the other girls thought she was different. She lived out on a ranch, but the ranch house was close enough to town that she could ride her bicycle in every day. The town girls visited each other and had parties and played hopscotch together, but they never invited her. Her parents were Irish and none of the town folks could understand their brogue. They were speaking perfectly good English, but for some reason the locals couldn't sort it out.

And Rollie was mean. He wasn't so bad lately, but he used to call her names and tease her when he met her on the street

"I'm going to call him 'Lard Bucket,'" she told her mother one day.

"Child! Child!" One could hear the shocked disapproval in Mother's voice. "Why would you say a hurtful thing like that to any human being?"

"He called us 'spuds'," Nora had told her. "Sometimes he even calls us 'half baked spuds'."

"Well, ignore him," Mother had directed her. "Don't bring yourself down to his level. Just raise your chin and continue on your way as though you didn't even hear him. He'll soon forget it if he gets no reaction."

Nora sighed. A rhyme was building in her head, but she put the words firmly aside. She wasn't the only one who was left out. The few Irish families who lived in town were mostly ignored, too. And the sheepherders—they were all Irish—they were *really* scorned. But the Irish community helped each other and she always felt welcome around them.

Rollie's voice interrupted her thoughts again.

"—and the sheepmen are complaining because FDR is thinking of taking the tariff off of the Australian lamb. Why, that would be wonderful. Everyone could afford to buy more meat—" Rollie continued.

"No one can afford to buy meat anyway," Nora thought. "American lamb isn't even selling, and they are practically giving that away!"

The rhyme crystallized suddenly in Nora's head.

Fat Rollie Fitch
Dumb son-of-a-bitch.

She closed her eyes and shook her head, willing the sinful poem to go away.

Mrs. Delfman stepped out of the telephone office next door. She fanned herself with a magazine and smiled at them as she approached her car. She tossed her purse through the open car window, but recoiled when she touched the metal door handle.

"Whoa," she said, "That thing is blistering hot." She opened the door carefully and put a tentative finger on the leather of the seat.

"It's too damn hot to sit on." Rollie spoke with authority. "It's been a'bakin' and a'cookin' there in the sun for an hour."

Mrs. Delfman hesitated for a moment. "I'll just spread out my magazine," she decided. "I'll sit on that."

She opened the *Saturday Evening Post* to mid-point, placed it carefully on the seat, then eased herself into the car.

Rollie closed the door with a gallant gesture and called out to her as she backed into the street. "Be sure you park it in the shade now, Missus, when you get home. Sun this hot is bad for that there leather."

Rollie barely paused for breath. "People don't have no idea how much damage the sun can do to them car seats. And you know something? Just awhile ago, I went right into the bank and told Bud Fitch—he's my uncle, you know. Well, anyhow, I told Uncle Bud his car seat was really steaming. I think he must have spilled something on it before he went to work, and that damn sun, it was just toastin' that upholstery."

Nora spun around to look at Rollie. She wondered how much of the story he would tell—and if he'd stick to the truth. He was a liar and a cheat, and she hated him.

Fat Rollie Fitch – the rhyme started again and she shook her head violently to put it away. Mother would have her chewing soap for a week if she ever heard her say anything like that. But, somehow, she couldn't help those sneaky thoughts that popped into her head.

"Well, Old Bud, he came running out," Rollie continued. "He still had a bunch of papers in his hand. He threw them in the car and drove it around to the alley behind the bank and parked it in the shade under the cottonwoods down there." Rollie gestured toward the grove of trees two blocks down the alley.

"Then he got out and gathered up all those papers and started to go in the back door of the bank." Rollie laughed and paused to look around at his audience, expecting some questions. Then he hurried on. "But, Old Bud, he had parked too close to the bank and he couldn't get the back door open far enough for him to squeeze into the back room!"

Rollie laughed and slapped at his leg with his hat. "I told him he oughta' move the car anyhow 'cause it was blocking the alley. Well. He tore around, threw those papers back in the car again, and pulled ahead and across the grass further down." Rollie turned away and put his hat back on.

"You didn't tell them about the papers blowing away," Nora snapped. The Benson brothers and Nathan Cox looked at her, puzzled. One never gave Rollie a chance to keep on talking.

"What?" Rollie looked pained. "Oh yeah. Well, a gust of wind came along and just lifted that whole stack of papers up and whirled them around and blew them every which way –" he hesitated and looked at Nora. She glared back at him.

"Well," Rollie continued, "I had to help Uncle Bud gather them up. They must have been awful important because he was a runnin' and a swearin' trying to get them." He hesitated uncomfortably and looked at Nora. "And Nora helped, too. She ran around and found some of them for us."

"I got most of them," Nora snapped. "They were blowing across the creek, and under the library steps. They were stuck to the park fence. They were all over the place.

"Yeah. You done really good," Rollie admitted.

"And when your Uncle Bud paid you, you didn't give me my half of the money," Nora finished triumphantly. "You'd both still be looking if I hadn't helped."

"No. No. That ain't so," Rollie looked hurt. "Did you really think that I

– that the money he gave me was for gathering up those papers? Ah—ah, now I see why you are so upset. No. No, I did some chores over at his house last night. Uncle Bud was just payin' me my quarter for that work I did." He spoke very earnestly. "Why, Nora. You don't think I'd – I'd – cheat you!" The hurt look intensified.

"It was more than a quarter," Nora stated. "And it was supposed to be half mine."

Nathan Cox and the Benson brothers turned accusing eyes toward Rollie.

"Ah, now," Rollie started, his face slowly reddening. "Nora, you know I wouldn't—I couldn't –" but everyone looked at him in silence. They didn't believe him.

Rollie you're so big and fat
Talk your way out of that!

Another poem! She clapped her hand across her mouth afraid she might speak aloud.

Georgie Lawson rode up on his bicycle. His route was the *Oregon Journal*. "What's going on?" he asked, looking around at the quiet group, bewildered. Even Rollie had stopped talking.

Nora wriggled to the very edge of the step. There was barely a sliver of shade there now. The heat seemed unbearable. She bent down and untied her shoes. Slowly she eased them off and then removed her stockings. The air, hot as it was, felt wonderful as it dried the sweat on her toes. Feeling guilty she tucked the shoes into her paper bag. Mother would have a fit if she saw her with bare feet. Nearly every kid in town went barefoot. Some even went to school without shoes. But it was a matter of pride with her mother.

"Why those town folk will think we can't afford to put shoes on your feet," Mother would say. "But use the brakes on your bicycle. Don't drag your shoes in the gravel to stop."

Nora sighed. Mother was hard to understand. She made a big point about wearing shoes but she didn't give a thought to the fact that Nora always wore overalls—and hand-me-down overalls, at that. No girl in town wore overalls.

The town folks don't give a damn
They don't even know who I am.

"Stop!" Nora told herself. The verse had appeared so suddenly and so unexpectedly that Nora was shocked. That's what she got for criticizing Mother. She was getting to be a really rotten person.

Mother, my brain works really slow
There's so much that I don't know.

She shook her head, trying to put the thoughts away, Another unbidden rhyme! The damn things kept sneaking into her head at the most unexpected times.

Uncle Jack had started the whole thing. He would sing off a rhyme about anything and urge her to make a poem, too. Out in the bunkhouse in the morning he'd get the sleepy, reluctant men moving:

Come on men, don't waste the day
Now's the time to go make hay.

The men would grumble, but they would laugh, too, as they filed in for breakfast, and they always got to the field early. Dad was up in the mountains with the sheep and the men might have taken advantage of Mother if Uncle Jack hadn't been there to keep them in line.

Even Mother had to laugh at him sometimes, and she didn't always get along with Uncle Jack. Mostly she thought he was setting a bad example for the children because he was always swearing. He couldn't seem to talk or carry on a conversation without peppering it with some profanity.

"Goddamn horses are out of the corral again," or "that lazy little son-of-a-bitch. I sent him back to town. Christ almighty, with people starving in this goddamned depression, you'd think he'd at least try."

Mother would set her face and pointedly send all the children upstairs, "out of harm's way," she would say, "until Uncle Jack takes his offensive language out of here."

Uncle Jack wasn't around much. He had his own band of sheep and was just finishing the shearing. He would be taking the animals to the summer range in a few days and then he would be gone until early fall. Nora would miss him. She loved him. He was always high-spirited and buoyant, teasing, and playing jokes on those around him.

Nora smiled. The poem making was something new. He used to occasionally make up a funny extra verse to a song or add a thought of his own to a poem they were required to learn at school—but now he'd call out a line to her and urge her to finish the thought and make the next line rhyme.

"How come you make up all those poems?" she asked one day.

"Hell. I get so damned bored out there with the sheep. Four hundred miles of sagebrush, not even a tree. Nothing to read—no one to talk to. I don't know. I just started—I just pick a word and away I go."

"How about…'sagebrush'?" Nora picked a word.

"Sagebrush? Singing thrush. Burned mush. He's a lush. Waters gush. Evening hush." Uncle Jack didn't even pause to think, but reeled the words off as though he were reading them from a page. Nora was impressed.

This morning when she jumped on her bicycle preparing to leave for town, Uncle Jack had been shoeing his horse. He called out to her, "Nora, don't you hit my poor old dog," and he looked at her expectantly. She answered, "He moves like a fat old hog."

"Good. Good," Uncle Jack smiled his approval and went back to nailing the iron shoe in place. She would miss him when he left with the sheep.

Last night she had pulled a good joke on him. She wriggled with pleasure at the thought. He was teasing her mother as she hurried to put supper on for the men. He sat at the table and called out, not intending to make a rhyme.

"Come along, Madam cook. We are all waiting here." Then Nora spoke up –

"Yes, waiting for Uncle Jack Shakespeare."

His eyebrows rose in surprise and he fell back in his chair clutching at his heart. Even Mother laughed. But really, the rhymes were getting to be a nuisance, especially when they came unbidden. And many of them were—well, unladylike. She was beginning to appreciate how concerned her mother was about the swearing.

Again Rollie's voice interrupted her thoughts and drew her attention back to the waiting group.

"—and Uncle Bud says this depression's gotta be over soon. FDR is taking steps to pull us out of it. Oh, here comes Phil."

Phil, Nora's older brother, rode up on his bicycle, surprised that they were still all there.

"I thought I was late," he said. "I figured all of you would be halfway through with your routes."

"Naw. The stage is late," Rollie pointed out. " – and it's a hell of a thing that it's late today. I wanted to go to the ballgame this afternoon."

"Who is playing?" Nathan Cox asked.

"Today it's the high school team," Rollie answered. "I don't know who is pitching."

"You miss playing, don't you?" Cox spoke again.

Rollie shrugged. "Yeah. Well, I play for the town team now that I'm out of high school. We're lucky, though. Ol' Clarence Quimby coaches both teams and he knows me from when I played for him last year in school. We're playin' tomorrow. Some big old town team from Burns."

"You are playing?" Phil asked.

"You bet your life I am," Rollie answered with pride. "I had the most home runs last year and I – I'm going to start pitchin' this year."

Nora went back to thinking about Uncle Jack. He never made verses with Phil or Katie, and one day when she asked him why. He answered, "They don't need it."

"Do you think I need to make rhymes?" Nora wanted to know.

Uncle Jack looked at her thoughtfully for a moment. Then he turned his head off to one side, raised an eyebrow and looking very solemn he said,

Hell. They couldn't make a rhyme
Even If I paid them each a dime.

Nora smiled. Somehow Uncle Jack understood her.

"I wish I were pretty like Katie," she said. "She has that black curly hair and not even one single freckle."

Uncle Jack was suddenly serious. "You're a fine looking girl yourself, and I love your freckles," he said. "Katie is a very nice girl, but—well, sort of—persnickety."

"But you—you're spunky! You've got enough spirit for both you and Katie!"

The sun stood straight overhead and the last bit of shade was gone. Phil settled down on the step near her.

"Better put those shoes on before you go home," he said. "Mother will have a fit."

"I'll put them on before I leave town," Nora assured him. "My feet were so hot—I was chasing those papers..."

Phil interrupted, speaking quietly. "Nickie is supposed to come in on the stage."

"Really?" Nora looked at him with interest.

Phil leaned closer, almost whispering. "We don't want Rollie to see him. He'll get all the other players upset."

"Why? What?"

"Tell him to go up to Grandma's and get cleaned up. I think he's going to pitch today!"

Nora's eyes widened. She nodded.

Nickie was a cousin of theirs. He was fifteen and would be a junior in high school next year. The problem was—he only made it to school about a third of the time, but he was an excellent student. His family was also Irish, of course, and very poor, so Nick had to go out caring for their sheep while his father took a job herding sheep for a townsman named Orrin Windell. Windell owned a fine house in town and also a ranch out near Ft. Bidwell, and he had bought into the sheep business only a few years ago. All the natives who invested in sheep always hired the Irish as herders. These foreigners, as the townfolks called them, were dependable and knowledgeable about sheep and very successful in managing the huge herds that were raised on the open range. Besides, no self-respecting cowboy would be caught dead in sheep camp. So, Nick's dad herded sheep for Windell, and Nick herded their own sheep and missed school most of the time. He came to school sporadically and always left with his arms full of books and the assignments for the next month. He was so shy that he rarely talked to fellow students and never volunteered to answer questions in the few classes he attended, but his test scores were always perfect.

"Rollie is always yelling about Nick not going to school," Phil spoke quietly as Rollie's voice echoed in the background. "He has such a big mouth."

"Why does Rollie want to make it hard for Nickie?" Nora wanted to know. "How come he doesn't help him? They are both good players."

"Because, Rollie wants to pitch!"

"But he plays out there by the fence!"

"Left field," Phil commented. He sounded a little annoyed that she didn't even know what left field was. "He plays left field, but he wants to pitch."

Phil played short-stop on the high school team, and one of the Benson boys played third base. They had played one or two games last season when Nick was in school and he had done a fair job of relieving the pitcher.

"He's a natural," Coach Quimby had said. "He'd be really good if he had a chance to practice every day like the rest of the team."

"Boy, are they in for a surprise!" Nora squirmed with delight. "Has the coach seen him pitch lately?"

Phil hissed for her to be more quiet. "He hasn't seen him pitch. But I just stopped and had a talk with him. I told him how much Nick's improved and he's willing to give him a chance." Phil hesitated. "Coach is worried because he's so—bashful—and he's missed so much school."

"Well he sure never misses when he throws that ball," Nora declared. "Did you tell him about the frame? I couldn't believe it when we stopped there last week. He gets that ball through that square every time."

"I told him," Phil admitted. "And Quimby is the one that suggested the frame. I explained that Nickie has almost nothing else to do out there in sheep camp. He practices for hours every day!"

They regarded each other. "The coach is afraid that—well, that Nick will be—uneasy—you know—nervous—with the crowd looking on and all."

But Nora was back thinking about the frame. She didn't quite understand the whole thing, but evidently there was a—a *zone*, where the ball had to go when the pitcher threw it. The ball must go over the plate, but not too high, not too close to the ground, not too far out from the plate and not too close to the batter. Nora understood the hits, the players running around the bases, and the foul balls, but she had never realized that there was an art to pitching.

Nickie and Phil, with Uncle Jack's help, had built a wooden frame that Nickie carried around with him all over the desert and sagebrush as he followed the sheep. The frame was mounted on a stake which he drove into the earth to hold the frame in the proper position. He then paced off the appropriate distance to an imaginary pitcher's mound. He had never possessed a real baseball, but he had a burlap bag half full of round rocks. As he walked the desert or took the sheep to some watering hole, whenever he found a rock that was about the proper size he would add it to the bag. When he set up the frame and started throwing the rocks through the opening, he could keep pitching until all the rocks were gone. Then he would take the empty bag and pick up all the rocks and start the routine again. Last week, when her father had taken supplies out to Nick's camp, Nora herself had found two rocks that were the perfect size and they had added them to Nickie's collection.

Nora looked back to Phil. "Maybe Nickie likes baseball so much, and is so good at it that he'll *forget* to be shy." She suggested.

I hope so," Phil looked at Rollie. "I'll keep old Big Mouth busy while you get Nickie off and up to Grandma's."

Rollie was still talking!

> *Stupid thoughts roll round his brain*
> *Pour out his mouth like the driving rain*

Nora winced. What if Nathan Cox and the others could hear what went on in her head? She felt consumed with guilt. Another rhyme had come, quick and unexpected, but she thought that Uncle Jack probably would approve of that one.

"Here comes the stage!" Benson shouted, pointing. The paper boys all jumped to their feet.

"They've got the big coach today," the station master observed. "Must have several passengers."

The bus pulled to the curb and the driver shut off the engine. No one moved for a full, quiet moment. It seemed that the driver, the passengers, and the bus itself were grateful and relieved that, in spite of the desert heat, they had finally arrived. The engine ticked audibly as the metal cooled. The radiator hissed and a small plume of steam escaped. A white film of alkali dust covered the full length of the cab and the luggage belted on top.

Lonzo Graham, the driver, expelled a deep, grateful sigh and opened his door. Old Cox stepped down and across the sidewalk to open the doors for the passengers. Rollie ran up, shaking hands with each person as they climbed stiffly out of the car. "Welcome, welcome," he said. "Hope you had a grand trip."

"Trip from hell," growled a salesman as he stretched and sighed. "Open the windows and you choke on the dust. Close them and you die of the heat. That was four hours of pure *hell*."

> *Crowded people sweat and smell*
> *No wonder it's a trip from hell.*

Nora closed her eyes and turned aside. Why couldn't the poems be nice? And not have all those swear words?

Lonzo climbed to the top of the stage and started throwing down the bundles of newspapers. Every day he threw them off before he unloaded a single suitcase or piece of luggage, and the paper boys loved him for his thoughtfulness. During the school year they delivered most of their customers on their lunch hour, and every moment was precious. They weren't pressed for time this week, however, because of the teachers' conference.

Nora stripped the cords from her dusty bundle and tried to fit the papers into her paperbag. She kept a wary eye on the passengers descending from the stage, but Nickie didn't appear! She removed her shoes from the bag, smoothed the papers into the canvas sack, then eased her shoes back in again. Now all the people were out of the bus, stretching, complaining and trying to find their luggage. Still no Nickie.

Georgie Lawson and the Benson brothers peddled away on their overloaded bicycles, struggling to balance the extra weight.

Nick's going to pitch. That's really swell
But he missed the bus—damn it all to hell!

She shook her head, blushing. Another sin, she thought.

"You'd better get going," brother Phil was beside her, lifting her paper bag and holding her bicycle upright. She felt confusion growing in her. She wanted so much for Nickie to be accepted, become part of the school, and to get over his painful shyness—and he hadn't come. Rollie was talking as usual, and walking toward them. She looked at Phil, disappointment in her eyes. Her brother shifted his gaze—two quick glances, across the street, one eyebrow raised, like Uncle Jack's. And there, hurrying away down the alley behind the hotel, was ragged Nickie.

"…and I'm glad you're not still mad at me," Rollie was saying. "You must know I wouldn't cheat you!"

"You would and did," Nora snapped as she pushed off from the curb.

"There's a couple of packages for the hardware store," Phil interrupted as Rollie sought to stop her, "and I think there is one for the drugstore, too. Better see if they want them delivered—or I could take them…"

"No, no." said Rollie. He was happy and hopeful as he rushed toward the freight office. "I didn't see none."

"I could be wrong," Phil steered him inside. "But I think I saw a couple."

Nora circled the block and met Nick near the back door of the hotel.

"How did you get here?" she asked. "I didn't see you get off the stage, and I was watching for you."

"I hopped in the very back with the luggage," Nick explained. "Just wedged myself in there with the packages and the suitcases and listened to the passengers whining about the heat. They didn't even know Lonzo picked me up. Thought he was adjusting the back window. Too miserable to even turn their heads—"

"Listen," said Nora. "Phil thinks you are going to pitch today. At least, you'll get a chance. And you are supposed to go up to Grandma's and…" she hesitated. She had almost said 'get cleaned up.' And Nick was a mess. Ragged pants, no socks, shoes barely holding together, only one button on his shirt, sunburned, peeling nose, and hair that hadn't been cut in months.

"Oh. Phil told coach Quimby how much you've been practicing," she stopped. "There's some of those damn papers—"

"What papers?" Nick was mystified.

"Some papers that belong to the bank. They blew away this morning."

Nick bent to retrieve the papers caught in the screen door to the hotel kitchen.

"We chased them all over down by the bank," Nora explained. "I thought we got them all. Oh! There's another one."

Nick gathered up the third page and studied the papers with interest.

"Where did you say they came from?" he asked, his voice sober.

"From the bank. Old Fitch had them in his car and they blew away. He and Rollie and I chased them all—what's wrong?"

Nick studied the papers quietly. He didn't answer, but folded the pages together carefully and put them in his pocket.

"I'll go up to Grandma's," he said.

"Wait a minute," Nora had an idea. She counted out five papers. "You take the bicycle and I'll deliver these on foot as I go up to her house. I'll get the bike there. You don't have a lot of time if you are going to pitch today. The game is early because of the Teacher's District Meeting—and there's no school."

Nick didn't argue. He rode off hurriedly as Nora headed down the block to where Mrs. Turner waited at her gate for the late newspaper.

A half hour later she let herself into Grandma's house. It was dark and cool in the front room, and she heard the excited voices from the kitchen

"It was April 12th exactly," Hugh O'Brien was saying. "Old Fitch came out and served the papers as I closed the gate at the stockyard. I had already made the deal for summer range over near Yancey." His voice shook a little as he continued. "Well, I won't be using that range. And you can be sure, Old Fitch waited until lambing was well over and the shearing crew paid. Then he foreclosed! He doesn't give a damn about the wool. Sure, the bottom has dropped out of the wool market. A man is lucky to get three cents a pound for it—"

"And out of the lamb market as well," another voice sounded.

Nora stopped at the door to the kitchen. O'Brien was cutting Nickie's hair, and the sheet that Grandma had wrapped around him and the floor beneath the chair were already dark with dusty curls. Nick's forehead that had been hidden by the long thick hair looked strangely pale while the rest of his face and neck were burned a deep brown by the sun. Paddy Larkin was carrying buckets of warm water to the tub that waited in the closet off the back porch and John Regan held soap, a soft brush and a fresh towel in his hands. Regan's brother Ned sat on a stool in the corner holding the papers Nickie had secured from the alley.

"Aye," he said as he studied the typewritten columns, "…and he waited until you had them safely delivered to the stock pens." He ran his finger down the page.

"And here is Red O'Connor's name. They foreclosed on his sheep the week of April first. He had just finished lambing and shearing also. Ah, Nora, I didn't see you there."

They all nodded their welcome.

O'Brien stepped back to survey his barbering. "Just a wee trim here, around the ears," he said. "Then I'm going to quit. Sure, I'm so mad I'll have you bald headed if I keep on."

"And didn't they ask O'Connor to go out as a herder for his own sheep that they sold to Fred Bowers? Yes. Here it is…" Ned Regan again referred to the papers in his hand. "O'Connor owed $7.50 a head. Bowers paid $8.10 a head, and he bought all the lambs, too. Sure, they didn't pay O'Connor for the lambs at all. He mortgaged the sheep before they ever produced a lamb, but when they took the sheep they got the new lambs free. The wee things were too young to separate from their mothers."

O'Brien, shaking his head in disbelief, rolled the barbering sheet carefully and stepped to the back door to shake the hair into the yard. John Regan took the broom in hand and started sweeping the floor as Nickie hurried out to his bath.

"In truth, I wasn't able to pay the interest, and I'm sure O"Connor hadn't the money for interest, either. Fitch said if we could only come up with the interest we could hold on for another year."

"Well. According to these papers, there are damn few, Irish or natives, that have paid their interest this spring. Here is Harry Bush, sheep mortgaged for $9.50 a head and Oscar Sims—he has nearly $11.00 owing on each of his, and he hasn't paid the interest—no, and he didn't pay the interest last fall, either. But *they* aren't slated for foreclosure! Not according to these figures!"

"Are you sure?" John Regan asked his brother.

"Isn't it written down here? Plain and simple. There's no misunderstanding!"

"They owe so much no one will buy them at that price," Larkin observed.

"Maybe," Ned Regan still studied the papers. "Look. They have it marked here. The sheep they are foreclosing on, and the ones they have already taken. Most of them seem to be Irish. Of course, most of the sheepmen *were* Irish, but…" He let the thought trail off.

"And not a damn thing we can do," Larkin said. "The bank is doing fine, though."

"Here are the names of Dan and Maurice Crowley. They think they are in good shape, and they are to be notified this week. And aren't Crowley's sheep already sold? It says here that Winfield is to be the buyer for their sheep. He'll take possession as soon as the boys are served the foreclosure notice. And here is Dan Dennahy and Charley Murphy, and Jack –" Regan stopped abruptly. He raised his head and looked at Nora.

She felt herself grow suddenly chilled.

"Jack?" she asked. "Not Uncle Jack?"

There was complete silence in the kitchen. The men looked at each other and then back at Nora. Finally O'Brien spoke. "Is your Uncle Jack home?"

"He was when I left," she answered. "He was shoeing his horse. But I think he was going out to the shearing corrals. They just finished up yesterday. I think they were going to start for the summer range today—or tomorrow. But he said he was trying to get a drainage ditch finished, too. It's out toward the west side. I – I – just don't know."

Nora walked to the chair Nick had just vacated and sat down, her thoughts in turmoil. Grandma stood quietly at the stove making fried bread and the other guests gloomily discussed the information they had learned from the documents Nickie had rescued from the alley. She remembered all the other pages she had gathered up and given to Bud Fitch. There had been many names on them. Those unknown people would soon be faced with the agony and despair that so many of her Irish friends had recently suffered. And most of them would be more of her Irish friends. No wonder Bud Fitch had thought the papers were so important. She struggled to pull her thoughts back to the conversation that had swirled around her.

"Maybe they won't be able to foreclose on any of the people written down there," Nora indicated the papers Regan still held in his hands. "They won't have the names if they don't have those pages."

"Indeed, they have other records," O'Brien shrugged angrily.

"Listen Nora," Paddy Larkin looked at the others for confirmation. "We'll have to make some plans here," he paused thinking of the words he should use to explain things to her. "Your Uncle Jack had a very early lambing. I remember. We all thought he was crazy to lamb in late February. But he did a great job. There were no storms, no cold weather. Sure, he has the finest bunch of lambs I've seen anywhere this spring."

The men nodded their agreement

"Nora," Larkin leaned close, his voice and manner very serious. "Nora. We think most of those lambs are big enough to wean. Some are already weaned, I'm sure."

The men nodded their agreement again, almost in unison.

"He mortgaged 800 head of sheep, and by the High Holy the bank shouldn't get more than 800 head when they foreclose. If we can rescue most of those lambs – hell, the bank can have the ewes. But the lambs stay with Jack." He paused to look around the quiet kitchen. "By God, if any of those lambs are big enough to make it on their own—and I think many of them must be—then old Fitch won't be quite as wealthy as he hoped."

He looked at Nora trying to fathom if she understood all this. "You go down and tell your Uncle Jack we'll be out to help him. He sheared at the Mud Creek pens and I hope he hasn't started them through the canyon headed for the summer range. Tell him to keep the sheep penned up there at the shearing corrals for one extra day." He threw his hands up in despair.

"Tell him to come in and talk to us," O'Brien said reasonably.

"I'll go right now," Nora jumped to her feet. "I hope he's there –at the ranch, I mean."

"Take these papers with you," Regan folded the pages and handed them to her. "And show them to your mother."

Nora hurried, almost running out the door. She rolled up her pant leg on the right side. This would be no time to get the cloth caught in the sprocket. She peddled furiously, standing on the pedals, her newsbag stored in the basket on the handlebars. She would have to ride all the way back into town to finish her route and for the ballgame, but she felt a terrible urgency to find Uncle Jack immediately before he started trailing the sheep to the mountains. The bicycle wheels hummed and gravel spurted beneath the tires. The two and a half miles home seemed like ten miles but her spirit lifted when she saw the ranch house appear in the distance. It slowly grew larger in size as she drew nearer.

She stopped in a rush of dust at the top of the lane. She threw the bike down, jerked her shoes from the paper bag and hurriedly pulled them on. She could see Uncle Jack down by the bunkhouse, sorting the supplies for the packhorses. She mounted the bicycle and hurried down the lane.

Uncle Jack turned, concern showing in his face. "What's wrong?"

"Come quick! Come quick!" Nora threw the bicycle down. The front wheel still spun as she leaped up the steps.

Uncle Jack dropped the harness he held and strode after her.

Mother turned from the stove as Nora burst into the quiet kitchen.

"Child! Child!" Her voice mirrored her concern as she reached toward her daughter.

Katie appeared from the dining room. "Nora! Be quiet. You'll wake the baby!"

"Look at these papers! Look at these papers!" Nora cried. She pushed the pages into Mother's hands. "They're from the bank."

Uncle Jack burst through the door.

"Nora!" Katie spoke in exasperation.

"What is it?" Uncle Jack demanded.

"Those papers," Nora pointed to her mother who had grown very still, her face losing color. "They're bank papers—about people losing their sheep!"

Katie spoke again, her voice sounding aggrieved. "Nora! Look at you. You're a mess and you're supposed to do the churning today." She pointed to the hand churn, half filled with cream, that waited on the table.

Uncle Jack stepped to read the papers over Mother's shoulder. Their faces gradually took on a look of utter dismay.

Nora grabbed the churn, threw herself down on the woodbox and started turning the handle furiously.

"Nora!" Kate spoke in exasperation. "Wash your hands!"

Nora jumped to the sink to splash water over her hands and arms, then she snatched up the churn again.

"Where did you get these papers?" Mother's voice shook.

"I found them in the alley behind the hotel," she began "They blew away from Bud Fitch at the bank."

"How did you know?" Mother interrupted, puzzled.

Nora spoke quickly above the whirring of the churn. "I helped Bud Fitch gather those papers up when they blew away at the bank. I thought we got them all, but then—Nickie and I found those three pages in the alley behind the hotel—"

"You shouldn't be in the alley behind the hotel," Katie interrupted. "That's right next to the saloon."

"Katie," Mother snapped. "Be quiet!" Anger sounded in her voice. "Nora. Begin at the beginning and tell me the whole story."

Katie bit her lip and stood pouting in the corner.

Nora took a deep breath. She told them everything, beginning with her ride into town. She described the frustration of Old Bud Fitch when he parked the car too close to the back door and couldn't get into the bank and how Pauline Fitch had stalked out and watched as Bud Fitch and she and Rollie gathered up the pages that blew away after he moved the car. Her voice shook with indignation as she told of how Rollie Fitch had cheated her and pocketed all the money himself. She explained that the bus was late, and that Nickie was supposed to pitch and that Rollie would have been mad and insulting to Nickie if he had seen him come in on the bus looking so—so—. Well, anyway, Phil had distracted Rollie, and Nick had slipped away and headed up to Grandma's house.

She paused, trying to think if she had forgotten anything. The dasher in the churn splashed the liquid rhythmically against the glass.

"Nora always gets to have all the fun," said Katie, but she looked very confused.

"Oh, Jack. I'm so sorry," Mother turned to Uncle Jack and put a hand on his arm. "I'm so very sorry!"

"What the God blessed hell—" Uncle Jack started and Katie gasped in mock horror.

"Stop!" Mother tried to make her voice sharp, but she still looked with pity at Uncle Jack. She turned to Nora. "Go on with your story," she said.

"Well. Nickie took the papers up to Grandma's and showed them to John and Ned Regan. Paddy Larkin and Hugh O'Brien were there, too. The bank just took Hugh O'Brien's sheep and Red O'Connor's and—oh, some others. They read those papers and said I should hurry down and tell you." She turned to Uncle Jack. "They said you should hurry right in and see them. They have a plan."

"I'll bet they have a plan," Mother sounded sarcastic. "Poor men." Her voice softened. "They've all been through so much. Aren't we all living on hope?"

"Goddamn it all to hell!" Uncle Jack smashed his fist down on the counter top. "That fat, grasping bastard. That slippery son of a bitch met me in town just a couple of days ago and asked me how shearing was coming along. And the next day he came out to the shearing corrals and looked all the sheep over and told me what a fine bunch of lambs I had. Good Christ almighty, he was friendly and as smooth – as smooth—as–as that goddamned cream the kid is churning. And all the time he knew he was just waiting until I got all the goddamned work done. And of all the names on that bitchin' set of papers—I owe the least! He and that goddamned Windell have a real game going there. He probably owns half interest in all of Windell's bitchin' herds."

Katie gasped in mock horror at every profanity, uttering a shocked "Oh," at each forbidden word Uncle Jack spoke.

"That goddamned little blackguard pup!"

Nora churned furiously and Mother swung around, the color coming back to her face. She stamped her foot and raised her voice.

"Stop it! Stop it right now!"

"He—he said…" Katie began.

"Katie! Kate! *Shut up!*" Mother's voice slashed through the kitchen like a whip. "And Jack, you know that language is not permitted here."

"Kee-rist on a crutch, Ellie," Uncle Jack shouted, throwing up his hands This is a goddamned *crisis!*"

"Stop!" Mother spoke again, her chin high.

"Great God!" Uncle Jack raised his arms as though in surrender and strode toward the door. "Great God. Sure isn't it my *prayers* I'm saying at a time like this?" The door slammed behind him.

Katie pouted, her feelings hurt, and looked with accusing eyes at Mother who had dared tell her to shut up, but Mother was having none of it.

"Kate. Go upstairs," she said.

Katie drew herself up, trying to salvage some of her pride.

"—and Nora was barefoot in town again today," she announced. "I saw her stop and put her shoes on at the top of the lane. Look. She didn't even bother to put her stockings on. They are probably still in her paper bag." She marched away into the dining room and they could hear her angry footsteps mounting the stairs.

Mother shook her head sadly, and sat down in a chair near the table. She closed her eyes and put a trembling hand to her mouth.

"Poor man," she mourned. "Poor Jack. And we could be next."

"Dad's name wasn't on those papers," Nora pointed out. "And they let him go to the mountains with the sheep. Wouldn't they have taken them from him when he finished shearing, if they were going to foreclose?"

"Yes." Mother looked a little hopeful. "You understand this situation better than Katie, don't you?"

"I heard the men talking in town," Nora explained. "And I think they do have a plan."

"We'll see," Mother sighed. They could hear Uncle Jack riding off on his horse, hurrying toward town.

"I have to go in and finish my route," Nora spoke almost afraid her mother would keep her home because of the bare feet. But Mother's mind was elsewhere. "Come straight home when you've finished," she said.

Nora hesitated, then spoke, her voice unsure.

"The ballgame at school," she began. "Nickie is pitching."

"No!" said Mother. "You come straight home."

Nora headed back toward town pedaling slowly, acutely uncomfortable in the afternoon heat. She felt herself to be the only thing on the landscape moving. The animals in the fields stood head down, patiently enduring. There was no shade. Even the sagebrush seemed stunted and defeated by the blazing sun and endless brightness.

She blinked, then closed her eyes for a moment. Even through her closed lids the light penetrated.

She felt tears gathering, but she was too old, too big, to cry. Disappointment filled her with bitterness. In a stern voice, Mother had told her again as she left. "Come straight home," and she meant it. Of course, that meant no ballgame. She wouldn't get to see Nickie pitch. That damn snotty Katie! It was all her fault! She blinked again and encouraged the rhyme that was building.

Tattle-tale Katie. The perfect little miss
Lips puckered like a prune, waiting for a kiss
Nora did that! Nora did this!
Tattle-tale Katie. Makes me want to-----

"No! No!" She shook her head, almost swerving off the road. That is a sin! She wouldn't say it. She'd think of another line—no, two lines:

Nora sneaking with Uncle Jack. Shooting off his gun
Tattle-tale Katie. Spoiling all the fun.

Yes. That would work. She pedaled along thoughtfully. She smiled. Secretly she liked the first version better.

There was no break in the weather. The next day was dry and hot, but the atmosphere around the stage office was hopeful and exciting.

"I'm not missing that game today," Nathan Cox announced. "I'm closing up. Putting a sign on the door sayin' I'll be back when the game is over. Look. I already have it printed."

"Did you see us play yesterday?" Doug Benson asked.

"No. But I heard about it. Everyone in town heard about it and I'll bet the whole town will show up!. Probably most of the merchants will close up shop, too, so they can go. They won't have any business anyway, to speak of. Everyone will be down at the ball field!"

Benson laughed. "Clifford Hill, the catcher—he's still in shock. When Nick threw that first warm-up pitch it surprised him so that—well, it knocked him flat down on his seat in the dirt with his mouth hanging open. Ol' Quimby had to tell him to get up and throw the ball back."

"Phil told us he did really good," Nora spoke with pleasure.

"Good? He was great! Man, that ball just *sizzled* coming across that plate. Old Hill, he was half afraid of it for the first inning or two."

"Aw, he wasn't *that* good." Rollie Fitch spoke for the first time. He had been strangely quiet, which was unusual for him.

"Yeah, he was so bad that they didn't get but one hit," Benson laughed, 'and he's pitching again today for the town team."

"Now that ain't fair," said Rollie. "If he's playin' for the high school team he shouldn't be playin' on the grownup team!"

"Yesterday you were saying that he shouldn't play for the high school team," Nathan Cox interrupted. "You said he missed too much school to be considered a student. Now you want him to be a student and not play with the grownups!"

"Rollie. You played for the town team last year, and you were still in school." Benson pointed out. "In a little town like this they don't care if you're out of school or if your grandmother plays, just so you can get a team on the field."

Rollie turned away, pouting. He reminded Nora briefly of Katie. She slipped her shoes and stockings off and put them in her newspaper bag. She wiggled her toes happily and considered how differently she felt today when she wasn't mad at Rollie.

"The coach says he throws so fast because he's been practicing with rocks

193

and they are heavier than a regular baseball," Nathan Cox explained seriously. "I never thought of it before, but it makes sense."

"Tom Watson, down at the creamery, he took Nickie out to supper last night," Benson told them. "He said when he worked that hard he deserved a good meal and said he'd take him out again tonight if he wins! Took him right down to eat at the hotel."

"And he won't be ordering any beans," Nora smiled.

Beans were a staple in every sheep camp. She remembered when Uncle Jack had trailed the sheep in from the high desert country a few weeks ago. He had ridden through the canyon and hurried to the bunk house to shave and get cleaned up. Then he came in to eat.

"I'm out of grub," he told Mother. "I've been out of flour for ten days or so. Even my sourdough starter died on me. I had no coffee, no sugar and no canned milk—and the nearest store was eighty miles away."

"Eat up. Eat up," Mother had encouraged him. "It's only plain old stew, but the bread is fresh today."

"By God, it tastes wonderful," Uncle Jack was enthusiastic. Mother winced and placed the butter on the table. "I'll give you another starter for the sourdough," she promised.

"Don't you have anything to eat in camp?" Nora asked. "Are you really starving?"

A slab of bacon and a sack of beans,
You don't know how much that means.

Uncle Jack recited, bitterness in his voice. "This goddamned depression…"

Nora let the matter drop.

"The stage is coming," Benson sang out, pulling Nora back from her daydreaming.

Lonzo Graham climbed on top and threw the paper bundles down.

"I hear Nick did a fine job," he called.

"Yeah, they didn't get a single run." Benson answered. "The whole town is going nuts. They'll all be at the town game today."

Lonzo laughed. "Do you suppose he'll ride up in the front seat now when I pick him up?"

Nora folded her papers into the newspaper bag and pedaled off on her route. She didn't want to be late today and miss the start of the game.

Both the Regans and Paddy Larkin were at Grandma's. They were the only ones she had met all day who weren't talking about the game. She felt strangely guilty that she had forgotten Uncle Jack's trouble. The men were ragged, tired and extremely dirty. Ned was washing at the sink while John and Paddy were shirtless on the back porch and scrubbing their arms, necks and torsos in a tub of sudsy water. Grandma was making sandwiches and the tea was already steeping in the huge teapot.

"The men are in a terrible hurry," Grandma explained. "They worked the whole night through separating the lambs from your Uncle Jack's herd."

"Did Fitch—?"

"He did," Grandma nodded, her eyes very serious. "He served the papers on him yesterday. Saw him ride into town and followed him right here and into my front room," her voice shook with indignation. "Then the boys got busy." She indicated the men now eating at the table." They borrowed a pick-up from—from—you know, that Irish lawyer from back East—"

"Sheehan," Larkin supplied the name, his mouth full.

"Yes. Sheehan. They drove right out there to the shearing pens—and worked all night. They just got back in a few minutes ago. They left O'Brien at Juniper Springs. He's driving the ark in, and the sheep are right behind him."

"Juniper Springs! That's not too far up the canyon," Nora said.

"No. It's fairly close," said Ned Regan. "The whole outfit will be in town soon."

"I'm going," Nora announced. "I want to finish my route and get the papers to the stores uptown before the streets are blocked with sheep."

"You might just make it," said Larkin. "It will be close."

Nora hurried away, desperate to finish and not be late to the game. She couldn't quite shake the feeling of guilt. Uncle Jack would be feeling—terribly upset—and she was worrying about being late for a ball game.

She rushed to each customer. The West Side was mostly spread out, each house having some acreage around it. The South End was easier because all the houses were closer together. Within a half hour she was pedaling toward the court house with only three papers remaining in her newspaper bag. And there, coming out of the mouth of the canyon was the sheep camp wagon, the ark, swaying and bumping over the ruts, brushing the sagebrush on either side of the trail as O'Brien guided the horses, trying to miss some of the bigger rocks.

Nora dropped her bike and hurried with a paper into the tailor shop and delivered another next door to the drug store. Only one paper left and that one went to the bank. She pushed her bicycle along the sidewalk in that direction.

Now she could hear the mellow ringing of the bell as the bellwether led the river of sheep down the trail from the canyon. She stopped, watching in awe. The sheep were so white! Usually they looked dusty and grey but these were so white and the black paint of the brand stood out remarkably.

Of course! They had only been shorn a day or two ago and the dusty old wool had been removed. But it was a grand sight to see that packed herd move forward in unison. Hundreds and hundreds of animals, bodies touching, moving and swaying like a frosty avalanche of snow, undulating, shifting, but always moving.

The white sheep, crowded together and moving at a measured pace, filled the street, hemmed in by the buildings on either side. The few people on the sidewalk retreated into the courthouse yard, behind the wrought iron fence, and closed the gates. They had seen these huge herds of sheep before. They were not an uncommon sight as they must pass through town on their way out to the high desert country for the winter, and again as they returned and were taken to the mountain meadows for the summer. When a band of sheep invaded the town, all traffic stopped. Cars were marooned in the middle of the street, surrounded by a mass of nonthreatening animals that parted as they approached and flowed together behind any vehicle in their way.

The herd reached the cross street and poured across the intersection. Some bleated and complained at the unfamiliar surroundings, but they remained tightly packed and doggedly followed the bellwether and the sounding bell.

Uncle Jack and his dogs stood at the intersection. He turned the sheep so they could head down Main Street toward the stock pens.

Bud Fitch came out of the bank followed by Orrin Windell. They laughed, pointed at the sheep, and shook hands.

Nora hurried across the street. She propped her bicycle near the bank entrance and adjusted her newspaper bag. The last paper would soon be on Pauline Fitch's desk.

A hand touched her shoulder and Ned Regan, wearing a clean shirt, bent to speak to her.

"Hold a minute, now," he said quietly. He stood and seemed to be watching Uncle Jack across the street.

"But—but—I have to get that paper into the bank before the sheep,"

"No, wait." He bent down to speak to her again. "You aren't afraid of the sheep, are you?"

Nora laughed. "Afraid of the sheep? Of course not." She couldn't believe he'd think such a thing.

Mrs. Windell and Mrs. Delfman came out of the dress shop across the street and hurried toward them. They wore large brimmed summer hats and lovely dresses. Mrs. Windell pulled on her gloves as they walked in shoes called pumps with high, narrow heels.

"I hope Pauline is ready," said Mrs. Delfman. "We want to beat those sheep down to the hotel." They swept along the sidewalk but stopped under the shade of the awning next door.

"She should be coming right away," Mrs. Windell answered. "I hope they have the fans on in the dining room."

"They go eat at the hotel every Wednesday," Nora told Regan, nodding toward the two women. "Don't they have the most beautiful dresses?"

Regan wasn't listening. He seemed tense and watchful. Something was going on down the street. Bud Fitch and Mr. Windell were shouting at Uncle Jack. They were shaking their fists and pointing at the sheep. Something about the lambs. And there were only a few lambs, very small ones.

Suddenly Nora understood. Yesterday the men had talked about Uncle Jacks fine large lambs. Big enough to make it on their own. Uncle Jack's friends had worked all night separating the half-grown lambs from the herd and had taken them away. Only the small lambs, those still nursing their mothers, were with the herd.

Regan leaned down a third time. "Now, Nora. Go along and deliver your paper, and when you come out, hold the door open for a minute – just until we get the sheep started in—"

"Get the sheep started in?" she began, but Regan was pushing her forward.

"Good. Old Fitch is going back into the bank," Regan observed. "Open that door wide," he said as Nora hurried away. She smiled. She laughed. She understood. She was part of a huge joke they were going to play on the bank, and on the Fitches. You bet she would hold the door wide open!

Pauline Fitch swept out of the bank at that moment. She adjusted her flowered hat and patted at the ruffles that cascaded down the front of her blouse. She also wore high heels and looked affronted at the milling, bawling sheep.

"You're late with that paper today," she told Nora as she swept past to meet her friends.

Nora marched into the bank and across the marble floor. She loved the feel of the cool tile on her bare feet. She pushed open the low, swinging gate that led to the area behind the teller's cages. She placed the paper respectfully on Pauline Fitch's desk. Several of the girls nodded and smiled at her, but Howard Kahn, the bookkeeper didn't even look up from the columns of figures he was studying. He wore a green, celluloid visor pulled low on his forehead.

Through the huge front window she could see the men signaling the dogs. She walked back across the empty lobby and opened the heavy front door.

Immediately the frantic sheep, urged by the barking dogs, veered into the opening. The swift press of frightened ewes hit her and thrust her back so suddenly that she nearly lost her balance. She felt herself flattened against the open door, unable to move, the metal doorknob thrusting against her ribs. The throng of frenzied animals, eyes rolling in terror, bleating and crying in dismay, burst past her filling the lobby in seconds. Some slipped on the polished marble floor and their momentum carried them across the room as dozens of other sheep closed in behind them. Chairs were shoved along with the reckless river of sheep and one old ewe jumped up and stood on the polished seat of a chair and seemed to survey the mad scene.

One ewe half fell against the low swinging gate and then staggered through it. Immediately she was pushed violently forward and the herd surged after her, displacing desks, overturning chairs and scattering papers that floated for a moment and then fell to be lost beneath the packed, churning animals.

Nora winced as one fat ewe stepped on her bare foot. The animal's sharp hooves slid across her instep and another kicked her shin as it struggled to escape the dogs.

The tellers screamed and climbed up on the high counters, atop the desks, and even the recessed windowsills. Viola Larson spilled her drawer of money and the bills and coins disappeared into the seething maelstrom. The inkwell on Howard Kahn's desk was dislodged and spilled over his hands, his trousers, and several sheep that pushed hurriedly past. His green eyeshade slid from his desk and settled like a collar around the neck of a struggling lamb.

Nora, pinned in her position by the press of sheep still fighting their way through the door, looked with amazement at the screaming women. How could they be afraid of sheep? Yet they crouched on hands and knees, without dignity, atop the high counters white with mortal terror. Nora felt a rise of anxiety herself as she clung to the edge of the door behind her. She had to hold desperately to keep from being pushed out into the milling herd. Two more sharp hooves landed on her bare feet.

Bud Fitch was swearing and kicking at the sheep, but soon he couldn't even raise a leg, let alone kick, as the throng pressed tight around him.

"Open the damn back door!" He roared at Howard Kahn, but Howard was crouched on top of his desk shaking his head helplessly.

"Quiet!" Fitch yelled above the pandemonium of bleating sheep, screaming women and crying lambs trying to be united with their mothers.

Nora looked at the noisy chaos in utter disbelief.

Bud Fitch turned toward the back entrance himself. "I'll open the damn door," he said. "They'll all run out. They'll go right on through." The employees looked hopefully toward him.

He turned toward the door. He stiffened his legs and pushed his way, sliding his feet along the floor, not daring to raise a foot to take a normal step. He made his slow way through the packed, struggling animals. He reached the door, pushed the lock aside and turned the knob. Triumphantly he pushed at the door. It opened—a few inches. A sheep camp wagon was parked outside, blocking the way. The sheep, glimpsing the narrow shaft of sunlight, surged toward it pinning him securely. With his fists he hammered at the wooden door in utter frustration.

Nora, trapped helplessly against the door in the lobby, watched in growing bewilderment at the chaos. The bleating, bawling, milling, panic-stricken sheep filled every inch of the floor space. They were packed together in a dense throng and one of the dogs walked, barking, across their backs frightening them even more.

The low dividing wall shuddered, swayed and broke loose from the floor where it had been nailed. Because of the densely packed animals the divider didn't fall, but one could see the top rail move drunkenly as the animals shifted about.

A large frightened ewe plunged through the door. Her two back hooves landed squarely on Nora's bare instep and the animal pushed with terror-inspired strength to propel herself forward. Other sheep struggled to enter the already densely-crowded lobby, and they stamped in helpless frustration because there was nowhere to escape.

Nora grimaced in pain as countless hooves now nicked, stamped and walked across her hidden feet. The terrified animals, lunging and surging to escape the dogs, were stopped short at the door—but they still struggled to enter, crushing her against the door and mutilating her bare feet.

Her toes, her feet, her ankles and even the nails on her toes were suffused in pain. Her feet grew more distressed by the moment, and now a burning sensation inched up her legs. She felt the outline of one of her shoes in the newspaper bag draped over her shoulder. Every time a sheep lunged against her, the shoe bumped her knee. The shoe was kicking her as she kicked herself for having taken them off.

She was pinned, completely immobilized by the pressing bodies, and dozens of ebony hooves stabbed, slashed and punctured her feet. She felt warm blood oozing between her toes. She realized that her own screams now joined the others.

Uncle Jack heard her agonized cries and spun toward her. He realized that she was caught and helpless behind the pressing, agitated herd. He spoke to the dogs and hurried toward her. With the dogs silenced, the violent commotion immediately started to quiet, and the herd outside partially separated as he strode across the sidewalk. He reached and lifted her straight up, above the backs of the densely packed sheep.

"Great Christ," he breathed as he saw her bloodied feet. He swung her into his arms, backed out of the entry way and started carrying her down the street.

The two Regans, Larkin and O'Brien whistled to their dogs and hurried after them.

"Don't cry! Don't cry," Uncle Jack crooned in her ear. "Sure, it will be alright. You'll be fine. Great holy God —" He pressed her head into his shoulder so she couldn't see the blood dripping from her lacerated feet.

"I couldn't move," she hiccupped. "I shouldn't have taken my shoes off. Mother said I should keep them on." She shuddered. "Oh, they hurt. *They hurt!*"

Pauline Fitch, Mrs. Windell and Mrs. Delfman strolled leisurely toward the hotel. They knew there was some sort of a commotion back there near the bank, but they were on the same side of the street and too far away to see what was going on. It was probably just that huge band of sheep milling about the intersection. They paused to look back and were astonished to see an Irishman rushing toward them, carrying the paper girl. She must have had some sort of an accident because both her feet were—were—*ghastly!* Covered with blood that dripped on the street. In unison they backed away and pulled their skirts aside.

Uncle Jack looked at them with cold, accusing eyes. "They might offer to help!" His voice was bitter but he didn't hesitate or miss a stride as he passed them. Nora felt his arms tighten around her as he hugged her close. He whispered,

> *Ruffles and lace and bright fancy stitches*
> *Don't make them ladies! They're just backyard bitches!*

Nora jerked in shock. She laughed. She cried. She became somewhat hysterical. Uncle Jack swerved across the street and, followed by his friends, took her into the White Dove Saloon.

He deposited her on the bar and turned her with her feet over the sink inside the bar. Hanrahan, the man standing at the bar with a cup of coffee in his hand, backed away in alarm. The bartender, Thad McAuliffe came from the back room with a stack of clean bar towels folded over his arm.

"Great God," he gasped as he dashed to help. "What happened to the child's feet?"

Nora only half heard them. She felt faint and sick. She clung to Uncle Jack and protested. "Take me out of here. Ladies—nice girls don't go into bars. Mother will have a fit—"

They poured water over her feet. They patted her knees and sympathized. They told Uncle Jack he should send for a doctor.

"I can't be in a saloon," Nora insisted.

O'Brien rushed forward with a large, clean bucket. They half filled it with warm water and McAuliffe threw in a handful of soap flakes. They lowered her feet gently into the water. Nora winced and her hands clinched into fists.

"Aaahhhh—" she heard herself groan.

"Those wounds are bad," McAuliffe said. "Some are quite deep and all are caked with dirt—"

O'Brien reached under the bar and came up with a bottle of Lysol. He squirted the liquid liberally into the suds. Her feet began to pinch and burn.

"They hurt. Ohhhh. They hurt *worse*." She tried to lift her feet from the bucket.

Hanrahan left his half-finished coffee on a nearby table and rushed out the back door.

"Take me out of here," Nora begged. "Someone will see me. Mother will be—humiliated." She covered her mouth with her hand to keep from screaming aloud.

Uncle Jack wasn't listening. He was giving orders. "Ned. Run and fetch Dr. Willard. Larkin. You'd best move the wagon from behind the bank. Bring it down the alley here. Thad. Pour a little more warm water in that bucket. Heat it up a little."

"I can't stay here," Nora moaned. She winced as the hot water was added. "They hurt. They hurt! My feet hurt all over!"

Michael J. Sheehan came through the entry. He was the lawyer from Boston and had his office next door. He always wore a suit, a white shirt, and a tie. Nora was impressed that he walked along the streets and spoke to the townspeople as casually as he spoke to the Irish. He was a friend of her parents and often came out to the ranch for a visit or a meal.

"He is a professional," her mother had once explained. "The townfolks don't intimidate him one bit. That's what an education will do for you."

Nora thought Sheehan to be a fine man. He held classes for the immigrant Irish and taught them Civics and American History so they could pass their citizenship tests. He encouraged them, counseled them and often loaned them money. He was accepted and respected by the local folks who mostly ignored the other Irish.

He called out as he entered. "Is anyone here going to the ballgame?" He stopped in consternation at the activity behind the bar.

"Nora?" He said. "Nora. Whatever is the matter?" He stepped behind the bar and looked at her feet immersed in a bucket of water that was slowly turning pink. Wordlessly he raised his eyes to Uncle Jack.

"Please. Please!" Nora begged. "Get me out of here." She tried to raise herself. "Mother will kill me. And you too, Uncle Jack. I can't be in a saloon!"

Uncle Jack restrained her, hugging her to his chest. "She's upset to be in a bar," he explained to Sheehan. "She's half hysterical—"

"I'm not hysterical," she objected. "Nice girls can't be in—in here."

"And where can we go then?" Uncle Jack's voice sounded gruff and angry. "Maybe we could go sit in the hotel lobby, or maybe the shoe counter at the Penney's store. The doctor is coming here."

"No. No. Mother will find out that I've been in a saloon." Nora fell back, sobbing. She lifted her aching feet from the bucket. She shuddered.

"Great Christ," she moaned, "the damn things hurt like bloody hell!"

No one paid any attention to her outburst except Uncle Jack. He stopped talking, mid sentence. His mouth hung open. He blinked, twice, and closed his mouth. He tried to speak, and blinked again.

"We'll just go next door to my office," said Sheehan, removing his keys from his pocket.

Uncle Jack picked her up in his arms. McAuliffe ran around the end of the bar carrying the bucket of water which he shoved up so as to again immerse her bleeding feet.

As they reached the door, Hanrahan rushed in. He held a quart bottle triumphantly in his hands He pulled the cork and poured a portion of the brown liquid into the bucket.

"Sheep dip!" he declared happily. "It will stop any infection within twenty miles." He went back to his coffee.

Nora sat on Sheehan's upholstered chair. Her feet seemed on fire and the water in the bucket had turned a milky color, gradually getting pink. The men looked at each other in consternation.

"My feet don't feel like feet," she said. "They burn so much."

Uncle Jack patted her shoulder. "The doctor will be here soon."

Nora felt herself growing chilled. Her teeth chattered. She shivered uncontrollably. The warmth of the burning feet seemed almost pleasant. The sun was brilliant outside and the men in their shirtsleeves seemed comfortable. Uncle Jack draped his coat around her and they carried her, chair, bucket and all, to a warm spot in the sun-filled window.

At last, Paddy Larkin and Dr. Willard came hurrying down the street. Uncle Jack stepped to the door and waved them into the lawyer's office.

"What have we here?" Dr. Willard came to Nora and lifted her feet out of the bucket. Her skin was puckered and drawn into deep ridges like a two-year-old shriveled apple. The skin was white. The dirt was gone.

What were you soaking these feet in?" Willard asked as he bent to look closer at the lacerations.

McAuliffe handed him a bar towel to protect his clothing. "Well. There's hot water, and soap flakes and Lysol," he enumerated as the Doctor nodded his agreement. "And there's—some sheep dip,"

"Sheep dip?" Dr. Willard seemed to stop breathing. He straightened, raised his eyes and looked in disbelief at Sheehan.

Sheehan frowned, puzzled. "What is sheep dip?" he asked.

Nora felt surprise. She thought everyone knew what sheep dip was. The stuff you dipped sheep in to make all the ticks, bugs, maggots or any other disgusting things drop off. But then, Sheehan was from back East somewhere. They probably didn't know about sheep dip there.

"We were afraid of infection," Ned Regan explained. "Sure, the feet were very dirty from all those sheep stamping on them—but—but Hanrahan threw in the sheep dip—actually, before we could stop him."

"Let's throw this out and get some cool water," the Doctor became very businesslike. "Warm water will keep those wounds bleeding." He pushed the legs of her overalls up above her knees as McAuliffe came with the fresh bucket of water.

Nora shuddered when the air hit her feet. She shuddered again when they were plunged into the cold water. She heard herself moaning.

Dr. Willard opened his bag. "Could you get me a large spoon?" he directed McAuliffe. "And bring a glass of water." He took a bottle from his bag and when McAuliffe returned he carefully filled the spoon and held it for Nora to swallow the liquid. "That will make you feel better," he soothed her. "Now, drink some water—"

Nora nodded and sipped the water, trying not to whimper.

Sheehan and McAuliffe retreated to the corner where they spoke in whispers.

After a few quiet moments, Dr. Willard opened his bag. Again, the water in the pail was turning pink. Dr Willard seated himself and lifted out one dripping foot. "They are certainly clean enough," he said, his voice dry. "That will save us some time." He produced a small kit from his bag. "We'll have to put some stitches in that cut across her instep, and that's a bad one there near her ankle, and a few others…"

Uncle Jack turned his back and walked away, cussing—or perhaps praying, Nora couldn't tell. He strode for a moment around the room and then came back to put his strong arms around her. Nora could scarcely feel the needle. Her feet, which had been on fire, now seemed strangely cool and almost removed, as though she were watching the doctor sew up someone else.

"Your feet will be very colorful," Dr. Willard said. "In a few hours they will be all black and blue and red, and very swollen. In a few days they will become purple and blue, and even a little green in spots—"

Nora nodded. She watched with interest as the doctor sewed up her cuts. The stitches were neat and even reminded her of her mother's embroidery. "That must be magic medicine," Nora said. "My feet don't hurt much now, and I can barely feel those stitches."

" —and you won't want to walk much." The doctor continued. "They will be pretty tender, and sensitive— and I'm afraid you'll miss some school—"

"I don't mind," Nora spoke with honesty, then added. "Just so I don't miss the game."

"The game?" The doctor frowned.

"Nick is pitching," she explained. "He's my cousin, you know. And he's, he's—" she paused, frowning. She forgot what she was saying.

"Well. No ballgame today, I'm afraid. It's home and to bed for you— when we've finished here.

"I *have* to go to that game!" she protested. "I *have* to!"

"No. No." Uncle Jack shook his head.

"I *have* to go!"

"Steady. Steady!" Uncle Jack reached to hold her leg and foot in place. In her agitation she had pulled her foot away.

"I *have* to go," she insisted, and the tears started.

Dr. Willard handed her a fat piece of gauze to use as a handkerchief. He started pouring Iodine over the feet. Nora was surprised. It didn't pinch and burn. Her feet just felt suddenly warm.

"Let me watch just one inning," Nora begged. "Even just a couple of pitches—"

"We'll see. We'll see!" The doctor continued with his work. Larkin and Ned Regan slipped in hurriedly through the door.

"Isn't 'his majesty' coming thundering down the street?" Regan addressed Uncle Jack.

"Fitch?"

"Himself! And not in good humor. He's seeking yourself, you know."

"Let him come," said Uncle Jack.

Bud Fitch, his face very red, hurried past the window. He entered the bar next door. Soon he reappeared on the sidewalk, looked around and discovered the men in Sheehan's office. Angrily, he strode through the entrance.

"I'll come right now and serve you," McAuliffe started for the door.

"I don't want anything from there," Fitch nodded toward the bar next door. "My sister told me this fellow here had taken the child into the White Dove."

"The little girl was brought here, into my office," said Sheehan.

"And I came here to treat her," Dr. Willard announced.

"*He's* the fellow I have business with," Fitch turned forcibly toward Uncle Jack. "You come and get those damn sheep out of town," he shouted. "They're wandering all over. Grazing on people's lawns, trampling their flowers, trying to drink from their sprinklers, eating their gardens—and my bank is—is—a *disaster*. I had to close it. A wall knocked down. Ink staining the tile floor. Manure everywhere! YOU'LL PAY!" he roared. "You'll pay to have it cleaned up and for all the damage!" He pushed closer, shaking his fist in Uncle Jack's face.

Nora cringed aside and cried out.

"And why should I pay for the damage your sheep did to your bank?" Uncle Jack stood to face Fitch.

"You'll pay!" Fitch strode closer, dislodging the chair where Nora sat. She cried louder.

"Stop it!" Dr. Willard and Sheehan spoke almost in unison.

"I'm treating a patient here," Dr. Willard spoke with anger. "Just step away please."

Sheehan stepped forward. "You burst into my office," he half shouted. "You don't even ask about the child who nearly lost her feet! You make unfounded accusations—"

Fitch took a step backward and looked at Nora, then turned his attention to her feet.

"Ah, ah..." He reminded her of Rollie, trying to talk his way out of some mistake. "Ah. I'm sorry about your feet—but you shouldn't have held the door for those sheep."

"Hold the door!" Sheehan spoke with authority. "The child was jammed against the door and couldn't move. She was at the bank, as she is at that same time every day, delivering the paper." The lawyer paused for a moment. "I understand you were pinned against the back door yourself, for a time, and you are three times her size!"

Nora tried to follow the conversation and to watch the doctor as he covered her feet with a soothing white salve. Now he was wrapping them in yards of thick gauze.

Sheehan continued to speak in his lawyer's voice. Fitch no longer shouted.

"You served the papers the day before yesterday foreclosing on the sheep. You owned them from then on. They belong to you." He held up a hand as Fitch started to protest. "Any damage they did—like nearly crippling a child, or destroying gardens in town, or upsetting your bank—is your responsibility. I'd advise you to get them out of town as soon as possible."

"I can't gather up all those sheep," Fitch declared. "I don't..."

Sheehan interrupted him. "Then you'd best hire someone to do it for you."

"But, but..."

"There are two fine sheepmen standing right here," Uncle Jack spoke, a gleeful smile on his face. "Perhaps you could strike a bargain with them."

Regan and Larkin looked surprised, but they nodded seriously.

Fitch hesitated. He seemed about to argue, but then threw up his hands in surrender. "I'll give you each a dollar," he offered, "just get the damn things down to the stockpens and see that they are fed and watered."

Larkin hesitated. "A dollar—?" he asked uncertainly.

"Yes. A dollar." Fitch clarified his offer. "Why, sheepherders are getting a dollar a day. This job won't take you more than a couple of hours."

"It's blistering hot out there," Larkin scratched at his head in indecision, " and we'd be pitching hay for more than an hour to feed that many. What is it? Eight hundred head?"

"It's over a thousand head," Uncle Jack put in. "There are more than two hundred small lambs."

"Hell. I'll make it two dollars." Fitch was disgusted.

Larkin scratched his head again, hesitating. "What do you think?" he asked Regan.

"Not me!" Regan was emphatic. "It's too hot for that sort of work!"

"Well. How the hell much do you want?" an angry Fitch demanded.

Larkin walked to the window. He scratched at his head again, thoughtfully. "I'd say—oh—five dollars apiece seems about right. What do you think, Regan? Would that suit you?" He looked doubtful.

Regan nodded. "But we must get the dogs to help us."

"Of course you'll need the damn dogs," Fitch was shaking with anger. "Now get out there and –"

"It will be a dollar apiece for the dogs," Larkin declared. "We each have two. That will be seven dollars apiece." He looked to Regan for confirmation, and Regan solemnly nodded his assent. Larkin turned back to stare out the sunny window while Fitch shouted and swore.

"By God, I'll hire someone else," the banker threatened. "Don't you know there's a goddamned depression on?"

"I heard that," said Regan. "About the depression, I mean. Do you think it's true?"

Nora saw Fitch's face turning very red. His mouth twitched in a strange manner. "I'll hire someone else!" he roared at the men.

"Well—do that, then," Regan counseled him, his voice serious. "I'm sure any Irishman in town will hurry to help you since most of them don't have sheep anymore." He paused thoughtfully. "Or maybe your friend, Orrin Windell will give you a hand. He's in town today."

"Look," said Larkin from his position near the window. "Some of those sheep have started back up the canyon."

"Alright! Alright, goddammit," Fitch roared. "I'll pay you. I'll pay you for the damn dogs, too—only get those goddamn sheep out of town!"

"In advance," Larkin demanded. "Pay us in advance."

Fitch tore at his pockets, sputtering with rage.

"I'll pay you, you stupid damn sons-of-bitchin' foreigners!" Fitch muttered and counted the money, dropping some on the floor and stooping to retrieve it. "I pay my bills. You damn well insult me making me pay in advance."

"Well. We're stupid, goddamned foreigners, and we only know enough to get paid in advance," said Larkin.

The two sheepmen counted the money very seriously, then pocketed it.

"You shouldn't swear in front of the child," Nora heard Uncle Jack speaking to Fitch, his voice very serious. "Christ Almighty. I'd think you'd damn well know better!"

In a rage, Fitch stormed out of the office, his face purple. Larkin and Regan followed him, smiling, and Nora heard her two friends whistle for their dogs.

"I'll have another patient if he doesn't calm himself," Dr Willard spoke, shaking his head. "But, we're finished here. And Nora, you've been a good patient."

Nora looked at her bandaged feet. "Wow!" she said. "I look like I'm wearing white galoshes." She wiped her face again with the piece of gauze. She couldn't quite remember why she was crying.

"We'll just give her another spoonful of this medicine," said Dr. Willard. "Those feet will be painful. And her mother must give it to her for a day or so."

Nora took the medicine obediently.

"I need to wash up," said Dr. Willard.

"Come along with me," said McAuliffe. "I've hot water and clean towels and plenty of soap—"

"And no sheep dip." Uncle Jack laughed as he gathered up the bucket, the bits of gauze and the bloodied towels and followed his two friends next door.

Hugh O'Brien passed him in the door coming in.

"And how is the patient?" O'Brien asked. His eyes filled with sympathy when he saw Nora's bandaged feet.

"She'll be fine," Sheehan assured him.

"You don't look too healthy yourself," Nora told the sheepman. Then she turned to Sheehan. "Uncle Jack's friends are all so tired," she told him. "Grandma said they worked the whole night through."

"That's right. That's right." Sheehan and O'Brien shared a smile.

"It was a desperate job," said O'Brien. "Making the sheep move in the dark is almost impossible in itself, and then separating out the lambs..." he threw up his arms in a gesture of futility.

"Ah yes," said Sheehan, "but Jack has a fine young herd now, and debt free!"

"But Fitch still gets more than he deserves," said Nora. "He has many more sheep than he loaned money on. I wish my feet weren't all bandaged up and I'd go right down to the stockyards and help you cut out a whole lot more. I'd leave him with only eight hundred head,"

"No. No. The lambs would be too small," O'Brien began.

"Take the baby lambs and their mothers," said Nora. "Uncle Jack's herd would be worth even more if he had some more ewes. Of course, you can't take them all, but you can cut out lots of mamma sheep and their babies and leave Fitch eight hundred head of whatever is left." She shook her head, trying to concentrate. "A lamb is a sheep," she hesitated.

She stopped. She shook her head. She couldn't remember what she was saying.

O'Brien stopped his pacing and looked at her, new respect growing in his eyes.

"Oh, yes. It's daylight now," said Nora. "It would be much easier to sort them out than in the dark."

Both men were quiet for a long minute.

"You could drive the ones you choose down to the ranch," Nora said. "It's only—it's not very far—and when they get the rest of the lambs down through the canyon, Uncle Jack can take the whole bunch off to the summer range."

"Well now," said O'Brien thoughtfully. He put his hat on and paced across the floor. He took his hat off and returned to stand by the door. "I think I'll just take my dogs and go down and give the lads a hand there at the stockyards." He chewed on his lip for a moment and then added. "Say nothing about this now to Jack. He's needed here, I think." He nodded toward Nora. "Just tell him I went to help the boys."

O'Brien was gone when Uncle Jack and Dr. Willard returned. Nora felt very tired. She watched as Sheehan took out his keys again in preparation of locking the door.

Uncle Jack picked her up and carried her across the street. He placed her on the high front seat of Dr. Willard's touring car and climbed into the back. The doctor eased himself behind the wheel and started the engine. "We'll just swing by and see what the score is," he said. Sheehan hurried across the street to join them.

When they arrived at the ball field Nora was surprised to see that the seventh inning stretch was in progress. Phil, seeing her in the doctor's car ran over to see why. He looked with alarm at her bandaged feet.

"They got all cut up," Nora told him. "I got stitches, and iodine and salve and everything. They don't hurt much anymore." She tried to read the scoreboard across the field while Uncle Jack told Phil about the excitement at the bank. She couldn't see the numbers. Even the board seemed blurred and wavering.

"How's Nickie doing?" she asked. "I can't see the score."

"Nick is doing—pretty well," Phil told them. "The score is four to three in our favor. And they shouldn't have got two of those runs, either. One of the players from Burns hit an easy fly, right out to left field—and dumb Rollie—he just stood right there and didn't even raise his glove or go ten steps to get it. Just watched the ball land right in the dirt. They scored two runs! Coach ran out there and asked him what was wrong and Rollie said. 'I'm not playin left field any more. I'm going to pitch!' Coach says, 'No. You aren't going to pitch. You're a valuable player. A good player. But Nick is the pitcher.' So Rollie took his glove and walked off the field."

"Really?" Nora could scarcely believe this story.

"He thought the coach would keep him on the team and let him pitch because he's such a good hitter. And then he hung around waiting for the coach to beg him to come back, I guess. But —"

Phil stopped. Rollie walked through the weeds in front of the car, a picture of dejection. He was pouting and morose and bent forward kicking occasionally at a stone in his pathway. They watched as he made his way to the weather-beaten dugout and then climbed to the top rail of the surrounding fence.

"That fellow better pick up his lip before he steps on it," Uncle Jack observed.

"Quimby sent Hank Metzger in as left field," Phil continued. "You know him. He drives the Standard Oil truck. He's been practicing with the team for several weeks. He did a real good job out there, too."

Nick stepped out of the dugout followed by Coach Quimby who talked earnestly in his ear.

When Nick saw Phil and Nora in the doctor's car, he hurried over to talk to them, still followed by a nervous Quimby.

"I'm not doing too well," said Nick. "I barely made it through that last inning."

"You ate too much at the hotel last night," Nora told him. "But you'll

210

have another wonderful meal tonight, and you don't have to pitch tomorrow, so you can eat all you want!" She wriggled in pleasure wishing she were going to the hotel.

"I can't believe Rollie would do something like that," Coach Quimby's voice was sharp with frustration. He started calling Nick some damn name—what was it? Ah, 'Irish Spud.' Quimby shook his head in disbelief. And then those players from Burns picked up on it, *they* started calling him that!"

Nick stood, looking dejected. "I'm sorry," he said. "I've lost my concentration—or something."

"That's just what Rollie *wants* you to do," Sheehan spoke suddenly. "You lose your concentration—you lose your ability—you lose your effectiveness. Are you going to let him do that to you? He's a sorry excuse…"

"He's a lard bucket!" said Nora, anger in her voice.

The men looked at her. They smiled and shook their heads. Nora felt ashamed. She should never have said that. Such poor sportsmanship. Men didn't act that way. They played, and even when they were fairly beaten they shook hands and smiled and said 'nice game,' and were friendly.

At least, *most* men. But, how about those Burns fellows that called Nick an 'Irish spud?' Yes. Rollie and the Burns team. They were surely poor sports.

"We've got to get back over there," said the coach. "The umpire is on the field. "And, Nick, these next two innings are—crucial." He looked at the men in the car. He shook his head and shrugged. He seemed consumed by anxiety. "The top of the batting order will be up soon. I wish the kid would lighten up."

Sheehan spoke to Nick. "He can't make you feel uncomfortable unless you let him," he said, his voice stern.

Nora patted Nickie's arm. "You deserve a great meal at the hotel," she said. "No beans and sourdough for *you* tonight. Throw those bums out!"

Nick looked at each of his friends thoughtfully and then he smiled. He walked back to the pitcher's mound and started his warm up.

"I think he feels better," Phil observed. He hurried back to the ball field.

"Batter up!" called the umpire.

The inning staggered along. The first batter hit an easy fly. The second hit a line drive that got him on first. The third batter struck out.

The town team didn't do any better when it was their turn to bat. They got two men on base but neither made it home. They missed Rollie's hitting.

Nora could see Coach Quimby talking earnestly to Nick. He restrained him a bit when he started to walk out on the field and gave him some further instructions. Nick looked tired and a little apprehensive. The men in the car sat forward, worry plain on their faces.

"Come on, Nick. You can do it," Phil was calling. "Come on. Come on." Then he seemed to be whispering to himself. Nora thought Phil was probably praying.

Nick rubbed at the ball. He watched intently to discern the signal from the catcher. He nodded. The crowd was very quiet. Nora inched forward on the seat, hanging out the window, willing Nick to succeed. She was having trouble seeing. She thought how sad it was that Nick would probably miss his fine meal at the hotel tonight.

Nick started his wind-up, and as he reared back to release his throw, Nora was surprised to hear her own voice ringing quite clearly across the field.

"Fried chicken," she shouted.

Nick jerked even further back. The ball left his hand. Nora couldn't even see it passing, but the catcher was standing, taking the ball from his mitt, smiling.

"Strike one," the umpire called.

The catcher threw the ball back to the pitcher's mound, and Nick was laughing when he caught it. The crowd looked at each other, seeking understanding.

Nick wound up again, and at the critical moment Nora shouted, "Mashed potatoes!" And again the ball smashed into the catcher's mitt.

"Strike two!" The umpire's voice soared.

The batter stepped out of the box, frowning. He looked at his teammates who looked back helplessly. They were as clueless as he.

Nick wound up again, but just before he released the ball, Nora called, "Brown gravy!" A few young voices in the crowd yelled 'Brown gravy' also, as the umpire called "Strike three!"

Quimby was laughing and slapping people on the back. He gave the 'thumbs up' sign to Nickie. He gave the 'thumbs up' sign to Nora.

The second batter came to the plate. He stumbled a little. He dropped the bat. He took his stance uncertainly

Nick wound up and, as his arm was about to start forward, Nora called, "Apple pie!"

"Apple pie!" the crowd yelled as the ball scorched past the batter. The people looked at each other, then shrugged. They weren't sure of this new twist but—hey! It seemed to be working.

"Strike one."

"Ice cream!" Nora called just before the next pitch.

"Ice cream!" the crowd chanted. They laughed and wondered and shook their heads.

"Strike two."

The fans were delighted. They cheered mightily, then quieted rather quickly so they could hear the next command from the childish voice.

Nick looked toward Nora. He was smiling. He seemed animated and suddenly vigorous. He rubbed at the ball and confidently stated his wind up.

"Lemonade," Nora called at the appropriate time.

"Lemonade!" the townsfolk roared.

"Strike three," the umpire was laughing himself now and gestured dramatically so the crowd would understand.

"One more batter," Nora thought. She felt very tired, but excited, too. She could see that Nickie was enjoying himself, and if her reminding him of food made him relax and pitch as he was capable of doing, she would keep reminding him. She thought he actually seemed to be waiting for her voice as he let the ball go for each wicked pitch. But now she was having trouble thinking of good things to eat. She had never dined at the hotel and she could only guess at what they might serve. She had to scramble to even think of 'lemonade' in time for that last pitch.

Port Porter was now at bat. He was the clean-up batter for the Burns team and his reputation as a hitter was well known. He stood nearly six-foot-four and was sturdily built. He was not intimidated. He whacked the plate with the bat and frowned at Nick, swinging the bat in a menacing gesture before he took his batting stance.

Nick was serious now. No smiling. The crowd was very quiet. Nora's mind spun in frantic frustration trying to think of some grand food as Nick started his wind up.

"Cinnamon rolls…" She squeaked the words out.

"Cinnamon rolls!" the crowd chanted.

"Strike one," the umpire said.

Nora felt desperate. What else would Nick be served? What other grand thing would be on hand at the hotel? Nick was starting his wind-up.

"Ah—chocolate cake!" she called out, almost too late.

"Chocolate cake!" the fans echoed.

"Strike two, foul ball," the umpire declared

"You got a piece of it," the Burns players called. "You've got his number. Now hit the next one over the fence."

Nora felt quite sick. She couldn't think of anything appropriate. She couldn't say boiled carrots or oatmeal. The catcher was throwing the ball back. The infield was talking it up, encouraging Nickie.

She saw Rollie leaning forward on the top rail. She knew he was hoping Nickie would stumble. He called down to the Burns players. "Irish spud! Irish spud!" Now the Burns players started to chant the hated words "Irish spud! Irish spud!" Nora felt herself stiffen in anger. Porter was completely confident. Nick was well into his wind-up

"Lard bucket!" she called looking at Rollie.

"Lard bucket!" the crowd roared.

Porter winced. He swung, much too late. Nora was filled with instant remorse. She didn't mean the batter. She meant Rollie!

"St-e-e-rike three!" the umpire's call was lost in the winning shrieks of happiness as the crowd spilled out on to the field to pound Nick on the back, shake his hand, tell him what a great pitcher he was, wish him further success.

Nick broke away from the crowd. He came running to the car. He reached to hug her close. He was swallowing, hard.

"I was afraid," Nora admitted. "I was afraid I would upset you—you know. Break your concentration or something."

"You did just right," Nick assured her. "You made me relax. Made me laugh. Made me—I don't know—made me see that Rollie is a—a—lard bucket."

"That stinking Rollie," Nora sputtered. "You don't see *him* celebrating!"

"Well. We'd best be on our way," Dr. Willard put the car in gear. He was smiling. Sheehan was smiling. Uncle Jack looked happy indeed. Nora settled back on the comfortable upholstery, waved goodbye to Nick.

"Who is this Rollie fellow anyway?" Uncle Jack asked.

"Oh, that's right," Nora observed. "You don't know too many people in town, do you?" She pointed. "That's Rollie sitting and pouting on the top rail."

"That's one job he'll never fail," said Uncle Jack.

They laughed.

Chapter 10

❦ HALFWAY THERE - 1935

Nora walked sedately along the sidewalk. She wanted to run but remembered her mother's admonition that it wasn't 'ladylike' to run about town. A lady should walk with quiet dignity. She wasn't sure she was ready to be a 'lady.' It was much more fun to be a kid.

She felt the noonday sun, hot, on her shoulders as though it were trying to burn through her cotton shirt. It was hard to believe that it was early April. Somehow it felt like August. The grownups were gloomily predicting another 'dust bowl' year and she felt inclined to agree. She looked about at the dusty, hot, deserted streets and sighed.

Ed Withrow sat under the awning at his service station. She used to deliver the newspaper to him daily until she gave up the paper route to Kevin. Ed looked as defeated as the other merchants in town who sat waiting for customers in their quiet stores. Even the barber pole in front of Stamford's barber shop stood motionless. Nora had never seen it when it wasn't twisting as though a giant peppermint stick that had no beginning and no end were thrusting up toward heaven.

"Hello there, Nora," Withrow greeted her.

"Hi." Nora stepped from the dusty walk to stand in the shade of the awning. "You have one of those N.R.A. signs in your window, too," she observed. "Every store in town has one."

"Yeah," Withrow shrugged. "All the merchants are supposed to put them up where people can see them. N.R.A. It means, National Recovery Act. It's supposed to make the depression go away, I guess. So far it don't seem to be working too well."

"N.R.A." Nora repeated the letters thoughtfully. "I wondered what they meant."

"There's an article there in the paper," Withrow told her. "It says this here is an 'alphabet government' that we got now. There's this NRA, the CCC's, the AAA, the FBI, the BLM, the TVA, and two dozen other big programs. I don't even know what most of them mean. I wonder if the big shots down there in Washington know."

"They even call the president by his initials," said Nora. "They call him F.D.R."

"Yep," her friend agreed. "Some of them agencies apply to our part of the country and some apply down south or back east, but F.D.R.—he gets recognized all across the world."

A car came speeding down the road. It was the first car Nora had seen since she arrived in town. Two young women sat in the front seat with the driver. He honked the horn and shouted and the girls giggled and waved. A cloud of dust followed the Ford roadster as it curved out of sight.

"Stupid damn bugger," said Withrow.

"Who was that? Nora asked. "Was that that Tanner fellow?"

"Yeah." Ed sat straighter in his chair and spit into the dirt of the driveway. "Young George Tanner, 'Kid' Tanner they call him—that arrogant little brat. He come in here, had me fill him up with gas a while ago, then drove off without payin'." Withrow's voice shook with indignation. "I know I can write it up on his brother's charge and Glenn Tanner will pay for it, but George's attitude—well—it just makes me do a slow boil. He ain't no kid no more, neither. He must be 27, maybe 28."

"Really? That's pretty old. I thought he was younger than that."

"No. He was in my wife's class there in school. He was a jackass, even back then." Ed spit in the dirt a second time.

"He is handsome, though," said Nora. "All the girls think so."

"He's a damned, spoiled, show off," Withrow growled. "His mom thought he could do no wrong. His grandma lived with them and she always took his part. But when them two ladies died—well, the whole world seemed to think they had to make it up to him. Those other Tanner men are good people, but they helped spoil him, too."

"Where does he live?" asked Nora

"Hell. He's supposed to be running that place on the West Side that his daddy owned. But, his brother Glenn pays Hank Harvey to run it. Kid is too busy chasing the girls."

"I know his brother Glenn," said Nora. "He's a nice man. He rents our house here in town."

"Yeah. I heard that. He got some new job with a big company in

Portland and is doing very well. I heard him and his wife were living in your new house."

"Well, my Dad says the price of wool and of lambs has gone down the well, so we are staying at the ranch again and renting out the house in town."

"Yeah." Withrow shifted in his chair. "That Glenn Tanner is a fine fellow. I wish he'd give that brother of his a good kick though, right where it would do the most good. That boy is headed for trouble and he's always making trouble for others, too."

Nora felt uncomfortable. She rather liked this adult conversation, but she worried that it was somewhat like gossiping. Mother said that 'ladies' shouldn't gossip, so she reluctantly changed the subject.

"How is Janie?" she asked.

"She's feelin' lots better," said Withrow. "Has to stay inside for a few more days but she's getting sassy and crabby so I know she's almost over them damn measles. The doc says she can't go out into the sun though and she hates having to stay inside. You can go in and visit her if you want. She'd like that…or maybe you ain't had the measles yet?"

"Oh, I've had them, and the chicken pox, too. But I've got to get on my way. Mother dropped me off at the school to pick up the report cards and she's waiting for me – up home – or I mean – up at Tanner's."

"Report cards," said Withrow. "I suppose I'll have to go down and get Janie's. Ain't it crazy? School's out for the summer and it's only the first of April. You kids are going to have a long vacation this year. Doc Hodges said he hated to close the schools, but with both chicken pox and measles making the rounds, he just didn't have no choice."

"Mr. Tanner's little boy, Billy—he got both the measles and the chicken pox. He's been sick for over a month," said Nora.

That's what I heard," Withrow agreed. "And in this heat the poor kids are so—itchy, so uncomfortable."

"Well, my mother is waiting for these report cards. She'd have a fit if any of us failed a grade."

"I remember when you and Janie started first grade," said Withrow. "You two little tykes weren't as big as a stunted sage brush. Janie was a cryin' and hangin' on my leg and wanted to go home, and you was demanding a book so you could read." He sighed. "And now you'll both be startin' high school. It just don't seem possible."

"I remember that day, too," said Nora, preparing to leave. "I believed that when I got to school that I would automatically be able to read. I was stunned when I found out that I had to learn all those letters in the alphabet, and then had to figure out how to put all those letters together to make a word."

Smiling, she said goodbye and walked out into the scorching sunlight.

Mother and Mrs. Tanner sat at the kitchen table, a pitcher of ice water between them. Grace Tanner looked pale and exhausted. Her eyes were red.

"I miss my baby," she told Mother. "I hated to send her home with my sister, but—Billy was so sick and I didn't want her to get sick, too." She wiped her eyes while Mother patted her arm and spoke in a soothing voice.

"Of course you miss her," Mother said, "but your son needed you, and you've done a wonderful job. He was so desperately sick, and you pulled him through. Your little girl will be home soon."

"I know. I know," Mrs. Tanner sighed. "It's just that I'm so tired. And Glenn—my husband, you know—he's insisting on buying this new place out there on Fort Rd. He says it's a beautiful home. We'll keep renting this house, you understand, so Billy can go to school, but he says this Bailey ranch is very special."

"The Bailey ranch is for sale?" Shock was evident in Mother's voice.

"Do you know the place?"

"Yes. Yes. It is a beautiful place." Mother struggled to control her dismay. "The house is only a few years old and very modern. And the land was – was quite profitable – until this drought hit."

Nora watched her mother in dismay. Mrs. Bailey was a good friend of Mother's. True, since the depression had taken hold of the country and people couldn't travel to visit as often as they had previously, her Mother and Mrs. Bailey hadn't seen too much of each other in the past year or so. But Nora knew that the loss of the Bailey ranch was a shocking piece of news.

"Nora, dear," her mother was saying. "Take a glass of ice water in to little Billy. Visit with him for awhile. The doctor should be here soon and that little fellow gets very lonely in there in that darkened room."

Obediently, Nora took the cool glass and retreated down the hall to the sick room. It seemed unreal to her to see strange furniture and different curtains in the rooms that had been so familiar. And the house was so quiet. It had always been noisy and busy when her family lived there.

The small room her father had used for an office had been converted into a bedroom. The green window shade was pulled down and the room was very dim. She paused at the door. Little Billy moved restlessly on the bed. He whined in frustration as she entered.

"Here is some nice, cool water," she offered. "It's such a hot day."

"Get out of here!" Billy's voice sounded petulant. "I don't know you. Get out of here."

Nora retreated into the hallway. "I'm Nora," she said. "I'm Kevin's big sister. You know Kevin. He's in your class in school."

"I don't care," said Billy.

Nora paused. She felt sorry for Billy. She knew how hard it was to lie in bed. The little boy looked so thin and – forlorn. She thought of the misery she suffered when she had the measles a few weeks ago. Evidently the measles weakened your eyes and one could lose their sight if you got into bright sunlight too soon after being sick. She had paced around her room. She had slept and wished she could sleep more. She was so bored that she even welcomed Katie coming in to tell her that her room was a mess. She could hardly wait until Uncle Jack came in from the fields and came to visit with her. She knew how frustrated little Billy felt.

Uncle Jack! She had a sudden idea. She marched back into the sick room.

Little Billy lived in our town and he was wondrous wise.
He stayed safe in a dim lit room to save his precious eyes."

"What?" Billy sat straight up from the pillows.

He missed his books, his friends—playing ball, but then—
His eyes were well and he was back—playing ball again."

"How'd you do that?" said Billy. "Can you do it again?"

Nora sat down near the bed. She told him about Uncle Jack and how they made rhymes all the time. She told him about when she was sick and how she loved it when Uncle Jack came to visit. She told him he had to eat and get strong and well again.

"Look at that stuff," said Billy. "Could you eat that?"

Nora looked at the bowl of cold oatmeal that stood untouched on the nightstand. She was glad when she heard the doctor's voice in the hall.

Mother and Mrs. Tanner ushered the doctor in. Nora squeezed out. She had never realized how small that room was.

"It's stuffy in here," she heard the doctor say.

Nora retreated down the hall. She could hear the voices of the adults but didn't bother to listen. She hoped Billy would be alright. He looked terrible —so thin, so distraught. And Mrs. Tanner didn't seem to be much help. She was weepy and unhappy and lonesome for her baby. Nora shuddered. Too bad that 'Kid' Tanner couldn't be more like Uncle Jack. He could help Billy and make him laugh and forget to be bored if he tried. Instead, he drove around town and charged all sorts of things to his brother. Nora shook her head.

Suddenly her mother was calling her. She hurried down the hall aware of all sorts of activity.

"Help us here, Nora," Mother said. "We are moving Billy out into the living room. We can pull the shades down there as well as in here and the room is three times the size of this one."

Billy was bundled into a chair. The davenport was moved into the dining room. The bed was dismantled.

"Could I hire Nora to help me with Billy?" Mrs. Tanner asked. "My husband will drive her home this evening, and Billy seems so happy to have her here."

Mother fit a bedrail into place.

"I'll be glad to pay her," Mrs. Tanner added.

"Nora will be glad to stay and help you out."

As the adults reassembled the sick room Nora took the bowl of oatmeal into the kitchen. She stirred up the fire and poured the cereal into a small pan. She added milk, a little sugar and cinnamon and searched through the cupboard until she found some raisins, which she added to the mixture. All the while she made rhymes in her head with which she could amuse Billy.

The doctor left. Billy was moved to the fresh cool bed. Although the green shades were pulled across all the windows, the large room didn't seem the least depressing.

When the adults returned to the kitchen, Nora took the bowl of cereal and hurried to Billy's new room. She sang out:

Billy had a little dog; his fur was soft and brown.
He made Billy laugh a lot, he was such a little clown.

"Make up some more," Billy demanded.

"Only if you eat your cereal." The boy took up his spoon.

No one else could see that dog. But Billy didn't care

He liked that pup, he loved that pup, Bill knew the dog was there.

Nora hesitated. Billy waited, smiling, his bowl half empty. What would Uncle Jack say? She had to think of an ending.

*"That's a stupid kind of dog to have," his Uncle Kid once said.
"He's smart," said Bill, "He doesn't bark, or bite, or even shed,
And when he sleeps with me at night, he doesn't wet the bed."*

Billy laughed and slapped at the clean sheet with his spoon.

"How do you do that?" he asked. "Do it some more."

"Finish your lunch. I have to have time to think, you know." Nora shook her head, laughing. "It takes time to make that stuff up."

When Mrs. Tanner came into the room an hour later, Billy was sleeping and the bowl beside his bed was empty. Nora roused from the easy chair.

"That's the first decent meal that child has eaten in a month," said Mrs. Tanner. "Nora, you are a marvel. I wish I – whoops. Here comes Velma Douglas. She's been 'stepping out' with Kid. My brother-in-law, you know. She stops in hoping to find him here."

Velma strolled in, chewing her gum. She always chewed gum and always wore lots of rouge on her cheeks. Nora thought her quite pretty. The two women went back to the kitchen where Mother was studying the report cards.

Nora wondered if her mother would ever allow her to wear rouge. Probably not. Katie was a senior in high school and her mother wouldn't let her wear rouge.

"He makes me so mad," Velma's voice came from the kitchen. "He takes me out, tells me how much he loves me, and then, the next thing I know he's driving around with Grace Pierson, or Maxine Downs, or someone else. Probably telling them the same thing."

"He can't be serious about anything," Mrs. Tanner murmured. "You mustn't take him seriously."

"I try not to, but he's so persuasive," said Velma. "He seems so sincere. When you are with him, well, you just have to believe him." Her laugh dissolved into a giggle. "And he has about five hands."

"Five hands?" thought Nora. "How could a guy have five hands?" She sat straight in the chair and listened more intently.

"Good Lord," Mrs. Tanner was saying. "You don't mean –"

"Yeah," said Velma. "I had to sew a couple of buttons back on my blouse the other day—*again*." She dissolved into more giggles.

Nora tiptoed down the hall. She looked into the kitchen. Velma's wad of gum was now stuck to the edge of her saucer as her hostess poured her a cup of coffee.

"Good Lord," said Mrs. Tanner, her tone outraged. "My word, child. You should be very careful."

"Oh, I'm careful," said Velma. "And it is kinda fun."

"Fun!" Mother's voice showed her outrage. "That man is a – a – an animal! A predator! Someone should take him out and shoot him." She paused, and her tone changed. "Well—not really. But Velma, dear. You should have more, more respect for yourself. Why bring yourself down to his level?"

"He's so good looking," said Velma. "All the girls think so. And he asked me for my phone number."

"Yes. And he has the phone number of every chippie in town," Mother snorted.

Mrs. Tanner changed the subject, and soon Velma prepared to leave. Nora hastened back to the sick room.

Velma waved to Nora as she strolled toward the front door, still chewing her gum. Nora wished she could talk to Velma. Perhaps that girl could explain how a fellow could have five hands and why she had to sew buttons on her blouse—again—whenever she went out with Kid. It was certainly a mystery.

Nora came each day to work for the Tanners. Billy continued to improve and Dr. Hodges allowed him to go out into the yard in late afternoon as long as he stayed in the shade. Kid Tanner came by a time or two, but she was always entertaining Billy and never spoke to him. She did look carefully though, from a distance, and he appeared to have only two hands and two arms as far as she could see.

"You like him, don't you?" said Billy. "Everyone likes him but me."

"I don't even know him," Nora shrugged. "Why don't you like him?"

"He pinches me," said Billy. "I'd like to have Max bite his nose off."

"He pinches you?"

"Yeah," said Billy. "He sneaks in a pinch every chance he gets. Usually when Dad is around. If I cry and run away Dad is—well, he's embarrassed—and Uncle Kid just shakes his head." Billy looked to Nora hopefully, seeking understanding. "I told my Dad he pinches me—but Dad doesn't believe old Kid would do such a thing. He makes me so mad."

"Don't get mad, get even!" said Nora.

"What?"

"Oh, that's just an Irish saying," Nora shrugged. "They say you shouldn't waste your energy being mad. Use that energy thinking up ways to get even. But—Mother says 'getting even' is a sin."

Billy remained silent and thoughtful for a long minute.

"It sounds like a good idea to me," he said.

Billy had decided to name his imaginary dog Max, and he and Nora included the animal in their play and conversation. The boy appeared happy and lively and was putting on weight. Mrs. Tanner also moved happily through the day. Her baby daughter, Sarah, had been returned to her, and her life seemed quite complete. Everyone agreed that it had been a good decision to close the schools early. Very few quarantine signs remained on the doorways of the homes.

Nora felt very fortunate. She was paid two and a half dollars a week for working for the Tanners and she got to come into town every day. Katie was green with envy.

In June, Glenn Tanner decided it was time to move the family to the Bailey Ranch he had bought recently. Mrs. Tanner was reluctant to leave town.

"We'll try it for a few days," said Glenn. "I'm sure you'll love it. Just pack up enough to last a week or so, and we can take it from there. Now that Billy can run and play in the sun it will be wonderful for him."

The Bailey Ranch was a lovely place. Nora loved it from the minute they moved in. She rushed about making up the beds, hanging the new curtains, setting the bread. Mrs. Tanner worked beside her and said that Nora knew much more about cooking than she did.

"We always had a cook when I was growing up in Portland," she admitted. "I'm trying to learn at this late stage of the game. You make me feel guilty. I depend upon you so much."

"Come sit here beside me," she said one day. "We're going to curl that hair of yours."

Nora was delighted. She sat patiently as Mrs. Tanner "put her hair up in rags," as she called the process. When the hair dried and the rags were removed, Nora could scarcely believe the change. She looked 'grown up,' and very pretty, she thought.

Kid Tanner drove his roadster out from town that night and stayed for supper. When he saw Nora he whistled in surprise and invited her to come and sit beside him. She demurred, blushing, and took her usual place at the table.

She felt flattered when Kid picked up his plate and moved around the table to sit beside her.

Mrs. Tanner frowned.

They were just starting to eat dessert when Nora felt Kid's leg pressing firmly against her thigh. Then his hand ran down her leg and squeezed her knee.

Startled, Nora dropped her spoon and sprang to her feet, bewilderment mirrored in her face.

Mr. and Mrs. Tanner looked up in confusion. Even Kid expressed surprise. He held his coffee cup in both hands and seemed innocent indeed.

"I'll bet he pinched her," said Billy.

Mortified, Nora stumbled out the door onto the porch. Looking back she saw Kid smiling.

Late one afternoon, Nora discovered a band of sheep moving through the ravine below the ranch. She snatched up a loaf of bread and she and Billy ran down through the meadow. The Breen brothers were moving their sheep from the winter range to the mountains for the summer.

"Nora, you're a darling. We haven't had a decent bite of bread since we left the desert. Only a sheepherder's daughter would know how grand it is to have real bread," Dennis Breen told her. "It's only eight miles to town, but this loaf is like an early Christmas."

Nora wriggled with delight.

"Haven't Joe and myself been busy propping up that fence there? We don't want the sheep getting into Tanner's meadow. Sure, it's the first green we've seen in days and the sheep are desperate to get at it."

"I'll tell Mr. Tanner that a section of the wire is down," said Nora. "He should be out from town tonight for supper."

"Aye. And sure, won't your Uncle Jack be along tomorrow? He's only a day behind us on the trail."

"Really?" Nora's voice showed her delight. "I've told Billy about Uncle Jack. Now he'll get to meet him."

"He will," Breen agreed. "But I'd best go help Joe with the fence or the sheep will overwhelm him and get into the meadow in spite of us. Thanks again for the bread."

The children returned to the house and Nora set about preparing supper. She put the pork chops in the oven and peeled the potatoes, ready for boiling.

When Mr. Tanner arrived, Nora remembered to tell him about the broken section of fence and how the Breen brothers had propped it up to keep the sheep from the meadow. She poured boiling water over the potatoes and pulled them forward on the stove.

Tanner strode to the window and looked out over the short grass of his property.

"That grass isn't going to be tall enough to mow," he said. "I wish they *had* let the sheep in to graze. It would be a good way to get some fertilizer on the land." He sighed. "Maybe next spring won't be so dry."

"Oh, good," Nora thought. "Uncle Jack can turn his herd in there when he comes tomorrow."

The next afternoon when she saw the cloud of dust coming from the East she shouted to Billy.

"That will be Uncle Jack bringing his sheep. We'll go down and tell him to turn them into the meadow. Your Dad said he wanted them to graze inside the fence."

Uncle Jack looked grizzled and unshaven. He shouted with delight at the fresh loaf of bread. The sheep rushed with enthusiasm in to the green meadow. Billy grinned happily as he was introduced to the bummer lambs and allowed to feed them from the bottle.

"They are so cute," shouted Billy. "Look how their little tails wag."

"They are hungry all right," Uncle Jack agreed. "And I'm nearly out of grub myself. It's a good thing we get into town tomorrow. Well, we'd best stick it out another day or two. The sheep haven't had this kind of grass for months."

"Where do you get the milk to feed these lambs?" Billy asked. "Do you use canned milk?"

"I don't," Uncle Jack answered. "Sure, I have a fine little goat that travels with us. Named *Queen Bess*."

"Queen Bess?" Billy frowned in thought. "That's a funny name for a goat."

"A fine name," Uncle Jack assured him. "Isn't she named after the Good Queen Bess of England."

"Queen Elizabeth of England!" Billy sputtered in disbelief.

"The same. And sure, isn't this Bess doing a fine generous thing for helpless creatures – something the first Queen Bess avoided her whole selfish life."

"But—we learned in history class that Elizabeth was a really good queen." Billy sounded doubtful.

"Aye. But you can be sure that no Irishman wrote that history," Uncle Jack told him.

Billy returned quietly to feeding the lambs. The smallest one tugged at the nipple, its tail pumping. The others crowded about, awaiting their turn.

"They are so cute," said Billy. "Max likes them, too, especially this little one."

"Max?" Uncle Jack questioned.

"Max is his imaginary dog," Nora explained.

Billy hung his head.

"Didn't I have a made-up dog myself when I was young?" said Uncle Jack. "I called him 'Ghost.' He was a great friend when I had no one else to talk to or when I was alone and hungry as a boy there in Ireland. But now I have a fine, fierce dog that is real."

He whistled and watched as a large, ugly brown dog raised himself from his place by the meadow gate and ran to his master.

"This is *Cromwell*," he introduced Billy. "I think he has been talking to your Max. He often talks to my Ghost. Ghost likes him better than he does me now. But dogs need friends, too." He stood aside and watched as Cromwell went to Billy and licked his hand, then his face. Billy fell down on his knees and hugged the dog to his chest. He forgot the bottle with which he had been feeding the lamb, and the milk spilled down his shirt. Cromwell calmly licked the milk from Billy's shirt and hands.

"Come now," said Uncle Jack. "We'll just hang that shirt here on the fence to dry. In this sun it will only take a few minutes. He reached to pull the shirt up over Billy's head, then halted abruptly.

"What happened to you there?" he asked and bent to look at the black and blue marks beneath Billy's arms and along his ribs.

"That's where Uncle Kid pinches me."

Nora stepped forward. She, too, stooped to look at the bruises. A terrible understanding filled her. She had not believed the boy. His father and Mother had failed to believe him. Yet here was the evidence. She resolved to tell Mr. Tanner that very evening as soon as he arrived from town.

The sheep, quiet and content, were bedding down when the children returned to the house. Mr. Tanner had driven from town early. He talked excitedly. He was being sent to Reno. He would leave tomorrow and drive as far as Susanville, and from there he would take the train. It was a wonderful opportunity for him. The company was placing much trust in him. He had hoped for this day but didn't think they would give him this much responsibility for several years to come. His enthusiasm lasted throughout the meal.

"I'll be gone for a week or ten days," he said. "I'll write you as soon as I get there and let you know how things are going."

"Then we'd better get packed up and go back into town with you in the morning," his wife said.

"No. No. You stay here with the children. They are much better off here than in town."

"But we are nearly out of supplies," Mrs. Tanner spoke. "We only brought enough for a week. We used the last of the meat for supper."

"I'll send out a load of groceries before I leave tomorrow," said Tanner. "I'll have Kid bring them out. He's always looking for something to do."

"And I can stay and feed the bummer lambs," shouted Billy. "You should see them, Mother. They are the dearest little things."

So it was decided that the family would stay on at the ranch.

Kid Tanner did not drive out from town the next day. They had no meat and the ice was completely melted. The vegetables and canned goods were gone. They had packed only enough for a week, and it had been almost two weeks since they left town. Mr. Tanner had brought fresh milk for the baby, but that was now almost at an end.

When Kid arrived on the third day, he became immediately defensive. He didn't know he was supposed to bring groceries, he said. No one told him. He seemed insulted when they ate only rice for supper.

"We'll ride into town with you this evening," Mrs. Tanner told him. "We are nearly out of milk for the baby—and there is nothing much else left around here, either."

"I used the last yeast cake yesterday," Nora told them. "We have less than a half loaf of bread."

"I promised to pick up a couple of fellows down at Bowers Meadows," said Kid. "They are going in to town to work at the mill. But I'll be out the first thing in the morning. I promise. I can bring supplies out, or you can ride in and stay."

"We'll go in and stay," Mrs. Tanner stated firmly. She picked up little Sarah and stepped out to put her in the baby buggy.

"I'm going to take this child for a walk," she said. "It's getting cooler and she has been fussy all afternoon. A little fresh air will make her sleep better tonight." Her voice betrayed her anger and annoyance.

Kid settled comfortably into the easy chair. Nora hurried to clear the table. She glanced at Kid who gave her a friendly smile and winked.

"You work too hard," he observed. "You are such a pretty little thing – you shouldn't have to work at all." He winked again, his long lashes lingering as he dropped them to his cheek. "Come here and sit beside me. Rest awhile. Better still, come sit on my knee."

"I'm no baby," said Nora. "Why should you bounce me on your knee?"

"Why are you afraid of me?" Kid asked, his voice soft. "I won't hurt you."

"You can be sure you won't," said Nora, almost surprised at the words that came out of her mouth. "I wouldn't let you close enough to me to hurt me."

"Someone has been telling you lies about me," said Kid. "I can't believe you would listen to such – such untruths. Why, I think you are something—well, something really special." He rose from the chair and walked toward her. "You don't know it yet, but you are becoming a beautiful young woman. We could have such fun. I could teach you soooo much." His voice sounded soft and persuasive. His eyes, innocent and sincere, looked deep into hers. He reached to touch her shoulder.

Nora threw the dishes she held into the sink and slipped sideways to avoid his hand.

"Get away from me," she said, trying to hold her voice steady.

But Kid apparently didn't hear her. Suddenly his hands were around her waist and he pulled her toward himself.

She butted his face with her head and pushed away, surprising him with her strength.

"You—you—*predator*!" She thought that was what her mother had called him. "Do you think I have no – no – self respect? Do you think I would bring myself down to your level? Every chippee in town has your number!"

"What the hell?" Red flared in Kid's face. He drew back his hand and slapped her.

Billy came running from the bedroom. He swung wildly with a baseball bat and hit his uncle a wicked blow on the upper arm.

"Let her alone," he screamed, and drew back the bat for another swing.

Kid reached and took the bat. He was looking at Nora and seemed alarmed and shocked at what he had done. "I'm s-s-sorry," he apologized. "I didn't mean—"

"Get out of here!" Nora spat. She felt blood on her inner cheek where the flesh had hit her teeth.

Nora reached for the pile of folded diapers. She took one with which to wipe her mouth. She was indeed bleeding.

"Please…" Kid began again, but he was interrupted by Mrs. Tanner's voice, calling from the yard.

"Nora, come help me lift this carriage up onto the porch."

Nora bolted out the door, her thoughts in turmoil.

Her heart raced. Her hands shook. A terrible, cold fright seemed to invade her body. She couldn't control the trembling that suddenly possessed her. She felt anger and resentment. But the awful terror that engulfed her was something she had never encountered before.

The buggy was wheeled into the kitchen. Mrs. Tanner shook her head, worry etched on her face.

"That baby is sick," she said as she lifted the child from its place.

The baby appeared listless. Her eyes remained closed. Her head fell forward, then rolled to one side.

"She is so pale," said Mrs. Tanner, "yet she's burning with fever."

The baby raised her head, let out a strangled sort of cry, and vomited almost into her mother's face.

There followed a shocked silence as the smell of bile and sour milk engulfed the room. Mrs. Tanner's neck and the front of her dress was covered. The baby vomited again, this time on the floor.

Feeling somewhat unsteady, Nora stepped forward. "Give Sarah to me," she said to Mrs. Tanner. "You go change your clothes and get cleaned up. I'll take care of her."

"Billy. Get out of here and into the fresh air," Mrs. Tanner commanded. "We don't want you getting sick again."

Billy hastened to the door. "I'll go feed the lambs," he said.

"And I'll get out of here, too," Kid spoke up. "I'll get out of your way."

"You'll do no such thing," said Mrs. Tanner. "You'll go over there in the corner and sit until we are finished here. You are taking us to town *right now*, tonight. This baby needs a doctor." She stripped off her soiled apron as she spoke and dropped it to the floor.

"Nora, wipe up the floor with this rag. That's all it is—a rag. Don't try to save it or wash it. This apron has been threadbare for weeks. Put it in a paper sack and throw it out there to be burned. Then scrub up the floor with lye soap. We don't want anyone else getting sick." She disappeared into the bedroom to select the clean clothing she would need.

When she came carrying the fresh change of clothes, Kid was again angling toward the door.

"I promised them fellows at Bowers Meadows, that I would pick them up," he explained. "Little Sarah will feel better now and..."

"Sit down and shut up!" Mrs. Tanner stormed. "You are going nowhere until we go in to the doctor. Two fellows that are going to work at the mill," she snorted. "They haven't hired anyone at the mill in months."

Nora gently cleaned the baby with warm water and scented soap. She felt surprise and a secret admiration for Mrs. Tanner. Usually her employer allowed Kid to do as he pleased, especially when her husband was around. Now Kid moved to sit again in the far corner, uncertainty evident on his face.

If Mrs. Tanner could stand up to Kid, Nora decided that she could, too. Her fear was now turning to fury. She was still afraid, but she was mad, too.

Little Sarah remained listless and burning with fever. She whimpered as Nora placed her again in the buggy and went to find the scrub bucket and lye soap. She dropped the dirty apron into a paper sack and dropped to her knees to scrub the soiled linoleum.

Kid called to her, softly, from the corner hoping not to alert his sister-in-law. Nora ignored him.

Soon Mrs. Tanner emerged from the bathroom, dressed and ready for her trip to town.

"Call Billy," she directed Nora. "Oh, I do hope we won't be put under quarantine again."

"Billy is down feeding the lambs."

"Oh, dear." Mrs. Tanner paused as she lifted the baby, consternation evident on her face.

"We'll be all right here," said Nora. "Take care of little Sarah. We can come in tomorrow."

"I don't want to leave you out here alone, but— Nora dear—What happened to your face? It's swollen!"

"We will be just fine," Nora assured her. "Uncle Jack is right down there by the creek. And it's only for tonight." She touched her cheek. "We'll talk about it later. Now hurry and get that baby to the doctor."

"Good Lord," Mrs. Tanner seemed ready to burst into tears. "Could anything else go wrong?" She hurried out the door, followed by a surly looking Kid.

Nora made pancakes for breakfast. They were not very good. She boiled sugar and water together for syrup and then added a little molasses.

"Those pancakes are terrible," Nora admitted. "But we only have flour and baking powder. There is no milk, and not even an egg."

"We can get some goat milk from Uncle Jack," said Billy, "and he probably has other stuff we can get."

"He has beans," said Nora, "and barely any of those. They don't have much left by the time they get in here from the desert. I hope your Uncle Kid gets out here early."

But Kid didn't show up. They had pancakes again at noon, then walked down to the sheep camp to see if Uncle Jack had some bacon grease. They couldn't cook pancakes without some oil to keep them from sticking to the pan.

"I have the end of a slab of bacon," Uncle Jack told them. "It's about six inches of solid fat. It was the worst slab of bacon I ever saw. Very little meat on it, but you can slice it up and render out some of the grease. That will keep the flapjacks from sticking."

Uncle Jack looked off across the meadow toward the grazing sheep.

"I think I'll have to pull the herd out of that field," he said. "They have eaten all the grass down, so I'll start them on into the ranch tomorrow. They've had a good rest and a fine feed, and I've had a grand rest myself."

The two children walked back through the afternoon heat. They had pancakes again for supper.

"I hate Uncle Kid," said Billy. "He makes me so mad." He stopped, syrup dripping from his fork. "We should think of a way to 'get even'."

Nora laughed. "Don't get mad, get even," she said. "We'll just have to work on that."

She became suddenly thoughtful. Her fear had diminished somewhat, but instead a slow, steady anger grew with every hungry hour that passed.

"He's just a—a—*toad*," said Billy. "He should know that we'd want to know about Sarah, and—well, he knew we were out of groceries."

The child's face wrinkled in worry. "Do you think we could possibly—walk into town?"

"Don't you worry," said Nora. "We'll ride in with Uncle Jack. That will be more fun anyway. He'll be going in tomorrow or the next day." She hesitated and smiled suddenly. "Come here, Billy. Let's work out a 'get even' plan.

She stepped to the mirror over the buffet and stuck her finger in her mouth. She slid it carefully between her teeth and her cheek, wincing a little as she disturbed the cut on her lip.

"Does that make my face look swollen?"

"Yeah. Maybe a little."

Nora inserted a second finger.

"How about that?" she asked.

"That's good. That's good," said Billy. "But why do you want to look swelled up?"

"I want the toad to think that he broke my jaw," Nora laughed. "I want to worry him into a bow knot."

Excitement and approval built on Billy's face.

"I'll have to roll up a rag or something and stick it in there," Nora explained. "Then I won't have to talk to him or anything."

"He'll be awfully mad," said Billy.

"Good!"

Nora rolled up a piece of cloth and positioned it inside her cheek. She took it out and refolded it and tried again.

Somehow the material didn't seem to work the way she had expected. Billy looked on skeptically and shook his head.

Next she tried a piece of paper that she rolled up to the appropriate size. That seemed to work better after she clipped the ends with the scissors. But soon the paper became soggy and uncomfortable and that idea was cast aside.

"Maybe we should forget it," sighed Nora. "Mother says that 'getting even' is wrong."

"But I'd sure like to see ol' Kid sweatin' a little," said Billy. "He always makes everyone else feel bad."

Nora nodded agreement and started picking up the sticky dishes from the table. They would have to eat pancakes again tomorrow if Kid didn't show up. How she feared and disliked that man.

Then she stopped half way across the kitchen. There on the work table lay the end of the slab of bacon. Beside it lay the sharp knife she used to slice away the rind.

"Wait a minute," she said, excitement growing in her voice. "This might work."

She took the knife, lay the two fingers of her left hand atop the solid white fat of the bacon, and using the fingers as a pattern, she carefully cut a solid mass from the slab.

Billy was aghast.

"Can you put that greasy chunk in your mouth?" he asked.

"I—I think so."

She picked up the piece of fat and stepped to the mirror. Shuddering, she slid the raw bacon along her jaw between her teeth and her cheek.

"Wow," Billy's voice was almost reverent.

"Wow!" he said again in rising excitement.

Nora looked at her reflection. A wave of satisfaction flowed through her. Her face looked grotesquely swollen. She could have had a monstrous toothache. She forgot the revulsion she felt from that disgusting piece of fat in her mouth. It wouldn't become soggy and fall apart. It wouldn't lose its shape. She smiled happily.

"Uh-oh," said Billy. "When you smile or when you talk, I can see white stuff bulging out."

"Yeah. We'll have to find something to color it with," The words slurred as they came from Nora's mouth. "Maybe I can cook it till it's a little brown. Otherwise, it's perfect."

"I'm going down to feed the lambs," said Billy. "I'll be back soon. I can hardly wait for Uncle Kid to get here."

Nora felt an uneasy twinge of fear. Maybe Kid would want to 'get even' himself.

"Ask Uncle Jack if you can bring Cromwell back here with you," Nora suggested. "And tell him we'll probably be riding into town with him tomorrow." She didn't want to alarm Billy, but she would feel safer with the big dog nearby.

She slid the piece of pork out of her mouth and watched as Billy ran down through the meadow. She felt a spasm of guilt, too, as she continued cleaning up the kitchen. She knew Mother would never approve of what she was doing.

She took out the frying pan and was about to try to brown the piece of bacon when she realized that the heat would render out the oil and shrink the original piece. It would be too small then. It was just right as it was. She would have to think of something else. If she only had some beet juice or some Easter egg dye.

Suddenly an idea seemed to explode in her brain. She hurried into the bathroom, opened the medicine chest, and took out the bottle of iodine. That would do the trick. She congratulated herself as she returned to the kitchen.

She put the chunk of bacon fat on a saucer and splashed the medicine over it. Immediately the meat started to lose its waxen white color.

"I'll let it soak there until it gets darker," she said and hastened about packing up the clothing that she and Billy would be taking back to town with them. Occasionally she would stop to turn the fat over in the saucer as it gradually darkened.

She heard the dog barking and Billy returned full of joy that Cromwell was his for the night. He was impressed by the color of the pork fat and gleeful as he thought of the great joke they were playing on Uncle Kid.

"You must be sure you don't laugh and spoil it," Nora warned him. "We have to act worried and—well, unhappy. We must make him think I'm really in bad shape and have to get to a dentist right away."

"I know. I know," Billy agreed. "And *you* have to keep from laughing, too."

They removed the pork fat from its iodine bath, called Cromwell in from the yard, and went to bed.

In the morning, the two were just finishing their pancake breakfast when Cromwell started barking.

Nora looked out into the yard.

"We forgot to burn the trash last night," she observed. "Cromwell is out there dragging that sack around—the one that has your mother's dirty apron in it. It must smell *terrible!*"

"It's time to go feed the lambs," said Billy. He opened the door and started across the porch. The dog turned suddenly and, rushing ahead, barked furiously at Kid Tanner, who strode angrily across the yard.

Billy dashed back into the kitchen.

"It's Uncle Kid," he shouted. "He's almost at the back door."

Nora jumped to her feet, rushed to the cupboard and slid the colored piece of fat pork beyond her teeth against her cheek.

Instantly her mouth burst into searing fire. Her eyes watered. Her injured lip hurt. Her mouth filled with ugly tasting saliva. Her throat seemed on fire. She leaned, gagging, over the sink. She couldn't swallow that fiery poison. How could she have been so stupid? So thoughtless? Of course the iodine would burn the tender tissue in her mouth. She had been so intent on fooling Kid that she hadn't thought of that fact. Iodine burned when you put it on a cut on your foot or your elbow. How much worse it burned on the inside of your mouth.

Billy watched her in wide-eyed amazement.

Uncle Kid stomped about the kitchen, swearing and furious. He hadn't even seen her discomfort.

"—into the ditch," he was saying. "I ran into the damn ditch and got stuck. I got that stupid damn sheepherder to take his team and pull me out. Had to pay him twenty dollars before he'd come near my car. Then I couldn't get it started and wanted him to tow me into town. He wouldn't do it. Said he had to take the damn sheep on the damn trail or some –"

Kid stopped abruptly in the middle of his tirade to look at Nora vomiting into the sink.

"What the hell?" Shock showed on his face.

"She's got a broken jaw," said Billy. "It's all your fault. You are the one that hit her."

Nora staggered a few steps to reach for a towel. Her eyes were watering so that she could barely make out where Kid was standing. She drew long, painful sounding breaths through her tortured throat. She stepped out onto the porch in search of fresh air.

"Holy damn!" said Kid, his voice rough. "I didn't do that. You musta' fallen or something," He rushed to Nora and swung her toward himself. "I didn't do that. I told you I was sorry. I didn't mean nothin'." He was babbling, and shaking her, looking with horror at her grotesquely swollen jaw. "I couldn't have done that." He jerked her back into the kitchen.

There came a low, savage growl. Suddenly Kid was no longer standing, but lying full length on the floor, screaming, as Cromwell stood over him nipping at his arm and shoulder.

Billy danced about shouting in delight.

"Call him off!" Kid shouted.

Billy laughed.

Nora leaned against the table. She wiped her mouth and eyes.

"Cromwell!" she called. The word came forth as a whisper.

She cleared her throat. "Cromwell!" she croaked a second time. The dog trotted reluctantly to her side, but turned toward Kid, growling.

Kid cowered on the floor. Nora wished Velma could see him now, and wondered where that thought came from.

"Put that damn dog out and lock the screen door," Kid ordered from where he lay. Cromwell turned, snarling.

Nora sank into a nearby chair. She leaned on the table, gathering her strength. The fire in her mouth made her feel faint. Her breathing slowly improved.

"Billy," she said at last. "Get the two bags of clothes we packed last night. We're going down to ride into town with Uncle Jack." Her slurred words seem to hang in the quiet of the kitchen.

"Now—just you wait a minute." Kid started to rise up from the floor, but a menacing growl from Cromwell stopped him. Billy scampered away, laughing.

"Nora, listen," Kid pleaded. "I meant to get out here yesterday. Really I did. And I need you to go down there and persuade your uncle to tow me into town. I'll pay him for it. He's probably—well, mad at me for swearing at him, but—" he hesitated, his voice turning soft and flattering, "*you* can talk him into it."

"You haven't even told us how little Sarah is," Nora struggled to get the words past her swollen tongue.

"Oh. She's better. She's sick. Got the measles alright. But she's feeling lots better. They got the quarantine sign back on their house, though."

"You knew we had nothing here to eat!" Nora managed. "We've had pancakes for two days!"

"Well. I *wanted* to come out yesterday," Kid excused himself. "I had a couple 'a other things I had to do and—"

Keeping a wary eye on the dog, Kid eased himself up until he was leaning on one elbow.

"Nora," he pleaded, his voice soft, "please put that damn hound out. I think I'm bleedin' here on my shoulder, where he bit me. And on my arm, too. You can tell your uncle that I have to get in to town to the doctor—from the dog bites. It's his dog and he's responsible!"

"You were shoving me around," said Nora. She felt anger rising.

"I'll shoot that damn cur," Kid said. "First chance I get." He hesitated, stopped himself and began in a softer, more persuasive tone. "But listen, honey. Get your uncle to take me in to town and—"

Nora rose to her feet. Her faintness seemed to be vanishing.

"Are you ready, Billy?" she called.

They took their packs and hurried across the porch and down the steps. Cromwell followed behind.

Billy bounced along gleefully. He looked at Nora with amazement.

"How could you do that?" he asked. "You really looked like you were dying. You belong in Hollywood." He swung his sack above his head and skipped, laughing, along the trail.

Nora took the offensive piece of pork from her mouth and threw it far out into the sagebrush.

"Wait! Wait!" Uncle Kid called from the porch. Cromwell turned back and growled.

"What am I to do?" Kid sounded almost pitiful. "There's nothin' here to eat, and my arm—it's really hurtin'."

"Eat pancakes," shouted Billy. "They'll taste pretty good for the first few days."

Uncle Jack was just loading the bummer lambs into the wagon when the children arrived at his camp. The sheep had already started out on the trail for town.

"I hear a bell somewhere," said Billy.

"That comes from the lead sheep," said Uncle Jack. "He wears a bell around his neck and the rest of the sheep follow him. They listen for the sound."

"Does he know the way into town?"

"He does." Uncle Jack explained. "He's made the trip back and forth from the desert to the mountains for several years now. He won't get lost."

"But we aren't goin' to the mountains, are we?" said Billy.

"We aren't. Not today, anyway. But that bellwether knows every stop along the road. Tonight we'll be at the home ranch and we'll stay there for a few days—"

Nora crawled gratefully into the wagon, glad that she didn't have to answer any of Billy's questions. She felt relief that she would be going to stay at the Tanners. Mrs. Tanner wouldn't think to ask any questions about her sore throat and mouth, while, if she went home, Mother would demand an immediate explanation.

Little Sarah was very ill for several days, and then began a slow recovery. Dr. Hodges again warned them that the baby's eyes must be protected from all bright lights for several weeks. Billy and Nora spent many hours entertaining the little toddler as the summer slowly passed.

The day finally came when Dr. Hodges came to remove the big red quarantine sign from their front door.

"We must be the very last ones in town who have a sign like that on their door," said Billy. "I think I'll roll it up and keep it for a souvenir."

"Yes. You are about the last people to be quarantined," the Doctor agreed. "But guess what! That uncle of yours, you know – Kid Tanner? We had to put a sign on his porch just last night. He has one of the worst cases of measles I've seen all summer. Of course, it's usually pretty serious when an adult gets one of these children's diseases."

He handed the faded sign to Billy and turned to Mrs. Tanner.

"The poor man is really uncomfortable. He keeps insisting that he got the disease from some dog that bit him out there on the Fort Road. Said all the infection started in a bite he had on his shoulder and arm. Wants me to find the dog and have him put down." He shook his head. "Poor fellow! But he'll have a good month, maybe more, to think it over."

Nora turned away and entered the house. She walked to the kitchen and started preparing a bottle for little Sarah, who was calling from her crib. Her mind raced as she measured the milk. She remembered Cromwell dragging the paper bag that held Mrs. Tanner's soiled apron around the yard out there at the ranch. He had ripped it apart with his teeth and then, shortly afterward, he had taken a nip out of Uncle Kid.

They had really 'gotten even.' She could hardly wait to tell Billy!

She smiled as she lifted the baby from her crib and settled into the rocking chair to feed the child the bottle.

"Return good for evil," Mother often said. Nora chuckled softly to herself.

"Ignore any wrongdoing," "Turn the other cheek," "'Vengeance is mine, sayeth the Lord." Nora thought of all these sayings that Mother often used as she instructed the children.

"I like the old Irish saying the best," Nora laughed. "Don't get mad, get even."

Chapter 11

🌸 JOB HUNTING - 1935

"Please, Mother." Nora tried to keep the quaver out of her voice. "Let me get a permanent for my birthday. I'll pay for it myself."

"Maybe later," Mother answered. She was busily ripping apart a dress that had hung in her closet for several years. She held the razor blade carefully in her fingers and concentrated on her work.

"Mother! Classes start next week, and I want to have my hair changed before I go back to school."

Mother murmured something. She didn't appear to be even listening. She had been somewhat sad and quiet for the past two weeks since Katie had left for college.

Nora burst into tears. She hated to have anyone see her cry, but the frustration she felt welled within her and spilled out in spite of her attempts to hold it in.

"I've grown so tall," Nora sobbed. "I'm the tallest one in my room. Even the boys are shorter than I am. I'm awkward. I'm gawky. I look like a freak. Katie always looks nice, but her hair is naturally curly. I look better when I put my hair up in rags to curl it, but the curls are gone by noon and—"

"Nonsense, child," Mother put the razor blade aside and picked the short threads from the sheer fabric. "Besides, who can afford to pay four dollars for a permanent? Your father isn't a banker, you know."

"I *have* the money," Nora cried. "I earned it watching little Billy and working for his mother. And I gave you twelve dollars that I had saved—you know, for Katie—when she left for college."

"I know," Mother began, but Nora interrupted.

"Dorothy Elliott got a permanent *months* ago, and so did Buelah Grange. They looked ever so much better, and Clarice Benson had *two* permanents last year, and she was only in the seventh grade."

"Hush!" warned Mother. "Here comes Billy and his mother now. Wipe your face."

The front door closed and footsteps sounded down the hall. Mrs. Tanner and Billy entered the kitchen.

"I should have knocked," said Mrs. Tanner. "I guess I still think I live in this house. We rented it for so long, and we were so happy here."

"How are things going down there in California?" Mother asked.

"Fine. Fine. Billy is a little worried about starting a new school, but the mister is happy with the promotion. We do miss our friends up here, though. We've only been gone two weeks, but it seems like two months. And I miss Nora. I'll never find another Nora." She turned to smile at the girl and then asked in quick concern. "What's the matter? What's wrong, Nora?"

"Nothing," said Nora. She wiped at her cheeks again and hastened up the stairs. She could hear Mother explaining about the permanent, about the dress she was making for Nora's birthday and about how empty the house seemed since Katie left for Oregon State.

"I read in the paper that Katie got a great scholarship," said Mrs. Tanner. "She'll do very well. I know she will."

"I hope she's not as lonesome for us as we are for her," said Mother.

Nora buried her head beneath her arms and thought about Katie. She wished *she* could be up there at Oregon State. She imagined all the new things Katie was seeing, all the adventures she was having, all the new friends she was making. There would be young people there from all over the state. What an exciting life Katie must be living! Katie, with her curly black hair and...

Mother was calling. Nora jumped from her bed and hurried down the stairs. Mother and Mrs. Tanner stood smiling in the hallway. Billy seemed to glow with happiness.

"We have a surprise for your birthday," shouted Billy. "You'll *love* it!"

"Mrs. Tanner has persuaded me that you should get a permanent," said Mother. "She wants to give it to you for your birthday. She has already called the beauty shop and they can take you right away. Go, change your clothes and she'll drive you up there."

"*Really?*" Nora squealed. She hugged Mother. She hugged Mrs. Tanner. She even hugged Billy. She dashed back up the stairs, then called down from the landing. "Do I have to wash my hair or anything?"

"No. No, of course not," said Mrs. Tanner. "They will wash your hair. That's all part of the process."

Nora changed her dress, then hurried to the bathroom. She didn't need to wash her hair, but she would scrub her neck.

The 'Chic' Salon was a small beauty parlor tucked behind a dress shop. Nora had delivered the paper there every day for several years. She had seen the women getting finger waves and shampoos and permanents, but she had never paid any special attention until the past year or so, and then she had found it wonderful that the women could step out onto the sidewalk looking entirely different from when they had entered.

Now she found it a thrilling experience to lean back in a chair and have Eva Teller shampoo her hair. It was then towel dried and she sat under the dryer while Eva pulled out that strange machine with little clamps dangling from electric wires.

Eva plugged in the machine.

A table nearby was topped with a bottle of 'wave lotion', as Eva called it, a scissors, a box full of little rollers and a slim wand-like instrument that tucked in any stray hairs that didn't lie flat when the hair was twisted around the rollers

Eva snipped and thinned. Then she opened the bottle of wave lotion and, using a piece of cotton, she saturated each small tuft of hair and wrapped the hair around one of the little rods and clamped it in place. The solution smelled terrible, and soon Nora's head began to feel extremely heavy with all the little rods of wet hair that circled her head. Now Eva pulled the machine forward and pulled at the little clamp that dangled on the end of each wire. She fit a clamp over each little rod and adjusted the heat. Soon the smell from the chemical solution seemed to fill the room.

Nora began to feel the heat from the clamps at the end of those wires. After all, the machine was electric.

The weight of the apparatus on her head made Nora feel as though she were sinking through the bottom of the chair. Eva came with a blower and directed cool air along her scalp as the rods and clamps grew ever warmer.

"Wow!" She never expected getting a permanent would be anything like this. The heat, the weight, the smell—she began to think that Mother had been right. But no, she had to go to school looking better than when she left it in the spring.

Finally, Eva put down the blower and selected a single curl which she unclamped, unrolled from the roller and tested by bouncing the hair, now partially curled, on her hand. She re-rolled it, re-clamped it and nodded in satisfaction.

"Looking good," she said cheerfully. "Just a few more minutes."

Nora sat miserably in the chair. She had the strange sensation that she was shrinking. The machine seemed to be glowing and growing larger while she grew warmer and smaller. She wished Eva would come again with the blower and cool her scalp. She felt sure that there would be nothing but a huge blister where her hair had been—a huge, bald blister.

Eva came with the blower. She selected another curl, unwound it and bounced it in her hand.

"Great," she said. "You have good, strong hair." She unplugged the machine but left the hot clamps in place as she went to adjust the dryer for another client across the room. Finally she returned and started removing the clamps.

Nora's hair was rinsed in cool water. Heavenly cold wave lotion was applied, and Eva added curlers, finger waves and 'spit' curls held in place with bobby pins. Nora was placed under a dryer and Eva handed her a magazine named 'Chic.'

"Same name as my shop," she said. "You'll enjoy it."

"Chic," Nora repeated. "'Chic.' It's spelled almost like 'chick,' a baby chicken."

"It's French, I think," Eva laughed. "It's pronounced 'sheeek', like in *meek*—with a 'sh' in the front."

Sheek, sheek. Nora whispered to herself as she leafed through the slick pages. There were portions devoted to new hair styles, new dress styles, new hat styles and new underwear styles. Nora was surprised. Underwear so blatantly displayed. But there were pages that showed new table wear, new dishes, new toasters and other kitchen gadgets. Some of the advertised items Nora had never seen. There were several pages of new shoe styles, and she learned that the 'button hook' for fastening the row of buttons up the side of a shoe was obsolete. None of the new shoes had rows of buttons.

Finally, Nora was moved to a different chair and Eva started combing out her hair. She brushed and combed and smoothed and used a bobby pin when necessary. She purred and complimented and seemed genuinely happy.

"This looks great," she murmured. "You have such wonderful hair to work with." Finally she turned Nora toward the mirror. A stranger stared back. Nora moved and looked around to find her own image somewhere in the room and the stranger in the mirror moved and looked around as she did. Her mouth fell open in surprise. That handsome, beautiful girl staring back at her was—was—herself!

Eva slid away and hurried into the dress shop to call to the clerks there to come and look.

"Who is it?" asked Mary Holt. "I know I should know her—but…"

"That's not—not—Nora!" said Mrs. Crandall. She seemed awestruck.

"That's Nora," Eva paced proudly across the room. "She came in here like a little tomboy and now she's a lady." They looked at each other almost unbelieving.

* * * *

The dress was blue. Not a dull, drab navy but a bright, sassy sky colored blue. Nora loved it. Mother had washed and pressed the pieces of her old dress and cut out a dress for Nora.

The fabric was light-weight and sheer and seemed to float on the air, but underneath was a heavy satin petticoat that reflected the same lovely color and kept the dress very modest. There were puffed sleeves and a Peter Pan collar and delicate little trims of the blue satin. Nora had never seen such a lovely dress and Mother had sat up far into the night to finish it in time for her birthday.

There was a Sodality meeting at the church that afternoon, and Nora dressed with care. She combed the new permanent so that the deep wave across her forehead feathered back into a nice wave above her ear. The curls underneath the wave added just the right touch. Eva herself couldn't have made her hair look better.

Then she put on the bright new dress.

"You look absolutely lovely," said Mother.

"What happened to my little girl?" said Dad. He sounded rather sad.

Nora walked out the door and down the street, feeling wonderful. She couldn't wait until her cousins and the other girls in the Sodality saw her. They would be so surprised.

She crossed Main Street and half a block further she saw two of her former newspaper customers chatting across the fence.

"Hi, Mr. Graham," she smiled. "Mr. Poindexter."

The two men stopped talking. Mr. Poindexter took off his hat and Mr. Graham tipped his hat respectfully.

"Nice afternoon," said Graham.

"Wonderful," Nora answered.

She proceeded a few steps further along the walk, but had to stop to allow little Danny Fetsch to pull his wagon through his gate.

"Who the hell was that?" she heard Graham ask. "I know I should know her but—"

"I can't place her, either," Poindexter answered. "I thought it might be that Katie Nolan, but she's gone off to college,"

Graham shook his head. "Damned if I know," he said. "She's prettier than Katie Nolan—and taller. Maybe she works downtown. Now it'll bother me all night."

Nora walked on, her confidence soaring.

The Sodality meeting was a huge success. Even Father O'Hagen didn't recognize her. He said she looked sixteen or seventeen. She had thought a permanent would be a great help to her self-esteem, but she had never believed that it could change her life to this extent.

Betsy Houle was leaving for San Francisco. Her aunt was ill and Betsy would help care for her and go to a private school down there. She wanted everyone to be sure and write to her. Yes. They would be hiring someone to take her place at the drug store. Betsy wouldn't put in a good word for anyone. She had too many friends, and some would surely be mad if she chose one of them.

Nora loved Betsy. They had been friends for a long time. When Nora had the paper route she could stop in at the drug store fountain and if she didn't have any change Betsy would give her an ice cream treat of her choice and write the amount down in a little book she kept under the counter. Nora would pay the bill when she collected for the papers at the end of the month. Some of the other kids also ran up bills that Betsy kept track of in her little book. Mr. Everett didn't seem to mind.

"I wish I could get her job," Nora thought. "She gets a whole dollar a day and I know I could do the things she does there at that fountain."

She laughed and talked and played games with the other girls, but the idea kept growing in her mind. If she went up there and applied for the job first—if she could impress Mr. Everett—maybe she could get the job. Betsy had just told her boss today that she would be quitting. And if Nora could impress him—

She moved to a chair at the far side of the room. She fell so deep into thinking and planning that she scarcely heard what was going on around her. She took her purse and counted the change that she carried there. She had eighty-five cents. She had babysat for Cronimillers on two separate nights, and she had found a quarter outside the gym at the school. Well that would have to do.

She would go in and tell Mr. Everett that she owed fifty-five cents that Betsy had written in her book. He would think her very honest.

She hoped her plan would work.

She said her goodbyes and hurried up the street. It was only two and half blocks to the drugstore. She found herself taking deep breaths to prepare herself. She hoped she wasn't going to make a fool of herself.

Head down, half muttering to herself, she started across the street. She bumped squarely into a man crossing from the other direction.

"Sorry, sorry," she apologized.

"Nora?" It was Uncle Jack. "Nora?" he questioned again.

"Oh, Uncle Jack!" Nora's voice showed her relief. "Oh, I'm so glad to see you. I need some advice. You see, I have this plan—"

"Come out of the street," Uncle Jack guided her back to the curb. "What have you done to yourself? I'm not sure I recognize you—"

"I got a permanent," said Nora. "And Mother made me a new dress. I want to get the job at the drug store. Betsy Houle is quitting. But I'm afraid – I'm worried—you know, about applying for the job. Mr. Everett will think I'm too young, although everyone thinks I look older and—oh, I want that job so bad…" she paused, almost breathless.

"Wait a minute. Slow down." Uncle Jack took her hand and looked at her for a long, quiet moment.

"Great God, girl! Yesterday you ran about wearing your brother's overalls, racing on your bicycle. You looked like a – well, like a gypsy. And now you—you are so…changed."

"Do you think I'm changed enough to get the job?" Nora's voice showed her impatience. "Let me tell you about my plan."

Standing on the sidewalk in the late afternoon sun, Nora explained how she would pretend to owe the store 55 cents. The druggist knew that Betsy wrote kids' charges in her little book all the time—and he would think that she, Nora, was very honest to come in and pay.

"No. No," said Uncle Jack. "Your name won't be written in the book. It will make Betsy look bad. And it may make old Everett suspicious." He looked at Nora, his face very serious.

"If you want the job, just walk in—calmly—and apply for it. Be quiet, and restrained – but show self-confidence. Show that you can handle the job, and the public that you'll be serving—and you will be showing the boss that you are mature. Self-confidence. That's what you need. Sure, aren't you as good or better than any of the others that will be applying?"

"Oh! Uncle Jack. I'm so glad I met you. I know Mr. Everett will be asking all kinds of questions, and—"

"Answer the questions. Look him straight in the eye and answer calmly, truthfully, and with self-confidence."

"But—he'll probably ask me how old I am! I can't tell him I'm only fourteen—today. Do I have to tell the truth when he asks me that? Everyone says I look older!"

Uncle Jack looked thoughtfully out into the street. He sighed and squeezed her hand.

"Tell the truth," he said. "When he asks you how old you are, you can say—well, you can say—'I'll be seventeen on my birthday." He paused dramatically. "You aren't really lying. Not technically. You will be 17 on your birthday. You just aren't telling him which birthday."

"Oh, Uncle Jack. I'm so glad I met you!"

"Off you go now," he said. "And remember—self-confidence. That's the key. Self-confidence."

Mr. Everett was behind the prescription counter when she entered the drugstore. Smiling, and hoping she was walking in a very ladylike manner, she approached the counter.

"Betsy Houle told me she was leaving for San Francisco," her voice was cool and confident. "I'd like to apply for her job."

"Oh, yeah. Yeah." Said Mr. Everett. "I have to get some job application blanks to be filled out. I meant to stop and do that today. I imagine there will be lots of young people applying."

"Possibly," said Nora. "But if you hire me, you won't have to bother with the application blanks." She could scarcely believe those words were coming so smoothly from her mouth. *Self-confidence,* Uncle Jack had said.

"Your name?" Mr. Everett was looking at her with that questioning look that other adults had seemed to have had all day.

"I know I should know—" he began, but Nora interrupted him.

"My name is Hanora Nolan," she extended her hand. Mr. Everett hastened to put down the pen he held and shook her hand.

Everyone in the town knows that scrawny kid name Nora, she thought. *Hanora is a new person.*

"You go to the high school here?" Mr. Everett asked.

"Yes," Nora answered. "School starts next week but I feel sure I can arrange to take the last hour off, just as Betsy did."

"And how old are you?"

"Why, I'll be seventeen on my birthday," she nodded her head, as though indicating sometime in the near future. Nora's voice remained calm and assured. Her heart seemed to have stopped, but her voice remained calm.

Other questions followed but her confidence was growing. She answered easily—convincingly, she thought. Mr. Everett seemed impressed.

Then Uncle Jack entered the store. He looked somewhat disheveled. His shirttail hung out and his hair stood out at odd angles. He made his way to the counter and interrupted the conversation.

"I need some Bull Durham tabacky," he said "and a tin of Carbolic salve."

Nora turned in surprise. Uncle Jack flashed her a warning look. Mr. Everett seemed ill at ease.

"I beg your pardon," said the druggist. "I didn't quite understand."

"Bull Durham tabacky," Uncle Jack repeated, "and Carbolic salve."

Nora listened, appalled. Uncle Jack's Irish brogue seemed so thick *she* could scarcely understand him. He had been in this country 12 years and had lost most of the brogue that the new Irish immigrants brought with them, but today he sounded as though he had just gotten off the boat. And he had never used the word 'tabacky' in his life.

Mr. Everett shook his head. "I don't understand," he admitted. "Here is a pen. Perhaps you could write it down."

"He said he wanted Bull Durham tobacco and a tin of Carbolic salve," Nora interpreted.

"Oh. Oh. Good," Mr. Everett sighed under his breath. He hastened to pull the two items from his shelves.

Uncle Jack put a bill on the counter and carefully counted his change when he received the package.

"Thank you," he nodded to Everett, and left the store.

"You can understand those—those—ah, Irish greenhorns?" Mr. Everett said to Nora.

"Well, of course," Nora answered. "He was speaking perfectly good English."

"Well, that's an asset," said the druggist. "I have a hard time understanding many of the Irish." He looked thoughtfully toward the door that Uncle Jack had just closed behind him. He looked at Nora.

"Well, why don't we give it a try?" he said at last. "You come in tomorrow and for the weekend, and Betsy can show you what's expected."

"I'm a fast learner," said Nora. She extended her hand again as though to seal the bargain, and then she walked *confidently* from the store.

On Friday, Nora started to learn the intricacies of serving the public. She learned to make milkshakes, ice cream sodas, sundaes, root beer floats and all sorts of sandwiches. Mrs. Sorman, who ran the fountain, was delighted to learn that she knew how to make potato salad, tuna salad, salmon salad and ham salad. Nora learned that some people preferred brown bread when one made a sandwich, and most people liked their sandwiches toasted.

When the work at the fountain was caught up and no customers were around, there was always cleaning to be done. Mirrors were polished several times a day. The exposed stainless steel parts of the storage bins had to be scrubbed and polished, and the glasses and serving pieces had to be washed in hot, soapy water and then polished to a bright shine. If the work at the fountain was caught up, there was always the glass on the front door, the front windows and the display cabinets that needed to be cleaned.

In the late afternoon, Nora worked on the display cabinet for the tobacco products. She stacked the green packages of Lucky Strikes on the top glass shelf and arranged the red cans of pipe tobacco on a lower shelf. The Camel cigarettes were given a prominent place—also on the top shelf, and then she set about stacking the little cloth sacks of Bull Durham on the second shelf. The booklets of tan papers for those who chose to roll their own were placed handily next to the Bull Durham sacks. As she was about to close the case, George Ellerby walked up to the counter.

Nora disliked George. He had a 'dirty mouth' and most of the girls at school avoided him. He flipped a quarter up on the polished glass surface of the tobacco case.

"Gimme a couple of packs of humps." he ordered.

Nora was perplexed. "What?" she asked.

"Gimme a couple of packs of humps, stupid," he said. He grinned happily. He had found someone whom he could belittle.

"I—I—don't understand," Nora managed.

"A couple of packs of Camels," said George. "You know, Camel cigarettes." He snorted and shook his head as though he couldn't believe anyone could be so dumb.

Nora felt herself blushing. She reached into the cabinet, set the cigarette packages on the counter and picked up the quarter. She was busily polishing the top of the cupboard before he had even left the store.

"Were his hands that dirty?" Betsy questioned. "Did he get the glass smeared or something?"

"I'd like to scrub where he stood," Nora said.

Later, a stranger came into the store. Nora assumed he worked at the mill, as bits of sawdust clung to his shoulders and hair. She helped him pick out tablets and pencils for his children and a jar of cold cream for his wife.

"And chewing gum," he said. "The kids love chewing gum, although the wife gets mad because she finds it squashed on the floor or even in their hair from time to time."

"Get them suckers," Nora suggested. "They don't stick to the floor and rarely get in their hair."

"Good idea," he agreed, laughing. Mr. Everett nodded his approval from behind the pharmacy counter.

The man bought several other items—a package of handkerchiefs, some razor blades, a wind-up toy top for one of the children. Nora stacked the purchases in a neat pile on the top of the counter. The man hesitated for a moment, looked around and whispered, "And a package of Sheiks—"

"Your wife will love it," said Nora as she stepped from behind the counter. "It's a wonderful magazine." She crossed the store to the magazine rack and looked carefully through the books displayed there.

"I'm sorry," she called back to him. "We don't seem to stock 'Chic,' here—But we do have *Mademoiselle*. I think that is very similar."

The man seemed to be shrinking against the counter. He looked embarrassed, or very ill at ease. Mr. Everett hastened from the pharmacy and spoke to the man. He placed a strange little box on the counter and started adding up all the purchases.

"I'll finish up here," he called to Nora.

Nora felt somewhat bewildered. She had rung up purchases all day and hadn't made a single mistake. Mr. Everett had watched her and nodded with satisfaction, and now he felt it necessary to ring up the items that man had chosen. Well, Nora shrugged, maybe he was a personal friend, or something.

The man took his sack and hurried from the store. He didn't say goodbye or make eye contact as he left.

Mr. Everett looked at her thoughtfully for a moment. He beckoned her toward the counter where he stood.

"I did something wrong," said Nora. "But I can't figure out what it was I did."

"No. No," the druggist assured her. "It was a matter of misunderstanding." He paused and glanced around. "The man wanted 'Sheiks,' " he said. "S-h-e-i-k-s." Everett spelled the word for her.

"What? What – are—"

"It's…it's sort of a—prescription," said Mr. Everett. He looked at his feet. "When anyone asks you for 'Sheiks' just send them to me or the other pharmacist."

"I'll remember," Nora promised. She turned away. Uncle Jack had told her to be self-confident, but there was so much to learn. She had heard of the Sheik of Araby, and the sheiks over there in the Egyptian desert, but she sure didn't know there was a prescription.

Chapter 12

❧ NORA GOES TO COLLEGE - 1935

Nora rushed from the post office. A nagging suspicion that had bothered her for several days began to loom large in her thoughts. All the other kids at school that she knew were planning to go to college had already received the appropriate papers from the colleges of their choice. She alone had not received the letter of acceptance.

But, Oregon State hadn't sent a letter of rejection, either. Something was definitely wrong. She suspected that she knew what that something was.

Mother was terribly busy. Nora admitted that. But Mother surely knew how important it was to write that letter asking that Nora be enrolled—after all, Mother had written letters for both Katie and Phil.

She stumbled a little as she hurried along. Her stomach felt strange. There seemed to be a hard knot in her chest. The depression still weighed heavily upon all the country. Money seemed almost nonexistent. But she was working. She could save—was saving—for college. She wished she had gotten a scholarship like Katie had, but still—she worked every day of her life. Even on Sundays. And why did her mouth feel so dry?

She turned in the gate at home. She hoped Mother didn't have company. She had to speak with her immediately.

She jerked open the front door, ran down the hall.

"Mother, did you forget to write that letter to Oregon State?" she blurted as she rushed into the kitchen.

Mother looked up in alarm.

"Did you send that letter?" Nora repeated. "All the other seniors have been accepted. They have all heard back from the colleges and…" Nora stopped mid-sentence. Mother seemed stricken. She looked guilty, then sad, then resigned, the emotions sweeping across her face in swift succession.

"Sit down, Nora," Mother finally spoke, her voice unsteady. She cleared her throat.

Nora felt glad to sit. Her knees seemed to have turned to water. She sank into a nearby chair.

"You got a letter and didn't tell me," she said. "They turned me down!" She hadn't known tears could come so quickly.

"No. No!" Mother reached toward her. "Nora, dear, we got no such letter." She paused thoughtfully. "You know that Dad and I are – well, we are very proud of you, and—and think you are a very outstanding person."

"Then what—what are you talking about? What do you mean, 'you're proud of me?' For *what*? And why haven't I heard from Oregon State?"

Mother sighed, then shrugged. "Nora, I didn't write that letter. There's no way we can afford to send you off to college." She spoke with sorrow in her voice. "We have more than we can do to keep Phil there."

Nora sat in stunned silence.

Mother continued, her voice soft. "We had to borrow money to get the sheep sheared," she said, "and now they are paying only 8 cents a pound for wool. By the end of the week the price may be only 5 cents a pound. We just can't afford anything more."

"But, I'm working. I'll pay my own way."

"No," said Mother. "You'll have to face it. You just don't make enough. Maybe if times get better, maybe next year—"

"NO!" Nora jumped to her feet. "I'm going. I'll get another job. Graduation is only a week away. I'll have more time to work then."

Mother interrupted. "Nora, dear. Another year isn't so long to wait, maybe then…"

"I'm *going*," said Nora. "I'm going, even if I— I have to go on my hands and knees." She turned and ran from the room.

She bathed and dressed hurriedly. She hoped Uncle Jack was in town. *Mother hadn't written the letter.* Mother wouldn't write it. If Uncle Jack wouldn't write it, she would write it herself.

"I'm going to work now," she called as she let herself out the door.

Uncle Jack was in the Blue Goose Saloon. She had never done such a thing before, but she walked boldly in. The conversation and rustling stopped momentarily because it was unusual for a woman to enter such a place. Uncle Jack stood up from the table where he sat and hastened to join her near the door. They walked out into the sunlight.

"Jesus Christ," he said. "Now what?"

Nora explained. She told him all the details. How Mother hadn't sent the letter asking that she be accepted. How the principal had sent her transcripts. How all the other kids who were going to college had already received an acceptance letter and how he, Uncle Jack, was going to write a letter for her. It had to be done today since it was already so late.

"But what will I say?" Uncle Jack seemed bewildered. "I don't even know what the hell is expected."

"Pretend like you're my mother," said Nora. "No. Pretend that you're my dad. You're writing to tell them that you want me to go to Oregon State. That you're planning for your daughter to attend there. You need to know how much it will cost—for the stuff I want to take—you know. That whole sort of thing."

"I haven't written a letter in two years," said Uncle Jack. "Not since my mother died there in Ireland. Great God! I don't know if I can even remember how to spell – to spell – 'yours truly.' "

"Of course, you can," Nora assured him. "Just pretend I'm your daughter. You do want to help me, don't you?"

"I do. I do. But I don't even know where to begin."

"Begin by going right there into Sheehan's office. He's a lawyer, and he's a good friend. He can help you. I have to get to work but I'll come down here on my break and see how things are going."

"Christ. I'm afraid I'll only make things worse!"

"Things can't get any worse," said Nora as she hurried away.

When she reached the drugstore she was surprised to see a group of boys from the high school and even a couple of men from the mill standing around a strange, shiny, streamlined car that was angle parked at the curb.

"Did you see all the excitement out there?" Dorothy asked, as Nora adjusted her apron. "Some fellow drove in here in that car and you'd think he came from the moon. I even went out and looked it over and I can't tell the difference between a Model T and a wheelbarrow."

"Who does it belong to?"

"Some stranger. He even gave a couple of the boys a ride in it." Dorothy took her purse and headed out the door. "See you tomorrow," she called. "The top of that car even flips back so you can get the sun in your face as you drive. It's really something."

Nora polished the mirror behind the blenders. When one made a

253

milkshake, it seemed the mirrors always received a smattering of the mixture when the container was removed.

She used a paste of Bon Ami to clean all the covers of the huge ice cream containers and then filled the wells of syrup. The chocolate and the strawberry were nearly empty, and the cherry was almost half gone. Dorothy must have been busy. She scrubbed the floor behind the counter and went to sweep up the portion of the room in front of the counter while the floor dried. And all the while she wondered how Uncle Jack was doing. She knew he would much rather be in the saloon with his friends. He would be worried that somehow her mother would find out that he had written the letter and that would lead to trouble. He was a dear man to help her out.

A man came in and sat at the counter. Nora turned to wait on him.

"I should probably have locked that car," he said, watching out the window. "Those kids will be piling into it, if I'm not careful."

"Lovely car," said Nora as she placed a glass of ice water on the counter in front of him. "Can I help you?"

The man turned back and reached for the menu.

Nora stopped, menu in hand and stared at him. He seemed a stranger, and yet—she felt she knew him from somewhere.

"What?" the stranger questioned, frowning.

"Do I know you?" Nora stammered. "Somehow you look so—familiar."

"I don't think we've ever met. I've never been to this town before."

Nora turned away as he studied the menu. She was puzzled and uncertain. She studied his reflection in the mirror and became more convinced that she should know him.

He ordered a toasted sandwich and a chocolate milkshake. She hurried to complete the order, but cast surreptitious glances at him as he watched the excitement surrounding his car. She became more convinced that she knew him.

Maxine Trost entered the store. She hurried to the back counter to pick up some supplies that she had ordered for her third grade class. As she hurried toward the door, she saw the stranger. She made a sudden dramatic stop.

"Rob?" she exclaimed. "Rob Lever! Is that you?"

"Maxine!" The stranger jumped from the stool and went to embrace her. "I was going to try to look you up this evening," he said. "Come and have some supper with me." He nodded toward the counter where Nora worked.

"Can't," said Maxine. "Have to be at a meeting at the school in about three minutes. How long will you be in town?"

"Oh, a couple of days. I'll be sure to see you before I leave, though."

"Call me! Call me! My number is in the book. Or ask anyone in town. I've been here so long—everyone knows me."

She hurried away.

Nora smiled as she placed the sandwich on the counter before the stranger. He reached to pick it up.

"Looks good," he said.

"I knew I knew you from somewhere," Nora told him. "You were engaged to Eleanor Gleason."

"What?" The man stopped, the sandwich half-way to his mouth. "How did you know that?"

"I saw your picture every day when I went to her apartment. She lived upstairs in Fisher's house—in an apartment that they rented out. She lived there with Maxine and they both taught school. She taught me in fourth grade and I saw her almost every day, even after that, because—"

"You went to her apartment after school and started the fire," Lever broke in. "You—you're Nora!"

"Yep. I'm Nora."

"She told me about you," he said. "She wrote about you in her letters, too. I was going to try to find you while I was here. But—but somehow, I expected a...a little girl."

"I grew up," said Nora.

"Of course you did," he said. "And I've got old and grey. After all, it's been nine years, since—since—"

"Since she died," said Nora. "I'll never forget her." They stared at each other, silent in their shared sadness.

"What do you do now?" Nora asked.

"I teach. Believe it or not, I'm a professor at Oregon State. I teach engineering."

"Oh, I so want to go to Oregon State this fall," said Nora. "I just don't know..." She paused, uncertain how to continue.

"Tell me about the job you had starting the fire for Eleanor," Lever said at last. "I never quite understood that operation." He laughed and reached for his sandwich.

"Well. She came from Portland. No one in that big city uses wood to cook with, or to heat their homes. Maybe they have a fireplace, but they use electric or gas stoves to cook on." Nora paused, then laughed.

"Here, in this town, everyone uses wood. They cook with it. They heat their homes with it—they never heard of a gas stove or an electric one. Some of them don't even have electric lights. They still use table lamps."

Lever nodded his understanding.

"Well, Miss Gleason and Maxine Trost rented that apartment together. Neither one had ever started a wood fire in a big old cooking stove. Miss Gleason got a whole newspaper and laid it in the firebox. She put the kindling on top of it, then the bigger wood and lit a match to it. The edge of the paper burned a little and then went out. None of the kindling caught fire. She tried and tried. It was cold up there and they were hungry, but they couldn't get the fire going." Nora shook her head at the memory.

"Then I came by to see if they wanted to subscribe to the paper. They looked desperate. They showed me how they were trying to start the fire. I took everything out of the stove. I pulled out that flat folded newspaper and took it all apart. I crumpled the newspaper up, page by page and put it in the firebox. I put the kindling in on top and lit it and the paper burned and the kindling caught fire, then the larger pieces of wood, and pretty soon the kettle was boiling and the place was warming up. Lord. All they had to do was crumple that paper up so they got some air in between the pages, and then it burned just fine."

"Well, I'll be damned," said Lever.

"To tell the truth, I had seen people start fires like that all my life," said Nora. "If I hadn't seen them wadding up the paper, I probably would have laid the whole newspaper in there and tried to light it, too. Fisher just told them to start with paper and lay the kindling on it. He never said to wad it all up so there would be oxygen trapped between all the layers."

Lever smiled and nodded his understanding.

"Well." Nora continued, "They subscribed to the paper, and since the bundles of papers to be delivered don't come in on the stage until noon or later, I would go by Fisher's apartment to deliver the paper every day after school. I'd take the wood up to their wood box and, as long as I was there, I'd start the fire and put the kettle on. It gets really cold here in the winter, and when they came home after a day at school, the place would be all warm and comfortable and ready for them."

"Well. I'll be damned," said Lever again.

When he said 'damned,' he reminded her of Uncle Jack.

Oh, Lord. Uncle Jack! How could she have forgotten about him? She was supposed to have gone back to see if he needed anything, but here was Uncle Jack now, coming through the door looking like a thunder cloud. She hurried from behind the counter.

"Oh, Uncle Jack, I'm sorry. I got busy and forgot—"

"Well, I didn't forget. I'm fit to be tied! I don't mind helping you out, but I'd rather work the whole day in the hayfield than try to get that letter out."

"Oh! I'm sorry. I'm sorry." Nora rushed behind the counter and drew a coke for Uncle Jack. She scooped in some ice and handed it to him.

"Too bad you haven't a 'stick' to put in it," he said.

Nora hastened to make the introductions. "This is my Uncle Jack," she said. "And this is Mr. Rob Lever."

Uncle Jack nodded and turned away. He didn't even offer to shake hands. He had stopped in at the saloon, Nora felt sure.

"What the hell was that stuff the principal there at school sent?" Uncle Jack asked. "I've got the damn letter written but for that one word and I can't bring it to mind. A postscript, or a dang ship, or something like that?"

"A transcript," said Nora.

"That's it." Uncle Jack snapped his fingers in satisfaction. "Haven't I tried for half an hour to call that to mind? Transcript. Transcript." He started for the door.

"Let me make you a sandwich," Nora hastened to offer.

"Nay, girl. I'm going to finish that letter and I'm going to do it now."

"Where is Mr. Sheehan? Can't he help you with it?"

"He's been gone most of the afternoon, and I don't need help. I've nearly finished." Uncle Jack swallowed the last of the coke and strode out the door. "And I need the address if I'm going to send it," he called back." He scowled at her as he passed the window.

Nora felt uncomfortable. What would Mr. Lever think of Uncle Jack? She wanted them to like each other, but Uncle Jack had been almost rude.

"I have to make a phone call," she told Mr. Lever. "I have to get that address he needs, and then I have to take it down to Sheehan's office."

"I'll see you later this evening," Lever promised. "I must go rescue my car."

Nora made several phone calls. Finally Julia Hermes found the address she needed and Nora wrote it gratefully on a scrap of paper. She called to the clerk in the other part of the store and told her she was going on break. She hurried the three blocks to Sheehan's office.

Uncle Jack sat impatiently behind the desk. Seven or eight crumpled pages littered the desk, and there were several on the floor. A dictionary stood ready at his elbow. He looked tired but also triumphant.

"I'm just finished here," he said. "I'll have to make a nice, clean copy of it, if you approve." He handed her a sheet of paper and sat back, looking proud and hopeful. The page was covered with stiff, awkward script. Several ink spots dotted the paper.

"It would need a nice, clean copy," she thought. She read the letter.

To whom it may concern,

My daughter, Nora, would like to enroll in your college beginning this fall semester. I would like to see her take nursing or become a teacher but she wants to become something called a dietician.

Please send me the necessary information on the cost of books, tuition, board and room, and any other expenses that we need to know about.

Mr. Hillman, the principal of our local high school, has encouraged her to go and has already sent you the transcripts of her high school courses.

Her older brother and sister are already students at your college and are doing very well.

Sincerely,

Mr. Sheehan, the lawyer, returned to the office as Nora read the letter. She handed it to him and watched as he read.

"Good," he said. "Very good."

"What do you think?" she asked, then hastened to add, "I think he's done a great job."

Uncle Jack beamed.

"Do you think we should leave the part in about him wanting me to take nursing or teaching?"

"Absolutely!" said Sheehan. "That sounds exactly like a parent. We want him to sound like a true parent."

Nora nodded. She had to get back to work. She started for the door. Uncle Jack followed her out to the sidewalk.

"Wait now, a minute," he said. "I'm your father now, you know—so I'm going to act like a father."

Nora stopped in confusion.

"That blackguard—that fancy fellow with his fancy car," he began.

"What?" Nora's confusion grew.

"I watched there, through the window," said Uncle Jack. "When I went down to find that word, and to ask you to get that address."

He waved a hand in the direction of the drugstore.

"Well I watched Mr. Fancy Car and his smooth way of talking, and you laughing and flirting like a—a—screen star, listening to every word he said. He's no good, I tell you. Have nothing to do with him. He's old enough to be your father. Don't even wait on him, if you can help it!" He turned and strode back into Sheehan's office.

"No. NO. Wait," called Nora, but the door slid shut behind him and she stood alone.

"I have to get back to work," she thought. "I'll straighten it out when I see him again."

The fountain was busy that evening. People stopped to look at that wonderful roadster and then stopped to have a treat and talk about it. Mr. Lever gave several of the bystanders a ride, sometimes with the top up, but mostly with the top down. The customers thought he was a fine, friendly fellow. He made a good impression on all. Finally, he came into the store and sat at the fountain again. He laughed as he told her about some of the young kids who were so impressed that he would give them a ride. One kid, Orville Swan, he had taken home and the child asked him to wait while he hurried his parents out of their house to see that he had really ridden in the wonderful car.

"Oh, the Swans," laughed Nora. "They don't even own a car. They have a couple of teams and a wagon that they get around in."

And then Uncle Jack came through the door. His face looked like a thunder cloud. He marched straight to the stool next to Mr. Lever and sat down.

"I'm Jack Nolan," he said. He didn't sound friendly.

"I—I think I met you," said the stranger. He seemed ill at ease. "I'm Rob Lever."

"As in 'Rob the Cradle'?" said Uncle Jack.

"Pardon me?"

"You heard me. Now Mr. Lever—just 'leave her' alone!"

"UNCLE JACK!" Nora exploded. She spilled the glass of water she was setting before him. Uncle Jack jumped away to avoid the wet cascade. Mr Lever staggered to his feet, also.

Nora dashed from behind the counter. She caught her uncle by the arm and swung him toward her.

259

"STOP IT!" She hissed as she jerked on his elbow. "This man is – was—engaged to Eleanor Gleason." She looked about in alarm. Mr. Everett would hear this commotion and come to find out the cause. Several of the customers in the booths had stopped eating and were watching with curiosity.

"So what's he doing here?"

"He came to visit her friends," said Nora. "You know. Maxine Trost and the other teachers, and—well, me."

Uncle Jack stiffened and looked at Lever.

"And he wanted to find me, because, I'm the little girl that used to start the fire in her apartment every day so it would be warm when she came from school. You remember. I told you about the lady who didn't know how to start a fire in her stove."

"Oh." Uncle Jack seemed to be relaxing a little. He looked at Lever and a slow flush crept up his face.

"Miss Gleason had written him about me—about Nora—and he expected to find a little girl that she had told him about in her letters," Nora continued in a quiet voice. "Of course, that was ten or so years ago, and I just plain *grew* up." She paused to look around at the other customers who now seemed to be going back to their previous conversations.

"He has a date tonight with Maxine Trost," said Nora. She hoped Mr. Lever wouldn't be offended by that little white lie.

"Now he's a—a—professor at Oregon State College," she said. "He teaches agricultural engineering." She knew that would impress Uncle Jack. "I talked to him and found all that stuff out," she continued. "I tried to tell you, back there at Sheehan's office, but you rushed off and closed the door."

"Oh." Uncle Jack said again. He looked at the floor. He looked at Nora. He looked at his feet. He turned to look at Rob Lever.

"Damn," he said. "I'm a stupid blackguard. I hope you'll forgive me."

He hesitated, then took a step toward Lever and offered his hand. "I wouldn't blame you," he said, "if you spit in that hand, but I offer it to you in friendship. Isn't life too short for a long face?"

"A couple of nice fresh coffees," Jack said to Nora. He produced a flask from his pocket and poured a stiff shot into each cup.

The two men moved to sit beside each other at the counter. Their conversation came uneasily at first, but soon they talked as old friends.

"I'll give her an address that she can write to," said Lever. "She can get a job working in the kitchens or in the food line somewhere. That always works well, because she won't have to miss any classes. She's working while everyone else is eating and there would be no classes then anyway."

Nora's heart leaped. She felt secure and happy and smiled as she went about her work. Mr. Lever would help her. He was a professor. He could tell her what to do. One week to graduation, 'commencement' it was called. And then her life would begin, would *commence*.

She could barely wait.